I0719206

Post-Mortem Narrative

A Mackenzie Nash Mystery

Ronald Lamont

Post-Mortem Narrative
First edition, published 2020

By Ronald Lamont

Copyright © 2020, Ronald Lamont

Cover art by Carli Hillman
Author photo by Tara Templeton

Paperback ISBN-13: 978-1-942661-78-8

Published by Kitsap Publishing
Poulsbo, WA 98370
www.KitsapPublishing.com

Acknowledgments

To my family, friends, and loyal readers for their overwhelming support throughout this journey. To Amber Gravett whose invaluable feedback keeps me on the straight and narrow with my story and the characters therein. To Carli Hillman for her amazing book cover art. To Kitsap Publishing for continuing to believe in me. And to the Kitsap (Slaughter) County community for inspiring the locations herein, and for the continuous support of its local authors.

Other Mystery Novels by Ronald Lamont

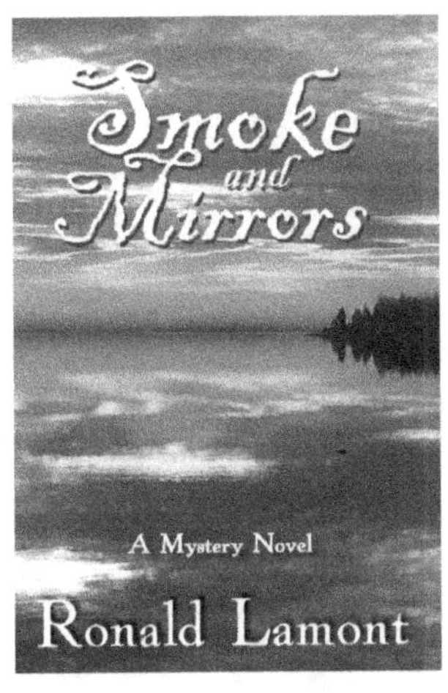

A Mackenzie Nash Mystery

A Pacific Northwest Mystery

A U.S. Navy / NCIS-themed Mystery

1

Saturday, October 26th, just before midnight

Traveling along a deserted country road in the dead of night… his mind wandered. Darkness defined the moment. Beware the dreams you conjure, for they might become a nightmare. The tormented or the tormentor: which version would lurk within?

Cresting a hill, the glow of civilization permeated the sky. He eased off the accelerator and began to apply the brakes in anticipation of the stoplight up ahead. This was the end of the road… literally; the meandering stretch of pavement had intersected with a well-traveled throughway. A glance at the clock on the dashboard showed *11:57 P.M.* He surveyed his surroundings—not another soul in sight… nothing before him, nothing within the confines of the rearview mirror. He exhaled; it was almost a sigh of relief.

The intersection would yield two options: head east toward town, or west to far-reaching corners of the county and beyond. He hit the blinker and merged to the right. The headlights of a fellow late-night traveler illuminated the scene to his left. He slowed to a stop as the midnight-rider cruised through the intersection. He eased off of the brake pedal and hit the gas… turning right onto Old Kitsap Highway, a four-lane boulevard, two lanes in each direction. He proceeded directly to the inside lane in preparation for a left turn at the next intersection. Up ahead, in the opposite direction, a parked vehicle's headlights sprung to life… it was a police cruiser. He glanced at his speedometer; he was safely below the speed limit. As the cruiser became nothing more than a reflection in the rearview mirror he mumbled, "Nice try,

Officer Speed Trap."

He clicked the blinker, transitioned to the left-turn lane, and rolled to a stop at the light. He glanced at the mirror: the police cruiser had made a U-turn and was pulling up behind him. *"I wonder what this clown is up to?"* he thought to himself. He grinned as the ironic nature of his statement dawned on him. Maintaining too much focus upon what lie behind him he failed to notice the light change to green; a short "whoop" from the cruiser's siren rang out. Startled, he returned his focus to the traffic light… a green arrow pointed the way. He hit the gas.

Midway through the turn he was lit up from behind by flashing lights. He scowled while he pulled off of the road and onto the shoulder; figuring the cop was going to spew some lame excuse for pulling him over, likely in the hopes of making a DUI collar. "Twice in one day?!" he vented, "You've got to be frickin' kidding me!" He killed the engine and sat motionless–keeping a bead on his side-view mirror.

The cop exited his cruiser and began to approach. The mirror revealed a spindly lad with an anxious demeanor–looking as if he was 'playing cop' for Halloween.

Continuing to look straight ahead while the Officer sidled up to the window and rapped on the glass, he rolled down the window and slowly turned to face the cop. The cop jumped back and reached toward his weapon at the sight–a face painted-up in the likes of Heath Ledger's "Joker".

The Joker glanced at the cop's trembling hand near his still-holstered weapon. He raised his gaze to the eyes. In a raspy voice as if he was playing a role, he grinned and said, "Good evening, Officer."

"Umm…" the Officer stammered through a nervous response, "When you made your right turn onto Kitsap you went directly across to the left lane."

"Well, Sir," the Joker continued his raspy voice while thumb-pointing back toward the intersection, "As you can see I had a left turn to make at the very next light."

The cop flinched at the man's simple gesture.

"Something the matter, Officer?"

"Just watch the quick movements," the cop replied.

"I was just…"

"I know what you were doing," the cop interrupted.

The Joker responded with a stern glare.

"Been drinking?" the cop probed.

"Nope."

"License and registration, Sir."

"In my gym bag on the seat here," the Joker pointed to the passenger seat and then turned away to reach for the bag.

The cop grasped and drew his weapon, "Hold it right there!"

"You said you wanted my license."

"And I told you to watch the quick movements."

"You *asked* for my license; I was *getting* it."

"Get out of the car!" the cop gestured with his gun.

"Why?"

"Are you refusing to cooperate?"

The Joker took a breath and scowled at the cop. "You know the gun is unnecessary," he nodded while slowly exiting the car.

"Wait up at the front of the vehicle."

The Joker trudged up near the fender, turned around, and crossed his arms.

The cop holstered his weapon. The car door still open, he leaned in and started poking around inside while he mumbled, "I hate Halloween weekends."

"There's no contraband in there!" the Joker yelled out. "Nor do you have permission to conduct a search!"

"Sounds like you're trying to hide something," the cop replied. He reached under the dashboard and engaged the trunk release.

"What are you doing?!" the Joker demanded as he began to approach.

"Stay there!" the cop pointed while he backed out of the driver's-side door and stood up.

The Joker ceased his approach, breathed heavily, and once again crossed his arms.

The cop trekked to the rear of the vehicle while periodically glancing back at the Joker. He grasped the trunk lid and raised it. He jerked back and flailed, "What the holy hell??" while fumbling to grab his weapon.

Smack! at the back of the cop's head.

The cop dropped his gun and crumpled to a knee. He winced and grabbed the back of his head. The pain was piercing, but there was no blood–yet. A rustling sound invoked a fight-or-flight reflex and he raised his hands to block any further blows, but all remained still. Attempting to regain his senses, a foggy halo of emptiness emerged. He began to rise and once again stumbled; this time to his hands and knees. Almost hyperventilating, he scanned his surroundings for his gun. He spied what appeared to be his weapon, grabbed it, and wobbled to his feet.

Not yet fully lucid, the cop froze at the sight of the contents of the trunk. It was a ghastly scene: a seemingly lifeless woman; beaten, battered and bruised… wrists, ankles, eyes, and mouth duct-taped… her throat slit.

The cop quickly turned away as he gagged forth a dry heave.

He exhaled and aimed his weapon toward the front of the vehicle; 'The Joker' had disappeared.

2

Homicide Detective Mackenzie Nash of the Slaughter County Sheriff's Office was awakened by the sound of her buzzing cell phone. She glanced at the clock radio; it read 1:34 A.M. "Crap," she said as she reached for her cell. She focused on the identity of the caller; it was Captain Sean O'Rourke of the Bennington Police Department, her former partner from her days back on the B.P.D.

"Hey Sean," Nash mumbled into her phone.

"Hey Kenz," said O'Rourke, "Sorry to wake you, but there's a case that might be coming your way if you want it."

Nash wasn't sure what to make of O'Rourke's statement, "A case that *'might'* be coming my way?" she replied, "And *'if I want it'*?"

"Officer Wilberforce pulled over a guy a little over an hour ago and discovered a woman in the trunk… throat slit."

"Son of a bitch."

"Yeah," O'Rourke concurred. "Her condition was so dire that she's been airlifted to Harborview."

"Harborview?" Nash replied, "She's still alive?"

"Barely," O'Rourke took a breath. "And the prognosis is not good."

"So, the 'might be coming my way' aspect rides on whether or not this woman survives," Nash concluded. "But what's the 'if I want it' angle?"

"Technically, the guy was pulled over outside of the city limits."

"My jurisdiction," Nash concluded.

"You got it."

"But if you've got the guy in custody…"

"Therein lies the problem," O'Rourke interrupted.

"You're shittin' me?"

"I wish I were," O'Rourke lamented. "Anyway… I'm at Harborview myself right now, waiting for her to get out of surgery."

"Were you able to get any info from her… a name or description of her attacker?"

"She made a garbled attempt to talk, but the sadistic bastard cut right through her windpipe."

"Damn," Nash exhaled.

"Yep."

Nash thought for a moment and then stated, "Well, at least you've got the perp's car," she said, "unless it's stolen."

"Not reported as such," O'Rourke replied. "Plus his I.D. was in a gym bag on the passenger seat, and it matches the registration, so I've got Officers on the way to the owner's residence."

"Not including Wilberforce though; correct?" Nash queried; her concern based on a previous interaction with the inexperienced, overzealous Officer.

"He was pretty shaken up by the ordeal, but he wanted to be the one to make the collar if the guy is, in fact, the perp."

"Sounds risky."

"Which is why I've got a seasoned veteran accompanying him."

❉ ❉ ❉

A streetlamp flickered overhead as a police cruiser pulled up to the curb outside of the home of Spencer Dunn, the registered owner of the vehicle whose trunk was the repository of a beaten, battered, and throat-slashed woman barely clinging to life. The home was dark and quiet, save for a low-wattage bulb illuminating the porch.

Two Officers exited their cruiser and beheld the stillness of the night surrounding them. They paused and listened. The silence was broken by the random disturbances of nocturnal animals: the rustling of a raccoon or a possum, the hoot of an owl, the pterodactyl-like shriek of a blue heron.

The Officers returned their focus to the objective before them, and trekked along the home's walkway while scanning the area.

Stepping onto the porch, one of the Officers leaned his head up near the door. He looked over to the other Officer and shook his head, indicating no sounds of activity within.

The Officers checked their weapons and readied themselves. They were startled when a vehicle emerged from the darkness and pulled up to the curb. It was another cruiser… their backup.

"Shit!" the Senior Officer whispered. He took a breath and glanced at the other Officer–Officer Wilberforce; who gave the Senior Officer a thumbs-up.

Two Officers exited the second cruiser and established a position in the background… a strategic distance from the two Officers at the home's doorway.

The Senior Officer made a fist and held it up inches away from the door. Officer Wilberforce, nearest to the opening, drew his weapon and nodded. The Senior Officer rapped on the door and then drew his weapon.

"Mister Dunn… B.P.D," the Senior Officer yelled out. "Open the door, please."

There was no response.

The Senior Officer looked over toward the backup Officers and gestured toward the house. The Officers scrambled through the side yard, establishing positions in the event that the suspect attempted to flee out the back.

The Senior Officer waited a few seconds and once again rapped on the door. A muffled, "Just a minute," was heard from within the home.

Time stood still as anticipation cast a shadow over the scene.

As the doorknob began to turn the tension grew among the Officers. Officer Wilberforce in particular was exhibiting a heightened state of anxiety: his hands shaking, his heart pounding, beads of sweat accumulating on his forehead.

The door slowly opened to reveal a makeup-smeared version of a 'Joker' face. Wilberforce jumped back and fired his weapon.

"Shots fired, shots fired!" rang out from the Senior Officer as the man doubled-over and fell to the floor. The backup team sprang into action.

"Man down! Suspect down!" the Senior Officer stated as the man lie bleeding on the floor.

Officer Wilberforce, shaking uncontrollably, fumbled to holster his weapon and stood frozen in a dazed stupor. "Dammit!" the Senior Officer said as he pushed Wilberforce out of the way in order to provide aid to the gunshot victim.

✻✻✻

Detective Nash's cell phone rang. She rolled over and looked at the clock—it was now 3:17 A.M.

"I had a feeling I wouldn't be getting any sleep tonight," she mumbled to herself aloud. Once again the Caller I.D. indicated Captain O'Rourke on the line.

"Hey Sean," Nash spoke into the phone.

"Everything just went to hell," O'Rourke proclaimed.

"The vic didn't make it?" Nash responded.

"She coded in surgery ten minutes ago," O'Rourke lamented. "And to make matters worse, Officer Wilberforce gunned down the person of interest when he answered the door."

"The guy drew a weapon?"

"Nope," O'Rourke exhaled, "I don't have the details yet, but it appears he may have been unarmed."

"Holy crap."

"Yep."

"But if he turns out to be the perp…"

"I concur," O'Rourke interrupted, "but even so, we're talking a potential public relations nightmare; this kind of crap makes it look like my Officers are executing vigilante justice."

"And if evidence shows this guy was NOT the perp after all…" Nash pondered.

"Then I'm totally screwed," O'Rourke responded. He took a breath, "After the whole ordeal with Roberson, this is the *last* thing I need."

"I hear ya," Nash replied. "You realize you'll have to get an outside agency to investigate the shooting."

"Don't I know it," O'Rourke concurred, "Which is why I already ran it by your boss."

Nash glanced back at the clock, "You just got off the phone with Sheriff Clarke?"

"I'd rather have you folks take the reins than the Seattle or Tacoma Departments."

"What'd he say?" Nash queried. Before Captain O'Rourke could respond Nash's cell phone rang. "Hang on, I think I'm about to get my answer," Nash added. "Detective Nash," she spoke into the phone. She listened and nodded, finishing with… "Yes, Sir… I'm on it."

Nash ended the call and got back to O'Rourke, "That was Clarke," she said, "Looks like I'm on the case."

"Perfect," replied O'Rourke. "I'm on my way to the scene; I'll text you the address."

"See you there."

3

Detective Nash's cruiser rounded the corner and was met by a cavalcade of vehicles with flashing lights. There was no need to check for a house number, the flurry of activity spotlighted the home of interest. She pulled up to the curb just as EMTs began rolling a victim-laden stretcher along the home's walkway. Nash jumped out of her car and jogged over to them, holding up her badge, "How's the vic?" she asked.

"Not good," one of the EMTs responded as they continued their trek; stopping at the open doors of their van.

Nash took notice of the victim's makeup job, "Halloween party?" she queried.

"That's our guess," replied an EMT as they loaded the victim into the van. "The Police Captain," he nodded toward O'Rourke standing near the home's doorway, "might have more info on that."

Nash was tempted to ask if the victim would be able to respond to some questions, but she already knew the answer—his mouth was covered by an oxygen mask. The EMTs closed the van's doors and sped away.

Nash turned her focus to the home's entryway. A quick glance yielded Captain O'Rourke and four additional police officers. One of the Officers stood out; he was standing silent a few feet away from the others. He resembled a toddler whom had been scolded and sent to sit in the corner. When Nash got up close to the group she realized the long-faced cop was Officer Clarence Wilberforce, and immediately understood his apparent exile.

The two 'backup' Officers stepped aside as Nash approached.

"Ma'am," one of them acknowledged.

"Mornin'," Nash responded.

Even though Captain O'Rourke had only been on-scene for a matter of minutes, he looked like he'd been run through the ringer. O'Rourke glanced over at Nash as she stepped onto the landing. "Hey Kenz," he sighed.

"Hey Sean," Nash replied. An Officer standing next to O'Rourke immediately caught Nash's attention; he was covered in blood, presumably from attempting to tend to the victim's gunshot wound.

O'Rourke turned to the blood-covered Officer and made introductions, "Sergeant Dale Johansen, this is Detective Nash with the Sheriff's Office."

Covered in blood, the Sergeant refrained from the customary handshake, "Detective," he nodded at Nash.

"Sergeant," Nash returned the nod.

"Considering the circumstances, Detective Nash has the lead on this investigation," O'Rourke explained to the Sergeant.

"Understood, Sir," the Sergeant replied.

"So gentlemen, what've we got?" Nash relayed to the Officers.

"Too be blunt, ma'am; it's a frickin' nightmare on multiple levels," the Sergeant replied.

"I got that impression," Nash responded. "How about we start at the beginning?"

"Officer Wilberforce!" Captain O'Rourke commanded.

Wilberforce just about jumped out of his boondockers, "Sir?"

O'Rourke gave Wilberforce the 'get your ass over here' finger gesture.

"We'll get into specific details when we get back at the Station," O'Rourke directed to Wilberforce, "but right now give us the Reader's Digest version of what exactly transpired, from the point you pulled over the vehicle… to the shooting."

"Yes, Sir," Wilberforce responded. "Around midnight I was parked on Old Kitsap Highway, keeping an eye out for impaired drivers, and

I saw the vehicle make an illegal lane change."

"An illegal lane change?" Nash asked.

"Yes, ma'am; he turned right onto Kitsap and immediately proceeded across the outside lane to the inside lane," Wilberforce explained, "instead of merging into the right lane… the outside lane, then signaling a lane change to the left, and THEN changing lanes."

Nash rolled her eyes. "Okay… proceed," she said.

"The guy then merged to the left turn lane at the next light…"

"Did he signal this time?" Nash interrupted.

"Yes, ma'am," said Wilberforce. "While he was doing that I spun around behind him, and when the light turned green I lit him up."

"You engaged your flashing lights?"

"Correct. He pulled over, I asked to see his license, and then he reached toward a bag on the passenger seat. I drew my weapon and told him to hold it right there."

"You thought he was reaching for a weapon?"

"I did… yes," Wilberforce replied. "I ordered him to exit the vehicle and wait up near the front end. I reached in, popped the trunk, and when I went to look inside I got hit over the head."

"From the suspect?"

"That's my guess."

"You didn't see him sneak around to your location?"

"I was too shocked by the sight of the woman in the trunk to pay attention to anything else," said Wilberforce. "When I got back up I grabbed my weapon and trained it on the area where the suspect was, but he was gone."

"Then you called it in?"

"Yes, ma'am," Wilberforce replied, "Not only to report the incident; but to get an ambulance for the woman."

Nash nodded. "Okay; let's move on to the events here at the suspect's home," she said.

"The Sergeant and I approached the door, knocked, and when the suspect opened the door I saw the same painted-up Joker face, so I knew it was him. It looked like he had a weapon in his hand so I discharged *my* weapon."

Nash noticed a gun in an evidence bag. She turned to the Sergeant, "He had a weapon on him?" She pointed at the gun, "Is that it… the Glock?"

"It turned out to be a cell phone," the Sergeant gestured toward a phone lying on the entryway rug. "The Glock," he pointed, "is Officer Wilberforce's service weapon."

"Damn," Nash replied. She scanned the Sergeant over, "And I assume you jumped in to save the victim?"

"Yes, ma'am," the Sergeant replied.

There was a moment of silence as Nash processed the information.

"Anything else for these two?" O'Rourke asked Nash.

"I'd like to see them later today, but that's all for now," Nash responded.

"Sergeant, you need to turn your clothes over to the forensics team here," O'Rourke directed to the Sergeant while gesturing toward Forensic Scientist Evan Lowell whom had been standing nearby. "They will provide you coveralls to wear," he added.

Forensic Scientist Lowell nodded concurrence with O'Rourke's statement.

"Yes, Sir," the Sergeant responded toward both O'Rourke and Lowell.

O'Rourke turned to Lowell, "Mister Lowell, do you have everything you need from Officer Wilberforce at this time?"

"Actually," Lowell replied, "We'll need his clothes as well to test for gunshot residue and blood spatter."

"Understood," O'Rourke said. He then turned to Wilberforce, "You heard the man."

"Yes, Sir," Wilberforce replied as he started to remove his shirt.

"Sergeant; when you and Officer Wilberforce are done with the forensics team, you are relieved," O'Rourke directed to the Sergeant. "However, I need to see both of you back at the Station later; tentatively at ten-hundred hours."

"Understood, Sir," the Sergeant replied.

"And tell the two other Officers that they can stand down."

"Yes, Sir."

While the Sergeant and Wilberforce were turning over their clothing to Lowell's forensics team, Lowell approached Nash. "Where's your sidekick?" he asked.

"Dirk?" Nash replied, "He gets a reprieve until morning."

Lowell looked at his watch.

"Okay; *normal* morning hours," Nash clarified.

"I heard you're taking the lead on this case."

"Both of them."

"Both?" Lowell's face scrunched up, "What's the other one?"

"You heard about the woman in the trunk of this guy's car?"

"Hard to miss," Lowell replied. "That's yours, too?"

"It occurred in my jurisdiction," Nash explained. "Plus, the Officer who discovered the woman… Officer Wilberforce… is going to be a bit indisposed for a while."

"Good point," Lowell nodded.

"So, what have you turned up thus far?"

"Not much," Lowell replied. "His cell phone, obviously," he nodded toward the cell and then reached down, grasped it, and dropped it into an evidence bag.

"His recent calls, possibly tracking his movements, relevant contacts, text messages…" Nash concurred, "A potential treasure trove of information."

"Agreed," said Lowell. "Plus, although the vic's face was covered in makeup, we didn't find any makeup within the home."

"So, he obviously got 'costumed' elsewhere," Nash concluded.

"And tracking his movements through his cell or via his contacts could lead us to the location, which would presumably provide us persons with knowledge of the guy."

"I concur," Nash replied. "Anything else?"

"Just the usual stuff."

"Well, don't forget that we are looking at this guy not only as a victim of a police shooting, but as a suspect in a murder. With that in mind, the suspect's car where the woman was found in its trunk will be coming your way… hopefully as soon as later today."

"I'll make sure that we're looking at all of the evidence in one large collective manner," Lowell replied. "Specifically, how it all dovetails together."

"Sounds good," Nash replied. She turned to Captain O'Rourke, "Anything to add?" she asked.

O'Rourke shook his head, "Nope. I'll be sure to get the car headed to the forensics garage, and I'll meet you later for further discussion with Sergeant Johansen and Officer Wilberforce."

"Sounds like a plan," replied Nash. "I'm going to head to my office and get Detective Brogan read in. The two of us will see you around ten o'clock."

4

Detective Nash's eyelids had grown heavy as dawn's early light began to overtake the dark of night. A yawn and a head-shake took center stage as Nash wheeled her cruiser into the parking lot of the Slaughter County Sheriff's Office. She steered into a spot near Detective Dirk Brogan's vehicle, placed the shift lever in PARK, and engaged the parking brake. Momentarily staring off into space, the first thought that came to mind was a simple one: hoping that Brogan had a pot of coffee brewing.

Walking through the office doorway Nash noted that her wish had been granted; the aroma of a freshly-brewed French Roast permeated the space.

"Hey Kenz," said Brogan as he spun around from a mostly-empty whiteboard. "I started the board… sorta kinda," he added.

"Yeah, I guess I didn't give you much to work with over the phone; did I?" Nash noted.

"Well, I got that we're working two cases which are essentially connected; but I wasn't sure how to lay them out on the board."

Nash removed her jacket and draped it over a chair. "Let's put one on the upper half of the board, and the other at the lower half," she commented. "That should give us space between the two timelines in order to identify any connection points."

"Got it," Brogan replied and then turned back to the board and began to write.

Nash grabbed her coffee mug. "I'll be right back; I'm in desperate need of a smack-in-the-face courtesy of a cup o' Joe."

Brogan grinned at Nash's descriptor while continuing to write.

As Nash was returning from her sojourn to the Break Room, Brogan hit her up with an initial inquiry, "Well heck," he gestured toward the whiteboard, "we've got two known connections right off the get-go: the cop who discovered the victim in the trunk of the suspect's car, whom he subsequently shot at the suspect's home. And, well… the suspect himself," he pointed at Spencer Dunn's Driver's License photo, "Correct?"

"Correct."

"And who was the involved cop?"

"Officer Clarence Wilberforce of the Bennington P.D."

"Wilberforce?" Brogan replied, "Isn't he the 'Barney Fife' newbie cop you kicked out of an interview a while back?"

"That's the cop."

"Holy crap," Brogan responded. "Was his shooting of the suspect justified?"

"That's one of the lines of inquiry we've been assigned to determine," Nash responded. She thought for a moment, "Actually, our assignment is to establish the facts around the incident and provide those to the County Prosecutor; who will then determine if charges will be filed."

"Charges to be filed against a cop who took down a murderer?" Brogan shook his head, "That bites."

"Did you already forget the first question you asked?"

Brogan looked confused, "What's that?"

"Whether the shooting was justified."

"Yeah, you're right," Brogan admitted. "It just seems that extenuating circumstances should be taken into account."

"And I'm sure they will be, by the Prosecutor, once we've determined and presented all of the facts."

"I suppose," Brogan exhaled. "But remember how Deputy Prosecutor Dansby was jumping to conclusions and playing all kinds of politics in our last case," he added. "I don't trust the guy."

"You've got a point there," Nash replied, "But a Judge isn't going to be a party to political B.S."

"Yeah, I guess," said Brogan. "So, what else have we got?"

"A date with Captain O'Rourke at ten o'clock."

"A what??" Brogan replied. It suddenly dawned on him that Nash was making an attempt at humor, "Oh, I get it," he said. "What's that about?"

"Getting specific details from Wilberforce about everything he was involved with last evening," replied Nash. "Along with details from the Senior Officer… his Sergeant… who was with him at the time of the shooting."

Brogan nodded.

5

Walking through the doorway of the Bennington Police Station, Detectives Nash and Brogan were greeted by Captain O'Rourke.

"Hey Sean, long time no see," Nash smirked as she shook his hand. "You remember Detective Brogan?" she added while nodding Brogan's way.

"Of course," O'Rourke shook Brogan's hand.

"Captain," Brogan responded and then released his grip.

"So, Kenz…" O'Rourke quietly began as he pulled Nash to the side, "I'm a little concerned about the optics of us collaborating on this case." He paused and added, "Or should I say these *cases*, as it were."

"I understand where you're coming from, but here's the way I see it," Nash replied. "Regarding the shooting: I need to obtain specific details from your Officers as to what all occurred, so in *that* instance they are merely *cooperating*, not collaborating."

"Hmm… okay," O'Rourke replied.

"And in regard to the woman found in the trunk," said Nash, "*that* case is under my jurisdiction anyway; and I need every detail from involved witnesses in order to help solve it." She then added, "It just so happens that an important witness is the Officer who discovered the victim."

"Two separate events," O'Rourke responded. "And my office is merely providing relevant information in support of your investigation," he concluded.

"You got it."

"Alright then," O'Rourke said, "I've got Officer Wilberforce and Sergeant Johansen standing-by in the Conference Room."

19

Nash, O'Rourke, and Brogan entered the Conference Room; Wilberforce and Johansen were seated at the table.

"Officers, you remember Detective Nash?" stated O'Rourke.

"Yes, Sir," the Officers responded in unison.

"Detective Brogan will be assisting her in the investigation," O'Rourke said as he gestured toward Brogan. "Detective, this is Officer Clarence Wilberforce, and Sergeant Dale Johansen."

"Gentlemen," Brogan acknowledged the Officers.

O'Rourke, Nash, and Brogan took their seats at the table. Nash opened the inquiry, directing a question to the two Officers, "My understanding is that you two approached the suspect's home, one on each side of the door, you knocked, did not initially receive a response, knocked again, and then a voice was heard from within. Is that an accurate depiction thus far?" she glanced between the Officers.

"Yes, ma'am," the Sergeant replied.

"And how about you take it from there?" Nash replied.

Wilberforce took the lead, "Considering what I found in the trunk of his car," he said, "we were in a heightened state of caution."

"Weapons drawn, a backup team strategically in place," the Sergeant added. "We weren't sure what to expect, but we wanted to be prepared for all eventualities."

"When the suspect opened the door I immediately noticed that same damn 'Joker' face," said Wilberforce. "And when I saw what I thought was a gun, I discharged my weapon."

"You didn't try to de-escalate the situation… tell him to drop whatever presumed weapon he was holding?" Nash probed.

Wilberforce dropped his head, "No ma'am, I simply reacted."

Nash crossed her arms and exhaled. A quick glance over to Brogan indicated that he couldn't believe what he'd just heard. Nash followed with a look at Captain O'Rourke; she couldn't tell if his mood had turned solemn, or if he was beginning to percolate.

Nash turned her focus to the Sergeant, "Your perspective, Sergeant?"

"Pretty much as Officer Wilberforce stated," the Sergeant replied. "It happened so fast," he paused to take a breath. "All I can say is that he, the suspect, looked just as surprised to see *us* as we were to see *him*."

"Are you saying that he displayed a look of recognition? Surprised that Officer Wilberforce, the Officer whom had pulled him over and discovered his captive, had tracked him down?" said Nash.

"Could be that," the Sergeant shrugged. "Could be that he wasn't expecting cops showing up at his door at o'dark-thirty."

"If you just ran from a crime scene," Nash postulated, "you'd think the possibility of cops showing up looking for you would be the first thing on your mind... especially if you ran straight home."

"I agree, ma'am," replied the Sergeant. "Obviously we won't know the answer to that question until we're able to talk to the suspect."

"Agreed."

Nash turned to O'Rourke, "Do we have body-cam footage of all this?"

"We do," O'Rourke replied as he grabbed a remote and pointed it at a wall-mounted television screen.

The footage from both Officers' body-cams corroborated their statements.

"I see what you mean about the suspect's surprise as he answered the door," Nash directed to the Sergeant. She cringed, however, a mere second later at the sight of the suspect being gunned down: Him hurtling back from the impact of the bullet and associated shockwave, his cell phone flying out of his hand, his body slamming onto the floor. The last portion of the footage was that belonging to the Sergeant jumping in and attempting to save the man's life.

Nash exhaled. "Anything to add, Sergeant?" she asked.

"No ma'am," the Sergeant replied.

Nash looked toward O'Rourke, "I think that's all I need from the Sergeant at this time, unless you wanted him to address anything further?"

O'Rourke shook his head and directed to the Sergeant, "That will be all for now, Sergeant… thank you."

"Of course, Sir," the Sergeant replied. He stood up and gestured toward Nash, "Ma'am," and departed the room.

Nash glanced around the room; the image of the suspect being gunned-down had taken a toll on the group. "Alright," she said to break the tension, "Are we ready for the dash-cam and body-cam footage from Officer Wilberforce's first contact with the suspect?"

O'Rourke nodded and once again aimed the remote at the screen. Officer Wilberforce's dash-cam footage was the first to emerge.

"Okay, Officer," Nash directed to Wilberforce, "You're up."

"There's probably not much to see here," Wilberforce replied as the footage began. "Here I'm pulling up behind him at the left-turn light, he fails to immediately proceed when the light turns green, so I give him a reminder 'whoop' on my siren. He then proceeds into the turn and I engage my flashing lights. He pulls over to the right, and I pull in behind him at a slight angle in accordance with procedure… you know…" Wilberforce turned to Nash to explain, "Angled such that the nose of my cruiser provides a safe-zone between me and any passing vehicles when I go to speak with the driver."

"Understood," Nash replied.

"Anyway," Wilberforce continued, "Now all you see is my backside coming into view as I proceed to the vehicle's driver-side window."

Nash turned to O'Rourke, "Can we switch to the body-cam?" she asked.

"Sure thing," O'Rourke replied.

The body-cam footage showed the entirety of Wilberforce's up-close exchange with the suspect. Due to the lack of a nearby streetlamp, the quality of the camera, and being the dead of night, it was a dark and grainy image throughout the sequence.

At the point where the suspect first appeared and spoke, Nash had the Captain pause the footage. She turned to Wilberforce, "Is he being a smartass and playing the role of The Joker? Or is that his normal voice?" she asked.

"Considering the smirk on his face, I think he was screwing with me," Wilberforce replied.

Nash was inclined to agree with the Officer, especially after viewing the footage and noting that any attempt by the suspect to screw with Wilberforce appeared to work… with the Officer fidgeting at every turn of The Joker's actions.

"The suspect is wearing something different here than when you encountered him at his home," Nash noted at the point in the footage where the suspect exited his vehicle.

"Yeah, I guess so," Wilberforce shrugged. "He must have changed when he got home."

Nash turned to O'Rourke, "Any idea if the forensic team gathered up the clothes he was wearing earlier; they could be covered in evidence of the attack on the woman?" Nash asked.

"I couldn't tell you," O'Rourke replied, "I was unaware of the difference in his outfit until the viewing of this footage."

"No problem; I'll make sure that Lowell includes this as part of his gathering of evidence."

The body-cam footage ran to the end. Nash directed a question to O'Rourke, "Can we go back and run through the rest of the dash-cam footage?"

O'Rourke complied.

The remainder of the dash-cam footage showed the suspect exiting his vehicle and standing near the front fender, the Officer perusing the interior and then stepping back out of the vehicle and walking toward the trunk. Due to the angle of the cruiser and associated dash-cam, the Officer disappeared out of sight when he rounded the rear fender near the vehicle's trunk. A small portion of the trunk lid, the driver-side of the vehicle, and the suspect off in the distance comprised the extent of the visual. However, as the footage ran it also showed the suspect disappearing out of the camera shot at the same moment the trunk lid was being raised by the Officer.

"This is where he hit me over the head," Wilberforce proclaimed.

"Are you sure he hit you over the head?" Nash commented, "Or could you have been startled by the sight of the woman, and jerked your head back into the trunk lid?"

"Uhh… I guess I hadn't considered that."

Nash sat in quiet contemplation as she processed what she had seen. The dash-cam and body-cam footage had painted a picture—a rather concerning portrait from Nash's perspective. She had mentally interwoven the multiple films to create a story; and would be doing so literally with the associated pieces of footage when she got back to her office—creating a True Crime documentary film of sorts.

Nash broke her silence. "I'm seeing some problems," she stated, "And I'm not just referring to the shooting of an unarmed suspect."

"Ma'am?" Wilberforce began to sweat.

"For one, regarding your initial interaction, you asked for the suspect's license and registration, yet you did not obtain either one of them before ordering him to get out of the vehicle."

"Umm…" Wilberforce grasped at a response. "Well, we did get them later, and everything matched," he said as he began to count on his fingers, "The license plate matched the registration, which matched the owner's residence, which is where we later found the guy."

"So, you got lucky?"

Wilberforce remained silent.

"And then you began to rummage through the interior?" Nash continued.

"I was looking for contraband," Wilberforce replied.

"Contraband?"

"Yeah, you know… liquor, drugs, and such. It's the weekend before Halloween, all kinds of partying going on… just look at the guy's face," Wilberforce pointed toward the screen.

"Was he driving erratically?"

"Uhh… no."

"Did he seem impaired?"

"You heard his voice," Wilberforce defended.

"You said he sounded like he was purposely screwing with you, not that he was impaired," Nash countered.

Wilberforce started to open his mouth in response, but stopped himself.

"And what made you seek out the contents of the trunk?"

"Umm… just a feeling I guess," Wilberforce replied. "And it's a good thing, too," he added, "Otherwise we may have never gotten the guy."

Nash thought for a moment and then commented, "I guess that's all I have for now." She turned to O'Rourke, "Can you send me the footage from all of the involved cameras?"

"Can do," O'Rourke replied. He nodded toward Wilberforce, "Officer, you may go now. Realize that you are on paid administrative leave. As such, also realize that you're subject to additional questioning at any time."

"Understood, Sir," Wilberforce replied and exited the room.

O'Rourke looked at Nash, "Can we have a moment?"

"Sure," Nash replied and then glanced over at Brogan.

Brogan got the hint, "I'll meet you outside," he said to Nash and then exited the room.

"You're beating him up over 'protocol'?" O'Rourke said to Nash in reference to Officer Wilberforce.

"Oh, it's much worse than that," Nash replied.

"What do you mean?"

"Watch the footage again… all of it… in detail."

O'Rourke gestured a plea for clarification.

"Sorry… that's all I can say," Nash responded.

Nash proceeded out of the Station. As she exited the building there stood Brogan, leaning against their cruiser. Brogan pushed himself away from the vehicle and trekked over to the passenger-side while Nash was jumping in and climbing behind the wheel. Nash paused in thought with her hand on the ignition.

Brogan broke the ice, "Are things as bad as they look for Wilberforce?"

"Technically, it depends on a number of factors," Nash replied. "But yeah, to put it mildly, it doesn't look good."

"He did have a point about the trunk, though," Brogan said. "If he doesn't look, who knows if the woman is ever discovered or the suspect caught."

Nash started the car, backed out of the space, shifted to DRIVE, and hit the gas… not uttering a word.

6

Detective Brogan was tempted to ask Detective Nash for clarification regarding her concerns with Officer Wilberforce's actions, along with the consequences that might result from those actions; but he could tell by her demeanor that it was a closed subject… at least for the time being. Detective Nash, on the other hand, was concerned that Captain O'Rourke might be viewing the actions of the Officer under his charge through rose-colored glasses. From Nash's perspective there were glaring issues that could be problematic… not only for the case, but for the Officer himself.

Brogan decided to break the silence with an unrelated question. "Where're we headed?" he asked as they were cruising along Olympic View Road.

"Forensics," Nash replied.

"Forensics?"

"To see what Lowell might have turned up."

"You think he's got something this soon?" Brogan responded. "I mean heck, the case is literally only hours old."

"Perhaps, but a little bit of something beats a whole lot of nothing," Nash replied. "Besides, don't you want to see the involved vehicle; it could be filled with scads of evidence?"

Brogan shook his head in the affirmative.

Gliding into a parking spot outside of the Slaughter County Forensics Lab and CSI garage, Nash and Brogan exited their cruiser, walked over to the backdoor entrance, and entered the facility. Forensic Scientist Evan Lowell was standing in front of a large Information Board that was covered with an equally large map. He spun around at the sound of persons entering the building and was surprised to see the detectives this early in the investigation… with the case in its infancy.

"Chomping at the bit already?" Lowell directed to the detectives. "Aren't you familiar with the adage, 'patience is virtue'?"

"Yeah, well…" Nash replied, "Apparently I'm not very virtuous."

Lowell grinned as he crossed his arms.

"Got anything of note yet?" Nash inquired.

"We've got a few random puzzle pieces that might pique your interest, but…"

Nash inadvertently cut Lowell off before he finished, "Great; but before you get to that I've got something for you."

"Okay," Lowell replied.

Nash grabbed her cell phone, "This outfit the suspect was wearing when Officer Wilberforce pulled him over," she held up the phone for Lowell to see, "Was that part of the evidence you seized?"

"Not that I recall," Lowell replied. "But we're still segregating everything, so they could be in there somewhere."

"How about you put a priority on it?"

"Since that's what he was wearing when he was pulled over it stands to reason that's what he was wearing when he placed the woman in the trunk, and thus there might be evidence of her on the clothes?" Lowell concluded.

"Bingo," Nash replied. "I'm especially interested in the gloves."

"You and me both," Lowell responded. "I'll move that to the top of the list."

"Great," Nash said, "What else have you got?"

"Well, speaking of evidence," Lowell replied as he began walking toward the car.

Nash and Brogan followed Lowell's lead.

Lowell stopped at the car's open trunk. "There's a lot of blood and DNA evidence in here," he gestured.

"Implying that she was attacked right here in the trunk?" Nash replied, "while she was restrained or something?"

"No; more like the trunk here has been used as a repository to transport someone who had been attacked elsewhere."

"You're sounding contradictory," Nash replied. "You said there's a lot of blood and DNA evidence, but then you said it's not enough to indicate that someone was attacked while lying inside the trunk?"

"The 'a lot of blood and DNA' that I'm referring to," Lowell said with air-quotes, "is that we're talking *multiple* individuals."

"More than can be explained from everyday cuts and abrasions you might receive from working on the car or changing a tire?" said Nash.

"That's our opinion… yes."

"You're not saying what I *think* you're saying, are you?" Nash probed.

Brogan jumped in before Lowell could respond to Nash's question, "We've got a possible serial killer on our hands?"

"That's a bit of a leap," Lowell replied, "but we definitely need to run down the sources. And who knows, perhaps there's a benign reason behind all of the evidence?"

Nash appeared skeptical, "Do you have some examples along those lines?" she directed to Lowell.

Lowell paused in thought. "A team of Extreme Sports attendees throwing all of their dirty, muddy, and bloody clothes in the car?" he shrugged.

"Extreme Sports?" Brogan replied.

"Yeah…" said Lowell, "like the Tough Mudder, Warrior Dash, Spartan Race, and other crazy-ass competitive events."

"That doesn't sound very plausible," Brogan added.

"Be that as it may, Dirk," Nash noted, "We all know that predetermining the potential outcome and trying to make the evidence fit that specific narrative can lead to a faulty conclusion."

"I know… 'Keep an open mind and drill down on the facts… following the evidence wherever it leads you'," Brogan said with air-quotes.

Nash was not amused, "You're making it sound like a punch-line."

"Sorry; you're right," Brogan responded. "All I can say is… thank God the guy's in custody."

"That's true," Lowell jumped in. "You don't usually have a suspect in custody before you start piecing together the evidence and building your case."

"Yeah, we almost have to reverse-engineer this one," Brogan noted.

"Not only that, but in this case we have to weave a murder around an Officer-involved shooting of an unarmed man," Nash stated, "who just so happens to be the suspect in the murder."

"When you put it that way," Lowell replied, "it sounds like the plotline to a Hitchcock film."

"No kidding," Nash conceded. "And one of the suspect's actions seems curious right out of the gate."

"What's that?" Lowell responded.

"Why would he go straight home after abandoning his car; a car with a beaten and battered woman tied-up in the trunk?" Nash replied. "He had to figure we'd trace the vehicle to him; not to mention that he left his driver's license in the car."

"I wondered the same thing," Lowell replied.

"Do we know his blood alcohol content?" asked Brogan. "People make really stupid decisions when they're under the influence."

"We haven't received specific results," Nash replied, "But remember Officer Wilberforce's statement that the suspect did NOT seem impaired."

"That's right," Brogan recollected. "Maybe the guy just wasn't thinking straight? Maybe he just freaked-out when the cop caught him and his instinct was to get the hell out of there and run home?"

"Yeah, well, we likely won't know that until we get a chance to question him," Nash replied. "Assuming he pulls through."

"In either case," Lowell stated, "I've got something related over here I've been working on," he nodded toward the board covered with the large map.

The trio trekked over to the map. The location of the suspect's car was highlighted, as was the suspect's home. "As you can see," Lowell relayed to Nash and Brogan, "I've traced-out and highlighted the most-likely path, or route, that he would've taken from his car to his home. I've also highlighted a couple of alternatives. Right now my team is traversing each possibility searching for evidence."

"Such as weapons, duct tape, along with the gloves and shirt he was wearing?" Nash replied.

"Yep; anything that might be relevant," Lowell replied. "Who knows; maybe he had a burner phone that he tossed?"

"I knew your team would be all over this," Nash responded. A thought struck her, "What if he caught a cab or an Uber instead of heading home on foot?"

"Since it's only about a mile between the two locations it seemed that walking would've been the most likely option. After all, you don't want to be standing around waiting for a ride when you're on the lam," Lowell replied.

"Good point."

"But just to be sure we talked to all of the local cab, Uber, and Lyft outfits and none of them dropped a guy off at, or anywhere near, his address," Lowell added.

"I guess that answers that," Nash replied, "Anything else?"

"A lot more evidence to sift through," Lowell said, "But no results at this time."

"Got it; thanks," said Nash. "By the way, you still have his cell that you found at his home, correct?"

"Yes, I do," Lowell replied as he walked over to a table rife with evidence and grabbed the phone.

"We can go through all of his calls, texts, and contacts if you'd like."

"That would save my team some work," Lowell handed the phone to Nash. "We already got prints from it, and they match the suspect, FYI."

"Sounds good," Nash replied. "We'll keep in touch," she turned around and headed out of the building with Brogan.

Brogan made note of the late afternoon sky as Nash and he climbed into their cruiser; it was not yet dusk, but shadows were growing long. He looked at his watch. Under normal circumstances the detectives would be heading back to their office to 'call it a day', but Brogan had a feeling that Nash might have one more stop in mind. He glanced her way; she seemed to be in a bit of a fog. He decided to venture a guess, "Next stop… the Coroner's Office?"

Nash broke out of her fog and started the car. "I reckon so," she sighed.

7

The drive to the Coroner's Office was far from typical for Detective Nash. Not that such an excursion was an abnormality; as a Homicide Detective one could say it was an all-too-often occurrence. But today was different; the image within her own mind, brought forth through the description of what she was about to bear witness, was weighing upon her. She had been provided nothing more than words—oral and written accounts of what would soon lie before her; but her mind controlled the narrative, and there was no escaping the image it had conjured.

Detective Brogan, riding shotgun, could sense that Nash was preoccupied. He was tempted to broach the subject, but her demeanor seemed more intense than mere contemplation while assessing aspects of a case. He opted to remain silent.

Arriving at the County Coroner's Office, Nash and Brogan were greeted by Deputy Coroner Doctor Valerie LaGrange—the Lead Medical Examiner for Slaughter County.

"Hey Val," Nash said to LaGrange.

"Hey guys," LaGrange responded as she acknowledged both of the detectives. "I've got the victim in autopsy," she gestured toward a nearby door. "You two know the drill," she added.

Nash and Brogan grabbed lab coats off of a rack adjacent to autopsy, and donned latex gloves.

LaGrange pushed the door open; the victim was lying supine on an autopsy table a few feet away. The trio surrounded the victim.

Nash gasped at the sight while her blood began to boil, "Dammit! I'm sick of this shit!" she yelled.

Both Brogan and LaGrange flinched; neither of them had expected such a reaction from Nash. Brogan was particularly puzzled. It was a disturbing sight, there was no doubt about that, but Nash and he had investigated much more gruesome scenes: a charred corpse whose teeth had been yanked-out in their most recent case, for example.

LaGrange saw things differently from Brogan. She knew there were aspects of Nash's most recent case that were much more distressing than a charred corpse, as crazy as that notion seemed. But she had an insight into Nash's psyche that Brogan was not privy to, so she was not overly surprised at Nash's outburst. "It *has* been a rough past couple of cases," LaGrange offered to Nash.

"Same bullshit… different victim," Nash huffed.

There was a moment of uncomfortable silence. LaGrange was aware that their previous case had dredged up long-dormant nightmares from Nash's past; she feared that this latest salvo could send Nash back into that dreaded hellhole. She contemplated her options and decided not to press Nash on the subject.

Brogan's attention had returned to the woman on the autopsy table. His stomach wrenched itself as reality sank in. Beyond the cuts, the bruises, and the pallor of her skin, he saw beauty thrashed by the likes of a demon. It was if he knew her, even though he'd never laid eyes upon her before.

One specific item about the victim's face caught both Nash and Brogan's attention—a frown had been drawn from the edges of her mouth, presumably via lipstick. It was smeared and blotchy—likely from removal of the duct tape that had covered her mouth.

Nash pointed at the disturbing image, "The bastard draws a Joker smile on himself, and a frickin' frown on his victim; what kind of a sick son-of-a-bitch are we dealing with?!"

Brogan and LaGrange were at a loss for words. Something suddenly hit Nash. "Hey Val," she said to LaGrange, "We need to get a sample of the substance used to make the frown and get it to the lab."

LaGrange nodded, grabbed a swab and vial, and obtained a sample while Nash extracted her phone and made a call.

"Captain O'Rourke," echoed through Nash's phone.

"Hey Sean," Nash spoke into her phone, "You're at the hospital with Spencer Dunn, correct?"

"That I am."

"Get word to hospital staff that we need to obtain a sample of the lipstick or whatever was used to make his Joker smile."

"Got it," O'Rourke replied.

Nash ended her call and turned to LaGrange, "Do we have a name yet?"

"No," LaGrange shook her head. "AFIS was our first stop—no match to her fingerprints."

"So, she's not in the system," Nash replied. She glanced at the victim's hands, "She spends money on manicures."

"And pedicures," LaGrange pointed at the victim's feet.

Nash glanced at the feet and then back at the hands, "A couple of broken fingernails I see," she pointed.

"Could be from attempting to fight off her attacker."

Nash perked up, "DNA under her fingernails?"

"No such luck," LaGrange replied while grabbing one of the victim's hands, "It looks like her hands were scrubbed clean."

"Forensic countermeasure?"

"Probably."

"Age range: twenty-something?"

"Yep: early-to-mid."

"What about any identifying marks: tattoos, birthmarks, broken bones, surgical scars?"

"I'll be documenting all of those types of things, including dental work and taking impressions… I'm just not there yet."

"Understood," Nash replied. She took a breath, "Sexual assault?"

"I'm afraid so," LaGrange sighed.

Nash's jaw clenched shut in anger and she began breathing heavily through her nose. She crossed her arms and stared into space.

"Early indications are that he wore a condom," LaGrange added.

"It figures," Nash growled.

Tension once again overtook the room. LaGrange glanced over at Brogan, who responded with a subtle shrug. Both of them knew that their best recourse was to let Nash dictate the pace of the discussion.

Nash soon realized that standing silent and fuming wasn't going to get the case solved; she looked back at the victim and gestured, "What do you make of these marks around her neck, wrists, and ankles?" she asked LaGrange.

"They're definitely indicative of some type of restraining devices," LaGrange replied.

"Restraining devices?" Nash responded. "They couldn't be from the duct tape being excessively tight?"

"No," LaGrange replied. "Note the sharp edges," she ran her fingers near each of the injuries, "it's more like some kind of shackle. Forensics swabbed the areas and Lowell said there were metal shavings on, and within, the wounds."

"Geez," Nash responded. "Including around her neck?"

"Yep; similar to a collar."

"Like some kind of medieval torture device?"

"I don't know if I'd go that far," LaGrange replied. "It's almost like a chained-up animal, but with the ankles and feet shackled along with the collar."

"Hogtied?" Brogan chimed in.

"Nah," LaGrange shook her head. "The variation in the abrasions, along with the location and depth of the cuts, would tend to indicate she had some freedom of movement."

"Son of a bitch," said Nash.

"No kidding," LaGrange replied. "It looks like we've got one sadistic bastard on our hands. Or should I say... handcuffed to a hospital bed." She paused in thought, "Speaking of... is there any news on the suspect's condition?"

"Still alive," said Nash. "Which I'm trying to reconcile is a plus, or a minus."

"But his condition is critical," Brogan added, "so it appears there will be no talking to him anytime soon."

"So in the meantime," Nash conveyed to LaGrange, "we follow the evidence that you and I, and Dirk, and Lowell gather, and build a case around it."

"And then we compare that to whatever story the suspect tries to tell us," added Brogan.

"If and when that occurs," Nash sighed.

"I'll do everything within my power that I can," LaGrange responded.

"I know you will, Val," Nash exhaled, "Thanks."

Detectives Nash and Brogan exited the building and headed toward their cruiser. Nash's pace was slow; an aftereffect of having been 'at it' since around one-thirty in the morning. In Brogan's eyes however, Nash not only looked exhausted, but beaten-down. "You want me to drive?" Brogan offered.

"Nah; I'm good," Nash replied.

The detectives climbed into their cruiser. While they were buckling-in something dawned on Brogan, "I just had a disconcerting thought," he said.

"What's that?" Nash replied.

"Do you think there could be another victim, another captive, out there somewhere?"

"We definitely need some answers regarding the extent of DNA that Lowell mentioned, but holding more than one person captive at a time seems like a stretch."

"You're thinking that the guy abducts a woman, does *whatever* with her, and then dumps her before moving on to the next?"

"If we're even dealing with a serial offender," Nash replied. "Right now we don't know *what* exactly we're dealing with; which puts a priority on following the evidence we have, and equally importantly, talking to this guy."

"Maybe it's a longer-term deal?"

"How do you mean?"

"Maybe it starts out as a relationship, at least in the woman's eyes, while he grooms her?"

Brogan's statement piqued Nash's curiosity, "Grooms her?" Nash replied. "Go on," she urged.

"He starts out as being Mister Nice Guy, says all the right things, makes her feel special…"

"Okay," Nash responded.

"But it's not long before he starts to show his true self. First with the putdowns and making her feel worthless; followed by outright verbal abuse," Brogan continued. "Then there's the first slap in the face, the apology, the 'good-guy' routine, with things ultimately escalating to beatings."

Brogan's words struck a nerve with Nash, "Who have you been talking to?!"

"Uhhh… no one," Brogan flinched, "I was just reiterating what we learned from our Domestic Abuse seminar."

Nash took a breath, "You're saying these two could have been in a relationship and things got out of control?"

"Maybe she tried to walk away, or said she wasn't going to take it anymore; and the guy went berserk?"

"With the shackles being some form of punishment?" Nash replied. "*'You mouth off or misbehave and you'll pay for it'*?" she punctuated with air-quotes.

"Exactly," Brogan replied. "In fact, maybe this is a recurring theme with the guy, which could explain the other DNA in the car's trunk?"

"Perhaps, but that would tend to eliminate the thought that there might be another captive somewhere."

"How do you mean?"

"If he's in a so-called 'relationship' until he either gets tired of her or she pisses him off," Nash explained, "it tends to reason that he'd end one relationship before starting a new one."

"I see what you mean," Brogan nodded. A notion hit him, "What if he has an accomplice?"

"An accomplice?" Nash's face scrunched up, "I'm not seeing indications that would lead to that conclusion."

"Yeah, I guess you're right."

"But if there *is* another such asshole out there, even if he has nothing to do with this case," Nash commented, "let's hope that karma deals him his comeuppance."

8

She stared at the ceiling—at least what she could make of it in the chasm of emptiness. Her stomach wrenched in knots... her heart racing... her breaths rapid and shallow. Sleep would not be an option—not this night.

Her head rested upon a pillow damp with tears. Or was it blood? Probably both. She had learned to weep without making a sound... a conditioned response borne out of self-preservation. She had become numb to the pain... physically; was there anything left emotionally?

She slowly turned her head to one side; her tormentor was fast asleep. Her gaze returned to the ceiling. She took a deep breath. She wiped her eyes.

Slowly and gently she pushed herself upright and spun around to a seated position at the edge of the bed. She paused and listened... all remained still.

Rising to her feet she glanced back at the monster—he lay motionless; the repetitive breaths of deep sleep interrupting the silence. Gingerly stepping away from the bed she maneuvered past the footboard and exited the room—a nightlight emanating from the bathroom drawing her in.

She entered the bathroom and gently nudged the door within the jamb and engaged the lock.

Positioning herself at the sink, she grasped its edges and stared into a void of nothingness. She contemplated the vanity light, but feared the reflection it would reveal. She wept in silence as she tried to summon the courage to face reality.

Taking a deep breath, she flicked ON the light. She gasped at the sight even though the bruised, battered, and bloodied image had become all too familiar. What she failed to recognize, however, was the essence of the soul buried deep within the reflection. *"Who is this person? How did I get here? What have I become? When do I make it stop?"* She paused in thought. She wiped her eyes. She repeated, *"What have I become? When do I make it stop?"* She took a breath and once again, *"When do I make it stop?"* She exhaled and glared into the mirror, *"NOW… is when."*

She flicked OFF the light, gently unlocked and opened the door, and slowly made her way back to the bedroom.

The demon lying motionless before her, she reached under the bed and grasped a baseball bat. She raised the bat over her head and… "Aaaaarrrrgh!"

9

"Aaah!" Nash jerked awake.

Ian leapt from his slumber at Nash's exclamation. He feverishly glanced around the room, "What is it, babe?"

"I killed him," Nash replied in rapid breaths.

"What?" Ian attempted to comprehend. Still in a fog, his heart racing, he once again scanned the room. "Killed who?" he uttered.

"Lyle."

The name wasn't clicking with Ian. "Lyle?" he asked.

"The uh…" Nash struggled to respond. "What I told you about…" she hesitated, "you know… what happened back in my twenties."

"The asshole who was beating the crap out of you?"

"Yeah," Nash sighed; her heart still pounding.

"You…" Ian paused in disbelief, "you *killed* him?"

"Yep."

"Back then?" Ian queried, "That's how you got away?"

"Ummm…" Nash pondered. She turned her head toward Ian. "Just now," she replied, "in my dream."

Silence overtook the room. Ian wasn't sure what to make of it all; wondering if there might be more to Nash's statement. She had explained that she was merely referring to a dream, or in this case, a nightmare; but it sounded like a confession.

"You just had a dream where you killed him?" Ian sought clarification.

"It was exactly how it happened all those years ago," Nash replied.

"It was *exactly* how it happened?" Ian questioned.

"Well… except the last part where I bludgeoned him over the head while he slept."

Ian found himself in stunned silence; he couldn't get Nash's former tormentor 'Lyle' out of his head. It had been only a matter of months since Nash had reached deep within her soul and shared the secrets of her past: how a strong and independent young woman had fallen victim to an abusive, manipulative monster. Ian's reaction at the time was to become enraged at the man whom had inflicted such harm upon her. The monster was nothing more than an image that materialized out of Nash's words, but Ian's rage was as if the specter stood before him. Blinded by that rage, Ian failed to recognize the courage it had taken Nash to share this painful part of her past… events she had kept hidden all those years, a vulnerability she had never shown to another. Ian did not want to make that same mistake with this new revelation. With that in mind he realized he needed to tread lightly as he attempted to comprehend the current circumstances.

"Wow; are you okay?" Ian offered.

"Yeah," Nash took a breath, "Must have been the sight of the latest victim dredging up old memories."

"Pretty bad, huh?"

"Even worse than the domestic abuse victims in my last case," Nash replied. "At least they survived their injuries."

"Do you want to talk about it?"

"Not really," Nash rolled over, "but thanks for asking."

"Of course," Ian replied. He ran the conversation through his head. He convinced himself that if Nash had truly gotten her revenge against Lyle that it would have been self-defense… *justifiable homicide* as they say. Was he jumping to conclusions? Was there more to the story? Or was it all exactly as Nash had explained… simply a bad dream? He rolled over and tried to go back to sleep, but it was an ill-fated endeavor.

10

Detective Nash trudged through the doorway of the Slaughter County Sheriff's Office. Detective Brogan was working on the whiteboard; he turned to acknowledge Nash, "Hey Kenz," he said.

"Mornin'," Nash replied.

"No offense, but it looks like you're still suffering from your sixteen-hour day yesterday," Brogan commented.

"Tell me about it," Nash sighed as she draped her jacket over a chair. When she turned back around Brogan was staring at the board; he seemed to be transfixed on the photo of Spencer Dunn. "Trying to get into the mind of the suspect?" Nash asked.

Brogan emerged from his fog and glanced back at Nash, "Something's not making sense to me."

"What's that?"

"Not that this guy is Quasimodo," Brogan nodded toward the photo, "but he's no Adonis."

"Is there a point you're trying to make?"

"You saw the victim; she's absolutely stunning," Brogan replied, "And this guy is… well… THAT," he pointed.

"She's the Homecoming Queen and he's your Average Joe," Nash gathered from Brogan's conundrum.

"Exactly."

"I hate to speak in generalities, but women tend to be attracted to more than good looks."

"Yeah? Then what's this guy got that attracted her to him?"

"She was ABDUCTED, not…" Nash stopped herself. "Wait a minute; are you trying to fit your 'relationship gone wrong' theory into the equation?"

"Well…" Brogan shrugged.

"Let's not put the cart before the horse, shall we?" Nash replied, "We know very little about the suspect at this point; and we know virtually nothing about the victim, so what say we avoid speculation based on a single superficial data-point?"

"Understood."

"Yeah?" Nash was not completely convinced.

"Yep," Brogan responded.

"Okay, how about we get back to the relevant items on the board?" said Nash. "You got anything new?" she added, "or are you just documenting what we've learned thus far?"

"Mostly what we got yesterday, but I do have some cell phone info," Brogan replied, "for what it's worth."

"I take it that means either his phone was off, or all we have are cell tower pings?"

"Correct," Brogan replied. He grabbed a map and laid it out on a table, "I've circled the areas where the various towers received signals," he pointed, "but as you can see it's a wide swath."

"Well, crap. Does he have any family or friends within these areas?"

"No family; they're all out of state. And as far as friends go, I haven't started a search of them yet."

"I'm thinking we may have to get Donnelly working on that aspect," Nash replied. "Were there any extended periods at one or more locations?"

"A couple," Brogan responded. "Including one particular area of note" he added.

"What's that?"

"It looks like he arrived at his home at 11:41 P.M. Saturday night and never left."

"You mean his *phone* never left?"

"That's true," Brogan replied. He pondered a notion, "So, he stopped at his home for something, set his phone down, and when he ventured back out he left the phone there for some reason?"

"Correct. In fact, leaving his phone could have been a purposeful act in order to keep it from being tracked to his intended dump site," Nash responded. "Remember, he also could've had a second phone… a burner."

"Good point," Brogan replied. A notion hit him, "Hey, maybe his home is where he held the woman captive, and he stopped at the house to get her in order to transport her to some predetermined disposal site?"

"A nice thought, but there were no shackles; nor were there indications that any restraining devices were used within the home or garage."

"Hmm…" Brogan pondered, "Maybe his home was just a weigh station?"

"How's that?" Nash wondered.

"Maybe he duct-taped her where he was holding her captive, threw her in the trunk, and was heading to his dump site when he got interrupted for some reason?" Brogan explained, "So he took her to his home, left to go take care of who-knows-what, came back home and got her, and was on his way to the dump site when he got pulled over?"

"Certainly a possibility," Nash replied.

Nash's cell phone rang, "What do you know, it's our favorite forensic scientist," she said as she glanced at the caller I.D. "Hey Evan," she spoke into the phone as she answered. She listened and then responded, "Nothing, huh? We've got cell tower pings, which has given us a general area regarding his movements, but no GPS. And interestingly enough, no movement past eleven-forty-one, so your thoughts about a burner may be correct; or he just left his cell at home when he took off around midnight with the victim." She listened and nodded her head, finishing with, "Got it… thanks."

Nash hung up her phone and commented to Brogan, "Lowell said that neither the clothes, nor the gloves that the suspect was wearing when

Wilberforce pulled him over, were within the items of evidence they bagged. And nothing along the routes he may have traveled between the car and his home."

"That sucks," Brogan replied.

"Yep," Nash responded. "He also said they've found no evidence of the woman anywhere in the home or garage."

"She was never there at the house?"

"So it appears," Nash replied. "Thus she may have been in the trunk the entire evening, or he placed her there sometime during his foray around the county."

"Which means his hideout could be somewhere within those cell tower locations," Brogan concluded.

"He could've turned his phone off, went to get her, and then turned it back on when he got to a certain location," Nash replied. "But I agree; we should start with possible hideouts in the area where we *know* he was."

Nash and Brogan's discussion was interrupted by Deputy Laura Donnelly entering the space.

"Hey Laura," said Brogan.

"Hey guys," Donnelly responded. "Sheriff Clarke assigned me to work with you two on this new case."

"Welcome back to the team," Nash replied. "Actually there are two cases; related, yet unrelated."

Donnelly looked confused, "Two cases?"

"Saturday night Officer Wilberforce of the Bennington P.D. pulled over some Joker; I mean the guy literally had a Joker face," Nash said, "for a questionable traffic violation on the outskirts of town. When he looked into the guy's trunk there was a duct-taped woman barely clinging to life. After Wilberforce nearly vomited on himself, he drew his weapon; but the suspect had vanished."

"That's the one I was aware of," Donnelly stated. "Out of curiosity, what made the Officer look in the trunk?"

"Although that action may have saved the day, the reason behind it is a matter of concern that I'm not going to get into at this point," Nash replied.

Donnelly nodded.

Brogan jumped in, "We got the case because it actually happened in our jurisdiction." He then added, "Plus the advent of the second case."

Donnelly looked confused, Nash filled in the blanks.

"By the way," Nash added, "My description of Wilberforce freaking-out is unofficial, so let's not promulgate that."

"Yes, ma'am," Donnelly replied. "And you mentioned a Joker-face," she added, "I'm assuming he was dressed up for a Halloween party or something?"

"That's our guess."

"Apparently that was a popular costume Saturday night," said Donnelly, "I pulled over such a guy around nine o'clock."

Nash was caught off guard, "Wait… what?" she commented.

Donnelly had a sudden feeling of concern. "He made an illegal left turn into the parking lot of the Quonset Hut Pub," she explained, "I let him off with a warning."

"Holy shit!" exclaimed Brogan. "The Quonset Hut is within the area of the cell tower pings," he gestured toward his map.

Nash pointed to a photo of the suspect's vehicle on the whiteboard, "A black 1999 BMW 7-series sedan?"

"No, this was a white E-series Mercedes… 2010-ish," Donnelly said with a sigh of relief.

"Damn!" Nash replied.

"Hell, there could have been a hundred people dressed like The Joker around town that night," Brogan commented.

"That's an unfortunate truth," Nash replied.

"But the guy is already in custody, right?" noted Donnelly. "So why does it sound like you're looking for him?"

"Trying to retrace his steps," said Nash. "Like I said, we have no idea where the victim was abducted or held captive. All we know is that she wasn't held at the suspect's home."

"Wow," Donnelly replied, "Where would you like me to start?"

"Right now we have no information regarding friends or family," Nash replied. "Anyone within the cell tower locations would be of particular interest, but leave no stone unturned."

"Understood," Donnelly replied. "I'm assuming you're talking social media, regular mail, email, and such?"

"Including his cell phone contacts," Nash handed Donnelly the cell phone.

"Got it."

11

Detective Nash pulled up near the home of her sister, Katelyn. The home was awash in the usual fare for this time of year: ghouls, goblins, witches, skeletons; along with *Happy Birthday* balloons. This was the first time that all of the balloons were black… indications of Katelyn having achieved a milestone. Numerous vehicles dotted the landscape, but luckily Katelyn had saved Nash a spot in the driveway. Nash smiled at the "Sheriff's Dept." sign that her sister had placed in the spot. She wheeled into the space.

As Nash was exiting her cruiser, Ian pulled up to the curb. He rolled down the passenger-side window. "I see you got preferential treatment," he nodded toward the sign.

"What can I say," Nash replied, "It's all about family."

"I think I saw a spot to park down the street," Ian replied, "I'll see you in a few."

Nash strolled up to the door, gave her customary 'boom-badda-boom-boom' knock, and opened the door. Katelyn ran over to greet her. "My big sis," Katelyn hugged Nash, "I'm glad you could make it!"

"Couldn't miss your Big Three-Oh celebration," Nash replied.

Overhearing the conversation, one of Katelyn's girlfriends yelled out, "Dirty thirty!"

Nash and Katelyn both laughed. "How many has she had?" Nash nodded and grinned.

"Who knows, but she's good… she's crashing here tonight."

"Good plan."

"Where's Ian?" Katelyn asked.

"Parking his car," Nash replied.

"You two rode together?"

"No such luck."

"That means you're in the middle of a case, doesn't it?"

"Two of them, actually," Nash replied. "But let's not talk about that; today's all about you."

"What can I get you?" Katelyn grabbed Nash's arm and led her toward the kitchen.

"Iced tea will work."

"One iced tea… coming up."

Katelyn poured and handed Nash her drink. "We've got all kinds of snacks… nachos, tacos, wings, veggies, fruit," Katelyn said. "Grab a plate and dig in."

"Sounds good," Nash replied. "By the way, thanks for the parking spot," she grinned.

"I thought you'd like that," Katelyn smiled.

The door opened. Ian stuck his head in and said, "Knock-knock."

Katelyn glanced over and waved Ian in. Ian walked over and gave Katelyn a hug, "Happy Birthday," he said.

"Thanks," Katelyn replied. "I can't believe my twenties are nothing more than a memory."

"Are you kidding, the thirties are the best," Ian said, "You'll see."

"I'm looking forward to it, actually," Katelyn responded. "I mean heck, just look at my big sister," she nodded toward Nash, "Mid-thirties, looks great, super smart, and kicks ass at her job… both figuratively and literally."

Ian glanced over at Nash, "I agree wholeheartedly," he said.

"Now go join her and grab some eats," Katelyn nudged Ian. "You're not avoiding alcohol tonight, are you?"

"Heck no," Ian replied, "What are tacos and nachos without a beer?"

"Now you're talkin'," said Katelyn.

Ian made his way over to the kitchen. "Hey, babe," he said to Nash as he gave her a kiss on the cheek.

Nash head-nodded toward Katelyn, who was mingling with her guests, "The girl sure knows how to throw a party."

"And look at all these friends," Ian said. He looked Nash over, "It's a good thing you don't wear a uniform, they'd probably be all prim and proper, possibly even paranoid."

"Too funny; I was thinking the exact same thing."

Ian eyeballed Nash's plate, "A few veggies and only one taco?"

"I'm watching my girlish figure," Nash winked.

"I've been watching your girlish figure too, and I'm sure it would be unfazed by a second taco," Ian returned the wink.

"Okay, Lover Boy," Nash nudged Ian.

Ian grinned like a mischievous schoolboy.

"Do you know any of Katelyn's friends here?" Ian asked.

"A couple of them," Nash replied. "And a couple more look familiar, but I couldn't come up with a name."

One of the women noticed Nash and Ian looking their way. She walked over to Nash, "You're Katelyn's sister, right?"

Nash extended her hand, "Mackenzie," she said, "Although most people just call me Kenz."

"Kelsey," the woman replied as she shook Nash's hand. "And I understand that you're a cop?"

"A detective," Nash said. "I'm off-duty, but still on-duty."

Kelsey looked confused. Nash clarified, "I'm not here to bust anyone's chops, but I am in the middle of a case, so…"

Kelsey lit up, "What's the case?"

"Sorry; I can't share anything at this time."

Kelsey was disappointed. She turned to Ian, "And you are?" she asked.

"A nobody," Ian grinned.

"He's with me," Nash explained to Kelsey.

Ian extended his hand to Kelsey, "Ian," he said.

Kelsey shook Ian's hand, "Kelsey," she said, "Nice to meet you."

"And you as well," Ian replied.

"Are you a detective, too?" Kelsey asked.

"No; just a not-overly-exciting Contracts Negotiator."

"Really? What kind?"

"Mostly Defense stuff," Ian replied. "Basically I'm a liaison between the D.O.D. and state and local jurisdictions."

"Oh."

"How about you?" Ian asked.

"I own a latte stand here in town," Kelsey replied, *"The Daily Grind."*

"Nice."

"Well, I should get back to the birthday girl," Kelsey said, "Nice to have met both of you."

"You, too," Ian and Nash replied in unison.

Ian filled up his plate and grabbed a beer. "This looks delish," he said.

"You talkin' about the tacos or the beer?" said Nash.

"Both," Ian replied as he bit into his taco.

Nash grinned.

Ian swallowed his bite of taco and took a swig of beer. "You seem to be doing pretty well after your long day yesterday," he said to Nash.

"I think I got my second wind, thankfully," Nash replied. "I was draggin' ass this morning."

"Are you expecting to have to go back in tonight?"

"I could use a night off, but who the hell knows?"

"Yeah," Ian replied. He crunched another bite of his taco.

Nash's cell phone rang. "You may have just jinxed me," she said to Ian. "Detective Nash," she said as she answered her phone. "Really? Okay, I'll be right there."

Nash turned to Ian, "Sorry babe… gotta run," she said. "The suspect just woke up." She gave Ian a kiss on the cheek.

"See you back at the house," Ian replied.

Nash rushed over to Katelyn, "I apologize, sis… duty calls."

Katelyn frowned; Nash gave her a hug. "Oh crap, I forgot your birthday present," Nash commented. "We'll meet up at *The Grill* within the next day or two," she added. "Happy birthday!" she gave Katelyn one more hug.

Nash bolted out the door, jumped into her cruiser, and sped away.

12

Ian was looking like a lost puppy dog. Now that Nash had departed Katelyn's birthday party and headed back to work Ian was contemplating his escape. Not that he was a party-pooper, but he was certainly out of his element with Nash being gone. He figured it was best to let Katelyn enjoy the festivities with her friends instead of worrying about him sitting all by himself. He was not quite ready to leave, however, as there was something important he wanted to discuss with Katelyn, if and when the opportunity arose. With that in mind, he decided to stay at least a little while in the hopes that he could catch a moment with her.

Katelyn was engrossed in the revelry when she looked over and saw Ian sitting alone. She wandered over to Ian's location.

"I bet you're feeling a little out of place?" Katelyn said to Ian.

"That's true," Ian nodded. "But there's also something important I wanted to talk to you about, if you've got a few minutes?"

Katelyn glanced around the room. "Everyone's busy chatting, so sure, I don't think they'll miss me for a few minutes."

"That would be great."

"Let's go to the spare bedroom," Katelyn said as she began to walk. Ian followed behind.

"So, what's up?" Katelyn asked once they got to the room.

"Do you know much about the guy named Lyle that Kenz was seeing back in the day?" Ian asked.

Katelyn was caught off-guard, wondering what Ian was up to, "Yeah… some," she replied. "Why do you ask?"

"Her last big case brought back some harsh memories for her; specifically related to things that happened between her and this *Lyle* guy."

"Really?"

"Yeah, for the first time in these past couple of years that we've been seeing each other, she shared some disturbing secrets about him… about how he treated her."

"About the abuse?" Katelyn whispered.

"Unfortunately, yes."

"We all had a feeling that something was going on, but she hid it well… either by providing an explanation regarding certain injuries, or by avoiding us for an extended period of time. You know… things like 'I'm too busy right now' or 'I'm under the weather'."

Ian nodded; Katelyn continued, "I mean heck, she's one of the strongest women… strongest *persons* I know; it never dawned on any of us that she could have been a victim of some abusive asshole."

"Don't I know it," Ian replied.

"And then one day things hit the breaking point and she got the hell out of there," Katelyn said. "That's when she finally shared everything with us."

"He never tried to track her down?"

"I have no idea; she went to stay with some friends in the city."

"The city?"

"San Francisco," Katelyn replied. "That's what the Bay Area locals call it."

"Oh yeah; I seem to recall Kenz telling me something like that."

"Anyway, the three of us… my mom, Bella, and I… had just moved to my grandparents' place in Los Altos, so there was no way he knew where we were, either… thank God."

"Where had Kenz and this guy been living; you know… when she took off?"

"South of Santa Cruz, near Monterey if I remember correctly," Katelyn replied. "Umm… Pacific Grove," she finger pointed as it dawned on her. She then added, "We were never invited over to their place, so I don't know exactly where it was."

"I don't suppose you remember his last name?"

"Casey; but why are you asking all this stuff about that jerk from ten or more years ago?"

"I think this new case is once again bringing back some bad memories, and I figure the more that I understand what she's going through the better I'm able to be there for her."

"That's awfully good of you."

"Well, to be honest, I kind of screwed it up when she shared everything with me the first time," Ian confessed.

Katelyn's curiosity had been piqued. She crossed her arms and awaited further details.

"I was so enraged at the guy for what he did to her that I let it consume me, and I failed to show compassion toward her," Ian continued. "Basically, I was a first class idiot, and I don't want to be 'that guy' again."

"I understand," Katelyn nodded. She grew wide-eyed, "But you can't tell her I told you all of this."

"My lips are sealed," Ian gestured.

13

Detective Nash entered the reception area of Bennington General Hospital. She held up her badge, "Detective Nash with the Sheriff's Department; can you give me the room number for Spencer Dunn, please?"

The administrator looked at her computer screen and responded, "Room two-forty-two; you can take the stairs or the elevator," she pointed.

"Got it… thanks," Nash replied.

While Nash was heading to the stairway, the administrator put in a call to the doctor assigned to Spencer Dunn.

Nash exited the stairwell and glanced up and down the hallway. She noticed a uniformed Officer standing post outside of one of the doors; nearby was a doctor. She made eye contact with the doctor, who gave her a nod; she proceeded down the hallway to greet him. The Officer took notice of Nash as she approached.

Nash held up her badge as she greeted the doctor. "Good evening, doctor; I'm Detective Nash," she said, "Any chance that I can speak with your patient?"

"Good evening," the doctor replied. "He seems to be out of the woods, but he's still in pretty rough shape, so you'll have to keep it brief."

"I understand… thanks."

"And go easy," the doctor added. "If he starts getting upset or agitated you're going to have to cease your interview."

"Understood," Nash nodded.

Nash began to enter the room and was immediately struck by something. "No handcuffs?" she said, glancing between both the doctor

58

and the Officer.

The Officer started to reply, but the doctor beat him to it. "He wasn't going anywhere," the doctor stated.

Nash looked at the Officer, whom shrugged concurrence with the doctor's statement.

The doctor took the lead entering the room, with Nash right behind. Nash noticed a couple of 'Get Well' balloons and cards. She wondered how word had gotten out about Spencer Dunn since there had been no release of his name—not as a gunshot victim, nor as a suspect in a murder.

The doctor sidled up next to Spencer and stated, "Mister Dunn, this is Detective Nash," he nodded toward Nash, "she is going to ask you a few questions."

Spencer looked over at Nash. Although Spencer's wound was not visible, and aides had cleaned the Joker makeup from his face, he looked awful. A phrase that Nash often used immediately came to mind: 'Death warmed over'.

The doctor continued with Spencer, "And you can stop the interview at any time," he said.

"Okay," Spencer replied in a raspy voice.

The doctor stepped back to a corner of the room.

Nash approached Spencer. As she was about to speak, Spencer beat her to it, "Do you know who it was that shot me?" Spencer asked. "It's all just a blur, but I think he was dressed up like a cop."

Nash was surprised that Spencer was apparently unaware that he had been shot by a police officer. Or was he faking it?

"Umm… yes, we know who it was," Nash responded.

"Is he in custody?"

"In a manner of speaking."

"What does that mean?"

"The gentleman wasn't *dressed-up* like a cop; he *is* a cop."

Spencer was flabbergasted, "What?? Why did he shoot me?"

"He thought you had a weapon."

"A weapon? You mean my cell phone?"

"I'm afraid so."

Spencer turned his head in stunned silence. His eyes appeared to become glassy. He took a breath. He reached up with his hand that was not connected to an I.V. and wiped his eyes. He turned back to face Nash, "Why was a cop at my door in the middle of the night in the first place?" he asked.

"That's one of the reasons I'm here," Nash replied. "So I'm going to just cut to the chase."

Spencer looked confused, "Umm… okay."

"Who's the girl?" Nash stated.

"What girl?"

"The one in the trunk of your car."

"What… what're you talking about?"

Nash grabbed her cell phone, scrolled, and then showed Spencer a picture of the victim.

"I've never seen her before," Spencer replied.

"Then how do you explain…"

Spencer cut Nash off before she could finish, "Someone must have put her there."

"You're telling me you had no idea there was a woman in the trunk of your car?"

"That's right."

"Then why did you run?"

"Run from what?"

"From the Officer who pulled you over and discovered the woman."

"What the hell?" Spencer was getting flustered, "I wasn't pulled over that night."

The doctor interceded, "Mister Dunn, do you wish to end this interview?"

"Not yet," Spencer replied. "I want to know what the heck she's talking about."

"Very well," the doctor replied. He turned to Nash, "But let's take it easy, shall we?"

"Yes, Sir," Nash replied.

Nash returned her focus to Spencer, "The Officer pulled over *your* car, sometime around midnight," she said. "The driver had your I.D. and looked just like you, including your 'Joker' Halloween makeup."

"What??" Spencer replied. "I was home before midnight and I never left."

"Then how do you explain your car getting pulled over?"

"Obviously someone stole it," Spencer replied. He then gestured toward his face, "And I wasn't wearing Joker makeup, I was the Mad Hatter, like Johnny Depp in that *Alice in Wonderland* flick."

Nash grabbed her cell phone. "This is a disturbing photo, so I apologize, but it's a picture of you right after you were shot," she held the phone up for Spencer to see. "Joker," she added.

"What the hell?" Spencer responded. "That wasn't my makeup; someone added the red lipstick, or whatever, to make me look like The Joker."

Nash gave Spencer the stink-eye, "Someone added the lipstick without your knowledge?"

"Everyone was partying, acting like a bunch of crazies, and I had a few drinks," Spencer replied. "So it's possible someone was messing with my makeup and I wasn't paying attention."

"Someone changed your makeup to look like The Joker, and then some guy, also made up like The Joker, just happened to steal your car and place a dying woman in the trunk?"

"I don't know!" Spencer yelled, "That has to be it!"

The doctor jumped in, "That's enough, detective."

"Yes, doctor," Nash replied. She then gestured toward the Officer standing outside the doorway. The Officer entered the room. Nash looked at Spencer, "I'm sorry to do this," she said.

The Officer extracted handcuffs and cuffed one of Spencer's wrists to the metal rail of his bed.

"You've got to be kidding me?!" Spencer said.

Nash turned to the doctor. "If any of your staff needs the cuffs removed in order to attend to Mister Dunn, an Officer will be stationed outside the door twenty-four-seven," she stated.

"I understand, detective," the doctor replied.

Nash looked back at Spencer. "We'll talk again," she said.

Spencer remained silent.

Nash exited the room.

14

Detective Nash pulled into her parking spot at the Sheriff's Office. Things were back to normal, time-wise anyway: Nash was the first to arrive at the office.

Walking through the doorway, the whiteboard caught Nash's eye. Although upbeat in regard to the progress made on the board, the memory of her discussion with the suspect the previous night dampened her mood.

Nash strolled past the board and headed directly to the Break Room. Number one priority: Get the coffee brewing. With the coffee trickling into its decanter she made her way back to the whiteboard. She wasn't expecting any new information; after all, she had departed to attend her sister's birthday party near the end of shift. Nonetheless, Brogan and Donnelly had left a few nuggets for Nash to chew on. She began attempting to decipher the notes when Donnelly walked through the doorway.

"Good morning," Donnelly said as she glanced over at Nash.

"Mornin'," Nash replied. "Where's your partner in crime?"

"Right behind me," Donnelly thumb-pointed just as the door opened and Brogan walked across the threshold. "Hey guys," Brogan commented.

"Hey," Nash and Donnelly replied in unison.

Nash nodded toward the board, "It looks like you two learned a few things before closing up shop yesterday?"

"Yep," Brogan replied. "By the way, how was your sister's party?"

"Nice, but brief," Nash said.

"Brief?"

"Yeah; I got a call that the suspect was awake, so I bolted out of the party and headed to Bennington General."

"You got to talk to him?" said Donnelly.

"Some," Nash replied. "He was in a pretty fragile state, so I only got a limited amount of time with him."

"How did he look?" said Brogan.

"Like he had one foot in the grave," said Nash.

"Yikes," Donnelly commented.

"What all were you able to find out?" asked Brogan.

"Believe it or not, he said it wasn't him."

"What?? He was caught red-handed, dead to rights, all that stuff, and he's pleading ignorance?"

"Yep. He said he got home around midnight and never left the house; and that he had no idea who the woman was, or how she got in the trunk of his car."

Brogan rolled his eyes, "How did he explain his car getting pulled over sometime after he allegedly was at home?"

"He said someone must have stolen it."

"And they just so happened to have Joker makeup like him?" Brogan shook his head.

"Interestingly enough," said Nash, "He said that someone must have made him look like he was The Joker."

"You've got to be kidding? Someone made up his face and he didn't know about it?" Brogan laughed.

"He said it was a crazy atmosphere and he'd had a few drinks, so…"

"Oh, brother," Brogan rolled his eyes.

"He said he was made up as the Mad Hatter, and someone must have added the Joker smile at some point."

Donnelly jumped into the conversation, "It looks like he was telling the truth about his makeup," she said.

"What're you talking about?" said Brogan.

"His cell phone," Donnelly walked over and grabbed Spencer's phone.

She scrolled through some pictures and then held it up for Nash and Brogan to see, "He took a selfie with his Mad Hatter makeup."

"Interesting that it's a selfie and not someone else taking the picture," said Nash.

"What difference would that make?" said Donnelly.

"With a selfie you are the writer, producer, and director."

"Come again?" Brogan responded.

"You set the stage, the camera angle, and take the shot."

"You dictate the parameters… you control the narrative," Donnelly concluded.

"Or in this case, the picture," replied Nash.

"You're saying that he wanted to have evidence of being this Mad Hatter character?" asked Brogan.

"Yep; what I'm seeing is a pretty lame-ass attempt at an alibi," Nash replied. "Heck, all he had to do was add the Joker smile himself and he pleads 'that can't be me, I was the Mad Hatter, not the Joker'."

"You make a good point, that's for sure," said Brogan.

"I'm still seeking out his friends," said Donnelly, "so maybe I can get more info along those lines?"

"True, but remember, they could've helped him with his Mad Hatter makeup," Nash replied, "but he still could've added the Joker smile by himself."

"But didn't Lowell say they didn't find any lipstick or other kind of red makeup at his home?"

"Hell, he could have chucked it in the bay for all we know," Nash replied.

"That's true."

"Hey, how about we show him the dash-cam and body-cam footage?" said Brogan, "There's no way he can refute that?"

"I wouldn't bet on it," Nash replied.

"No?"

"Considering how he's pleaded ignorance thus far, how much you wanna bet that he'll simply say 'that's not me'?"

"That seems crazy."

"Yeah," Nash sounded exasperated. "When was the last time you had a complete denial in the face of irrefutable evidence?"

Brogan thought for a moment. "Roberson?" he replied.

"Okay, I'll grant you that," Nash conceded. "But that was all circumstantial; we've got this guy, and his victim, on video."

"Speaking of the video," said Brogan. "How did he sound?"

"All raspy."

"Just like the footage," Brogan concluded.

"Something like that," Nash replied.

"Aha!" Brogan responded. "Did he happen to say anything about where he was that night so that we can either try to corroborate, or debunk, what he says?"

"No, the doctor cut me off after Dunn started getting worked-up," Nash huffed.

Brogan and Donnelly looked at each other, waiting to see if Nash was going to provide any additional information.

"Was that it?" Brogan questioned Nash.

"Pretty much," Nash replied. She turned her focus to the board. "A photo, and a drawing, of the victim?" she nodded.

"The photo is the one taken in autopsy," Brogan responded.

"Yeah, I've got that one," Nash held up her cell phone.

"The drawing is an artist's rendition that Public Affairs released to news outlets and social media."

"Smart move," Nash replied. "Any hits?"

"I've been fielding calls and pulling up I.D.'s to go with the names," Donnelly jumped in. "No matches thus far."

"If you start getting overwhelmed with calls let me know; I'll ask Clarke to provide us some assistance."

"Will do."

15

There was a feeling of nervousness, that certain level of angst one encounters when creeping around questionable territories, especially those that pertain to someone else's life. Curiosity can lead to great discoveries. It can also lead to disappointment; or worse… to disaster. For one whose career revolved around cost-benefit analyses, he seemed oblivious to the potential consequences of this undertaking. Was he looking for answers to a question that should've never been asked?

He sat at the edge of the sofa, elbows resting upon his thighs. On the coffee table before him lay a folder to his left, a pen and notepad to his right, a laptop dead-center. He flipped open the laptop and began the journey.

"Thank God for the internet; a researcher's Holy Grail of sorts," he said to himself.

"So, let's see what the name Lyle Casey turns up," he typed. "Damn; more of them than I expected. And I have no middle name," he pondered his first roadblock.

"Let's try narrowing it down. I'll start with the state of California since that's where he and Kenz were living back-in-the-day.

"Whoa, an obituary!" his eyes grew wide. "Nope; too young. Poor kid," he commented. "And here's an old fart… that can't be him.

"Wait, here's one whose most recent address is Pacific Grove. The age is right; that's got to be him.

"What? This isn't making sense; the date of this guy's 'most recent address' is twelve years ago?"

He slid against the back of the sofa and crossed his arms. "Son of a bitch," he said as he attempted to comprehend the information.

"Okay, I'm jumping to conclusions," he realized as he sat erect and scooted up to the edge of the sofa cushion.

"Now that I've got a middle name let's check obituaries in the area," he began to type. "Hmm… none that match; I guess that's a good thing. Let's extend the search-criteria to the entire state just to be sure. Nope; he's not there, either.

"Well, I have the address, let's see what this place looks like," he said as he sought out a street-level view of the property.

"Wow, this isn't what I was expecting," he said as he viewed the property, "A downtown street scene of Victorian-style buildings; with the upper floors a home or apartment, the bottom floor a street-level business." He scanned through the description, "No wonder, these were built between 1880 and 1910; kind of reminds me of certain areas of San Francisco."

He found himself sitting and staring at the photograph; his mind wandering. His level of angst and nervousness grew as he realized he was viewing more than a piece of Pacific Coastal history, but the former residence of his beloved; one she had shared with another man. He found his heart racing, his palms sweating, and his stomach twisting itself into a knot. Was his anxiety due to an unexpected feeling of jealousy? Or did he find himself grappling with the notion that he was violating the sanctity of his beloved's past, and more importantly, her trust?

As he contemplated his next move he was suddenly interrupted by the sound of the front door opening. He glanced toward the door and abruptly closed the lid of his laptop just as Nash entered the home.

Nash noticed Ian's curious movement.

"Hey, babe," Ian blurted out before Nash had a chance to say anything, "You decided to come home for lunch?"

"I needed a break," Nash replied while making her way to the kitchen. "Plus, I wanted some of that leftover taco stuff you brought back from

Katelyn's party last night."

"That dish she calls Taco Mess?"

"Yeah, that's it," Nash said as she opened the refrigerator door, grabbed a sealed container along with a bottled-water, and elbowed the door shut. "I think she just puts all of the taco ingredients into a casserole dish: ground beef or turkey, rice, refried beans, adds chunks of tortilla chips, and then bakes it."

"I don't blame you, it's delish."

Nash placed the container in the microwave, selected the requisite amount of time, and hit 'Start'. She turned to face Ian, "So, what are you doing here?"

"I get to work from home today."

"And you decided to pick my home over yours?"

"Yeah, that's gotten to be a bit of a habit, hasn't it?"

"No worries," Nash replied. She removed the cap from her bottled-water, took a swig, and set the bottle on the counter. "So, what's up?" she said.

"What do you mean?"

"You seem a bit preoccupied."

"I do?"

"Yep."

"Just one of those days, I guess," Ian shrugged.

"There's nothing specific on your mind?"

"Not really."

"Hmm… okay," Nash responded. She had doubts about Ian's proclamations; he seemed to be hiding something. But she wasn't sure if she wanted to press the issue at the moment, either.

The *ding* of the microwave rang out; the conversation would have to continue at a later time.

16

"Hey Kenz, how was lunch?" Deputy Laura Donnelly inquired of Detective Nash when she strolled into the office.

"Different," Nash replied.

"Different?"

"Well, the food was good," Nash responded, "but Ian was there."

Donnelly wasn't sure what to make of Nash's comment, "I don't mean to pry, but isn't that kind of the norm?"

"Not during work hours on a weekday."

"Oh."

"What's really weird is how he was acting," Nash continued. "As soon as I walked through the doorway he looked up at me and immediately closed the lid on his laptop."

"Like you caught him in a compromising position?"

"Precisely," Nash replied. "And he was acting strange the entire time that I was there; like a toddler with chocolate all over his face trying to convince Mom that he didn't get into the Halloween candy."

"Hmm…" Donnelly murmured; being at a loss for words.

"Anyway; it is what it is," Nash exhaled. "What say we change the subject?" she added. "Got anything new to report?"

Donnelly gestured toward a photo on the whiteboard; it was posted alongside the artist's rendering and the autopsy photo of the victim. "I think we may have an I.D. on our victim," she replied.

"Holy crap," Nash responded, "That definitely looks like her."

"Yeah; a woman named Tiffany Fairchild called in response to the artist's rendering. She gave me the name of Natalie Copeland," Donnelly replied. "When I came across Natalie's DMV photo I thought that we just might have a match."

"What was the story you got from Tiffany?"

"She had quite a bit to say," Donnelly replied as she grabbed her memo pad. "She identified herself as Natalie's roommate, and hadn't seen her in a couple of weeks."

"I thought we didn't have any Missing Persons Reports that matched our vic?"

"We don't," Donnelly replied, "Tiffany never reported her missing."

"Did she say why she failed to make a report?"

"Even though she and her friends were concerned, they assumed Natalie was spending all of her time with her new boyfriend."

"Concerned?" Nash responded, "About what?"

"The new boyfriend," Donnelly replied. "Tiffany said that he seemed to be very controlling, with Natalie spending more and more time with him… essentially backing away from all of her friends. She said that such behavior was very out of character for Natalie."

"And we're talking about our suspect Spencer Dunn being this new boyfriend, correct?"

"I have no idea."

"What do you mean?"

"Unfortunately, none of them ever met the guy."

"But Natalie had to at least mention his name, right?"

"Nope," Donnelly shook her head.

"What the hell?" Nash crossed her arms. "Who doesn't get all excited when they have a new love interest, and subsequently share every excruciating detail about them to their friends?"

"Which was one of the reasons her friends had a bad feeling about this guy," Donnelly replied.

"If we didn't already have a suspect in custody I'd be inclined to think her secrecy about the boyfriend is because he's married," Nash said.

"That's the first thing that would've crossed my mind if it were one of my girlfriends," Donnelly responded.

"Did Natalie share *anything* about this guy?"

"Yes; but only generalities: successful, good looking, drove a nice car."

"No specifics like whether he was tall or average height, his body type, hair color, clean shaven, what he did, or anything along those lines?"

"Not that Tiffany identified."

"Hmm… Spencer Dunn drives a Beemer; but nothing else she shared gives us much to build on."

Donnelly was confused, "But we've got the guy on video; and the victim in the trunk of his car. So is it that big a deal that none of her friends knew the guy?"

"Sure, we may have enough with what we've got; assuming DNA fills in the blanks," Nash replied. "But you know me; I want a boat load of evidence when I present a case to the Prosecutor."

"Understood," Donnelly nodded. She then continued, "Tiffany added that the reason she didn't consider Natalie to be missing is because even though she hadn't seen her in a couple of weeks, she *had* talked to her. Plus; she knew Natalie had been at the apartment."

"What was her basis for coming to that conclusion?"

"Natalie had picked up some of her makeup, along with a change of clothes."

"How do we know it was Natalie and not her abductor?"

"I had the same question," Donnelly replied, "and Tiffany said that Natalie had either called or left a note saying that she'd stopped by."

"Does Tiffany still have the notes?"

"I didn't think to ask; sorry."

"We need to get those notes if she still has 'em."

"Got it."

"What else?"

"Concerning Natalie's backing away from her friends," Donnelly replied. "Tiffany said that the group started getting concerned when Natalie seemed to be making up excuses for not getting together;

almost as if they were rehearsed responses."

"Or she had something to hide," Nash concluded.

"Exactly," said Donnelly, "Like wanting to hide any signs of physical abuse."

A notion hit Nash, "Wait a minute; were Natalie's 'stopped by the apartment' messages always left after-the-fact?"

"Do you mean were they "I stopped by" in lieu of "I'll be stopping by"?"

"Correct."

"Yes; I believe that's the case."

"So, maybe it wasn't Natalie who stopped by, but instead was her abductor?"

"And thus perhaps there's evidence of our suspect having been there?" Donnelly concluded.

"Precisely," Nash replied. Something dawned on her, "By the way, where's Dirk?"

"He's been running down info on our suspect."

The office door opened and in walked Brogan.

"Speak of the devil," Nash thumb-pointed at Brogan.

"What did I do?" Brogan replied as he entered the space.

"I was just wondering what you were up to," Nash replied.

"Digging up dirt on Spencer Dunn," Brogan responded. He looked to Donnelly and inquired, "Hey Laura, did you let Kenz know that it looks like we've I.D.'d our victim?"

Donnelly nodded in the affirmative.

"So, what's the dirt on Mister Dunn?" Nash directed to Brogan.

"Not so much 'dirt' actually, just a few details: Makes a decent living as a salesman with Premium Motors."

"A used-car lot?"

"Yep; but they specialize in nicer cars like BMW, Mercedes, Audi, Porsche, Lexus, and the like," Brogan replied, "Which is why he does okay financially."

"What else?"

Brogan grabbed his memo pad, "Obviously you already know his age and address, and the fact that he has no family in the area," he flipped a page. "I talked to a female friend of his who said she did his Mad Hatter makeup Saturday. She said he told her that he was going bar-hopping, but didn't say where."

"What was her name?"

"Candace Olsen," Brogan replied. "She also said that Spencer didn't have any girlfriends; at least not that she knew of. She said he was one of those guys who's 'always the guy friend; never the boyfriend'," he added with air-quotes.

"Hmm… that could definitely mess with one's ego," Donnelly chimed in.

"Agreed," Nash added.

"I also asked Candace how Spencer was with others; specifically, with women," said Brogan. "And she said he was always 'the nice guy'."

"No occasions where he went off the rails?" Nash said.

"Not that she ever saw."

"And I take it that she lives within the area of cell tower pings that you mapped out?"

"Correct; and he was at her place in the eight o'clock to nine o'clock time frame, give or take."

"Anyone else there at the time?"

"A couple of Candace's girlfriends: Cindy Bergman and Gillian Shields," Brogan replied. "But I haven't had a chance to follow-up with them." He closed his memo pad, "And that's all I've got."

"You're going to add all of that to the board, correct?" Nash said.

"Of course."

Nash's cell phone buzzed. "Hey Evan, I've got Dirk and Laura with me, I'm going to put you on the speaker," Nash said as she answered her phone.

"Just a minor update on the evidence in Spencer Dunn's car," Lowell stated. "The DNA evidence in the trunk includes both female and male specimens."

"Are we talking the perp's DNA? Or is there a male victim out there somewhere?"

"No telling at this point," Lowell replied, "but since you've got a suspect in custody we should have at least a part of that answer fairly soon."

"Would that really tell us much?" Nash responded. "After all, as the owner of the car it would be normal for his DNA to be there?"

"That's true; along with any previous owners, auto shops, detail shops, and others," Lowell responded. "But aspects such as quantity, locations, and whether there is a mixing of DNA specimens can help us paint a portrait."

"Mixing of DNA specimens?" Nash replied. "Do you mean something like a blood sample that indicates it's a mixture of two individuals, thus tending to imply an altercation between them resulted in a shared blood pool?"

"Exactly."

"You and your team never cease to amaze me with your investigative abilities."

"I appreciate that," Lowell responded. "And that's all I had for you at this time."

"In that case, I have something for you," Nash replied. "We got a promising lead concerning the possible identity of the victim. The name is Natalie Copeland; I'll send both you and Val her photo and associated info. I'm thinking dental records will be the best bet for a positive I.D."

"Forensically, I concur," said Lowell. "And I assume you'll be hunting down her next of kin?"

"Absolutely," Nash replied. "Let me know how things go on your end."

"Will do."

Nash hung up her phone.

"What do you think?" Brogan asked Nash.

"When you put a name to the face a whole new reality sets in," Nash sighed.

"Ain't that the truth," Brogan responded.

17

It had been several minutes since Nash exited her home and headed back to work following her lunch break. Still within the home, Ian stood silent–frozen in a moment of reflection. His heart was pounding, courtesy of the close encounter he'd had when Nash showed up unexpectedly.

He sat and stared at the closed lid of his laptop computer. Within its screen resided the mystery of Lyle Casey; and it was taunting him. He grappled with the potential consequences of continuing his attempts to unravel that mystery.

He took a breath. "Well, hell; it can't hurt to do a little more digging," he raised the lid on his laptop. "Let's see what Monterey County records show," he clicked and scrolled.

"Whoa; here's a stroke of luck–the same person has owned the Pacific Grove property for the past thirty years. Let's hope you have a good memory, or good records, or both," he said as he punched the owner's number into his phone. He stopped himself just before he hit 'Send'. "Shit; I need to come up with a backstory, a reason for my call, a script."

He grabbed a sheet of paper and commenced jotting-down notes. After several minutes of putting pen to paper he grabbed his phone. "Okay; let's do this," he said as he hit 'Send'.

"Hello," echoed through the phone.

"Mister Charles Titus?" he asked of the gentleman.

"Who wants to know?" the man replied.

"My name is Ian Monroe, I got your name through Monterey County property records," Ian responded.

"If you're a real estate agent I'm not interested."

"No Sir; I'm actually trying to find information about a former tenant of yours."

"You're a debt collector?"

"Not at all; I'm merely looking for some general information about a Mister Lyle Casey."

"Lyle Casey?" Mister Titus was befuddled, "That was over ten years ago; what are you… a cop?"

Ian had not expected such a response. "Uh… no," he stammered, "What… what makes you ask that?"

"His disappearance; and the scene at the apartment," Mister Titus explained, "I thought maybe his body, or that of his lady friend, had been discovered after all these years and you're a cop looking into the case."

Ian's heart nearly jumped out of his chest. He suddenly regretted his decision to delve into Nash's past. He hadn't truly believed that Nash had killed Lyle as she had articulated as being nothing more than a dream, but his curiosity had gotten the best of him. He now found himself in a quandary: Should he end the search now, thank the gentleman for his time, and hang up? Or had he ventured so far down the rabbit hole that the only option, in his mind, was to continue digging in the hope that an exit would reveal itself? He also realized that the ruse behind his inquiry had gone off-script. He stood in stunned silence as he pondered his dilemma; forgetting the fact that there was someone on the other end of the line awaiting a response.

"Uh… Mister Monroe?" Mister Titus probed.

"Sorry," Ian replied and then tested the waters, "Actually I'm a… a Private Investigator looking into Mister Casey's disappearance."

"So, I was essentially correct."

"Yes, Sir," Ian responded with increased confidence as his subterfuge appeared to have passed its first step. "With that in mind, I was wondering if you could share any details you might recall surrounding Mister Casey and… well… his disappearance?"

"Hard to forget," Mister Titus replied, "Considering the condition of the apartment," he paused in thought, "along with the events that had led up to that point."

Ian stood silent–the intrigue building.

"I remember the rent had come due... well, overdue... which had become a recurring theme," Mister Titus continued. "And it never made sense that I constantly had to hound him for the rent; judging by his car and his wardrobe he was doing very well financially, unless..." he stopped himself as a notion hit him.

"Unless...?" Ian prodded.

"Unless he was spending all of his money on a fancy wardrobe and nice car in order to impress others," Mister Titus said, "To portray himself as being more successful than he actually was." He pondered the notion, "Now that I think of it; that would explain a lot."

"How do you mean?"

"He had this way about himself; you know... a smooth-talker... a schmoozer even. The guy had the looks, the sense of style, the attitude... the kind of guy that could 'work a room' as they say," Mister Titus replied. "In fact; do you know what most people said about him?"

"What's that?"

"They said he was *the guy that every woman wanted; and that every man wanted to be*," Mister Titus responded. "But I was on to him."

"You were on to him?"

"Yeah; his act," said Mister Titus. "His whole persona was a 'sales pitch'. Most folks seemed to fall for it, but once they got to know him they began to see through his façade."

"Really?"

"It would start with subtle jabs. For example: because I was always having to hound him for his rent he started referring to me as 'Tight-ass' instead of 'Titus'. Not a super big deal, right? But a pattern was beginning to emerge; it wasn't hard to see that he considered everyone else to be beneath him," Mister Titus said. "He also tended to get a little too '*friendly*', if you know what I mean, with the ladies; even when their boyfriends or husbands were around… who I heard had grown quite agitated about his actions." He thought for a moment and added, "Not to mention that he was obviously disrespecting his own lady friend with his behavior. And that wasn't even the worst of it."

The statement drew Ian's concern, "That wasn't the worst of it?" he probed.

"There had been complaints of yelling and verbal abuse, along with worries about possible physical abuse," Mister Titus replied. "Other tenants and adjacent shop owners thought he might be roughing her up… his lady friend… based on the fact that the abusive language was always his voice–never hers. And then no one would see or hear from her for days."

"Son of a bitch," Ian sighed. His protective instinct suddenly took over, "Wait a minute… are you telling me that no one called the authorities on the woman's behalf?"

"To be honest I don't really know. Those with first-hand knowledge might have, or perhaps she herself called," Mister Titus replied. "Everything I knew was second or third-hand; and I didn't think to ask the cops when they showed up."

"Wait, what… the cops showed up?"

"Yeah; after I entered the apartment and was thrown for a loop by what I discovered: The bedroom was a disaster-zone; like someone had hurriedly gathered up belongings and scattered. There was blood on the sheets and pillowcases, and more blood on a washcloth and towel in the bathroom–along with the sink. The first thought that came to mind was that a jealous boyfriend or husband decided to teach '*Mister Dreamboat*' a lesson," Mister Titus explained. "Or maybe they were aware of his treatment of his lady friend and decided to intervene."

"You don't think his lady friend had anything to do with his disappearance, do you?"

"I… uh… that thought never crossed my mind," Mister Titus replied.

"I just figured she took off to get away from the guy, not that she went into hiding so that she wouldn't be implicated in his disappearance."

"Hmm…" Ian took a moment to process the information. "So, if the cops came out and investigated, why am I coming up empty in regard to his disappearance?"

"You'd have to ask them," Mister Titus replied. "All I can tell you is this: They came out and went through the place, but determined that there wasn't enough there to consider it a crime scene; not unless a Missing Persons Report came in or some other evidence of foul play turned up."

"And that was it?"

"Yep; never heard from either one of them again; nor from the cops for that matter," Mister Titus replied.

"What about his work; did you or the cops check with them?"

"I called them while I was waiting for the cops to arrive and they said he never showed up there, either; didn't even stop in to collect his last paycheck, which was one more reason I thought something happened to the guy," Mister Titus replied. "I have no idea if the cops ever talked to them."

"Do you remember where he worked?"

"He was a sales rep for a local furniture store. They went out of business about five or six years ago."

"Damn," Ian responded.

"Anything else?" asked Mister Titus.

"Uh… no," Ian replied. "Thank you for your time."

Mister Titus responded with a simple, "Yup," and hung up.

Ian sat in a stupor–staring at his phone. "Holy shit," he exhaled and slumped back against the sofa. He glanced down at his hands–they were shaking.

18

The morning sky was afire, courtesy of the burgeoning sunrise. "Red sky at morning, sailors take warning," Detective Nash said to herself as she stood next to her cruiser and embraced the scene. She trekked to the door of the Sheriff's Office, grasped and turned the handle, and walked across the threshold. Entering the office she was struck by a curious sight: Sheriff Steven Clarke perusing the whiteboard.

Sheriff Clarke glanced back toward the entryway. "Since I was stuck in Court yesterday afternoon I figured I'd get here early to get an idea as to how your case is going," he said to Nash. "I see you have a possible I.D. on the female victim," he added.

"Yeah; looks promising," Nash replied. "If you call the single act of a murder victim getting identified as 'promising'," she added with air-quotes.

"It's all relative; unfortunately," Clarke responded.

Nash nodded.

"Natalie Copeland," Clarke said as he stared at the trio of images.

"Yep," Nash said.

"A call just came in from her parents, Gary and Nancy Copeland."

"How did that go?"

"Not good; as you might imagine," Clarke replied. He looked at his watch, "They're planning to show up at the Coroner's Office at nine o'clock to make the identification."

"I'll be there," said Nash. "Hopefully they'll feel up to sharing information about their daughter."

"That could be a tough one; you may have to resign yourself to being nothing more than a source of information and of moral support at this point."

"Understood," Nash replied.

"And how goes your investigation into the Officer-involved shooting?"

"I've been working it under the radar," Nash replied. "In fact, my plan is to focus primarily on that case this morning before heading to the Coroner's Office." She paused and added, "I also plan to take another crack at our suspect-slash-victim, Spencer Dunn, this afternoon."

"Sounds good," Clarke responded. "Keep me posted," he added as he turned and headed toward his office.

Nash stared at the board. A timeline was coming together, but the gaps within the overall portrait were significant. She grabbed a pen and commenced to jot down a list of open action items. After several minutes she pushed the list aside and broke out her investigative notes regarding Officer Wilberforce's shooting of an unarmed man. To complement her notes she grabbed her copy of the Officer's official report. She then logged onto her computer and brought up the various dash-cam and body-cam videos related to the incident.

Nash was knee-deep in memos, folders, and reports when Brogan and Donnelly arrived. She glanced up from her desk, "When you two get settled we need to go over the plan for the day." She looked at her watch, "I have to meet Natalie Copeland's parents at the Coroner's Office at nine o'clock."

Brogan and Donnelly doffed their jackets, grabbed their memo pads, and met Nash at the whiteboard.

"We've got a lot on our plate today," Nash started, "We'll be adding to the board, utilizing maps, talking to knowledgeable parties, jotting down facts, compiling notes, you name it."

"Understood," Brogan and Donnelly replied in unison.

"For the chronology and timeline on the board," Nash gestured, "be sure to include everything we already know, and start peeling the onion on the various leads we've gotten thus far."

"For both Dunn and Natalie; correct?" Brogan responded.

"And Officer Wilberforce," Nash replied. "Remember that we've got two lines of investigation. Also note that there will be at least two intersects between them."

Brogan nodded.

Nash looked to Donnelly, "Laura, we need to get everything we can from Natalie Copeland's friends, starting with Tiffany."

"Do you want me to ask her about the notes that Natalie left, if she has them?" Donnelly replied.

"Yes; along with any voice mail messages she left, all calls made between the two of them, plus those with any of Natalie's other friends."

"Can't we just get Natalie's phone records from her cell provider?"

"Remember, a positive identification has not yet been made, so all we can do at this point is request information from her friends. Once we've got the I.D. we'll delve into her cell phone records."

"Got it," Donnelly jotted in her memo pad.

Nash turned her focus to Brogan, "Dirk, take the map we have of Spencer Dunn's cell phone pings, along with the map Lowell built regarding the likely options that Spencer took from the point he was pulled over, and overlay the two."

"Looking to dial-in all of his movements, and possibly get an idea as to the location of his hideout where Natalie was held captive?" Brogan said.

"Correct." Nash pointed at Donnelly, "And along those lines: Laura, go through county records and dig up all properties owned by Spencer Dunn and his family."

Donnelly nodded, and jotted.

Nash gestured toward her desk. "As part of developing the chronology and timeline related to Officer Wilberforce, go through his official report of the incident, which is on my desk," Nash stated, "and all of the dash-cam and body-cam videos, which I have up on my screen."

"I'm assuming you want us to note the specific places, and the durations, that he and Spencer Dunn were at those locations?" Brogan asked.

"You got it," Nash replied. "And when going through the Officer's report, make sure you don't confuse his 'opinions'," she said with air-quotes, "with the facts."

"Understood," Brogan replied.

Nash looked at her watch. "Okay; you two get at it," she directed, "destiny awaits me at the Coroner's Office."

19

Detective Nash was dreading this next stop. With rare exception, a seasoned investigator has an ability to view a crime scene's sheer hideousness through a technical lens. However, two related aspects of a case can leave a gut-wrenching impact upon even the most hardened detective: next-of-kin notifications, and a parent looking upon their now-lifeless child in order to provide a positive identification.

Nash wheeled her cruiser into the parking lot of the Coroner's Office and scanned the area. All indications were that Natalie Copeland's parents had not yet arrived. She pulled into a spot, exited her cruiser, walked to the doorway, and entered the facility; she was immediately met by Deputy Coroner Valerie LaGrange.

"Hey Val," Nash said to LaGrange, "I'm assuming you heard that Natalie Copeland's parents should be here any moment to identify the victim?"

"Yes," LaGrange replied. "And it will be a mere formality since we've already made a positive I.D. via dental records."

"I had suspected as much," said Nash. "Under the circumstances, when the parents arrive, how about we make them aware of that fact?"

"In the hopes that they might reconsider viewing their daughter in her current state?" said LaGrange.

"Exactly."

A buzz rang out at the entryway. Nash reached over, grasped the door handle, and opened the door. A very well-dressed couple in their mid-to-late forties entered the facility. Once inside, Nash extended her hand, "Mister and Misses Copeland?" Nash said, "Detective Nash with the Sheriff's Office."

The gentleman grasped Nash's hand, "Gary Copeland," he said. "This is my wife, Nancy," he added.

"I'm sorry we have to meet under such circumstances," Nash said as she shook hands with the couple. She turned to LaGrange, "This is Deputy Coroner Valerie LaGrange, the County Medical Examiner."

LaGrange extended her hand to the couple. "My condolences," she said.

Gary Copeland made an astute observation, "If you are offering condolences before we've even identified the body I assume that means you've already made a positive identification?"

"Through dental records," LaGrange replied, "Yes, Sir."

Nancy Copeland let out a muffled groan as she buried her face in her hands.

"With that in mind," LaGrange nodded toward Nash, "Detective Nash and I were thinking there is really no reason for you to view the body."

Nash jumped in, "You should remember her the way she was; not in her current state."

Gary glanced over at Nancy; an unspoken request for her thoughts.

"I have to see her," Nancy declared.

Gary looked back at Nash and LaGrange; no words were necessary.

"I understand," LaGrange stated. She nodded toward a door that separated the Waiting Area from Autopsy, "If you'll follow me," she began to walk.

Nash stood aside and offered an 'after you' gesture to Gary and Nancy, and the three of them followed LaGrange into the autopsy area.

LaGrange led the group to, what appeared to be, a body covered by a sheet. Nancy grasped Gary's hand and squeezed with a grip borne of fear and anxiety.

LaGrange, Nash, and the couple gathered around the body. LaGrange, at the head, grasped the sheet and stated to the couple, "I'm going to pull back the sheet for only a second or two; long enough for you to give me a nod of recognition."

Gary looked at Nancy. "Okay," Nancy said. "Okay," Gary mimicked.

LaGrange pulled back the sheet. "Yep," Gary said and then turned away.

"Oh my God! Nooooo!!" Nancy yelled and buckled to her knees. She began to sob incessantly.

Gary knelt down and wrapped his arms around his wife in an attempt to comfort her. He tried to remain stoic, but he was unable to hide his quivering chin and the tear running down his cheek.

Nash glanced at LaGrange. The two of them walked over to the couple. "Let's go back to the Waiting Area," Nash said to Gary and Nancy.

"Come on, dear," Gary said to Nancy as he helped her to her feet.

Gary turned to Nash, "You've got the bastard in custody, correct?"

"Yes, Sir," Nash replied.

"What's his name?"

"I'm sorry, Sir; but that information cannot be shared until the suspect is officially charged."

"And when will that be?"

"That's up to the Prosecutor," Nash stated. "But I assure you, he is not going anywhere."

Gary stood silent.

Now in the Waiting Area, Nancy eased herself into a chair; Gary sidled up next to her.

"I realize you might not feel like talking right now, but it would be of great assistance to our case if you're able to provide us some details about your daughter," Nash said to the couple.

Gary looked at Nancy; Nancy nodded 'okay'.

Nash took the hint, "We learned a fair amount from Natalie's roommate, Tiffany," she said.

"They both attend the Tacoma campus of the University of Washington," Gary stated. "They've been friends since junior high."

Nash jotted in her memo pad. "Tiffany said that she and her friends were concerned about a new boyfriend of Natalie's; that she became distant ever since she started seeing him."

"We noticed that as well," Gary nodded toward his wife.

"Apparently Natalie shared very little about him; not even his name," Nash commented.

"Same here," Gary replied. "All we got was that he was 'older'," he added.

"Did she say how much older?"

"No."

"Tiffany also said that she hadn't seen Natalie in a couple of weeks, although she had heard from her."

"We've been on vacation," Gary replied. "Even when we're around we try to avoid being helicopter parents; providing her a certain amount of space."

"So, you hadn't heard from her recently?"

"No."

Nancy clenched Gary's arm and then gazed upon his eyes. "I can't go through this right now," she sobbed.

"Yes, dear," Gary said and then looked over at Nash.

"I understand," Nash responded.

"Perhaps we can try again later," Gary said to Nash, "Maybe tomorrow?"

"Of course," Nash replied. "Thank you very much for your time."

Gary helped Nancy up, and the two of them exited the facility.

Nash turned to LaGrange. "The worst part of the job," she said.

"I agree," LaGrange replied.

20

Detective Nash was fighting a range of emotions as she made her way along a backcountry road between the Coroner's Office and Bennington General Hospital. Considering her current state, she wasn't sure if taking another crack at her suspect Spencer Dunn at this time was a smart move. She was normally laser-focused in the performance of her duties, but the heart-wrenching breakdown of Natalie Copeland's mother was weighing heavily upon her. Could she maintain her composure during the interview? Or would the responses from Spencer stoke the embers of rage burning within?

As she entered the second floor corridor of the hospital it dawned on Nash just how much of a fog her mind had been in: the trek from her cruiser, through the entryway, past the reception area, and her climb up the stairs was nothing but a blur. She stopped in her tracks to gather her thoughts. She checked to make sure she had her cell phone, and then grabbed her memo pad and flipped through the pages. "Okay, let's do this," she said to herself.

"Good morning," Nash said to the Officer standing post outside of Spencer Dunn's room.

"Detective," the Officer acknowledged.

Nash entered the room and was pleased to see that no doctor was there to potentially impede her interview.

Spencer Dunn looked up from his bed. "Are you here to get rid of these shackles?" he said to Nash as he pointed to his handcuffed wrist.

Nash was taken aback by Spencer's descriptor. "That's an interesting term you used there," she said.

"What's that?" Spencer replied.

"Shackles."

"Isn't that what they call these things?"

"Most people refer to them as handcuffs."

"Whatever."

"And sorry," Nash said, "Neither you nor your shackles are going anywhere at this time."

"Then why are you here?"

"I mentioned the other day that I'd be back with more questions."

"And I already told you that I'm innocent," Spencer replied. "Which means you must be here to eliminate me as a suspect so that you can go find the REAL killer."

"That would be all well and good, but the evidence suggests otherwise."

"I told you my car was obviously stolen, so whatever evidence you found there is bogus."

"Oh yeah?" Nash replied and then extracted her cell phone. "Then how do you explain this?" she said as she showed Spencer a compilation of the dash-cam and body-cam videos from the moment that Officer Wilberforce pulled him over.

"What the hell?!" Spencer commented in disbelief. "That's… that's not me," he said. "It can't be."

"And how about the fact that the trunk of your car contained not only the woman the Officer discovered, but blood and DNA from several *other* people?" Nash piled on.

Spencer looked bewildered. He grasped for a response, but before he had a chance to speak a gentleman in a suit suddenly entered the room. Unbeknownst to both Nash and Spencer, 'the suit' had been standing within earshot outside the door. "I'm Trent Lang, Mister Dunn's attorney," the gentleman said to Nash. "Mister Dunn will not be answering any more questions without the presence of counsel."

This was an unexpected turn of events for Nash. She glanced over at Spencer, whom appeared to be just as surprised as Nash.

"I'd like to see the video you claim is that of my client," Attorney

Lang nodded at Nash's cell phone.

"I'm sure the Prosecutor will gladly share it with you once charges have been filed," Nash responded.

"You're refusing to let me see it right now?" Attorney Lang replied. "Do you have something to hide?"

"Not at all," Nash responded as she held up her phone for the attorney.

Attorney Lang viewed the video and then commented, "I look forward to receiving my copy."

Nash turned to Spencer, "Now that your attorney is here; do you wish to continue this interview?"

Spencer glanced at his attorney and then responded, "Uh, no; not at this time."

Attorney Lang turned to Nash, "And to answer your question about blood and DNA in the trunk of my client's vehicle: He is an assistant rugby coach and all of the team's uniforms get tossed into a mesh bag for laundering."

Nash responded with a hint of skepticism, "And subsequently into the trunk of your client's car, I assume?"

"That's correct."

A thought came to Nash's mind, but she stood quiet; maintaining a poker face.

"In addition," Attorney Lang continued, "My client had several drinks that evening, and as you can see by your own video the gentleman in question seemed unencumbered. In fact, the Officer did not even administer a breathalyzer test."

"There are plenty of highly-functional drunks out there," Nash responded.

"You've experienced a few, have you?"

"Yes I have; including my own father," Nash replied. "And an Officer failing to administer a breathalyzer test is hardly exculpatory," she added. "Besides; your client could have drunk himself silly after he got home."

Attorney Lang paused in thought and, realizing he had no reasonable response, changed the subject, "We will also be requesting the Prosecutor to levy charges against the Officer who shot Mister Dunn."

"The involved Officer is currently under investigation by an outside agency," Nash responded. "Once that investigation is concluded, the results will be presented to a Grand Jury for determination as to whether the Officer shall be indicted. That is standard procedure."

"I understand you are the one performing the investigation of the Officer's conduct?"

"That's correct."

"But aren't you also investigating the woman who was killed?"

"Yes."

"Isn't that a conflict of interest?"

"Not at all," Nash replied, "they are two separate incidents."

"Are they?" Attorney Lang pushed back. "The Officer who gunned-down an unarmed man… my client, is the same Officer who pulled over my client's vehicle without cause; a vehicle that my client wasn't even driving at the time, having been stolen."

"As you are well aware, we have him on video," Nash countered.

"You mean the video of my client being shot in cold blood by an overzealous Officer?"

"I mean the video of your client with the vehicle in question that *you just watched*," Nash responded with a 'what the hell?' scowl.

"And I'm sure that my client has stipulated that it was not he who was driving the car, and thus not he whom is on your video?"

"He did," Nash crossed her arms. "And he wasn't very convincing on that point. In fact, he sounded more like he was surprised that he'd been caught."

"I'd say you are reading more into his statement than is actually there."

"And I'd say that neither you, nor I, are Judge or jury."

"Nonetheless, the issue sounds like a conflict to me."

"It appears that you and I may have to agree to disagree."

"I guess we'll just have to see what a higher authority has to say about that."

Nash walked to the door and turned back to Spencer. "Until next time," she said.

When Nash got to her car she jumped in, grabbed her phone, scrolled through the contacts, and hit 'Send'.

"Captain O'Rourke," echoed through the phone.

"Hey Sean; it's Kenz," Nash said, "Spencer Dunn just lawyered-up."

"He's unwilling to talk?" O'Rourke replied. "Or was he starting to incriminate himself?"

"You know I can't talk about that."

"Then why the call?"

"For one, it looks like his lawyer's defense tactic is to 'go on the offensive'."

"What does that mean?"

"He said that he'll be requesting the Prosecutor to levy charges against Wilberforce."

"Trying to muddy the waters by disparaging the arresting Officer?"

"I informed him how such investigations work, so that aspect should be a non-starter," Nash replied. "But it could be a political nightmare if he starts talking to reporters and trying the case in the Court of Public Opinion."

"Public opinion?!" O'Rourke began to rail, "We've got the victim in the trunk of his car; not to mention him on video behind the wheel and subsequently fleeing the scene!"

"I'm with you on that," said Nash. "But hey, I'm just the messenger."

"Yeah, I know," O'Rourke sighed.

"And I hate to say it, but there's more."

"I was afraid of that."

"On that same subject, his lawyer is also looking to have the investigation into the shooting taken out my hands and given to another jurisdiction."

"What the hell's the basis for that?"

"He says that I have a conflict of interest," Nash replied, "with me also working the murder of Natalie Copeland, the woman found in the trunk of Dunn's vehicle."

"That doesn't make any sense."

"Not to you and me, but if he gets the ear of a sympathetic Judge…"

"Oh crap," O'Rourke interrupted, "What if he gets it to Judge Wentworth?"

"Wentworth? Is he the one who was barred from hearing criminal cases by the County Prosecutor?"

"That's the Judge."

"What was the deal with him?"

"Wentworth had a disagreement with prosecutors over whether charging papers should explicitly say a crime occurred in Slaughter County."

"Okay, you've lost me."

"Wentworth ruled a drunken-driving suspect *not guilty* because he, the Judge, objected to the police report that gave the address or milepost, but did not specifically state that the alleged crime occurred in Slaughter County."

"You've got to be frickin' kidding me?"

"Nope."

"A drunk-driver got off because the charging papers identified an address that is located within Slaughter County but did not specifically say 'the crime occurred in Slaughter County'?"

"Go figure, huh?"

"Unbelievable," Nash shook her head. "Well, kudos to the County Prosecutor for barring this guy from hearing future criminal cases."

"I agree, but his ban may have been lifted by now."

"I guess we'll have to cross that bridge when we get to it."

"So, if your investigation into my Officer gets taken out of your hands, then what?"

"My concern is another jurisdiction going beyond the relevant facts."

"How do you mean?"

"The only actions relevant to Officer Wilberforce's culpability regarding the shooting of Spencer Dunn are those which occurred immediately leading up to, and at the moment of, the shooting."

"I agree."

"Well, another jurisdiction might take what occurred earlier in the evening, when Wilberforce pulled him over," Nash replied, "and add that to the events resulting in the shooting."

"Why would they do that?"

"From my perspective," Nash explained, "the purpose would be to paint a broad and unflattering picture of the Officer when presenting the case to the Grand Jury."

"You think another jurisdiction would throw a police officer under the bus?"

"I don't know if they would go that far, but they could be concerned about the optics if it appears they're going easy on someone simply because he's a cop."

"Well, that's a load of crap."

"You took a fresh look at the dash-cam and body-cam footage when Wilberforce pulled the suspect over, didn't you?"

"Yeah," O'Rourke sighed.

"So you understand my concern?"

"I do, but they'll have to get the current case files from you," O'Rourke replied, "which would only include what occurred at the time of the shooting, correct?"

"Potentially," said Nash. "But if they ask if there were any other interactions between the Officer and the gunshot victim I'd be compelled to provide that information."

"You're telling me my Officer won't be getting a fair shake?"

"Not at all; I'm just letting you know to be prepared for all possibilities."

"Understood," O'Rourke replied. "Thanks for the heads-up."

Nash ended the call and then scrolled through her phone's contacts and hit 'Send'.

"Evan Lowell," echoed through Nash's phone.

"Yeah, Evan; when you searched Spencer Dunn's car and home, did you come across a mesh bag?" Nash said.

"A mesh bag?" Lowell replied. "Like the kind I threw my laundry in back when I was in the Navy?"

"Precisely," Nash said. "In fact, it may have even had clothes still inside."

"I don't recall off the top of my head, but I'll go through the inventory and get back to you."

"Sounds good; thanks."

21

It had been a rough day for Nash, with her emotions running the gamut from empathy, to anger, to feeling disillusioned. Right now she was emotionally numb. She knew she could use some time to escape the madness and forget about work, even if only for an hour or two, but she wasn't sure she was up for it. Not that she wanted to sit and wallow in self-pity or self-reflection, but sometimes trying to 'put on a happy face' is an ordeal in and of itself. She knew, however, that canceling her committed meet-up with her sister would not be an option. After all, Nash had requested the get-together; trying to make up for having departed early from Katelyn's birthday party a few days prior.

Entering the lounge area of The Boat House Grill, Nash noticed Katelyn seated at a small hi-top table; she was swirling a glass of wine as if she was attending a tasting event. Nash spied a second glass of wine sitting patiently nearby. She took a seat and pointed to the glass, "Are you doubling-up, or is this one for me?" she asked Katelyn.

Katelyn smiled, stopped swirling her wine, and raised her glass. "Cheers," she said.

Nash got the hint, grabbed the nearby glass of wine, held it up and mimicked, "Cheers."

The two sipped their respective glasses of wine.

Nash set down her wineglass, "Sorry I had to bail out of your birthday bash the other day."

"Hey, you had to go out and save the world," Katelyn replied, "I get it."

"Not even close," Nash responded, "but thanks for the vote of confidence."

Katelyn was surprised by Nash's somewhat benign response; it was completely inconsistent with her typical humorous comeback.

"So hey," Nash continued, "Did you hear from your mother?"

"You mean YOUR mother?"

Nash grinned at the long-running joke between the two sisters.

"She sent me a Happy Birthday e-mail."

"No card, no call, just an e-mail?"

"I've pretty much given up on any expectations beyond that," Katelyn shrugged.

"You and me both," Nash sighed. "What about Bella?"

"She called," Katelyn replied, "Both to tease me about being an old lady now; and to bemoan the fact that she's only a year-and-a-half away from the big three-oh herself."

"YOU are an old lady now?" Nash responded, "Then what the heck does that make me?"

"You know you've always been a 'mother figure' to Bella," Katelyn replied, "much more than Mom."

Katelyn's revelation struck a chord with Nash. It dawned on her that being the eldest, the one whom everyone counted on for stability in the family, meant that no one had ever been there to catch her if she fell. She had to be the rock. It was an enormous responsibility to be placed upon someone in their youth, but if she had to do it all over again she wouldn't change a thing.

Nash emerged from her moment of reflection and asked, "Are those two still not speaking?"

"Bella hasn't forgiven Mom for the whole creepy-stepdad thing; and Mom's too proud to reach out to Bella."

"So the impasse continues," Nash shook her head. "I mean heck, Mister Creepy has been out of our lives for over twenty years."

"She seems scarred for life, unfortunately."

"Her and Mom, both," Nash replied. She took a sip of her wine and stared off into space.

Katelyn sat quiet for a moment and then asked, "So, what's up?"

"What do you mean?" Nash became defensive, "I was just looking to catch up since I missed most of your birthday celebration."

"I wasn't talking about that," Katelyn explained. "You just seem a bit out of sorts, not quite yourself."

"Oh, that," Nash sighed. "Today was just another bad day on top of several previous ones," she said. "Like getting kicked in the shin on a daily basis, and when you think it's finally over you turn around and get sucker-punched right in the face."

"Wow," Katelyn grew wide-eyed, "I'm sorry to hear that."

"It started Sunday at the Coroner's Office," Nash explained. "The sight of that girl who is not much younger than you and Bella," she took a breath, "Well, I pretty much just lost it."

"How do you mean?"

"I didn't break down in tears or anything like that, but believe it or not I actually yelled 'I'm sick of this shit'," Nash said. "Both Dirk and Val, the Deputy Coroner, were so surprised that they about jumped out of their shoes."

"Sick of it?" Katelyn replied. "Your job?"

"Sometimes," Nash confessed, "But that's not what I was referring to at the moment. It was seeing what all had happened to the victim."

"That bad, huh?"

"Yeah," Nash replied. "And then today the parents showed up to identify her," Nash took a breath. "The mother screamed in horror and literally fell to her knees." Nash shook her head, "It was awful."

Katelyn remained silent; unsure of how to respond.

"Anyway," Nash took a sip of her wine, "Enough about me; how was your party?"

"It was great," Katelyn replied. "It's amazing how big of a deal turning thirty is; it was like a rite of passage."

"In a sense you could say that it is," Nash replied. "Right up there with sixteen, eighteen, and twenty-one."

"Twenty-one; ugh, I gave up drinking for a month after that one."

"Yeah, we trolled quite a few bars in Seattle, didn't we?" An aspect of Katelyn's comment suddenly hit Nash, "Wait a minute," she gave Katelyn the stink-eye, "You gave up drinking for a month? You'd only been of legal age for a month; had you indulged in alcohol before you turned twenty-one?"

"I plead the fifth."

Nash grinned and shook her head.

"Anyway," Katelyn continued, "I had friends show up that I hadn't seen in years."

"Any old boyfriends hoping for a second chance?"

"Geez, I can't take you anywhere," Katelyn rolled her eyes and then took a sip of her wine.

"Well?" Nash prodded.

"A couple," Katelyn admitted. "But they were unsuccessful," she smiled like the Cheshire Cat and took another sip.

Nash grinned and took a sip of wine as well. "Oh geez, I almost forgot," she reached into her jacket pocket and extracted a card. "Your birthday present," she handed the card to Katelyn.

Katelyn's eyes lit up as she opened the card. "A Spa Weekend for you, me, and Bella at Harrison Hot Springs up in B.C.?"

"Canada's finest," Nash smiled.

"You're the best!" Katelyn gave Nash a hug.

Nash held up her wine glass, "Cheers!"

The two sisters toasted the moment.

"Oh hey, guess who stopped by?" Katelyn said.

"Who's that?"

"Aunt Ellie."

"Nice. What's she up to?"

"Livin' the dream. You know; retirement and all."

Nash nodded, "Can't argue with that one."

"She had some news," Katelyn commented.

"News?" Nash replied, "Good or bad?"

"It kinda depends," Katelyn hesitated; realizing her news could add to her sister's already-bad week.

"On what?"

"On one's perspective."

Nash's face scrunched-up. "What's with the evasive - deflective routine?"

Katelyn shrugged.

"Just out with it," Nash prodded.

Katelyn reached into her purse and extracted a piece of newsprint. "Dad's obituary," she said, "Aunt Ellie thought I might want to know that he died, and that I also might want a copy of his obit."

Nash grabbed the paper. "Last month," she observed while perusing the notification. "Did Aunt Ellie know the cause of death?"

"Alcohol poisoning."

"Somehow that doesn't surprise me," Nash shook her head.

"Look at the list of survivors," Katelyn pointed at the obituary. "Who are Todd and Bonnie?"

"Half-siblings I suppose," Nash replied. "But no wife listed I see."

"And no Bella, either," Katelyn said. "What's up with that?"

"Mom was pregnant with Bella when Dad left," Nash said, "so maybe he never knew about her?"

"Mom wouldn't have told him about Bella?"

"Who knows," Nash shrugged. "Or worse; maybe Dad thought Mom had an affair, and that Bella wasn't his?"

"Do you think that's why he left?"

"I have no clue on that one," Nash shook her head. "He was always drinking, hanging out with his buddies, coming home at all hours of the night. I think he just couldn't handle the responsibilities of being a husband and father."

"Geez," Katelyn shook her head and sipped her wine. "The whole thing sounds like some kind of trailer-trash Soap Opera," she added.

Nash sat and stared off into space. Katelyn realized that perhaps she had gone too far with her descriptor.

Nash broke out of her fog and grabbed her wineglass. "You could be right," she nodded and took a sip.

"You uh… you seem a bit more troubled by the news than I thought you might be," Katelyn said to Nash.

"To be honest, I'm a little surprised by my reaction as well," Nash replied. "It's weird," she started and then paused in thought. "I knew this day would come eventually. And since he'd been gone for so long I always figured it wouldn't really hit me; not like someone you'd spent your entire life with and then suddenly they have an accident, or get sick, and they're gone." She took a breath, "The thing is; you and Bella only knew him from stories, from the visions that grew out of your imagination. But for me, I have actual memories of him… of our time together."

"I see what you mean," Katelyn replied.

"Don't get me wrong," Nash responded, "I hated that he walked out on all of us without a word; and worse, letting the years pass by without an explanation or an apology, leaving us to grow up feeling the sting of rejection." She crossed her arms and shook her head, "What a horrible thing to put impressionable and vulnerable young kids through."

Katelyn was at a loss for words; she had never considered the perspective of her father as seen through the lens of her older sister's eyes.

"I guess it's just the finality of it all," Nash continued. "But now, whatever questions we might've had will never be answered," she sighed.

"To be honest, I'm glad I don't have the memories that you do; I'm not sure how I'd manage," Katelyn said.

Nash snapped out of her momentary malaise, "Sorry about getting a bit melancholy there."

"Not at all," Katelyn replied, "I probably shouldn't have brought it up."

"I'm glad you did; it's not like there's a good time for such news," Nash responded. "We'd have had to deal with it at some point."

"That's true." Katelyn thought for a moment, "What should I say to Bella?"

"Tell her that Aunt Ellie informed you of Dad's death," Nash replied, "but I wouldn't mention the obituary; Bella's had a hard enough life as it is."

"Yeah," Katelyn nodded and sighed.

22

Lying in bed, staring into the darkness, she reflected upon the past eighteen hours. Sleep is but a notion within the abstract when the mind is a jumbled mess: thoughts ranging from the facts, leads, and road blocks of her current case; to various 'what if' scenarios pertaining to her personal life. In regard to the latter: if she'd had a crystal ball perhaps a different path would have been taken, another choice made, an attempt to find answers by reaching out to ghosts from her past; but now it would be all for naught. Reconciliation, a concept which had been considered to be nothing more than "maybe someday" idle chatter shared with her sister, was gone forever.

23

In the wake of a restless, sleep-deprived, night Detective Nash trudged through the doorway of the Sheriff's Office and headed directly to the Break Room. She reached into the refrigerator and extracted her own personal stash, a Sumatra blend, and dumped a generous amount of grinds into the filter basket. She added water and hit 'Start'. She was seemingly fixated on her morning java as it began to trickle into the decanter, but that wasn't the case; she was pondering life in the face of adversity. Sometimes it defeats you; sometimes it's a catalyst for renewed determination.

Her concentration was broken by the sound of the office door opening. She looked at her watch, and then made her way toward the whiteboard.

"Hey Kenz," Donnelly said to Nash.

"Good morning," Nash replied, "Where's Lurch?"

Donnelly's face scrunched up, "Lurch?"

"The Addams Family," Nash responded. "My lame attempt at humor; it is Halloween after all."

"Ah…" Donnelly nodded. "He was right behind me."

The office door opened and in walked Brogan. "There's Lurch right now," Donnelly snickered as Brogan entered.

"Lurch?" Brogan responded.

"Kenz was asking where you were," Donnelly replied.

"Hey, it's Halloween," Nash said. "At least I didn't say 'Uncle Fester'."

"Lurch was cool; I'll take him over 'Uncle Fester' any day," Brogan replied.

"Speaking of Halloween," Donnelly said, "Is everyone all ready for the hobgoblins this evening?"

"Are you talkin' trick-or-treaters?" Brogan replied, "Or the hordes of nut-jobs who will potentially be out on the roads tonight?"

"Since it's the middle of the week I'm thinking we've already experienced the majority of nut-jobs this past weekend," Nash replied as she gestured toward the whiteboard.

"Good point," Brogan nodded.

"Okay," said Nash, "Are we ready to go over some status?"

"Absolutely," Donnelly responded. "In fact, both Dirk and I are interested in what all you got from Spencer Dunn yesterday."

"I had a feeling that would be your first line of inquiry," said Nash.

"Yeah," Brogan jumped in, "Were you able to get anything; or did you get derailed by his doctor once again?"

"Actually I got derailed by his attorney."

"His attorney?"

"He popped-in out of thin air just as I was blowing holes in Spencer's claims of innocence," Nash replied. "In fact, Spencer himself seemed to be surprised that an attorney showed up on his behalf."

"Sent by Dear Old Dad without even making Spencer aware of it?" said Brogan.

"That's how it came across to me," said Nash.

"What were the things he was saying before his attorney showed up?" Donnelly asked.

"Not much," Nash replied. "The one thing that was noteworthy concerned his response when I showed him the video footage."

"What was that?"

"He said, 'that can't be me, can it?'."

Brogan grew wide eyed. "Effectively admitting that it was him, but trying to claim ignorance as if he was drunk or stoned or otherwise impaired?"

"Yep," said Nash. "But an 'I don't remember' excuse does not negate physical and video evidence."

"That's a fact," Brogan replied. "Anything else?"

"Not from Spencer; but his attorney fired a few shots across the bow."

"Whoa; what were those?"

"I'm not going to go into all of the details, but we might lose the investigation into the Officer-involved shooting; you know... Wilberforce."

Brogan was not pleased at this news. "Are you kidding me? I've been busting my ass going through Barney Fife's dash-cam and body-cam footage frame-by-frame in order to capture every aspect of it and lay it out for you and the Grand Jury."

Nash gave Brogan the stink-eye, "Let's not get overly wound up over some blowhard attorney trying to make a big first impression with his new client," she replied. "For one: Nothing along those lines is going to happen anytime soon no matter what the attorney thinks; and right now we still own the case, so we can't cease momentum based on 'what ifs' or 'maybes'. And for two: Even if the case does get reassigned to someone else, anything we turn up will merely get transferred to whoever happens to draw the short straw."

"The short straw?" Brogan commented.

"You've watched the videos."

"Understood."

"And lastly: Aspects of your research are most certainly pertinent to Natalie Copeland's case."

"That's true," Brogan nodded.

"So, with all that behind us," Nash glanced between Brogan and Donnelly, "what have you two got?"

"As far as Wilberforce's actions go based on the videos, I've captured a chronology on the board," Brogan thumb-pointed.

"Since I've gone through the videos myself a couple of times already, I'll peruse your chronology later," Nash replied, "What else?"

"I looked into his family's properties," Donnelly stated. "Spencer Dunn doesn't own any, but his parents do, and they happen to be located within our area of interest: Spencer's home, which hasn't provided us with much, if any, evidence; and the Used Car lot where he works."

"His family owns the business?"

"They used to, but they sold it and moved to Arizona," Donnelly replied. "However, they still own both the property and the building, which they lease to Carl Jenkins, the current business owner."

"Crap; we need to check out that property."

"That's what I was thinking."

Brogan jumped in, "I actually talked to Carl Jenkins about Spencer Dunn. He does not yet know that Spencer's a suspect; just that he's in the hospital and is unable to have visitors outside of immediate family members. He gave me generic info about him being a personable guy, good salesman, no issues that he was aware of. He also said that Spencer worked Saturday from nine until six–took lunch from noon to one."

"Hmm… when we go to search the property we may have to make Jenkins aware that his employee is a suspect in a murder, otherwise I don't think he'd be too obliged to comply," Nash noted. "Either that or we just show up with a warrant."

"I think we need to keep in mind that his 'employee the suspect' also happens to be the son of the guy he leases the property from," Donnelly stated.

"Good point, Laura; that might make him somewhat hesitant in regard to his cooperation," Nash replied. "I'll go ahead and draft a warrant."

Brogan wasn't sure if he wanted to broach a certain subject, but he felt compelled to do so, "Hey Kenz; I heard that Natalie Copeland's parents made a positive I.D. of her remains yesterday."

Nash's demeanor turned solemn. "The mother's breakdown was so distressing that I had to grit my teeth and put up a façade in front of the two of them," she explained.

"It was that bad, huh?"

"The most heart-wrenching I've ever experienced."

Silence overtook the room. Brogan and Donnelly glanced at each other. Donnelly decided to take the conversation on a semi-related path, "After getting the positive I.D. I looked into Natalie's phone records," she said. "Her phone went silent two weeks ago; around the same time that she was last seen by her friends."

"What the hell?" Nash responded.

"And here's a red flag," Donnelly added, "The number that Tiffany currently has for Natalie is a burner. Tiffany said that Natalie lost her phone, but she and her other friends thought that the boyfriend may have had something to do with it."

"He took it? Or got jealous and tossed it?" Nash replied.

"Or he was that controlling," said Donnelly.

"Why are we getting personality descriptions of Natalie's boyfriend that don't seem to jibe with the version we're getting from friends of Spencer Dunn?" Nash commented.

"You've talked to him," Brogan directed to Nash. "What impression have you gotten from the man himself?"

"He's suffering from the physical and emotional trauma of a gunshot wound, and is on pain meds, so I haven't been able to get a good bead on the guy."

"Well hell, maybe he's a Jekyll and Hyde type?"

"Or worse," Donnelly added, "Ted Bundy?"

"Let's hope not," Brogan replied. "Otherwise we need to start looking for more bodies."

"But Bundy was charismatic," Nash noted, "Spencer Dunn has been described as 'always the guy friend never the boyfriend'."

"Maybe that's how he gets women to let their guard down; he comes across as non-threatening?" replied Brogan.

"Could be," Nash pondered. She turned to Donnelly, "Laura, did you get anything else from any of Natalie's friends?"

"Not really," Donnelly replied, "Other than Tiffany stating that she and Natalie attended U-dub Tacoma."

"That's the same word I got from Natalie's parents," Nash responded.

"Have you talked to the University to get info on her attendance… whether she had missed classes lately?"

"Not yet; I'll add that to my list."

"Spencer Dunn's not a student there, is he?"

Brogan jumped in with a response, "No, he's not."

Nash nodded. "Back to Natalie's phone records," she directed to Donnelly, "Any calls between her and Spencer Dunn before she quote-unquote lost her phone?"

"Not the cell phone number we have for him, or his work phone," Donnelly replied.

"Any calls between her and a burner phone?"

"I haven't gotten a chance to dissect all of her calls yet."

"Understood."

"Oh crap, I can't believe I almost forgot," Donnelly said as she headed toward her desk.

Nash looked at Brogan; he shrugged.

Donnelly returned with an evidence bag. She held up the bag and handed it to Nash, "Tiffany still had all of the notes that Natalie left at their place."

"Sweeeeet!" Nash replied. "Did she say whether they appeared to be in Natalie's handwriting?"

"She thought so, but couldn't say for sure."

Nash's cell phone rang. She glanced at the Caller I.D. It was Forensic Scientist Evan Lowell. "Hey Evan," Nash said as she answered the phone.

"Yeah Kenz, I've got some updates for you and your team," Lowell replied.

"Great; let me put you on the speaker," Nash replied as she made such a selection. "Okay; go ahead," she added.

"The blood and DNA in the trunk," Lowell started, "Some of the samples match Natalie Copeland. No surprise there of course, but we also have three other unidentified females."

"Three more women?"

"Yes."

"And 'unidentified' means no match in CODIS," Nash concluded.

"Unfortunately."

"Were you able to glean anything from the amounts of blood and DNA?"

"It wasn't a blood bath, so we cannot immediately jump to indications of a homicide," Lowell replied. "But blood and DNA from multiple persons in the trunk is, at the very least, odd."

"What about Spencer Dunn's lawyer saying that Dunn had routinely tossed dirty and bloody uniforms from an entire rugby team in the trunk?"

"That could be one explanation," Lowell replied. "But if that were the case you'd expect DNA from a whole team of individuals. And of course it would also imply that Spencer Dunn is coaching a girls team; is that the case?"

"His lawyer didn't provide specifics," Nash groaned.

"In addition," Lowell said, "we found no mesh bag or rugby uniforms that the lawyer described; not within the car, not at the home."

"What the hell?? The damn lawyer was throwing out a bunch of B.S. in order to try to cover for his client??" Nash vented.

"Obviously that's outside of my wheelhouse," Lowell replied, "But one could come to that conclusion."

Something dawned on Nash, "Hey, didn't you say earlier that there was DNA from a male as well?"

"I was just about to get to that," Lowell replied. "And yes; there is also blood and DNA from an unidentified male."

"Someone other than Spencer Dunn?"

"That's correct."

"And that's the blood and DNA that we were speculating belonged to Mister Dunn?"

"Correct again," Lowell replied. "Spencer Dunn's DNA is in the trunk as well, but only minimally, and only on the side areas, not the floor area; which is the exact opposite of the DNA of the unidentified male."

"I'm not quite getting what you're saying or implying," Nash admitted.

"I don't want to put the cart before the horse, or to jump to conclusions," Lowell replied. "But the placement of the unidentified male DNA is consistent with that of the female DNA."

"If I'm reading you correctly," Nash said, "We cannot positively state that the evidence indicates foul play, but in the off chance that such is the case we are potentially looking at four victims: three female and one male?"

"That's a great way to put it."

"Well crap; I wonder if that means we need to start digging into cold case files?"

"Don't you think that might be a bit premature?"

"I guess you're right," Nash replied. She thought for a moment, "What do you make of Spencer Dunn's DNA being solely on the side areas of the trunk?"

"We know he was wearing gloves when he was pulled over, so one might conclude that certain acts would dictate their use," Lowell responded, "and everyday run-of-the-mill acts would not."

"Good point," Nash replied. "Anything else?"

"Something that should make your day," Lowell responded, "The substance used to draw the frown on Natalie Copeland's face was lipstick; and it matched Spencer Dunn's 'Joker' smile."

"Son of a bitch," Nash replied. "Now I've got ya, you bastard."

"Yeah, hard to see how he can explain his way out of that one," Lowell concurred with Nash's proclamation. "Anyway, that's all I had," Lowell added, "How about you?"

"One more thing," Nash replied. "During the two-week timeframe when no one had seen Natalie Copeland; she allegedly stopped by her apartment, on more than one occasion, and left a note for her roommate."

"Was there something concerning about these notes?"

"Nothing obvious within their content; they were merely stating that she had stopped by."

"I'm assuming you have custody of them?"

"Correct; and I was going to drop them by, along with some of Natalie's handwriting samples."

"You want my team to check for DNA, fingerprints, and to analyze the handwriting?" Lowell asked.

"Yes; looking for potential evidence of her killer, and also that perhaps someone other than Natalie wrote one or more of the notes."

"Sounds good; I look forward to receiving them."

"I'll drop them by this afternoon," Nash said and hung up.

24

"I take it you're thinking these notes might have been a ruse to keep Natalie's friends from filing a Missing Persons Report?" Forensic Scientist Lowell said as Detective Nash handed him an evidence bag.

"That's one option," Nash replied. "But they also could be nothing more than Natalie simply making her roommate aware that she had stopped by the place."

"And you also have some known handwriting samples of Natalie's?"

"Yes," Nash replied and held out a second bag. "These are various notes, a birthday card; stuff like that."

"That should work."

"Any chance that the notepaper originated from Spencer Dunn's home?"

"Your guess is as good as mine; it's not something that was on our radar screen when we went through his place, so we'll have to take a fresh look."

"We should check his place of work as well; I've already drafted a warrant."

"I agree," Lowell responded. "Have you presented the warrant to a Judge, yet?"

"That's my next stop," Nash replied. "Assuming the Judge signs off on it how about we plan to hit up both Spencer's work and home tomorrow?"

"Sounds like a plan," said Lowell.

* * *

With a freshly-signed Search Warrant in-hand Detective Nash

glanced at the clock on her cruiser. She weighed the idea of heading back to the office, but the timing would have her arriving after the majority of personnel had departed for the day. Considering that she had put in extra hours for several days in a row, she decided that a relatively normal workday was a reasonable change of pace. She veered her cruiser toward home.

Various aspects of the case ran through her head as she traversed the local thoroughfares. She realized that one's own mind dictates when your workday is over, not some clock on the wall or the dashboard. So much for a brief reprieve from work.

Approaching her driveway she was surprised by the sight of Ian's car; this was the second time in just a few days that he was at her house at an abnormal time. It was not unusual for Ian to swing by her place, but it would typically occur around dinnertime or later; and seldom would be unannounced. She wondered if perhaps it had something to do with it being Halloween.

She walked through the doorway and scanned the living room—no sign of Ian, simply his laptop sitting open on the coffee table with various papers scattered nearby. She glanced over at the dining room and kitchen—nothing.

She made her way to the coffee table. What first caught her eye were the papers lying near the laptop; they consisted of handwritten notes detailing personal information, conversations, and historical data. As she shuffled through the pile she also noted printouts from various official websites. Her eyes grew wide and her heart began to race. She glanced at the laptop. She knelt down in front of the screen and began to scroll through various search modems. Her blood began to boil as she went through site after site.

Her search was interrupted by the whoosh of the bathroom toilet, followed by the rushing water via the sink. She stood up, grasped the stack of papers that had been lying on the coffee table, and awaited the bathroom visitor. Ian entered the room, took sight of Nash, and abruptly stopped in his tracks. Observing the stack of papers in Nash's hand, and her proximity to the laptop, Ian's face became flushed with anxiety.

"What the hell is this?!" Nash held up the papers. "You're looking into my past?!" she added.

"I uhh…" Ian stammered.

Nash threw the papers on the coffee table. "How do you even know this stuff?!!" she interrupted.

"I've been worried about you; the things you shared with me a while back about what happened to you in your twenties," Ian attempted to explain. "And then you had that nightmare the other night."

"And what the hell does that have to do with you sticking your nose into my past?!"

"That Lyle guy," Ian started.

"Lyle?" Nash interrupted. "Are you kidding me?!? You're jealous?!"

"No; that's not it."

"Then what?!!"

"He apparently just up and vanished off the face of the earth."

"Yeah? So?"

"So, I'm not talking a week ago or a month ago or even a year ago," Ian replied, "I'm talking twelve years ago."

"What're you getting at?"

"His last known residence was the place you two shared in Pacific Grove."

"Big frickin' deal," Nash glared.

"All indications are that the day he disappeared…" Ian took a breath, "is the same day that you took off."

"Okay, so his ego couldn't handle me walking out on him; surprise-surprise."

"There's more to it than that."

Nash crossed her arms; awaiting Ian's explanation.

"I talked to the landlord," Ian continued, "and when I asked about… you know… what's his name… he figured the guy's body had been discovered and I was a cop looking into it."

This news caught Nash's attention, "What would make him think that?"

"I kind of told him I was a Private Investigator."

Nash's eyebrows furled, "That's not what I meant."

"Oh, um, of course," Ian replied. "It had to do with the circumstances surrounding the guy's disappearance."

Nash's patience was running thin. "Okay; let's hear it," she pressed.

"He, the landlord, said that when he entered the apartment it looked like a crime scene," Ian explained. "The place was ransacked; in particular, the bedroom: there was a pile of clothes and hangers on the floor of the closet–nothing but empty hangers still on the rod. Dresser drawers were open–most of the clothing gone, the rest strewn about. There was blood on the sheets and pillowcases, with a trail leading to the bathroom and more blood… on some towels and the sink. The weirdest thing in the bathroom was that the shower curtain rod was lying in the tub–the curtain itself was gone."

Nash was skeptical, "Old Man Titus remembers that level of detail from something that happened a dozen years ago?"

"He provided a lot of the info," Ian replied, "the rest was from the police report."

This revelation drew Nash's ire, "Police report?!! What the frickin' hell?!!"

"Well, what I got from Titus sounded bad enough; but every place I turned in search of answers just made things worse," Ian defended. "He left no forwarding address; not with Titus… not with the Post Office. And according to Titus it was the same thing with his job; just up and vanished, didn't even stop to pick up his last paycheck." Ian took a breath, "So yeah… I called and talked to the local P.D."

Nash's glare increased in intensity.

"They said that they came out and surveyed the scene, noting the issues I had mentioned," Ian continued, "but did not see enough to consider it to be a crime scene… not unless a Missing Persons Report was filed or some additional evidence surfaced; which apparently never occurred."

"I assume you're going somewhere with all of this?"

"Like I said, the guy just up and vanished without a trace the same day you disappeared."

"Yeah… so?"

"You… umm…" Ian struggled, "You said you killed the guy."

"It was a DREAM!"

"But what about all the blood they found within the apartment?"

"It was probably mine, you jackass!"

Ian was shocked at the descriptor Nash threw his way, but he also realized he was treading on thin ice and one more ill-advised word would plunge him into a frigid abyss. Unfortunately he couldn't help himself… "But…" he stammered, "then what happened to him?"

"I don't know… and I don't WANT to know."

Ian stood silent.

Something suddenly dawned on Nash. "This is the crap you were trying to hide the other day when I came home for lunch, isn't it?" she said.

"I just…"

Nash cut Ian off before he could finish, "You can go now."

"What?"

"You heard me," Nash gestured.

Ian scooped up his papers, grabbed his laptop, and slowly trod to the front door. As he opened the door Nash threw a final shot his way, "By the way, *Sherlock,* did you consider that perhaps the landlord blurted out something about Lyle's body being discovered because HE is the one who made him disappear?"

Ian looked back at Nash. He realized that he had no response to the point that Nash had just made. He crossed the threshold; closing the door behind him.

25

A stone-faced Detective Nash walked through the entryway of the Sheriff's Office. She'd been beaten down and mired in emotional muck for the past several days, but her malaise had been overwhelmed by a single defining event: her discovery that Ian had been digging into not only her past but her personal life, and had unearthed questions within memories she had long since buried and had no desire to exhume. Her initial response to this revelation was anger, a powder keg ready to explode; but now her emotions were ranging from 'walking a tightrope between numb and walled-off' and 'simmering just below the boiling point'. She was suppressing the issues, for the moment, attempting to focus solely on her primary objective: bringing a killer to justice.

Brogan and Donnelly, working the whiteboard, turned to acknowledge Nash as she entered the space. "Mornin'," Brogan said.

Nash nodded a response; remaining silent. Brogan and Donnelly exchanged curious glances.

Nash removed her jacket and draped it over a chair, and then uttered, "Coffee?"

"Just made some," Brogan responded.

Nash disappeared toward the Break Room.

As soon as Nash was out of earshot Donnelly turned to Brogan and whispered, "What do you think is up with Kenz?"

"I have no idea," Brogan replied, "but it can't be good."

"Should we ask her what's up?"

"I'm not stepping onto that landmine."

Nash approached with coffee mug in hand. She stopped at the board, took a sip, and then stated, "What've we got?"

"I talked to the college," Donnelly replied, "They said Natalie's attendance had been sporadic in recent weeks."

"And I talked to her roommate Tiffany about the notes; asking if perhaps they originated from their apartment," said Brogan. "She said that she was pretty sure that was the case."

Nash's fuse got lit, "Are you kidding me?! I told you that Lowell and I were going to search the home!"

Brogan realized he had inadvertently stepped on one of the landmines he was hoping to avoid. "That's why I called," he began to explain before Nash cut him off.

"You purposely interjected yourself and potentially impeded an aspect of the investigation that I specifically stated was under my purview?" Nash interrupted.

"Not at all," Brogan clarified, "I was afraid that if the notes *did* come from their place that Tiffany might contaminate or use or toss the notepad and I wanted to make sure that didn't happen."

Nash realized she had jumped to conclusions and was taking out her frustrations on her team. She glanced between Brogan and Donnelly, took a breath, and responded, "Good call."

A hush of silence overtook the room as Nash appeared to stare into a void of quiet contemplation.

Brogan decided to test the waters, "Anything wrong?"

Nash broke out of her fog, "It's been frickin' hell-week and I'm sick of it! Not just the fact that every time we turn around we're dealing with some sort of B.S. on these two cases: Wilberforce and his rookie-like, borderline-incompetent, actions; Spencer Dunn's lawyer and his attempted bravado, not to mention apparently feeding me a line of crap about the rugby uniforms," she vented, "but other frickin' garbage on top of garbage I've had to deal with outside of these cases."

"Anything we can do?" Donnelly asked.

Nash hesitated for a moment and then responded, "Nah; just know that if I come across as being an ass-hat it has nothing to do with you two."

"Understood," said Brogan.

Nash paused in thought, glanced between Brogan and Donnelly, and then said, "What…" she took a breath, "What else do we have?"

"While I was talking to Tiffany she thought of something she had not previously shared," Brogan replied.

"What's that?" Nash inquired.

"Even though Natalie didn't share much about her new beau, when pressed as to how the two of them met, Natalie said it was while she was on vacation."

Nash perked up, "Did Tiffany recall where Natalie vacationed?"

"She was pretty sure it was along the Oregon coast, but that's as much as she knew."

"I'll see if I can get anything more from Tiffany when I stop by, in the meantime…"

"I know…" Brogan jumped in, "See if we can figure out a location via Natalie's credit card activity."

"Correct. And while you two are working that angle I'll see if her parents are feeling up to talking," Nash said, "They became emotionally frozen-in-silence the other day when reality set in."

"Anyway," Brogan said, "That's all I had."

Nash turned to Donnelly.

"I've done some research on Spencer Dunn's lawyer Trent Lang," Donnelly commented, "and your read on him might be spot-on."

"Oh yeah?" Nash replied, "What did you find?"

"He takes care of the family's business deals and properties. His website says he specializes in Real Estate, Business Law, Estate and Trust, Wills and Probate. As near as I can tell he's never represented a client in a criminal case."

"Hmm… he may have bitten off more than he can chew," Nash responded. She thought for a moment and added, "Which could actually be a double-edged sword."

"How's that?" Donnelly wondered.

"On one hand he could be so 'out of his element' that he gets crucified in court by a seasoned Prosecutor," Nash replied. "But on the other hand, if that ends up being the case, Spencer could hire another lawyer and appeal for a new trial based on ineffective counsel." Another thought took hold, "Then again, his attorney's inexperience could steer him clear of one of my biggest items of concern, and thus help our case. But that would also be one more item open to an appeal." She crossed her arms and summed up the conundrum with an expletive, "Shit!"

"Ah, the nuances of jurisprudence," Brogan chimed in.

Both Nash and Donnelly looked at Brogan with surprise.

"Hey, I've learned a thing or two about the process over the years," Brogan defended.

"I guess so," noted Nash with a grin; her first such gesture in days.

"So hey, I found out that Spencer had lunch at the B-Town Bar & Grill on Saturday," Brogan commented.

"You're kidding?" Donnelly interjected. "I noticed a number of Natalie's calls on her old phone were to that restaurant, so I talked to the manager, and she said that Natalie worked there part-time."

"Son of a…" Nash started. "Was she working that Saturday?"

"Nope; she hadn't worked a shift in a couple of weeks."

"Spencer told me he'd never seen Natalie before," Nash said. "Any idea if he was a regular at the restaurant?"

"I'll have to run his financials and-or check with the wait staff."

"What else did you get from her phone?"

"There were numerous calls between her *old* cell and a burner phone, and it provided quite the eye-opener," Donnelly replied. "It's the same burner that subsequently became her NEW cell phone."

"Holy crap!" Brogan jumped in, "That's got to mean that Spencer gave her *his* phone when she lost, or he took, *her* phone."

"That was my thought exactly, but both her old phone and her burner are nowhere to be found, thus far," Donnelly replied. "And the burner has been silent since Saturday."

"What about cell tower pings for those calls we are aware of?" said Nash.

"They all fall within our target area, but the calls are sporadic at best… it looks like he almost always had the phone off except when he wanted to call Natalie."

"So, trying to compare Spencer's movements with the time and location of the various cell tower pings is next to impossible," Nash concluded.

"Especially since he lives and works within the target area, which means he can claim that everything is all part of his normal daily life… on the up-and-up."

"Good point," Nash replied. "We need to see if we can find evidence of Spencer purchasing one or both burner phones."

"Got it," Donnelly replied.

Nash looked at her watch. "Time for my road trip with Lowell," she said.

26

Detective Nash and Forensic Scientist Lowell came up with a few answers in their search of Natalie Copeland's apartment, but the overall results were minimal. It was determined that the "I stopped by" notes that Natalie had left for her roommate Tiffany did, in fact, originate from the home. Forensics had previously determined that the notes were written by Natalie and not her abductor, so that potential lead evaporated. Tiffany had no new information regarding her thought that Natalie might have met her unnamed beau, presumably Spencer Dunn, while on vacation along the Oregon coast. Nash and her team had run Natalie's financials and, unfortunately, there was no indication that she had even been in Oregon within the past year. Along those lines, Spencer Dunn's financials were intriguing, yet inconclusive. He had no credit card activity along the Oregon coast, but he had numerous excursions within a reasonable driving distance: from north along the Washington coast; to east down the Interstate-5 corridor, including both Portland and Eugene, Oregon. At this point the information would be nothing more than notes within the case file.

Nash and Lowell's subsequent stop, Spencer Dunn's place of work, was even less fruitful than Natalie's apartment. Nash showed a hint of frustration as she exited the facility, "Well, that was a wasted Search Warrant; all we got was a whole lot of nothing," Nash commented to Lowell.

"When you think about it we shouldn't be too surprised," Lowell replied. "Spencer's family may own the property, but someone else owns the business; so it's not like Spencer could easily hide a secret room containing a torture chamber somewhere within the grounds."

"Yeah, I knew it was a longshot; but I'm getting tired of running into dead ends at every turn."

"I don't think it's so much 'running into dead ends' as it is 'struggling to tie up loose ends'," Lowell replied. "After all, you've got the guy dead to rights."

"You always manage to have the 'glass half-full' perspective, don't you?" Nash replied.

"I try," said Lowell, "But I've had my moments… as you well know."

Nash nodded, "Ah yes, I do recall you succumbing to the myriad of contradictions concerning the evidence in the Wagner case."

"Yeah, that one really tested my mettle."

Nash's cell phone rang just as she climbed into her cruiser–it was Donnelly.

"Hey Laura," Nash answered her phone. She listened intently as Donnelly provided her with a new piece of information.

"It's about time we got something concrete on Spencer Dunn's travels Saturday night," Nash responded to the news. "I'll stop by and visit our suspect as soon as I get Lowell back to the lab," she finished and then ended the call.

27

As Detective Nash entered the second floor corridor of the hospital she caught sight of a man walking away from the vicinity of Spencer Dunn's room. Even though she only caught a glimpse of the man, there was a familiarity to him. She wasn't one-hundred-percent sure, but it looked like Gary Copeland, the father of the victim discovered in the trunk of Spencer Dunn's car. What added to Nash's intrigue was not only the possible identity of the man, but that he seemed to notice Nash and immediately look away as if he did not want to be recognized.

Nash approached the Officer standing guard outside of Spencer Dunn's hospital room. "Officer," Nash started, "Did the man who just walked by stop and talk to you?"

"Yes, ma'am," the Officer replied. "He asked who was in the room; I told him that I was not at liberty to say."

"That was it?"

"Pretty much; I guess he was just curious."

Nash nodded. She then proceeded to open the door and enter Spencer Dunn's room.

Spencer was on his cell phone when Nash entered. "Yep; she just walked in," Spencer spoke into his phone as he glanced up at Nash.

Observing Spencer, Nash realized that her suspect was well on the road to recovery and would soon be well enough to be released–trading-in his hospital gown for an orange jumpsuit; unless, of course, a Bail Hearing determined otherwise.

"Got it," Spencer spoke into his phone, ended the call, and placed the phone on a table adjacent to the bed. He looked back at Nash, "Here to finally release me?" he said.

"That would be up to a couple of people above my pay grade: your doctor; and a Judge," Nash replied. "Assuming bail is even an option in your case," she added.

Spencer pointed to his cell phone, "That was my lawyer; he said I don't have to talk to you."

Before Nash had a chance to respond Spencer added, "He's on the way, by the way."

"In that case, how about I give you a little something to chew on while we wait?" Nash replied.

"As long as I don't have to talk."

"Fine by me," Nash responded. She grabbed her memo pad and began to read aloud the items of interest she had planned to address with Spencer. As she was finishing, in walked Spencer's lawyer, Trent Lang.

Lang focused on Spencer. "You didn't tell her anything," Lang nodded toward Nash, "did you?"

Spencer shook his head in the negative. Lang turned his focus to Nash.

Nash provided clarification to Lang, "I merely informed your client as to my areas of interest for today."

"I see," Lang replied. "Understand that I might instruct my client to avoid answering certain questions."

Nash nodded and turned to Spencer, "How about you provide me a detailed breakdown of your activities last Saturday, the twenty-sixth?"

"I got off work at six and went straight home," Spencer replied. "I kicked back for a bit, drank a cold one, and scarfed-down some leftover pizza. Then I grabbed my 'Mad Hatter' duds and headed over to Candi's place around, I don't know, maybe seven-thirty or so."

"I take it that Candi is your friend Candace Olsen?" said Nash.

"Yep. I hung out at her place for an hour or two while she…" Spencer began counting on his fingers, "…and Cindy and Gillian did my 'Mad Hatter' makeup."

"You left Candi's place around nine o'clock – nine-thirty?"

"Something like that," Spencer replied, "and went to the West Pacific Sports Bar."

"How long were you there?"

"Just long enough to down one beer; then I drove over to the Quonset Hut," Spencer replied. "I hung out there for maybe an hour and then headed home."

"So you drove home and, after you got there, according to *you*," Nash emphasized, "your doppelganger stole your car, loaded the victim's body into the trunk, and subsequently got pulled over by the police officer?"

"No; that's not it," Spencer replied.

"No?" Nash glared.

"At that point I realized I'd had too much to drink, so I got an Uber," said Spencer.

Attorney Lang jumped in, "So, as you can see, detective; my client's car was stolen from the parking lot at the Quonset Hut Pub & Ale House while my client was at his home." He paused and added, "A rock solid alibi."

"Have you ever noticed that a rock doesn't float?" Nash responded. "Well, neither does your alibi."

Both Spencer and Lang remained quiet; awaiting Nash's explanation.

"I'll concede that you called for an Uber from the Quonset Hut," Nash directed to Spencer, "but when the Uber driver showed up, you were nowhere to be found."

Spencer became defensive, "What?! No; that's not right!"

"I'm afraid so," Nash replied.

"No way… they're lying."

"I have corroborating reports: The guy showed up, couldn't find you anywhere, asked around–nothing," Nash declared. "And the coup de grace: We have the driver's GPS movements–he was nowhere near your home that night."

Spencer went to speak, but his lawyer gestured for him to cease on the particular subject.

"And don't forget we've got you on tape, in and around your vehicle," Nash added.

"And we told you…" Lang started.

"Yeah, yeah, yeah," Nash interrupted, "that was the doppelganger in the car; not your client."

Spencer and Lang stood silent; Nash then segued, "And while we're on the subject, we found *no* mesh bag full of rugby players' outfits to be laundered… not in the car, not in your home."

"The guy must have tossed it," Spencer responded.

Nash rolled her eyes, "We're back to that, are we? Okay, then let me ask you this: Is your rugby team male, female, or co-ed?"

"Male."

"Now see, we have a problem… and it's twofold," Nash replied. "For one: There was not a whole team's worth of blood and DNA in your trunk—only a handful."

"Well, not everyone gets all bloodied during a match," Spencer interrupted. "Plus, the bags aren't just tossed in the trunk; they're placed inside a cardboard box, so that would also explain why there are only a few specimens in there."

"A cardboard box?"

"Yeah; I don't want a bunch of blood and mucus and stuff all over my trunk."

"No such box has been uncovered," Nash replied.

Attorney Lang jumped in, "Since the bag of clothes was in the box, it stands to reason they were tossed together."

Nash shook her head and crossed her arms. "And back to my previous point concerning the blood and DNA: Besides *yours*," Nash emphasized to Spencer, "only one other sample was male; all the rest were female."

Spencer began to speak, but his lawyer once again silenced him.

"I guess I'll let you two chew on that one for a while," Nash commented. "Back to your whereabouts on Saturday: Where did you go for lunch?"

"Who said I went out to lunch?"

"You're really going to play that game?"

Lang nudged Spencer. "The B-town Bar & Grill," Spencer responded to Nash.

"Was that to see Natalie Copeland?"

"What're you talkin' about?"

"She works there part-time."

"I told you I don't know the woman!" Spencer exploded, "I've never seen her! Not here, not there, not anywhere!"

"Do you frequent the place?"

"I go for lunch on occasion," Spencer huffed.

"Not for dinner or drinks?"

"Not in a long time," Spencer replied, "Probably over a year."

"Okay; one last question for today," Nash said. "Do you own a burner phone?" She stopped and added, "Let me rephrase that: Have you *ever* owned a burner phone."

"Why would I need a burner phone?"

"Beats me," Nash replied, "but you didn't answer my question."

"Nope… no burner phone."

Nash glanced between Spencer and his attorney, "Do you two have anything for me?"

The two men looked at each other and then back to Nash. "Not at this time," Lang said.

"Alright," Nash responded, "Enjoy the rest of your day."

Nash turned around and walked to the door. She stopped, looked back at Spencer and his lawyer, and said, "By the way, don't forget to come up with an explanation for there being blood and DNA from several women in the trunk of your car." She grabbed the door handle and added, "Oh, and a little something that blows your whole 'doppelganger defense' to smithereens: The lipstick 'frown' drawn on Natalie Copeland's face…" she paused for dramatic effect, "matched YOUR 'Joker' smile… same tube of lipstick." She opened the door and exited the room.

28

Detective Nash stood on the landing of an upscale home. She seemed frozen in a moment—fixated upon the antique door-knocker staring back at her. She reached for the doorbell and stopped herself. She took a breath and hit the buzzer.

The door slowly opened to reveal a heartbreaking sight. The woman's eyes were red and puffy, her hands shaking ever so subtly. She looked frail; as if she had aged twenty years in the past two days.

Nancy Copeland gazed into Detective Nash's eyes. "Oh, hello detective," she said through a raspy voice.

"Good afternoon, ma'am," Nash replied, "I… I was hoping you and your husband might feel up to answering a few questions."

"Gary is out running errands, but I'll try to answer what I can."

"Speaking of your husband," Nash said, "I thought I might have seen him at Bennington General Hospital earlier this afternoon."

"That would be news to me; I don't know of any reason he would have been there," Nancy replied. "Are you sure it was him?"

"That was my impression at first glance; but to be honest, I'm not 100-percent sure."

"So, um…" Nancy hesitated, "what would you like to talk about?"

"When we spoke the other day I asked about Natalie's new boyfriend," Nash replied. "We believe the person we have in custody is, in fact, that gentleman; but we have been unable to confirm our suspicion."

"How is that possible?" Nancy responded. "Aren't there people she talked to, people who saw them together, texts or phone calls between them?"

"Not that we've been unable to uncover thus far."

"Did you check that new phone number she had?"

"We did, but it was an untraceable pre-paid phone."

"Untraceable? They make such a thing?"

"Unfortunately, yes," Nash replied. "But I assure you, even though we are still trying to piece everything together, we do have direct evidence against the gentleman in custody."

"So, you're here to try to find some of those missing pieces?"

"That's correct."

"Well, I don't see how I can be of much help."

"People often think that some small item might be insignificant; but it can end up being an important cog in the wheels of justice, so please bear with me," Nash responded.

"Okay."

"When we last talked you said that Natalie did not provide any specific information about the guy: not a name, not a description, not where he lived, or what he did for a living?"

"That's correct," Nancy replied. "It was so out of character for her; she would usually gush about a new man in her life, but not this time," she stared off in space. "She was so secretive; I should have... I should have pressed for more," Nancy began second guessing herself. She looked at Nash, "But how could I have known?"

"Not just you," Nash replied, "she didn't share anything with her friends, either." Something dawned on her, hearkening back to a statement that Brogan had made after he first caught sight of Natalie. "Can you tell me what kind of guy Natalie was normally attracted to?" she asked.

"Tall, dark, and handsome... successful," Nancy responded. "A guy with presence," she added, "You know; where everyone notices him when he walks into a room."

"I see," Nash replied.

"I know that sounds somewhat superficial; but one's youth is all about learning from life's experiences," Nancy said. "It's like the saying...

'Sometimes you have to kiss a few toads before finding your prince'," she added. "And when we're young we don't necessarily realize that it's 'the person within' that actually determines the difference."

"I hate to ask," said Nash, "but is there any chance that Natalie was mum about the new guy because he didn't measure up to her usual standards?"

"I hadn't thought of that," Nancy replied. "At first Natalie claimed that he was nothing more than a friend and thus there was nothing to tell; but the more time she spent with him, the more secretive she got," she said. "Gary and I thought there was something else… like he might have been married."

"Did Natalie happen to share how or when she met him?" Nash inquired. "Her roommate Tiffany said she thought the two met while Natalie was on vacation on the Oregon coast, but…"

"That's what Natalie told us as well," Nancy inadvertently interrupted.

"But we found no credit card activity that would have placed her there," Nash said.

"That's probably because she was there with her father and me."

Nash perked up, "With you and your husband?"

"A little family escape," Nancy replied, "At least that's what it was supposed to be."

"She met this guy while you were on vacation, but you never met him or at least caught sight of him during your stay?"

"We rented a cabin at Arch Cape, but Natalie spent most of the time up at Cannon Beach," Nancy replied. "Not overnight, but she was away from the cabin most of the time."

"When was this?"

"Last May," Nancy replied. "We also gave her some spending money, so it's no surprise that she didn't rack up any credit card debt." Nancy's eyes lit up as she relived the good times with her daughter, "It would be pretty lame of us parents to invite a broke college student on vacation and make her pay her own way."

Nash nodded; Nancy directed a question her way… "Do you have any children, detective?"

"No ma'am."

"Let me tell you; it's a fine line a parent walks between wanting to spoil your sweet, innocent, child…" Nancy began to choke up, "while still allowing them some independence."

Nash attempted to provide an expression of understanding while remaining silent.

Nancy took a breath; her lower lip began to quiver. She tried to maintain her composure, but could not hold back a flood of emotions… "This is all my fault," she began to sob while staring off into space, "I was supposed to be there for her, to protect her, to lay down my life for her if need be; this is a parent's worst nightmare!" She looked toward Nash, "She was our everything!" She took a moment and added, "Gary and I may still have each other, but Natalie was the glue that held us all together—our reason for being!"

Nash wasn't sure how to respond; or if she should even make such an attempt.

"Now what do we have to life for?! For seeing the monster who took her from us brought to justice?!" Nancy continued to plea, "And then what??! She's still gone—he's still here…" her voice trailed-off.

Nash stood silent, realizing that there was no good answer to Nancy's question, and hoped that Nancy was merely venting.

"I, uh… I don't want to talk anymore," Nancy said.

"I understand, ma'am," Nash replied.

29

"What are you two doing here?" Nash said to Brogan and Donnelly as she strolled into the office at ten o'clock Saturday morning.

"Every day's a workday when we're in the middle of a case," Brogan replied.

"Generally, that's true," Nash conceded. "But we've got the suspect in custody, which means we're not in the twenty-four-seven mode of running down clues in an attempt to point us in the direction of a suspect."

"Makes sense," Donnelly jumped in.

"Yeah; so let's not work ourselves to exhaustion here," Nash directed.

"But shouldn't that apply to you as well?" said Brogan.

"Touché," Nash replied. "But now that we know Spencer was at the Quonset Hut last Saturday I want to get out there and see if anyone saw him, and what they might recall."

"And after talking to you yesterday afternoon," Donnelly said to Nash, "I've been expanding my phone records search."

"Speaking of yesterday afternoon," Brogan turned to Nash, "How did your visit with our suspect go?"

Nash grinned, "You should have seen the look on the faces of Spencer and his lawyer when I told them that there was DNA from multiple women in the trunk of Spencer's car, AND that the lipstick on Natalie's 'frown' matched that of Spencer's 'Joker smile'."

"Oh man, I would've loved to have seen that," Brogan responded.

"Yeah, I think they both realized that the lipstick match is going to be the nail in Spencer's coffin."

"What do you think, Kenz," said Donnelly, "with this latest piece of evidence he'll try to work out a plea bargain with the Prosecutor?"

"A plea bargain?!" Brogan retorted. "Screw that; this guy needs to get thrown in the slammer and never again see the light of day."

"I don't disagree with you, Dirk; but we've got a long way to go," Nash responded. "Heck, we haven't even gotten through a Bail Hearing yet."

"Are you planning to attend?" Donnelly said to Nash. "You know… the Bail Hearing?"

"As you well know, my last such venture was due to special circumstances set forth by a Deputy Prosecutor who was about to withhold relevant facts," Nash replied. She paused in thought and mumbled to herself aloud, "Hard to believe trying to do the right thing got my ass chewed-up one side and down the other courtesy of political B.S." She emerged from her fog and got back on point, "Anyway, I'm thinking that the Deputy Prosecutor and I are actually on the same page this go-round."

Donnelly nodded and then changed the subject, "So hey, expanding my phone records search provided us with a little bit of something, but mostly nothing."

Brogan turned to Donnelly, "Since when did you start talking in riddles?"

"The only activity on Natalie's cell phone during the timeframe of the family vacation in Oregon was with her mother's cell phone."

"I'm assuming that's the 'mostly nothing' part?" Brogan said with air-quotes.

"Correct," Donnelly replied. "The 'something' was that the calls between her and the burner phone began a couple of weeks later."

"That would make sense, actually," said Brogan. "They meet one day at Cannon Beach, there's a bit of a connection between them, they end up spending time together while they're there, and when it comes time for one of them to leave they exchange phone numbers," he added.

"That's true," said Donnelly, "Each day before Natalie headed back to the cabin she and Spencer could have pre-arranged when and where they would meet up the next day."

"I agree," Nash joined the conversation, "although there's another possibility you may not have considered."

"What's that?" said Brogan.

"That her story about meeting her new beau while on vacation in Oregon was nothing more than that–a story."

"Why would she lie about that?"

"I have no idea," Nash replied. "And I'm not even saying that such is the case here; I'm just saying there's often an alternative that we may not have taken under consideration."

"You're right; that option never crossed my mind."

Nash turned to Donnelly, "And Spencer Dunn?"

"Can't specifically place him there at that time," Donnelly replied, "and can't rule out that he could have been there."

"I'm confused," Brogan chimed in. "Considering all of the evidence we have, what's the importance of determining where and when Natalie Copeland met her mystery man?"

"You're right, Dirk; we've got direct visual and forensic evidence tying our suspect to the victim; but you know me, I don't like gaps in my timeline," Nash replied. "And sure, the genesis of their relationship in this particular instance is almost immaterial, but if we can catch Spencer in yet another lie…"

"Understood," Brogan nodded.

"Back to the burner phones," Nash said to Donnelly. "Any luck determining the buyer, or buyers?"

"Nope," Donnelly shook her head. "We know that Spencer didn't make such a purchase via credit card, but if he had done so via cash Lowell had hoped he made a rookie mistake."

"A rookie mistake?" said Brogan.

"Hanging onto the receipt of purchase," Donnelly replied.

"That would be pretty bad to try to hide the sale by using cash, only to forget to toss the receipt."

"Yep," said Donnelly, "but no such luck."

"I wasn't holding out much hope on that one anyway," Nash stated. She extracted her cell phone and made a call, "Hey Evan," she spoke into the phone, "Sorry to bother you on a Saturday, but are you up for a trip to the Quonset Hut?" She listened, nodded, and said, "Great; I'll see you in a few."

Nash ended her call and turned to Brogan and Donnelly. "Well, you two know where I'm headed; do you know where you're headed?"

Brogan and Donnelly glanced at each other and then back to Nash. "Uhh… no," Brogan shrugged.

"Anywhere but here," Nash replied. "Take the rest of the day off."

"Copy," Brogan and Donnelly responded in unison.

30

Detective Nash wheeled her cruiser into the parking lot of The Quonset Hut, a pub located on the outskirts of town where city life transitions to countryside. Pulling into a spot next to the building she spied Forensic Scientist Lowell's car in her rear-view mirror as he rolled to a stop in an adjacent parking spot.

"Good timing," Nash said to Lowell after the two exited their respective vehicles.

The duo entered the establishment and were greeted by a woman in her mid-thirties, "Good afternoon," she said, "Welcome to the Quonset Hut."

Nash flashed her badge, "Good afternoon; I talked to someone named Teresa earlier about a box discovered in your parking lot that contained a bag full of clothing."

"That was me," the woman replied, "I've got it back in the office," she nodded and disappeared through a doorway. She promptly reappeared with the box in hand and placed it on an empty table.

"Perfect," Nash replied as she and Lowell eyeballed the box and bag. "Did you or anyone else happen to touch the bag or the clothing at all?" Nash asked Teresa.

"I can't speak for anyone else, but I only handled the box itself," Teresa replied. "Considering how grungy and grimy the clothes are I can't imagine anyone would've rummaged through it, but I can't say for sure," she added, "Why do you ask?"

"DNA," Nash responded. "We will be analyzing the contents, and it would be nice to know if anyone handled it so that we can eliminate them."

"Eliminate them?" Teresa grew concerned, "Do you mean as a suspect in a crime?"

"Not at all," Nash replied. "When performing an investigation, if someone's DNA shows up that is unexpected it's important to know that there was a valid reason for it to be there; such as them being the person who discovered this box, for example."

"I can ask my employees if you'd like."

"Actually," Nash started, "can you provide me a list of those who worked over the past week?"

"It would probably be easier if I just gave you a list of all of my employees since some of them could've come in to get a paycheck or for some other reason."

"Good idea," Nash replied.

"You also asked about a customer who was possibly here last Saturday," Teresa said while handing some receipts to Nash. "I can't say for sure, but this might've been him," she added.

Nash started to scan the receipts. "MH?" she said. "That doesn't make sense; his name is Spencer Dunn."

"That was for Mad Hatter," Teresa said as she pointed to one of the receipts that had 'Mad Hatter' written on it. "The bartender kept it simple after his first order," she added.

"Of course," Nash replied, feeling a bit the fool for not making the connection. She handed the receipts to Lowell and returned her focus to Teresa, "Was Mister Dunn, or the Mad Hatter, here with anyone?"

"Sorry; the place was a madhouse that night with almost everyone in costume," Teresa replied. "Both the bartender and I remembered a Mad Hatter, but that's all."

Nash extracted a photograph and showed it to Teresa, "How about this woman… Natalie Copeland?"

Teresa shook her head, "Doesn't look familiar, but if she was in costume then who knows."

Nash sighed–she knew the answer to that question.

Lowell held up the receipts toward Teresa. "A couple of these receipts show more than one drink," he said.

Teresa shrugged.

Nash and Lowell looked at each other and then back to Teresa. "Can you show us exactly where the box of clothes was found?" Nash gestured toward the parking area.

"Sure," Teresa replied as she headed out the door–Nash and Lowell right on her heels.

The trio ventured to the far end of the parking area, adjacent to a field.

"The box was right here," Teresa pointed to a spot in the field a few feet from the parking lot.

"Did anyone happen to see the person remove the box from their vehicle and place it on the ground here?" Nash asked Teresa.

"No; we found it the next morning."

Nash nodded.

"Umm…" Teresa pointed toward the building, "I'm gonna go get you the list of my employees," she said to Nash, "unless you need anything else from me right now?"

"We're good; thanks."

Teresa departed and Lowell turned to Nash, "Something isn't making sense."

"What's that?" Nash replied.

"Spencer Dunn's car has a decent-sized trunk, so I'm sure that both the box of clothes and Natalie could have fit inside… no need to toss the box."

"Maybe he opened the trunk, saw the box, and simply tossed it to get it out of the way?"

"But why here?"

"What do you mean?"

"The box being here near the parking area would seem to imply that this is where he placed Natalie in the trunk."

"Shit, you're right; and we know that's a virtually impossible scenario."

"Wait a minute…" something jumped out at Lowell, "Natalie's car…" he pondered, "Where is it?"

"Holy crap," Nash scanned the lot. She stopped and took a breath. "It hasn't turned up yet," she sighed, "but it's on our radar screen."

"I'm thinking there's suddenly a greater sense of urgency on that front."

"That's a fact," Nash replied. "And something else just hit me."

"About Natalie's car?"

"No; about the bag of clothing," Nash said. "We're assuming that it's exactly what Spencer Dunn and his lawyer says it is…"

"But if the blood and DNA matches what we found in the trunk," Lowell inadvertently interrupted, "then it's tied to one or more victims and not a rugby team?"

"Precisely," Nash replied. "Also, don't forget about the unknown male DNA," she added, "he could be associated with the team."

31

It was a day where one could have imagined an angry sky of gloom and doom… of dark clouds, fierce winds, and pelting rain; a vision so bleak as to evoke a feeling that the wrath of God was about to bear down upon the soul of humanity. But that was not the case. Instead, a brisk, cloudless morning had given way to a beautiful early-November afternoon. It was as if fate had pierced through the darkness and shone a light on this otherwise solemn occasion.

Nash, Brogan, and Donnelly sat quietly in Nash's cruiser. The upside of one's status as a detective: no uniform, no visible badge, and a nondescript sedan. In the circumstance that lay before them, the ability to fade into the background was paramount. Not from a 'stakeout' or 'undercover' perspective; but in reverence to the moment. There were times, of course, when Detective Nash had attended a Memorial Service in an official capacity–seeking out a suspect, the type of demon that would bask in the grief and heartache courtesy of their evil deed and show up to witness the impact of their carnage. However, with a suspect in custody, today would not be one of those times.

"We're not cops today; we're here to pay our respects," Nash directed to Brogan and Donnelly. "That means no badge and no service weapon," she added as she began to exit her cruiser. "You can maintain your backup piece if desired, but only if it remains out of sight."

"Understood," Brogan and Donnelly replied in unison while exiting the vehicle.

Nash stood next to her cruiser and watched the gathering crowd as they assembled for the outdoor observance.

Brogan and Donnelly sidled up to Nash. "We're not going to stand way over here by ourselves, are we?" Brogan said to Nash.

"No," Nash replied, "then we really *would* look like cops surveying the scene." She scanned the growing throng of mourners and added, "Let's go join the crowd, but stay in the background away from family and friends who deserve to have their special moment with their dear departed loved one."

The Service was both beautiful and heart-wrenching. The scent of dozens of floral arrangements permeated the air; large photographs of Natalie documenting her young and vibrant life graced the scene. Friends and family shared stories of their moments with Natalie–her mother Nancy unable to finish as she broke down in tears; her father Gary tried to remain composed, but ultimately broke down as well. Nash attempted to maintain a stiff upper lip, as did Brogan. A teardrop flowed down Donnelly's cheek. The majority of the crowd wept as the Service concluded with a heartfelt rendition of "Amazing Grace".

"Whew, that was tough," Donnelly exhaled and wiped her eyes.

"I'll say," Brogan responded.

Nash remained quiet; with two younger sisters not much older than Natalie she couldn't help but to imagine the "what if it were one of them?" scenario.

Someone off in the distance, deep within the crowd, caught Donnelly's eye. "There's something familiar about that guy," she nodded.

Both Nash and Brogan focused their attention in the direction of Donnelly's nod.

"Officer Wilberforce," Brogan recognized a face in the crowd.

"I wasn't expecting him to be here," Nash added. "But then again, he was the person who discovered Natalie."

Wilberforce, in civilian attire, stood in reverence with his hands clasped in front of himself even though the service had ended. He appeared to be frozen in the moment. He gazed upon the row of mourners stopping to convey their condolences to Gary and Nancy Copeland. He seemed conflicted; his attention shifting from the couple, down to his clasped hands, back to the couple, back to his hands. He took a breath, turned, and exited the area.

In the midst of receiving condolences Gary Copeland caught sight of Detective Nash. When the crowd began to disperse Gary leaned over and whispered to his wife Nancy; she nodded. Gary made his way toward Nash.

The first thought that came to Nash as Gary approached was to ask if he was at the hospital two days prior, but realized this was not the appropriate time or venue to broach such a subject.

"Detective," Gary said to Nash as he arrived, "Thank you for coming out to honor the memory of my daughter."

"Our condolences," Nash replied. "Detective Brogan and Deputy Donnelly are working the cases with me," she added as she nodded toward Brogan and Donnelly.

"Cases?" Gary responded. "Are you saying that there is more than one victim?"

"No, Sir," Nash replied. "But the Officer who discovered your daughter was subsequently involved in a shooting; and thus our office, being a separate jurisdiction, was assigned to investigate."

"The Officer shot the bastard who killed my daughter?"

"I'm sorry, Sir; but I cannot speak to the Officer-involved shooting in any way."

"Well, all I can say is: thank God for that Officer," Gary replied, "he deserves a medal."

Nash was struck by Gary's comment; as if he knew that the Officer whom had discovered his daughter was the same Officer that shot Spencer Dunn, even though that information had not been made public. There was no indication that Wilberforce had introduced himself to Gary at Natalie's Memorial Service, and Gary seemed to be merely referring to a generic police officer, so how could he have known? Or was Nash seeing something that wasn't really there?

<h1 style="text-align:center">32</h1>

Detective Nash sat in quiet solitude reflecting on the emotions that Natalie Copeland's Memorial Service had brought forth. She had maintained her composure throughout the service–barely; but now the onslaught of recent events were cascading over her. If she didn't have the intestinal fortitude borne from a lifetime of adversity her inner strength could have easily been replaced by inner turmoil. Even so, she felt as if she was teetering on the edge.

It wasn't the Memorial Service itself that was weighing upon her; instead, it had served as a catalyst to unleash her own Pandora's Box of recent travails, and they hit her like a montage of images flashing before her eyes. It began with the vision of Natalie Copeland on the autopsy table; and, as if it were a scene from a film, the camera within Nash's mind panned back to reveal the gut-wrenching breakdown of Natalie's mother at the sight of her daughter's lifeless body. Suddenly Nash found herself at the Boat House Grill as her sister Katelyn handed her their estranged father's obituary: Nash was now a happy-go-lucky four-year-old as Dad pushed her on the backyard swing, then a grief-stricken six-year-old as he walked out of her life forever, and back to the restaurant as a mid-thirties woman wondering 'what could have been'. And finally, she found herself in the midst of the nightmare that had prompted Ian to wonder if it was more than simply a dream. Her breaths grew rapid and her demeanor turned to anger as she replayed the discovery of Ian digging into her past and unearthing memories she had long since buried. It was a moment that had triggered two specific responses: she hadn't spoken to Ian since then; and her nightmares had returned.

She was startled back to reality by a knock on the door; finding herself sitting in total darkness. She had been so entranced that she hadn't noticed the filtered light of dusk had given way to the dead of night.

She paused and listened. Another *rap-rap-rap* rang out. She stood up, walked over and grasped the doorknob, and slowly opened the door. "What are you doing here?" she said.

33

Detective Brogan and Deputy Donnelly glanced up from their respective desks as Detective Nash entered the Sheriff's Office. Brogan looked at his watch–Nash's arrival was much later than usual; and she seemed to be in a bit of a fog.

Donnelly was equally curious as to Nash's state of mind. "Everything okay?" she offered to Nash.

"What?" Nash attempted to comprehend. "Uh, yeah... I guess," she said.

"Busy morning?" Brogan uttered to Nash.

"That's one way to put it," Nash replied. "And not all that productive," she added.

Brogan was unaware of any early morning plans Nash might've had, so he wasn't sure what to make of her statement. He opted to remain silent in the hopes that Nash might provide clarification.

Nash removed her jacket and draped it over her desk chair. "By the way," she glanced between Brogan and Donnelly, "I appreciate you two taking time during your day off to attend Natalie Copeland's Memorial Service yesterday."

"It was an honor," Brogan responded.

"Absolutely," Donnelly concurred.

"Speaking of..." Nash said, "is it just me, or did Gary Copeland seem to know that the Officer who discovered his daughter was the same cop who shot the suspect in her murder?"

"That's the impression I got," Brogan replied, "but he might have been merely speculating."

"Is there any way he could have known the two Officers were one in the same?" Donnelly asked Nash.

"Not unless someone spilled the beans," Nash replied. "And I just came from Captain O'Rourke's office and he said neither he nor Officer Wilberforce had spoken with Mister Copeland."

"So that's where you were, eh?" Brogan said.

"That and the West Pacific Sports Bar."

"The West Pacific?"

"Spencer's last stop before the Quonset Hut that night."

"Any luck?"

"He used the ATM right outside and then wandered into the bar for one drink," Nash replied. "He was alone… no female friend, no Natalie Copeland."

"Damn the luck," Brogan responded.

"Yep," said Nash. "How about you two," she added, "any items of note while I was out running into dead ends?"

"Spencer Dunn's release from the hospital this morning," Donnelly replied. "And his subsequent Bail Hearing."

Brogan jumped in, "Apparently mommy and daddy came to the rescue."

"How do you mean?" Nash responded.

"He made bail."

"What the hell??" Nash blurted out. "Some Judge disregarded the brutal murder of a defenseless young woman and set an amount of bail equivalent to a ham sandwich?"

"Not at all," Brogan defended, "the bail was set at half-a-mil."

Nash was confused, "Spencer's parents are retired; what'd they do, put up some of their properties?"

"Your guess is as good as mine," Brogan shrugged.

"Well crap," Nash took a breath, "Gary Copeland's gonna be pissed when he gets the news."

"Say what?" Brogan attempted to comprehend.

"I told him that the suspect wasn't going anywhere."

"Why'd you tell him that?"

"I was trying to alleviate his concerns about the previously-unnamed suspect getting away."

"Jumping bail and going on the run?" Donnelly interceded.

"Well; his parents do live out of state," Nash responded, "so I'm thinking there's a certain risk there."

"And now that Spencer has gone before a Judge everything will be a matter of public record," Brogan noted. "Which means the suspect will no longer be 'unnamed'," he added with air-quotes.

"What about Officer Wilberforce?" Donnelly asked.

"What about him?" Brogan countered.

"Is his involvement going to be a matter of public record as well?"

"You'll have to ask Kenz on that one," Brogan deferred to Nash.

"Eventually," Nash said, "but not while the investigation into his actions is ongoing." She thought for a moment and added, "Unless someone leaks that info to the press."

"What's the status on him?" Donnelly wondered.

"Captain O'Rourke has him currently on desk duty," Nash replied.

"And how about *our* investigation," said Donnelly, "are you ready to submit your findings to Sheriff Clarke?"

"Pretty close," said Nash.

"What do you think is going to happen to him… to Wilberforce?"

"It could go anywhere from a suspension to the end of his career," Nash replied. She thought for a moment. "Or worse," she added.

"What could be worse than the end of his career?"

"If a Grand Jury decides to indict based on his actions."

"But he's the cop who not only found Natalie, but who also captured her killer," Donnelly lamented.

"And who Gary Copeland refers to as a hero," Brogan added his two-cents-worth.

Nash glanced at Brogan and then focused on Donnelly, "You haven't seen the body-cam and dash-cam videos?" she said to Donnelly.

"You've only had me working the Natalie Copeland case," Donnelly replied, "not anything specific to Officer Wilberforce's actions."

"In that case, it's high time we had a teachable moment," Nash responded. "Watch the videos, in detail, and let me know what you think."

"I will," Donnelly beamed, "Thanks!"

Nash turned to Brogan, "And Dirk…"

"Uh… yeah?" Brogan replied.

"Since you've viewed the footage," said Nash, "no providing Laura any personal insights."

Brogan glanced at Donnelly and then back to Nash. "Roger that," he said.

34

It had been a working-lunch for Detective Nash—putting the finishing touches on her assessment of Officer Wilberforce's actions, and providing her findings to Sheriff Clarke. As she sat awaiting the Sheriff's feedback Donnelly rambled over to Nash's desk.

"So hey, I watched the video footage when Officer Wilberforce pulled over Spencer Dunn and all I can say is: Wow!" Donnelly said as Nash gestured for her to take a seat.

"A lot to take in from an investigator's perspective," Nash said.

"I agree," Donnelly responded. "One thing I have to say is that the dash-cam video is so dark and grainy that it's hard to get a good visual of Officer Wilberforce."

"You're not implying that it could be someone other than the Officer, are you?"

Nash's comment caught Donnelly off-guard, "Not at all," she said, "I was just thinking from the perspective of the familiar face I saw at Natalie Copeland's Memorial Service."

"How do you mean?"

"This guy… Officer Wilberforce… looks skinnier than the guy I was talking about," she thought for a moment, "but maybe that's just the video and the poor lighting?"

Nash opened up her case file and extracted a photograph, "Here's Officer Wilberforce's official B.P.D. photo."

"That's definitely not the guy I was referring to yesterday," Donnelly pointed. "This guy was older, taller, and more…" she pondered, "manly-looking I guess you could say."

"So, when Dirk and I thought you were talking about Wilberforce you were actually talking about some guy in that general area?"

"Apparently so," Donnelly shrugged.

"Any idea why the guy looked familiar to you?"

"I didn't give it any more thought when it appeared we were all talking about Wilberforce," Donnelly replied, "but it could be something as simple as seeing him at a local bar or restaurant on one or more occasions."

"I see," Nash replied. "Now, about the details of the footage itself…" Nash prompted.

Donnelly went through the video footage point-by-point with Nash.

"Obviously you see why I'm concerned," Nash said to Donnelly after providing her feedback.

"Yes, ma'am," Donnelly replied.

Nash and Donnelly's attention was broken by Sheriff Clarke entering the area.

"Sorry to interrupt," Clarke said to Nash. "Can I have a few moments of your time, detective?"

"Of course," Nash replied as she got up from her desk.

"I'll get back to the case," Donnelly said to Nash as she also got up and headed toward her own desk.

Nash followed Sheriff Clarke to his office. The Sheriff had Nash's report on a table. He gestured to the report. "Very thorough assessment," Clarke commented. "It doesn't paint Officer Wilberforce in a very good light, I must say."

"It's difficult when one has to take a fellow law enforcement officer to task, but…" Nash began to respond.

"But he gave you no choice," Clarke interjected. "He made his bed…"

"Precisely," Nash replied.

"How do you think your old pal Captain O'Rourke will take it?"

"He knows what went down, so hopefully he'll be open-minded; but I think it's all going to ride on a Grand Jury's decision."

"Well, ideally the fact that the Officer both discovered the victim, and caught the perpetrator, will have some sway in their decision," Clarke said.

"I concur."

"And on that note, how's *that* case coming along?"

"I've got an almost overwhelming amount of evidence, but I still have my concerns."

"Concerns?"

"Have you seen Wilberforce's dash-cam and body-cam footage when he pulled over Spencer Dunn?"

"No; just his body-cam when Dunn was shot."

"It's a procedural nightmare."

"That could impact the case?"

"Potentially."

"Well, crap!" Clarke lamented.

"Do you want to see the footage?"

"Hmm..." Clarke contemplated the question. "Not right now; I'm afraid it might piss me off."

"Understood," Nash replied.

35

Detective Nash reflected upon her conversation with Sheriff Clarke the previous afternoon as she poured her morning cup of java. With the investigation into the Officer-involved shooting featuring Officer Wilberforce of the Bennington Police Department out of her hands and into those of a Grand Jury, her focus was now solely on the murder of Natalie Copeland. Unfortunately, Officer Wilberforce played a starring role in that investigation as well, and those actions provided both strong evidence, and potential obstacles. *"Talk about a conundrum,"* Nash thought to herself. She took a sip of her coffee and headed toward her desk.

"Ah, the posse has arrived," Nash said to Brogan and Donnelly as she approached them.

"Another day in paradise," Donnelly commented.

"So hey, I just had a thought…" Brogan directed to Nash.

"You're lucky I'm feeling generous this morning," Nash grinned.

The light-bulb clicked with Brogan, "I almost walked into one, didn't I?"

"Yep," Nash replied, "but go ahead."

"Spencer Dunn's lawyer," said Brogan.

"What about him?"

"He failed to get you removed from the Wilberforce investigation."

"I never could figure that one out," Donnelly jumped in. "What was he implying; that you'd withhold evidence simply because you used to work with Wilberforce's boss?" she said to Nash.

"Which would be a pretty stupid implication on his part," Brogan interjected. "I mean hell, it's all right there on not only Wilberforce's body-cam, but his Sergeant's as well," he added while shaking his head.

"I'm thinking he was merely trying to pump up his chest in front of his client," Nash replied.

Nash's cell phone rang–it was Forensic Scientist Evan Lowell. "Hey Evan, what's the good word?" Nash spoke into her phone as she answered.

"Deoxyribonucleic acid," Lowell replied.

"That's a pretty big word for this early in the morning," Nash responded.

"I have a symposium to attend this week, so I've been practicing," Lowell explained.

"You're one of the speakers?"

"I am."

"You realize you just jinxed yourself."

"You're saying I should stick with the acronym?"

"That would be my recommendation," Nash responded.

"Hmm… you could be right."

Nash figured that Lowell had something more noteworthy to share, "So, I'm assuming you've got something DNA-related to report?" she said.

"That's true," Lowell said. "The DNA and blood from the bag of clothes does NOT match those found in Spencer's trunk. In other words, outside of obtaining a DNA analysis from everyone on his rugby team it appears that he was telling the truth."

"On that one item anyway."

"Correct."

"So much for hoping for some major breakthrough," Nash lamented.

"Like what?"

"Like figuring out who the hell that DNA belongs to."

"Remember that the quantities are relatively minor, and they're limited to a small area of the trunk," Lowell responded. "Has your team tried tracking down the vehicle's previous owners; maybe there's a benign reason for the samples being there?"

"Since I can't see how it would be relevant to this case I don't want to expend resources chasing a possible red herring," Nash replied. "I just hate unanswered questions," she added, "even if they *are* irrelevant."

"Understood."

"Anything else for me right now?"

"Like you I don't stop digging until the case goes to the Prosecutor, but that's all I've got at the moment."

"Roger that," Nash replied and ended the call.

Donnelly had been pounding away on her computer keyboard, oblivious to Nash's phone conversation; but Brogan had been eavesdropping. "No tie between the bag of clothes and the DNA in the trunk?" Brogan queried Nash.

"That's correct," Nash replied.

"Got 'em!" Donnelly yelled out from her desk.

Donnelly's outburst immediately caught Nash and Brogan's attention. "Got who?" Nash responded.

"The person or persons who provided Spencer Dunn's bail," Donnelly replied.

"Mom and Dad?" said Nash.

"Don't know yet."

Brogan jumped in. "Are you talking in riddles again?" he said to Donnelly.

"It's an LLC," Donnelly glanced between her computer screen and her contemporaries. "You know… some company."

"What's the name?" said Nash.

"OPAG," Donnelly replied, "Olympic Peninsula Advocacy Group."

"An advocacy group?" said Brogan. "What are they advocating?"

"It says: Advocating for transparency and equal justice under the law."

"Like those groups that advocate for people who they believe have been falsely imprisoned?"

"That's one example I suppose… yeah."

"How the hell could anyone think that Spencer Dunn is being falsely accused?" Brogan huffed.

"An advocacy group doesn't seem to align with the typical nuts and bolts businesses of the Dunn family," Nash commented.

Donnelly scrolled and clicked on her computer. "You're right, Kenz; this company is not listed within the Dunn family financial statements."

"Well, *somebody* felt Spencer needed assistance beyond what the family could provide," said Brogan.

"Or *would* provide," Nash added her two-cents-worth.

"What're you getting at?"

"As far as I know they never even showed up to visit him in the hospital," Nash replied

"Are you telling me we're supposed to feel sorry for this murderer?"

"Not at all; but his family dynamics could provide us a window into his psyche," Nash replied. "And who knows where that might lead."

"So Laura," Brogan inquired of Donnelly, "Who all is part of this advocacy group anyway?"

"Let's see," Donnelly replied as she manipulated her keyboard. "As near as I can tell it's a bunch of local business leaders," she said as she scanned her screen.

"No surprise there," Nash said.

"Wait a minute," Donnelly said as she eyeballed the screen. "This can't be who I think it is; can it?"

"Who's that?"

Donnelly glanced up at Nash. "If I'm right you're not gonna believe it," she said.

Nash gave Donnelly a 'cut to the chase' gesture.

"One of the members is a *'Garrison Copeland',*" Donnelly said. "You don't think that Garrison is *Gary* Copeland, do you?"

Brogan couldn't believe what he was hearing, "Natalie Copeland's father?"

Donnelly shrugged.

"Can't you verify one way or another?" Brogan asked.

"Umm… I think so," said Donnelly as she began to search. She stopped and glanced between Brogan and Nash, "Gary Copeland's given name is Garrison."

"Son of a bitch," Nash responded.

Donnelly was dumbfounded, "Why the heck would he bail out the guy who murdered his daughter?"

Nash took a breath, "The only thing that makes sense is too mind-boggling to even consider."

"He can't get at Spencer Dunn while he's in the slammer, but if Spencer's out on bail he's an available target?" Brogan offered.

"As crazy as it sounds that's the first thing that popped into my head," Nash replied.

"So, *that's* why Gary Copeland was sniffing around Spencer's hospital room?" Donnelly said.

"To 'take him out' right there in his hospital bed?" Brogan responded to Donnelly.

"Remember that Spencer Dunn's name had not been released to the public, only that there had been an Officer-involved shooting," Nash replied. "So I'm thinking Gary Copeland put two-and-two together and went looking for a room with a cop posted outside."

"Looking to I.D. the suspect?"

"That's my guess."

"But didn't Nancy Copeland say that her husband was not at the hospital?"

"Actually it was only an *'I don't know why he would be'* response, not an out-and-out denial," Nash replied. "And remember at the Memorial Service Gary seemed to know that the suspect had been shot? How would he have known that?"

"Well, crap…" Brogan responded.

"Crap is right," said Nash. "I should have listened to my gut and followed up on the guy I saw at the hospital; but who could have known that Gary Copeland might have been considering vigilante justice?"

"But you said you weren't positive that it was Mister Copeland you saw," said Donnelly.

"You think it's just a coincidence that I see someone who looks like Gary Copeland near Spencer Dunn's hospital room and then BOOM… Spencer gets bailed out of jail via some company partially owned by Gary Copeland?"

"I see what you mean."

"So, what do we do now?" Brogan asked Nash.

"Well, we can't just turn the other cheek and let Gary Copeland do something that he'll regret for the rest of his life," Nash replied.

"We go confront him?"

"No," Nash shook her head. "We can't just dive in head first."

"Why not?"

"For one: we're only speculating as to the motive behind providing Spencer's bail," Nash explained.

"What else could it be?" Brogan interrupted.

"And for two…" Nash glared, "technically, he… Gary Copeland… hasn't done anything illegal."

"Then what's the plan?"

"I'm going to go have a nice little chat with Mister Copeland before he does something stupid," Nash replied. "And then I'm going to pay Spencer Dunn a visit."

"What's the purpose of your visit with Spencer?"

"We'll see what I get out of Gary Copeland; but no matter his explanation a warning to Mister Dunn will surely be appropriate," Nash replied. "Plus, Spencer and I have some unfinished business."

"I can't believe it's our responsibility to protect a cold-blooded killer," Brogan responded.

"You're joking, right?"

"Yeah," Brogan lamented.

"What should the two of us do?" Donnelly said to Nash while head-nodding toward Brogan.

"You two go park near Spencer Dunn's home until I get there."

"Won't it be a bit odd for us to just sit right out in front of his house?" said Brogan.

"Treat it like a stakeout," Nash replied. "Select a strategic spot some distance away where you've got a sightline from all angles."

"Keeping an eye out for Gary Copeland or any suspicious vehicle or person showing up?"

"Precisely."

"Understood."

"What if we're parked down the street but Spencer still sees us and comes over and asks why we're there?" Donnelly asked Nash.

"Tell him you are merely following orders and that I will be there shortly to explain the situation."

36

Detective Nash found herself in uncharted territory. Not only was the current situation a rarity for a seasoned detective; it was one she had never even heard of, let alone experienced. Why would the father of a murder victim post bail for the prime suspect? Was this a grieving father's act of desperation—a precursor to vigilante justice? Considering the oddity of such an act, what else could it be? Nash was grasping for answers to a question she could barely wrap her head around.

As she stepped onto the landing of the Copeland residence Nash was running the impending conversation with Gary through her head.

Rap-rap-rap Nash engaged the doorknocker. The door creaked open to the sight of Gary Copeland.

"Detective," Gary said, "what can I do for you?"

"Good afternoon," Nash replied. "Certain information has come to light which has given me cause for concern."

Gary grew pale as he braced himself for troubling news. "Uh… okay," he responded.

"Along those lines," Nash continued, "I have some questions regarding the actions of one of your companies."

"One of my companies?" Gary was relieved, yet perplexed, "I thought you were a homicide detective?"

"I am," said Nash. "This relates to Spencer Dunn."

"Who?"

"You're really going to play that game?"

"I have no idea what you're talking about."

"I'm talking about your company, Olympic Peninsula Advocacy Group, posting Spencer Dunn's bail."

"It's not my company," Gary replied. "I'm merely one of the members and am not involved in the day-to-day operations of the group, nor do I make the decisions as to whom the company decides to support."

"Then who does?"

"I don't have to share my specific business information with you."

"That's true," Nash replied. "But maybe you can tell me why you would bail out the person who is the prime suspect in your daughter's murder?"

"Wait… what? That's who the firm is supporting?"

"You're telling me that you had no idea?"

"That's what I'm saying."

"Then how do you explain your presence right outside of Spencer Dunn's hospital room?"

"Who says I was at the hospital?"

"I saw you," Nash replied. "And I know you saw me."

Gary remained silent.

"And the Officer posted outside of Mister Dunn's room told me that you asked who was in the room," Nash added.

"It's not every day that you see a cop guarding a hospital room," Gary explained, "I was simply curious."

"So, why were you at the hospital?"

"I was there to visit a friend."

"Who would that be?"

"That's none of your business," Gary replied. "And why am I being interrogated as if I'm some kind of criminal when, in fact, I'm a victim?" he added. "You should be out there prosecuting the monster who killed my daughter instead of standing around here giving me the third-degree."

"I realize that I may be coming across as being a bit harsh; and I apologize," Nash replied. "The purpose of my visit is to stress to you one simple, yet extremely important thought," she said, "Do NOT do something that you'll regret for the rest of your life."

Gary stood in quiet contemplation.

"I promise you that I will do everything in my power to bring Natalie's killer to justice," Nash added. "Please; let the wheels of justice do its job."

Gary paused in thought, and then provided a subtle nod.

"Thank you," Nash said and then turned and walked away.

❈ ❈ ❈

Detective Nash was replaying her conversation with Gary Copeland through her head as she traversed the various thoroughfares that paved the way to Spencer Dunn's residence. In light of recent events she was considering calling an audible in regard to her impending meeting with Spencer. She'd had a line of inquiry in mind, but prevailing winds had impacted her anticipated course. She realized that there were times when the path forward was dictated by the ability to read a situation and react accordingly; counterpunching when necessary.

Pulling up to the curb outside of Spencer Dunn's home Nash caught sight of Brogan's sedan parked down the street. She exited her cruiser, directed a nod of acknowledgment Brogan's way, and negotiated the path leading to Spencer's front door.

Nash stepped onto the landing and reached for the doorbell, but the door opened before she hit the buzzer. An unexpected sight greeted her—Spencer Dunn's lawyer, Trent Lang.

"Good afternoon, detective," Lang commented.

"Mister Lang," Nash replied. "I wasn't expecting to see you here."

"I'm sure you weren't."

"And what, may I ask, has prompted your visit with Mister Dunn?"

"I could ask the same of you," Lang responded. "But in my case, it was when my client noticed your goons parked down the street," he head-nodded toward Brogan's sedan. "I hope this isn't a part of your standard operating procedure or I'll have to consider filing charges of harassment."

"They were merely holding down the fort until my arrival since I had some business to discuss with your client."

"You mean with both my client and me."

"Fair enough," Nash commented.

Lang turned around and motioned for Spencer to join him in the conversation.

"Mister Dunn," Nash acknowledged as Spencer approached.

"Alright," Lang said to Nash, "We're both here," he nodded toward Spencer, "what's on your mind?"

"Your mesh bag of rugby uniforms," Nash directed to Spencer. "We found it."

"Where was it?"

"In a field next to the parking lot at the Quonset Hut Pub & Ale House," Nash replied. "Exactly where you tossed it," she added.

"I did NOT toss it there!" Spencer railed.

"Then how do you explain…?"

"It must have been the guy that put the woman in the trunk," Spencer cut Nash off before she could finish.

"We're back to the doppelganger defense, are we?" Nash responded. "That must mean you have an answer as to how the tube of lipstick used to make your 'Joker smile' matches that of the victim's frown?"

Spencer began to respond, but his attorney gestured for him to remain silent.

"Anyway," Nash continued, "I'm assuming you're interested in the lab results concerning the clothes in the bag?" she glanced between Spencer and Lang. "None of the DNA within the clothing matched what was found in the trunk of your car."

"The bag was lying out in a field," Lang came to Spencer's defense, "the DNA is obviously contaminated."

The apparent naiveté exhibited by the attorney took Nash by surprise, "The State is not looking to utilize the contents of the bag to implicate your client," she paused to clarify, "at least not in regard to this specific crime." She then continued, "The evidence therein merely refutes your assertion that the DNA in the trunk is a result of the bag of clothing."

Spencer looked at attorney Lang; Lang stood silent.

Nash went for the jugular, "So, now that your previous explanation has evaporated, are you ready to explain the DNA from three women and an unknown male in the trunk of your car?"

"We, uh…" Lang began to fumble for a response as he glanced at Spencer and then back to Nash. "Considering all of the evidence…" he continued to stumble, "we were thinking about an Alford plea."

"A what?!" Spencer jumped at Lang.

"We'll talk about that later," Lang replied to Spencer in a hushed voice.

Nash could barely believe what she just heard from an attorney who's supposed to be looking out for his client's best interest. "For one…" she directed to Lang, "that's a discussion to be had with a Prosecutor, not a detective. And for two: it's a subject that needs to be fully understood and agreed-to by your client," she nodded toward Spencer.

Spencer provided a furrowed-brow gesture toward Lang.

"Well…" Nash glanced back and forth between Spencer and Lang. "It looks like you two need to talk," she said as she turned and walked away.

37

As Detective Nash entered the lounge area of The Boat House Grill she spied Deputy Coroner Valerie LaGrange and Sheriff's Deputy Laura Donnelly seated at a small round table–a high-topper with three stools.

"How come I'm always the last to arrive?" Nash said to LaGrange and Donnelly.

"Because you're a workaholic," LaGrange responded with a grin.

"Or that I have no life outside of work," Nash replied.

"No life outside of work?" LaGrange responded. "What about Mister Dreamboat?"

Nash remained silent as she took a seat.

LaGrange glanced at Donnelly. Donnelly shrugged–she had no idea if Nash was implying something or not.

"What're we drinking?" Nash inquired.

"Chard," LaGrange pointed at her wine glass. "Pinot Noir," Donnelly held up her glass.

The server arrived and Nash pointed to Donnelly's glass, "I'll have one of those," she said.

"Of course," the server replied and departed.

"So hey," LaGrange started, "I know our general rule is to avoid shop talk with exception of funny stories…"

Nash interrupted, "Like the streaker who thought he was running butt-naked through his ex's wedding and it turned out to be a church service?"

"What??" Donnelly interjected.

"Yep," Nash responded to Donnelly, "he had the wrong location."

"Oh my gosh, that's hilarious!"

Nash returned her focus to LaGrange. "Anyway, I'm assuming you wanted to suspend the 'no shop talk' rule?"

"Not completely," LaGrange replied, "but I have to admit I'm chomping at the bit as to what Gary Copeland had to say."

"No problem," Nash responded. "As far as Mister Copeland goes, he pleaded ignorance about his Advocacy Group posting bail for Spencer Dunn."

"You're kidding?" said LaGrange.

"Nope; and of course I wasn't necessarily buying it, but at the very least now he knows we're onto him."

"What if he doesn't care?" said Donnelly.

"That we're onto him?"

"Yes."

"For him to give up on the criminal justice system and take matters into his own hands simply because Spencer Dunn made bail would be absolutely ridiculous."

"Yeah, but then why did he post Spencer's bail?"

"Like I was saying, he said that he was not involved in the decision," Nash replied. "Now if Spencer somehow gets acquitted we'd have a major reason for concern."

"Acquitted?" LaGrange responded, "I was thinking the clincher was the chemical match between his Joker smile and the disgusting frown he drew on Natalie?"

"I agree," Nash replied, "but as you well know, as much as we'd like to think otherwise, justice is an inexact science."

"True," LaGrange nodded. "Nonetheless, the whole thing with Gary Copeland's Advocacy Group posting bail for his daughter's alleged murderer sure is an odd situation," LaGrange shook her head.

"The exact reason I went to have a chat with Mister Copeland," Nash responded.

"And you also talked to Spencer Dunn, correct?"

"I did; and with all the evidence we've got against him it looks like his lawyer is ready to throw in the towel."

"You're kidding?"

"Nope; he actually mentioned making an Alford plea," Nash said and took a sip of her wine. "And I'm positive that this was the first Spencer had heard of it," she continued. "I'm also ninety-nine percent sure that Spencer has no clue as to what an Alford plea even is."

LaGrange turned to Donnelly, "Were you aware of all this?"

"Oh yeah," Donnelly replied, "Kenz gave Dirk and me the rundown this afternoon."

LaGrange returned her focus to Nash. "An Alford plea," she said, "Isn't that kind of a guilty plea without actually admitting guilt?"

"Sort of," Nash replied. "Basically, the defendant is maintaining their innocence, but they've determined that the evidence is so strong against them that they would likely be found guilty by a jury."

"So, they're looking to get a lesser sentence than if found guilty in a trial?"

"Pretty much."

"But if you're essentially taking a plea bargain, yet not admitting guilt, then that means no allocution, correct?"

"Correct," Nash replied. "No 'standing before the court and explaining exactly what you did, and why you did it'."

"I can't see any way, shape, or form that Gary and Nancy Copeland would be okay with that."

"I doubt they'd want to hear the gory details; I mean hell, Nancy almost fainted at the sight of her daughter on the autopsy table," Nash responded. "But I'm sure they want to know why the bastard did what he did… his motive."

"You don't think Spencer would truly offer to make such a plea, do you?" Donnelly asked Nash.

"Oh, hell no," Nash replied. "Nor do I think the Prosecutor or the Judge would accept such a plea." She thought for a moment and added,

"To put it mildly, in my opinion Spencer's lawyer is in WAY over his head."

LaGrange nodded understanding, "And what about your related case: Officer Wilberforce?" she said to Nash.

"My best guess…" Nash replied, "Next stop–a Grand Jury to determine if charges should be brought."

"So, it's out of your hands?"

"As of the moment; that's correct."

"Do you have a gut-feel as to the outcome?"

"All I can say is: I wouldn't want to be in his shoes."

"Doesn't sound very good for him," LaGrange said.

"So, hey," Nash changed the subject, "Evan Lowell said he's going to be attending some kind of symposium this week."

"I'm going to be there as well," said LaGrange. "It's all about forensics; so there will be a lot of shared information relating to past cases, the latest techniques, stuff like that."

"Evan said he was one of the speakers; he was practicing saying deox… umm, deoxyribo…"

"Deoxyribonucleic acid?" LaGrange interrupted.

"Yeah; that's it," said Nash, "I told him he should stick with the acronym."

"Good advice," LaGrange grinned.

"Any idea what he's going to be discussing?"

"I think the Wagner case."

"That'd be a good one," Nash replied, "And how about you?"

"I'll be there to answer any questions related to his discussion, but I have no presentation of my own."

The server arrived with a veggie plate and some smoked salmon.

"Looks like a cue to cool it with the shop talk," Nash proclaimed.

"You ordered smoked salmon?" LaGrange said to Nash. "Ian's going to be treated to 'Mackenzie Salmon Breath' later?" she said with air-quotes. "How romantic," she added with a grin.

Nash remained silent, but provided a look that drew concern from LaGrange and Donnelly.

"Is something up between you two?" LaGrange queried.

"Ugh; don't ask," Nash replied.

"Really?"

"Yeah," Nash swirled her wine and took a sip. "We're not exactly on speaking terms at the moment."

"Wow, what happened?"

"He crossed a line," Nash replied. "One that I'm not sure he can uncross."

Silence overtook the moment. LaGrange and Donnelly glanced at each other and then returned their gaze to Nash.

"It all started with a dream… well… a nightmare," Nash said, "a week ago Sunday."

"Isn't that the night…" LaGrange started.

"That we first saw Natalie Copeland's sad, lifeless, body," Nash interrupted.

"Was the nightmare about her?"

"No; it was about Lyle and me," Nash replied, "umm… you know… *that* night."

LaGrange nodded. Donnelly, on the other hand, was unfamiliar with the name; but had an inkling that it might relate to the story Nash had shared on a prior occasion.

"It was the middle of the night, he was fast asleep, and I was staring at my bruised and battered face in the bathroom mirror," Nash continued. "And I was saying to myself *'When do I make it stop?'* over and over." She took a breath, "The next thing I know I'm jerking awake so hard it startled Ian."

"He didn't react like he did when you first shared the whole thing about that night, did he?" LaGrange asked.

"No; actually he was very comforting and understanding," Nash replied, "It wasn't until several days later that the shit hit the fan."

LaGrange and Donnelly remained silent, hoping that Nash would elaborate. Nash took a sip of her wine and then continued, "I got home last Thursday night and discovered Ian looking into my past," she said.

"What?? You're kidding?" LaGrange replied.

"No joke."

"What do you mean by *'looking into your past'*?" LaGrange asked, "Or is that prying too much?"

"Although it was *my* past he was looking into, his specific focus was on Lyle."

"Really? I never thought of Ian as being the jealous type."

"Me neither. And he started freaking-out because apparently Lyle disappeared the same day that I escaped from his abuse."

"Why would he get freaked out about that?"

"Well, there's more to it than someone just 'up and leaving'," Nash said. "Ian turned into some kind of amateur investigator, and according to his research Lyle literally disappeared without a trace."

"What??"

"Yeah; he said that any evidence of Lyle's existence stopped on that date," said Nash.

"Are you saying what I think you're saying?"

"I don't know if I'd give it too much credence," Nash replied. "I'm sure Ian's investigation is full of holes; but he sure was, or maybe even still is, obsessed about the whole thing."

"Have you looked into it at all?" asked LaGrange.

"Me? No," Nash replied. "I mean hell; why should I care if the bastard fell off a cliff? That means he could no longer verbally and physically pummel any other poor defenseless woman."

"He fell off a cliff?" Donnelly responded.

"I… uh… I don't know; I was just providing an example," Nash replied. "You know, a figure of speech; like the saying 'fell off the face of the earth'."

"Any idea why Ian was so obsessed with looking into this guy?"

"Well; in the dream I was bludgeoning Lyle with a baseball bat," Nash replied. "I guess Ian took that as being some kind of confession in lieu of being nothing more than a nightmare."

Donnelly grew wide-eyed. "Whoa," was all she could muster.

"He actually thought you murdered this guy?" LaGrange said to Nash.

"Apparently the whole thing raised his curiosity, and then his so-called 'research' tended to add fuel to his suspicion," Nash replied.

"Holy crap."

"Yeah," Nash shook her head.

The more LaGrange heard the more things weren't quite adding up. "But don't you think the fact that Lyle was never seen nor heard from again is rather strange?" she commented. "I mean in this day and age with all of the technology at our disposal?"

"You're giving Ian's investigative abilities way too much credit," Nash responded. "I'm sure he didn't do much more than Google his way around the name *Lyle Casey* and ran into not-too-surprising dead ends."

"You've got a point there."

"Hell, according to Ian the local authorities didn't think there was anything to pursue," Nash said. "And no Missing Persons Report was ever filed."

LaGrange nodded.

"I cannot even imagine how I'd react if I found someone digging into *my* past," Donnelly commented.

"I gave him a piece of my mind and then told him to get out," Nash said.

"And you haven't spoken to him since?" LaGrange asked.

"He showed up out-of-the-blue a couple of nights ago," Nash replied. "I said that I wasn't ready to talk… that I needed time to process everything," she added, "and that's where we stand."

"Sorry to hear that," said LaGrange.

38

It was 6:20 Wednesday morning and the Sheriff's Office was mostly quiet. Sheriff Clarke was holed-up in his office, Detective Nash had not yet arrived, and Detective Brogan and Deputy Donnelly were in the middle of a hushed conversation in an otherwise-empty Break Room. The discussion revolved around Donnelly sharing information learned the night before.

"Ian was looking into this guy Lyle from Kenz's past?" Brogan quietly responded to Donnelly's news as he glanced around the area to ensure no one was within earshot, "Holy shit!"

"And get this," Donnelly said. "The day after Lyle beat the crap out of Kenz he was never seen or heard from again."

"Wait… what; he beat the crap out of Kenz?"

"You never heard about that?"

"Not a word."

"Shit; I thought you knew," Donnelly began to sweat, "You can't share any of this with her!"

Brogan stood in stunned silence—seemingly oblivious to Donnelly's statement.

Donnelly glared at Brogan. "Dirk!" she elbowed him.

Brogan snapped out of his fog, "Uh, yeah… of course… not a peep."

"What do you think about the fact that this guy was never seen or heard from again?"

"You said that this was all according to Ian, right?"

"Correct."

"C'mon Laura, Ian does some amateurish online search and thinks he's unraveled some unknown crime?"

175

"Yeah, you're right," Donnelly nodded.

"Out of curiosity, what was this guy's last name?"

"Casey… Lyle Casey."

Brogan and Donnelly were startled by the sound of the office door opening and closing. "Crap, that's probably her!" Donnelly said. "Remember… not a word of any of this!"

Brogan gave Donnelly the thumbs-up and then grabbed his coffee mug. Donnelly followed suit just as Nash entered the room.

"Hey, what are you two up to?" Nash said as she spied the duo.

"Uhh… just grabbing some coffee," Brogan replied.

"Ditto," Donnelly added as she held up her mug.

Nash headed straight for the coffee decanter, "I'm right there with ya," she replied.

Brogan and Donnelly headed out of the Break Room while Nash poured herself a cup of java. She took a sip and pondered Brogan and Donnelly's 'looked like the cat that just ate the canary' demeanor when she had shown up. *Must have been discussing something personal,* Nash thought to herself.

Returning to the office area Nash noticed both Brogan and Donnelly staring at the murder board.

Brogan caught sight of Nash and said, "With Natalie Copeland's case to the Prosecutor, and Wilberforce's actions to a Grand Jury, I'm guessing we should start taking everything off the board and placing it in the associated case file?"

"I take it you didn't get anything new after Laura and I left yesterday?" Nash replied.

"I attempted to get some updates, but all I got was a whole bunch of nothing," Brogan responded. "Natalie's car is still missing, Lowell's team has not uncovered the clothes and gloves that Spencer was wearing when he was in the car, and there's nothing on the unknown DNA samples in the trunk."

"In that case, it looks like you're right," said Nash. "Let's grab a couple of boxes and start loading them up."

Brogan's cell phone rang. "Detective Brogan," he answered the call. "Really? Don't let it go anywhere; we'll be down soon to check it out." He turned to Nash and Donnelly. "Belay my last," he said, "Natalie's car was just found in Mason County."

"Whereabouts?" said Nash.

"The Thriftway parking lot in Belfair."

"Any idea how long it's been there?"

"Deputy Myers of the Mason County Sheriff's Office said he'd fill us in when we got there."

Nash grabbed her cell phone and made a call. "Hey Evan," she spoke into the phone, "Natalie Copeland's car turned up in Belfair, can you meet us there?" She nodded as she listened to Lowell's response to her inquiry. "That's today?" she said. "Well crap; I guess we'll check it out and then have the car towed to the CSI garage." She turned to Brogan and Donnelly, "Obviously the board stays as-is for the moment," she grabbed her jacket, "Let's roll."

❄❄❄

Nash wheeled her sedan into the Thriftway parking area and immediately spotted a Mason County Sheriff's Office cruiser at the far end of the lot. Near the cruiser sat a blue Subaru Impreza matching the description of Natalie Copeland's car—a check of the license plate confirmed the car as hers.

Exiting Nash's sedan the detectives were greeted by Deputy Myers of the Mason County Sheriff's Office.

"You just discovered the car today?" Nash said to Myers.

"We got the call yesterday and spent the time between then and now trying to find out if it had a reason to be here such as an employee of the store and, if not, whether any of the employees might have known the owner," Myers replied. "We also attempted to determine how long it had been here."

"What did you come up with?"

"As you know, the plate and the VIN identify Natalie Copeland as the owner, and none of the employees knew her or recognized the car," Myers said. "As far as how long it has been here: we've got a fairly large window of possibility–anywhere from a few days to a week-and-a-half."

"You're not able to narrow down the timeline any further?"

"Unfortunately, there are two factors working against us," Myers replied. "The store is open twenty-four hours-a-day, so there would always be cars in the lot," he said. "And the parking lot is adjacent to a Park-and-Ride, so everyone who saw the car on a daily basis thought it was there for one of those two reasons."

"What about surveillance cameras?" Nash said as she thumb-pointed toward the front of the store.

"The store manager said they don't cover this far out in the lot, but we haven't gone through them to verify that claim."

"No problem, we've got that," Nash replied.

"Yes, ma'am."

"Who called it in?"

"One of the employees thought it was strange that the car was always in that exact spot, and with those flyers," Myers pointed, "on the windshield over several days."

"Thanks, Deputy; we'll take it from here," said Nash.

After the Deputy departed Nash reached for the flyers on the car's windshield and said, "Not to disparage the Deputy, but let's see if he failed 'Investigative Techniques 101'."

"How's that?" Donnelly replied.

"If any of these flyers are advertising events that occur on a specific date," Nash flipped through the flyers.

"Ahh… like a pre-Halloween sale would tell us the car has been here over a week."

"Bingo."

"Hmm… these all are either for events this upcoming weekend, or that cover the entire month," Nash finished flipping through the flyers. "So much for narrowing the timeline down based on these."

"I know it's a longshot," Donnelly started, "but I could talk to each of these businesses and see if they can tell us exactly when they were placing flyers here in the parking lot."

"Sounds good," Nash replied.

"I guess that means I get the videos to review?" Brogan chimed in.

"Yep," said Nash. "See if this area of the parking lot shows up, if Natalie's car comes into view anywhere within the frames, if Natalie herself shows up, and if Spencer or his car appears."

"Got it."

Nash turned to Donnelly, "Laura, get some exterior shots of the car and the surrounding area, and then we'll got some of the interior."

"Yes, ma'am," Donnelly replied and then reached into Nash's sedan and grabbed the camera.

"If the car showed up after Saturday the twenty-sixth we've got a whole new mystery to unravel," Nash noted.

"What's that?" said Brogan.

"Natalie was in the trunk of Spencer's car, and Spencer was either at home getting gunned-down by Wilberforce, or in the hospital recovering from his gunshot wound."

"In other words," Brogan recognized, "how would the car have gotten here?"

"Precisely."

"Any chance that there's a sufficient window in the timeline for Spencer to have gotten away from Wilberforce, dumped Natalie's car here, and then back home before officers showed up and Wilberforce shot him?" Donnelly interjected.

"That's something for you and Dirk to work on when we get back to the office."

"Roger that," Donnelly and Brogan replied in unison.

39

Venturing into the office Detectives Nash and Brogan noticed a handwritten note on the murder board which read 'Retain' and was signed 'Clarke'.

Brogan turned to Nash, "Do you think Sheriff Clarke added the note based on the discovery of Natalie Copeland's car?" he said, "or maybe he has some new information that would keep the case active?"

"Your guess is as good as mine," Nash replied just as Sheriff Clarke entered the area.

"Detective," Clarke said to Nash, "we need to talk."

"Yes, Sir," Nash replied. As she began to follow the Sheriff back toward his office she glanced back at Brogan and shrugged.

Grabbing a seat in his office Clarke gestured to Nash to take a seat at the table adjacent to his desk. He crossed his arms and leaned back in his chair. "So, what's the latest with the Copeland case?" Clarke said. "You found Natalie's car, correct?"

"Yes, Sir; it's on its way to the CSI garage as we speak," Nash replied. "One of the things they'll be looking for is any evidence of Spencer Dunn having been in the vehicle."

"Looking to add to the evidence against Mister Dunn that we already have in-hand, I assume?"

"Yes."

"That's good because we may need that," Clarke replied, "and a whole lot more."

Nash was befuddled. "Sir?" she said.

"I'll get to that in a minute," Clarke responded. "What else have you got?"

"In relation to the car: Brogan's going through Thriftway's surveillance videos," she thumb-pointed behind her. "It was Thriftway's parking lot where it was found."

Clarke nodded.

"There were a bunch of flyers on the windshield, but none of them helped us dial-in the timeline as to how long the car has been there," said Nash. "So Donnelly is visiting each of the associated businesses in hopes they can tell us when they posted the flyers."

"I take it you got nothing definitive from the Thriftway employees?"

"Correct."

Clarke nodded once again, this time adding an exhale.

"So, you were saying we may be in need of any additional evidence that might surface from Natalie's car?" said Nash.

"Possibly more than that," Clarke responded.

"Why?" Nash replied, "What's up?"

"Spencer Dunn's lawyer filed a motion to suppress all evidence found in his car."

"A motion to suppress; does he even know what that means?! Yesterday he was ready to prod his client into making an Alford plea for crying out loud!"

"That guy's out; his family hired a new lawyer."

"Well, crap; we could be screwed."

"The 'procedural nightmare' captured by Officer Wilberforce's dash and body cams you were warning me about?"

"That's it exactly," Nash replied. "There would be no reason to file a motion to suppress unless they are basing it on Wilberforce's actions as shown on the videos."

"Some defense attorneys file a motion solely because they have no legitimate defense for their client and are merely attempting to throw a Hail Mary," said Clarke. "But it sounds like you think their motion is valid?"

"I may not be a lawyer, but I've been around the block enough times to recognize a potential evidentiary problem when I see it," Nash said. "I've been worried about it from the first time I viewed the videos."

"Well, shit," Clarke replied. "Obviously I need to watch them so I can see what we're up against."

"We can go over them as soon as we're done here."

"Give me about ten minutes," said Clarke. "In the meantime, you and your team need take a fresh look at the case from a dual lens: Digging up new evidence; and seeing what existing evidence might still be relevant even if what was found in the car is ruled inadmissible."

"As far as existing evidence goes: you're talking about anything that might fall under either the Independent Source or Inevitable Discovery Doctrines?"

"Are you sure you're not a lawyer, you're starting to sound like a Prosecutor?" Clarke grinned. "And you're exactly right."

"Got it," Nash said, "Anything else?"

"That's all I had for now."

Nash got up from her seat. "I'll get those dash-cam and body-cam videos ready for your review," she said and then departed Clarke's office.

Nash returned to her area of the office–Brogan was staring at his computer screen. "Reviewing surveillance footage?" Nash said to Brogan.

"Yep," Brogan replied. "I'm coming up empty thus far–no Spencer Dunn, no Natalie Copeland, neither one of their vehicles."

"Got any theories?"

"A few."

"Let's hear 'em."

"I'll start with the obvious," Brogan replied. "Either Spencer got lucky, or he was aware of the cameras and purposely avoided them."

"Assuming that Spencer was the one who parked the car," said Nash.

"Right," said Brogan. "Natalie could have parked the car there for some reason and left with Spencer."

"Maybe the adjacent Park-and-Ride lot was full and Natalie parked where we found her car and then caught a bus?"

"Crap; I hadn't thought of that," Brogan replied. He thought for a moment and added, "Heck; under that scenario Spencer could have done the same thing."

"Very true."

"I'll check bus schedules to see the various destinations from that Park-and-Ride."

"And then compare all of those with the timeline on the board."

"Got it."

"What else?" Nash said.

"Back to the idea of Spencer dumping the car," said Brogan. "He obviously had to do so before Wilberforce pulled him over that Saturday night."

"Unless, like we said earlier, there's a sufficient window from the time he bolted from his car until Wilberforce showed up at his house," Nash reminded. "Or have you already determined that scenario is not possible?"

"Nah; I simply had a brain-freeze regarding that option," Brogan replied.

"When you lay it out, let's not rely on a guesstimate, we need to actually drive the route from the point he took off in front of Wilberforce, to Belfair, and back to his house."

"Drive the route?" Brogan questioned. "But he was on foot when he got away from Wilberforce?"

"We can't assume he walked or jogged home, we have to consider that he could've gotten a ride somehow."

"But Laura said there were no Ubers or taxis to his home that night?"

"What if he hitched a ride?"

"Oh yeah, I hadn't thought of that."

"And just to be sure you understand where I'm coming from on this endeavor," said Nash. "We're not trying to prove whether he dumped the car within this window, we are merely attempting to determine if it's *possible* that he did so."

"Understood," Brogan replied. "But if we *are* able to prove it…?"

"All the better," Nash interrupted.

"Got it," said Brogan. "So, what did Sheriff Clarke have to say?" he added.

"I'll go over that with you and Laura as soon as she shows up," Nash responded. She glanced at her watch, "In fact, shouldn't she…"

The office door opened and Deputy Donnelly entered the room.

"Never mind," Nash said as her question had been answered.

"Nice to see you could join us," Brogan flipped Donnelly crap.

"What can I say, Deputy Myers and I had a few businesses to run down," Donnelly defended.

"I was just yankin' your chain," Brogan responded. "Any luck?"

"Not really," Donnelly replied. "They had all printed their flyers prior to Saturday the twenty-sixth, but they weren't sure if all of them had been placed at local businesses or on any vehicles at that time, or if they were delivered later."

Nash's cell phone rang—it was Evan Lowell. "Hey Evan," Nash spoke into her phone, "are you all done spinning 'tales of suspense and awe' with your fellow forensics experts?"

"Yes I am; and they were blown away by the details of the Wagner case," Lowell replied.

"So was I," Nash said, "And I lived it."

"What's the news on Natalie Copeland's car?"

"It will be waiting for you at the garage when you get to work in the morning," Nash replied. "Our initial look-see is inconclusive."

"I'll see what my team and I can come up with."

"Go through it with a fine-toothed comb," Nash responded, "We may need all the new evidence we can get."

"How's that?"

"Let me put it this way," Nash replied, "Assume you had to build a case without relying on the evidence discovered in Spencer Dunn's car."

"What??"

"I'll stop by and provide you details tomorrow morning," Nash said and then ended her call.

Brogan and Donnelly were stunned by Nash's statement to Lowell. "What... what's the issue regarding evidence?" Brogan said to Nash.

"Sheriff Clarke just gave me some potentially troubling news," Nash replied.

40

Detective Nash entered the CSI garage to the sight of Evan Lowell and his latex-gloved team crawling all over both Natalie Copeland's and Spencer Dunn's vehicles. Lowell was at the driver's seat of Spencer's car.

"Hey Evan," Nash said to Lowell as she donned a pair of gloves.

"Hey Kenz," Lowell replied as he climbed out of the car.

"I thought for sure you'd be working over Natalie's car; not Spencer's."

"You said we should be looking for all new evidence, so we're going over both vehicles," Lowell responded. "Plus, something I discovered about Natalie's car prompted me to make a similar check with Spencer's."

"What was that?"

"Natalie's driver-seat position is too far back for her to have been behind the wheel," Lowell said.

"Meaning she could not have been the one who parked the car," Nash concluded.

"Not unless she moved the seat back for some reason."

"And what was the deal with Spencer's car?"

"The as-found position of the driver's seat was different than the 'memory' positions."

"In what way?"

"Spencer is just over 5'9"," Lowell explained. "The seat position would tend to indicate someone around six-feet tall or so was behind the wheel."

"What if he always moves the seat back when he gets out of the car, and then hit's the 'memory' button after he climbs in?"

"That's certainly possible," Lowell replied. "But we also measured the distance from the pedals to the seat in Natalie's car, and they are approximately the same as that found with Spencer's."

"In my mind that would seem to confirm that Spencer does exactly that when getting in and out of *any* car he's driving," said Nash, "and that he was behind the wheel in both vehicles."

"Perhaps; but don't you think his attorney would argue that it indicates it was someone *else* behind the wheel?" Lowell replied. "You know… his so-called 'doppelganger defense'?"

"I think his whole 'doppelganger defense' blew up in his face with the lipstick match between his Joker smile and Natalie's frown," Nash replied. "I mean hell; it was that particular evidence that caused his previous attorney to cry uncle."

"You make a good point."

"Along those lines though…" Nash had a disconcerting thought, "You don't think the lipstick match could be ruled inadmissible if the motion to suppress goes through; do you?"

"That's way outside of my wheelhouse; you'd have to talk to someone in the Prosecutor's Office."

"The Prosecutor was salivating over that piece of evidence, so I'm sure they'll fight like hell for it," Nash said. "In fact, now that I think of it, at the very least it should fall under the Inevitable Discovery Doctrine."

"Makes sense," Lowell shook his head.

"So, what else have you got?"

Lowell's demeanor turned grim. He head-nodded toward the rear of Spencer's car and trekked to the trunk; Nash followed Lowell's path. Lowell raised the trunk lid and said, "I screwed up."

"What're you talking about?"

Lowell pointed to the trunk mat, "Do you see the difference in the fabric of the trunk mat and that of the other areas of the trunk?"

Nash shook her head, "Not really."

"We didn't either," Lowell replied. "But look what we find when we lift up the edge," he said as he grasped a corner of the mat.

"Another trunk mat," said Nash, "So?"

"It provides an explanation as to why the blood and DNA pattern on the mat found under the victim did not match that found on the other areas of the trunk."

"And the mat underneath?"

"It's consistent with the rest of the trunk," Lowell replied, "no match to the samples found on the upper mat."

"So, what are you telling me?"

"To be honest, I'm not really sure."

"C'mon Evan, do you know how many people use aftermarket floor mats and trunk mats in their vehicles?"

"Yeah, I know; it's probably in the millions."

"Precisely," Nash responded. "So I wouldn't get all 'wrapped around the axle' on something you didn't catch initially that's likely irrelevant."

"I suppose," Lowell replied, "but we should still pass it on to the Prosecutor so that he can decide if it needs to be included as part of the Discovery process."

"Hey; do what you gotta do," said Nash. She took a breath and shifted her focus. "Back to Natalie's car," she thumb-pointed, "Do you have anything other than the seat position?"

"No navigation system, so we can't track where her car has been… her various destinations."

"That sucks."

"Yep," Lowell nodded. "Other than that, we're collecting samples, swabbing surfaces, and dusting for prints virtually everywhere in there; but we haven't gotten a chance to analyze anything as of yet."

"Understood."

Nash and Lowell's conversation was interrupted by a familiar sight— it was Deputy Coroner Valerie LaGrange approaching.

"Hey Val," Nash said to LaGrange, "what prompts your excursion this way?"

"Evan told me about Natalie's car before he left the symposium,"

LaGrange replied. "Plus, the M.E. from Grays Harbor County went over a very intriguing case that occurred there about a year ago."

"Relevant to our case?"

"There are some eye-opening similarities."

"Really?" Nash perked up. "You've got my attention."

"Grays Harbor County Sheriff's Deputies received a call about a homicide inside a small cabin on a remote piece of property about eight miles north of Hoquiam," LaGrange said. "Not too far from Wynoochee Lake."

"What did they find?"

"A twenty-nine year-old woman, Samantha Dalton, with injuries consistent with those of Natalie Copeland."

"Are you kidding me?"

"Not only did she have abrasions on her wrists and ankles," LaGrange explained, "but she had been silenced, just like Natalie, by cutting through her windpipe."

"Son of a bitch," Nash exhaled.

"There were no shackles found within the cabin, but there were large eyebolts that could have been used as anchors for such restraining devices."

"Holy shit," said Nash, "We've got the bastard!"

"This one," LaGrange nodded, "Yes."

"Wait," Nash was befuddled, "What do you mean?"

"The perp was also deceased at the scene."

"You've got to be frickin' kidding me?!" Nash vented. "You're telling me that this was not the handiwork of Spencer Dunn?"

"Unfortunately," LaGrange shrugged.

"Maybe he's a copycat killer?" Lowell interjected.

"Was this homicide publicized at all?" Nash asked LaGrange.

"I hadn't heard of it before the symposium," LaGrange replied, "but it may have been covered by the local press."

"What's the perp's name?" Nash retrieved her memo pad from her jacket pocket. "I want to see if I can tie this guy to our suspect."

"Greg Wilson."

"What was his cause of death?" Nash began to write in her memo pad.

"Severed carotid artery," LaGrange replied. "By the same knife used to slit the victim's throat."

"So, he bled-out?" Nash continued to write.

"Exsanguination… that's correct."

Nash suddenly stopped writing mid-sentence, "Wait a minute… the same knife?"

"Yep."

"How is that possible?!" Nash replied. "How does he slice her throat and then have his own throat slit by the same knife? Or did he die by his own hand… committing suicide after killing her?"

"I haven't seen the official autopsy report, all I've got is what was presented at the symposium," LaGrange responded. "But what investigators concluded was that after her throat was cut Samantha managed to get the knife and slashed Wilson right in the jugular."

"The victim managed to take out the perp before she succumbed from her injuries?" Nash shook her head. "At least she was able to get her revenge… even if she wasn't able to see it."

"She probably *was* able to see it, actually," LaGrange replied. "Carotid artery…" she nodded, "He likely bled out before she did."

"Wow," Lowell responded to LaGrange's statement. "You realize that you're dying, but you get to exact your revenge and see your killer die before you do."

"Good for her," said Nash. She turned to LaGrange, "Hey Val; is there any chance you can get hold of a copy of Samantha Dalton's autopsy report?"

"Considering the similarities between their case and ours, I can't see why they wouldn't want to help us out," LaGrange replied. "I'll give them a call and let you know."

"Perfect," Nash responded.

41

"Why don't you just ask Spencer if he moves the seat back whenever he gets out of his car, and then repositions it after he climbs back in?" Detective Brogan said to Detective Nash after she shared the details of her visit to the CSI garage.

"You're kidding me, right?" Nash replied.

"Uh, why do you say that?"

"What if he does, in fact, move the seat back when he gets out of the car," Nash responded. "Do you think he would actually admit that?"

"Why wouldn't he?"

"Because he could lie and say 'NO' in order to perpetuate his 'someone else was in my car' defense."

"Even though we have him on camera?" Donnelly chimed in.

"I can't speak for his current lawyer," Nash replied, "but remember that his first lawyer tried that con even in the face of the video footage."

"I see what you mean," Donnelly nodded.

"And here's another option," Nash said. "What if he purposely moved the seat back in order to make it look like he was not the driver?"

"Hmm… then we'd have a second reason for the seat being in that position," Brogan responded.

"Correct," said Nash. "Thus the extent of our involvement is to share the possibilities with the Prosecutor so that they can provide reasonable explanations for the seat position," she added, "if it comes up in the trial."

"Understood."

Nash then updated Brogan and Donnelly about the murder in Grays Harbor County.

"Holy crap!" Brogan responded to Nash's news.

Donnelly had a thought in regard thereof; "I realize it's a closed case in another county," she said, "but do you think there's any chance that the unidentified male DNA in Spencer's car could be that of this Greg Wilson guy?"

"You'd think we would have gotten a match when we ran the DNA from the trunk through CODIS," Nash replied, "but since Grays Harbor County authorities had an open and shut case maybe they decided there was no reason to go to the expense of running Wilson's DNA?"

"So, we should check, right?"

"I'll take that on," said Nash, "I want you two to try to find any ties you can between Spencer Dunn and Greg Wilson."

"Are you implying that they could be accomplices?" Brogan wondered. "How could that be the case when Wilson has been dead for almost a year?"

"Just because Wilson wasn't involved in Natalie's death doesn't mean he and Spencer weren't co-conspirators in Samantha Dalton's death," Nash replied. "I don't know about you, but I'm not ready to write these two murders off as one-in-a-million coincidences."

"One in a million?"

"Okay, that may be an exaggeration; but you get the picture..."
Brogan nodded.

"If so," Donnelly chimed in, "Then wouldn't it be possible for Spencer Dunn's DNA to be inside Wilson's cabin?"

"That's a good point," Nash replied. "I should try to take a peek at their case file."

"How about taking a look at the cabin itself?"

"I'll attempt to make a run at both."

"Something just hit me," said Donnelly. "Remember when we were trying to place Spencer along the Oregon coast when Natalie was there?"

Nash saw where Donnelly was going; "You turned up activity showing him both near, and along, the *Washington* coast," she said.

"Do you know the exact location of the cabin?" Donnelly asked.

"Not off hand," Nash replied, "but I can get it from Val."

"Great; I'll see if I can place Spencer in the vicinity."

Nash gave Donnelly a thumbs-up.

Brogan turned to Nash, "If you didn't have anything else, we," he nodded toward Donnelly, "have some info for you."

"Go for it," Nash replied.

"While you were at the CSI garage we drove the path from where Spencer ditched Wilberforce, to Belfair, to Spencer's home," Brogan responded. "And we laid out the timeline on the whiteboard."

"Let's see what you've got," Nash said as she began to trek to the whiteboard—Brogan and Donnelly following suit.

Once at the board Brogan began… "Wilberforce pulled over Spencer just past midnight," he said and then turned to Nash. "About what time did you get the call from Captain O'Rourke?"

"One-thirty-four A.M."

"You remember the exact time?"

"Don't you look at the clock when your phone rings at o'dark-thirty?"

Brogan nodded and then added the time to the associated item on the board.

"How does my receiving a call have anything to do with Spencer's window of opportunity?" said Nash.

"It doesn't," Brogan replied. "It merely puts everything within the timeline in perspective."

"Got it."

"Now according to the files, supported by statements and body cameras," Brogan continued, "Wilberforce and Sergeant Johansen arrived at Spencer's house at 2:33 A.M.," he pointed at the board.

Nash scanned the board and stated, "So that gives us about a two-hour window… from around twelve-fifteen to two-fifteen… best case scenario."

"Correct."

"It would be tight," Donnelly said to Nash, "but do-able."

"I take it your assumption has Natalie's car at Spencer's home?" said Nash.

"Yes; but it could have been anywhere within the drive path," Donnelly traced out the path on a map, "so long as Spencer got a ride to wherever Natalie's car was parked."

"We should talk to his neighbors to see if Natalie's car was at or near his house that night."

"I concur."

"Does the timeline work if Spencer ran home in lieu of getting a ride?"

"Possibly," Brogan chimed in, "but it would be real tight, and I'm not sure that Spencer is that much of a physical specimen."

"Wait a minute," something dawned on Nash. She turned to Donnelly, "You came up empty when you checked cabs and Ubers that might have picked someone up near Spencer's car and dropped them at his home, correct?"

"Correct," Donnelly replied.

"We didn't take into account that he had to dump Natalie's car…"

"Damn, you're right," Donnelly interjected, "We need to expand our search all the way to Belfair."

"Precisely," Nash responded.

Nash's cell phone rang–it was Deputy Coroner Valerie LaGrange. "Hey Val," Nash spoke into her phone.

"Hey Kenz, I just got off the phone with the Grays Harbor County Coroner's Office and they're sending me the autopsy results for both Samantha Dalton and Greg Wilson," LaGrange replied. "I should have them either later today or early tomorrow morning."

"That's great," said Nash, "You'll let me know when you've completed your review?"

"Of course."

42

Deputy Laura Donnelly wasn't all that surprised to see Detective Dirk Brogan's car already in its parking spot when she arrived at the Sheriff's Office; she figured he had likely just arrived himself and was either getting coffee brewing or reading the morning paper before the official start of their shift. However, entering the office to the sight of Brogan pounding away on his keyboard had her wondering what he was up to.

Brogan glanced up at Donnelly. "Hey Laura," he said and then returned his focus to his computer screen.

"What, you woke up early and couldn't get back to sleep so you decided you might as well come to work and be productive?" Donnelly commented.

"Something like that," Brogan replied while still staring at his screen.

"Or are you merely reading the online version of the local paper?"

"Nah," Brogan continued to focus on his screen, "Just doing some research."

"Spencer Dunn? Natalie Copeland? Samantha Dalton? Greg Wilson?" Donnelly asked.

"I was planning to start with Wilson, but I got sidetracked."

"Sidetracked?"

"Yeah; curiosity got the best of me."

"What're you talking about?"

"It looks like Ian was right," said Brogan.

"Ian?"

"Kenz's Ian."

"What?!"

"Lyle Casey," Brogan responded. "His digital footprint ended in July of 2007," he looked up at Donnelly, "The guy's a damn ghost."

With clenched teeth and a hushed voice Donnelly gave Brogan a piece of her mind, "What the hell are you doing?! I told you to keep this under wraps!"

"I'm not planning on sharing anything with Kenz," Brogan defended.

"Then why look in the first place?"

"I just figured I could easily discover that Ian was freaking-out over nothing and we'd get a good laugh out of it."

"Who's this WE you're talking about?"

"Oh… uh… yeah," Brogan stumbled, "I guess that would only be the two of us."

"You didn't really think this through, did you?" Donnelly said at the same moment that the office door was opening.

"Didn't think WHAT through?" Detective Nash remarked as she entered the area and glanced between Donnelly and Brogan.

"Oh, nothing," Brogan blurted-out before Donnelly had a chance to provide a response to Nash's question.

"Hmm… okay," Nash replied as she draped her jacket over her desk chair and then grabbed her coffee mug. "Coffee," she said as she headed toward the Break Room.

Donnelly glared at Brogan. Brogan sighed relief and logged out of his search.

Nash re-entered the space and said, "So, what's on the docket?"

"Seeing if we can place Spencer Dunn in the vicinity of Greg Wilson's cabin," Donnelly replied.

"And if we can find any ties between Spencer and Wilson," Brogan added.

"Oh; and expanding our cab and Uber search in the early morning hours of the twenty-seventh," Donnelly finished.

"Sounds good," Nash responded and took a sip of her coffee.

"Any news on autopsy reports and the case files from Grays Harbor

County?" Brogan asked Nash.

"Val was hoping to receive the autopsy reports either late yesterday or early today; she said she'd call once she's finished her review," Nash replied. "As far as the case files go, I talked to the lead investigator yesterday and he was going to run it by his boss… no news yet."

"Any chance we can take a look at the cabin where the crime occurred?" Donnelly asked.

"That's a tricky one," said Nash. "The cabin is still owned by the Wilson family… Greg's widow Madelyn to be specific."

"Yeah, that could be a tough subject matter to broach."

"Agreed; thus my plan is to review the case file and decide which way I want to go from there."

Nash's cell phone rang—it was Deputy Coroner Valerie LaGrange. "Hey Val," Nash answered her phone, "Some autopsy results to share, I hope?"

"Good guess," LaGrange replied. "In summary I can tell you this: Samantha Dalton's wounds are similar to the marks around Natalie Copeland's wrists and ankles. Nothing around her neck though."

"So, if Spencer is an accomplice, a protégé, or otherwise involved, he must have decided he needed that additional restraining device," Nash responded.

"Or he read about this case and got an idea to be even more brutal and add the neck restraint."

"Perhaps due to Natalie struggling and fighting back, and the collar was her penance for doing so?"

"That's certainly a consideration," LaGrange replied. "Also, unlike Natalie, either Samantha didn't fight back, or did not have an opportunity to do so."

"*Except…*" Nash emphasized.

"Oh yeah," LaGrange conceded. "*Except* her grabbing the knife and slashing his jugular."

"So, in other words, she was likely caught off-guard and didn't have a chance to fight back until she was already mortally wounded when she grabbed the knife?"

"That's my hypothesis," said LaGrange. "Is that consistent with their case file?"

"I haven't received it yet," Nash replied. "And Samantha's slit throat?"

"Also consistent with Natalie's; and nothing like Wilson's."

"No?"

"Wilson's wound would have almost immediately incapacitated him," said LaGrange. "Samantha got him good."

"That's one saving grace I guess," Nash responded, "Anything else?"

"Not to impugn their Coroner, but it wasn't an overly-thorough examination."

"What are the issues?"

"They apparently didn't examine for possible sexual assault," LaGrange said. "Could be that they figured they had an open and shut case as to the murder, or they figured any sexual conduct was consensual."

"Consensual?!!" Nash exploded. "The guy's married, the woman… his victim… has obviously been previously restrained, and her damn throat was slit!"

"Like I said," LaGrange sighed, "not overly thorough."

"Understood," Nash exhaled. "Anything else?"

"Not at this time."

"Okay… thanks," Nash said and ended her call. She turned to Brogan and Donnelly, "Did you two get all that?"

"Yep," Brogan replied. "And all I can say is: Wow."

"Let's hope that's just the first of a few revelations today," Nash commented.

Brogan and Donnelly nodded and then headed to their respective desks.

Nash's computer chimed. She proclaimed aloud, "It looks like the Dalton-Wilson case file just arrived; give me a couple minutes and I'll fill you in."

"Roger that," Brogan responded.

Logging onto her computer, Donnelly had an incoming message that was also related to the Dalton-Wilson case.

"Not a whole lot to report on the case file," Nash stated.

Brogan and Donnelly scurried over to Nash's desk.

"Samantha's prints were on the knife, which was also lying on the floor next to her hand; hence the investigators concluding that she got the knife away from Wilson and slashed his jugular before she succumbed from her own injuries," Nash said. "Also, Grays Harbor authorities collected, but did not run, DNA from Samantha and Wilson."

"Did they say 'why' they failed to run the DNA?" asked Brogan.

"No; but in the lead detective's accompanying email he did say that, because of the similarities with the Natalie Copeland case, they've agreed to run them now."

"Well, that's something I suppose."

"I just received news that the Grays Harbor Gazette *did* run the story about the Samantha Dalton-Greg Wilson case," Donnelly interjected. "They don't know if any other newspapers picked up the story."

"So, Spencer Dunn could have gotten cues from this case," Brogan commented.

"If he had no involvement in this one; that's true," said Nash. She turned to Donnelly, "Do you think you can dig up if any local papers ran the story?"

"Absolutely," Donnelly replied.

"Do you have a plan for what's next in this case?" Brogan asked Nash.

"It looks like a talk with Greg Wilson's widow is in order," Nash replied.

43

Detective Nash stood on the porch of the home of Madelyn Wilson, the widow of Greg Wilson… the presumed killer of Samantha Dalton. She glanced back at her cruiser parked at the curb; Brogan and Donnelly sat quietly within, awaiting Nash's return. Nash knew the impending conversation was best left to her and her alone; realizing that it would be a potentially fragile exchange. She gathered her thoughts, took a deep breath, and rang the doorbell. A mid-forties woman answered the door.

"Madelyn Wilson?" Nash said to the woman while holding up her badge, "I'm Detective Nash with the Slaughter County Sheriff's Department."

Madelyn's demeanor was that of both skepticism and suspicion. "This is Grays Harbor County," she said, "Why would you be asking questions here?"

"It's more a matter of a request, ma'am," Nash replied.

"A request for what?"

"I'd like permission to visit your property up near Wynoochee Lake."

"For what purpose; to trample on my husband's grave some more?" Madelyn responded. "Haven't you people done enough?!"

Nash attempted to respond, but Madelyn wasn't finished, "This whole thing against my husband was a stinking rush to judgment!" Madelyn continued, "There's NO WAY he held that girl captive and killed her! Did anyone care that he himself was murdered… slashed right through the throat?! Of course they didn't; they just went for the easy answer to justify not doing a legitimate investigation and to close their damn case!"

"I'm sorry ma'am, but I'm not here to cast further dispersions on your husband or to re-litigate his case," Nash responded.

"Then why do you want to go back to the scene of this horrible travesty and crawl all over our cabin?" Madelyn replied. "Why do you want me to re-live this nightmare?!!" she snarled.

"To be honest, we have a murder in Slaughter County with a similar M.O."

"See, I told you this wasn't my husband!"

"Ma'am, it's possible that the deaths are merely similar, but unrelated," Nash replied. "And I hate to say it, but it's also possible that your husband had an accomplice, or a third option is that our killer merely copied what was reported about the incident at your cabin."

"Then why the hell should I help you?!"

Nash reached into her jacket pocket and extracted a picture of a smiling and vibrant Natalie Copeland that had been taken just weeks before her murder. "We know your husband had nothing to do with this girl's death, but your cabin could hold clues as to the person who did."

Madelyn stood silent, her breaths so deep you could see the expansion and contraction of her chest. She grasped the photograph and studied it intently. A tear rolled down her cheek. "I'm sorry," she said as she handed the photo back to Nash.

As Nash approached her cruiser Brogan and Donnelly tried to get a read as to the outcome of her conversation with Madelyn Wilson—they were unsuccessful.

"How'd it go?" Brogan asked as Nash jumped into the car.

"She's obviously in denial," Nash replied.

"Denial?" Donnelly responded. "How can she discard all the evidence: the eye bolts, the shackle-like marks and abrasions on Samantha, her husband and Samantha lying dead inside the cabin with wounds from the same knife?"

"That's what we often see with loved ones: complete denial in the face of overwhelming evidence to the contrary," said Nash.

"So, I guess we're out of luck concerning the cabin, huh?" Brogan lamented.

Nash held up a key.

"Damn you're good," Brogan commented.

As Nash, Brogan, and Donnelly cruised along the heavily-wooded vista surrounding East Hoquiam Road, north of the city of Hoquiam, Brogan made an observation, "If you didn't know better you'd have no idea there was any sign of civilization in these backwoods."

"The beauty of owning property in the Pacific Northwest: you can escape to the mountains, woods, lakes, rivers, streams, the ocean, or all of the above," said Nash.

"Ain't that the truth," responded Brogan.

Nash steered her cruiser onto a dirt road near milepost 8. The road was blanketed by leaves. "Doesn't look like anyone's been out here in quite a while," Nash commented.

After about a quarter-mile of driving through woods of poplar and maple trees Nash pulled up near a small rustic cabin. To her surprise the cabin still had fragments of 'Crime Scene' tape dangling near the front door.

The trio exited the vehicle. Nash stopped and listened. "There's a brook or stream nearby," she said. She then approached the front door of the cabin and unlocked the deadbolt. Swinging open the door revealed what appeared to be the remnants of a crime scene untouched by the passage of time.

"No one has been in here in a very long time," Nash said as she glanced around the space while still standing at the doorway. Brogan and Donnelly, crowding behind Nash, strained to take a peek.

"Hang on a sec," Nash said to her eager subordinates while she grasped and began to don latex gloves. "Let's treat this as an active crime scene even if it's not," she added. Brogan and Donnelly donned gloves.

Something caught Nash's eye almost immediately below her feet just inside the doorway. "Watch your step," she said to Brogan and Donnelly as she took a giant step.

"What is it?" Brogan responded.

"If I had to venture a guess," Nash replied, "Madelyn Wilson or another family member's first visit to the scene once it was released from the custody of law enforcement was so disturbing that they took one look, vomited at the sight and smell, and locked the place up and never returned."

"Wow," Brogan replied as he stepped over the remnants of vomit—Donnelly followed his lead.

Scanning the one-room cabin, a distressing story emerged: Two faded, dust-covered, crime-scene-victim chalk outlines marked where the victim and her alleged perpetrator took their final breaths. One outline was interrupted by a large swath of rust-colored stain denoting the blood loss from the severed jugular of the perpetrator; the second outline showed a much smaller stain surrounded by multiple droplet-sized stains.

One corner of the cabin yielded four large heavy-duty eyebolts; two on each wall. The eyebolts were strategically placed at the exact same spot on their associated wall: one ankle-high, the other approximately four-feet above the floor. A close examination of the eyebolts showed indications of metal-to-metal wear. Nash extracted an evidence bag and a swab; collecting several samples of metal shavings from each of the bolts. "I'm no forensic scientist," she commented, "but these bolts look much newer than the rest of the cabin."

"Do you mean 'recently added'?" Brogan responded.

"No; they're visible in the crime scene photos," Nash replied. "I'm merely speculating that they were likely installed only a few days, weeks, or months before Samantha's murder."

"What do you think of the specific placement of them?" Donnelly asked Nash.

"Apparently one anchor for each of the four limbs," Nash replied, "Left ankle, right ankle, left wrist, right wrist."

"You don't think the chains were so short that the victim, Samantha, was forced to stand with her arms spread wide like a crucifixion on a cross, do you?" Brogan interjected.

"Good God I hope not," said Nash. "Val didn't share anything about her autopsy report that would indicate such a thing, so I'm assuming the chains were long enough to at least allow her some freedom of movement." She shook her head and added, "As disgusting as it is to consider that to be some degree of an upside."

Brogan looked around and commented, "I'm not seeing much of anything that wasn't captured in the photos and descriptions in the case file."

"Let's take a few pictures of our own, including inside of the drawers and cabinets, just in case there's something that Grays Harbor authorities may not have captured."

"What about the fact that it has no longer been a sealed crime scene for over ten months," Donnelly said, "Someone could have been inside and added, moved, or taken something?"

"That's true; but it's better to look and find nothing than to not look at all."

"Understood," Donnelly replied and then began taking a series of photographs.

"Hey, Dirk," Nash said to Brogan. "Can you scrape up a sample of what appears to be vomit?"

"I can," Brogan looked perplexed. "What are you thinking?"

"For one: we're only speculating that it was left after the crime scene was released…"

"Oh, so it could have been left by Samantha or Wilson?" Brogan interrupted.

"Or a third party… such as an accomplice," Nash said. "And for two: what if it was left after-the-fact, but not by a member of the family?"

"Damn, you always come up with something I hadn't thought of," Brogan responded.

The trio completed their search of the cabin and locked the deadbolt.

"Return the key and then head back home?" Donnelly asked Nash.

Nash scanned her surroundings. "Let's take a look around the property," she said.

A short trek placed the detectives near a small stream. They followed the stream for several hundred yards, noting heavy brush in some areas, large trees crossing the stream in others, and multiple deep spots within the stream.

"It seems like you could stash a body almost anywhere out here and it would never be found," Brogan commented.

"I agree," Donnelly responded. "In fact, it makes you wonder why Wilson didn't just kill Samantha and bury her in the woods, or find a deep spot in the stream to submerge her body."

"Maybe that was his plan," Nash replied, "but Samantha foiled it when she grabbed the knife and slashed his throat?"

Brogan and Donnelly nodded.

44

Detective Nash yawned as she wheeled into the parking lot at the Sheriff's Office. It was mid-morning on a Saturday, and she had gotten plenty of sleep–a rarity of late; but she had not yet availed herself of her morning coffee. Restful night or not, a cup of java was always the jump-start to her day.

Pulling into her parking spot Nash noticed Sheriff Clarke's cruiser. She entered the office and headed directly to the Break Room. As the fresh brew trickled into its decanter she extracted her memo pad and reviewed the items of note that would soon be adorning the whiteboard.

Her coffee mug topped-off Nash began a trek to her desk. Her sojourn was short-lived–Sheriff Clarke emerged from his office.

"Got a minute?" Clarke said to Nash.

"Of course," Nash replied.

Nash followed Clarke into his office. Clarke grabbed a seat at his desk; Nash took a seat at the adjacent table.

"Any luck digging up new evidence in the Natalie Copeland case?" said Clarke.

"We've got a few irons in the fire that could prove noteworthy."

"What about the case in Grays Harbor County," said Clarke, "Is there anything there, or was it nothing more than a last gasp hope in support of our case?"

"Too early to tell, but there are some striking similarities," Nash replied. "Right now we're trying to tie Spencer Dunn and their perp, Greg Wilson, together; but who knows... Spencer could've merely copied the M.O. of Wilson's crime."

"Understood," said Clarke. He took a breath, "It looks like we're going to need to up the ante," he added.

"Sir?"

"The Judge ruled on the motion to suppress evidence in the Natalie Copeland case yesterday."

"I take it that things did not go well?" said Nash.

"That would be an understatement," Clarke replied. "Virtually everything found within Spencer Dunn's car has been ruled inadmissible."

"Son of a…" Nash started. "Wait… everything??"

"There was one saving grace: the lipstick match between Natalie's frown and Spencer's 'Joker' smile. The Judge ruled that it fell within the Inevitable Discovery exception."

"Just as we'd hoped… thank God."

"I concur," said Clarke. "Needless to say, there's a heightened urgency to essentially build a brand new case now that charges against Spencer Dunn have been dropped."

Nash grew wide-eyed, "Charges were dropped?"

"The Judge told the Prosecutor to come up with more evidence before re-filing charges."

"Damn," Nash responded. A distressing thought hit her, "Holy shit!" she added, "Gary Copeland…" her voice trailed off.

"You think Copeland will go after Dunn when he gets the news?"

"I'm afraid it's a possibility," Nash replied. "He'll think that the criminal justice system failed him."

"It's not like the case was dismissed with prejudice, we just need to build new evidence around the very strong lipstick match, which is what you're already doing."

"You know that… and I know that… but Copeland might not believe us, or have the patience to wait for justice."

"Well, then you need to intervene," said Clarke.

"Yes, Sir," Nash replied. "Should we also provide Spencer Dunn some protection, at least in the interim?"

"Let me talk to Bennington P.D. on that one," said Clarke. "Considering we're in this predicament due to the improper actions of one of their Officers, they need to take some responsibility for fixing this mess."

"Police protection for a stone cold killer... irony at its finest," Nash shook her head.

"Yep," Clarke replied.

"And having charges dropped due to the procedural misconduct of one of his Officers could not have gone over well with Captain O'Rourke."

"He told me that he ripped Officer Wilberforce a new one," Clarke replied. "Along with giving him a new assignment: Latrine Orderly," he grinned.

Nash returned the grin as she visualized O'Rourke's comment and Wilberforce's new task. Sometimes a hint of levity is needed to keep one from getting mired in the muck.

"Well, I'll let you get back to work," Clarke commented.

Nash nodded and departed Clarke's office. Approaching her desk she was pleasantly surprised to see that both Brogan and Donnelly had arrived. "I'm glad you two are here; we've got a lot on our plate today," she said.

45

Detective Nash found herself in deep contemplation as she cruised through town on her way to the Copeland residence. She had anticipated the prospect of a follow-up discussion with Gary Copeland concerning the prime suspect in his daughter's murder, but that didn't make the task any easier.

She pulled up to the curb, exited her cruiser, trekked along the home's pathway, and stepped onto the landing. She reached for the doorbell—the door opened before she had a chance to press the buzzer.

"How did I know you'd be showing up at my door once again?" a stern-faced Gary Copeland said to Nash.

"I'm assuming that means you have an idea as to why I'm here?" Nash replied.

Gary crossed his arms. "You're here to tell me that your case is falling apart because incompetence runs rampant within the local law enforcement agencies?" he responded.

Nash considered providing an explanation, but determined that any such response would likely fall on deaf ears. She decided to remain on point, "Like the last time we talked, I don't want you to do anything that you'll regret for the rest of your life."

Unlike the restraint and composure Gary Copeland had exhibited previously, he hit the breaking point, "Regret for the rest of my life?! What life?!!" he railed. "My daughter has been murdered, my wife and I were barely able to cope BEFORE her murderer got off scot-free, and now you're here to tell me, *'Sorry… we screwed up',"* he began to breathe heavily. "We're holding on by a thread here, lady!!" he screamed—his eyes becoming glassy.

"I understand your concern, Sir," Nash started.

"You understand??" Gary interrupted. "You promised me that the wheels of justice would prevail; so what kind of spin are you trying to sell me now that charges have been dropped against the monster who killed my child?!"

"Charges were dropped pending the discovery of new evidence," Nash replied. "And we've already uncovered such, and continue to follow new leads."

"Like what?"

"You know that I'm not at liberty to discuss specific evidence, but I can tell you that we've uncovered another homicide with a similar M.O."

"You're telling me that this guy has already gone out and killed someone else?"

It was obvious to Nash that Gary was implying that law enforcement had failed to protect the general public from Spencer Dunn. She was tempted to remind him that it was HE whom had posted the bail that had gotten Spencer back on the streets, but she realized such a comment would serve no useful purpose.

"No Sir," Nash responded, "This homicide occurred almost a year ago, and in a separate jurisdiction."

"A similar M.O. in a separate jurisdiction almost a year ago?" said Gary.

"That's correct," Nash replied. "We don't know if it's merely a coincidence, or if Spencer Dunn was involved," she added, "But if anything happens to Mister Dunn we may never know the answer to that question, and the parents of that young woman may never see justice done."

An impact to the family of another victim had Gary pondering a situation he had not previously considered. He found himself at a crossroads. After several seconds of silence he merely responded, "Is that all?"

"Umm... I guess so," Nash replied. She turned and walked away. Gary watched as Nash climbed into her cruiser and drove out of sight.

Now driving toward her next destination, the home of Spencer Dunn, Nash was perplexed as to Gary Copeland's response to her plea. In reality Gary's response wasn't a response at all, it was his way of saying he'd had enough of the conversation. Had Nash's words made an impact? There was no telling at this point.

Nash rounded the corner to the sight of a Bennington Police Department patrol car parked across the street from Spencer Dunn's home. She pulled up to the curb.

Rap-rap-rap Nash knocked on Spencer's door.

"You've got to be kidding me," Spencer commented as he opened the door to the sight of Detective Nash.

"Mister Dunn," Nash acknowledged.

"What's the deal, you cops decided unmarked cars were too inconspicuous and you needed to announce to the whole world that you're sitting on me... harassing me in plain sight now that charges have been dropped?" Spencer nodded toward the patrol car.

"There's more to it than that," Nash replied.

Spencer remained silent. Nash decided her only recourse was to start at the beginning and convey the ugly truth. "Do you know who posted your bail?" she said.

"My parents," Spencer was caught off-guard; trying to figure out the reason behind the question.

"Actually, that's not the case."

"Well, then I have no idea," Spencer replied. "Does it matter?"

"It might," Nash responded. She then added, "Your lawyer didn't mention the details regarding the posting of your bail?"

"Nope," Spencer crossed his arms. "And what's with all this cloak & dagger stuff?"

"Your bail was posted by a local Advocacy Group."

"It's nice to know that someone believed in me."

"Maybe yes… maybe no," Nash replied. "One of the principals in the company is the father of the woman discovered in the trunk of your car."

"What??" Spencer was befuddled. "Why would he do that?"

Nash feigned ignorance via a shrug.

Spencer read between the lines, "Are you telling me that he bailed me out so that he could hunt me down and kill me?"

"Well, I…"

"And now that charges have been dropped he has even more of a motive to seek revenge at my expense," Spencer interrupted as he connected the dots.

"We don't know that," said Nash.

"Well, did you talk to this guy… put him under surveillance… arrest him?!"

"Yes, I talked to him."

Spencer had anticipated additional information from Nash, but none came. "That's it? All you did was talk to him?"

"He made no specific threat toward you, so there's not much more we can do," Nash explained. "But these Officers," she nodded toward the patrol car, "will remain outside; at least for the time being."

"For the time being?! And then what??!" Spencer replied. "This is frickin' crazy! I didn't do anything! I'm innocent!" he railed. "And yet I'M the one whose life is in danger?!" he continued, "Where is the justice??!"

"Well, if you decided to make a plea you'd be safe and sound back in our custody," Nash said.

"Oh I get it… this is just some scam, some trick, some way for you to get me to confess," Spencer glared. "Screw you!" he slammed the door in Nash's face.

46

"How were your talks with Gary Copeland and Spencer Dunn?" Brogan said to Nash when she entered the Sheriff's Office.

"I don't know if my concerns struck a nerve with Gary Copeland or not," Nash replied, "but Sheriff's Clarke's going to put him under surveillance just to be sure."

"And Spencer?" Donnelly asked.

"He was professing his innocence at the top of his lungs and portraying himself as the victim," Nash responded.

"The victim?"

"Of now being in the crosshairs," Nash replied, "and thus a potential murder victim himself."

Donnelly nodded understanding; Brogan rolled his eyes and said, "A victim? …that's ripe."

Donnelly turned to Brogan, "I can see it from his perspective."

"What're you talking about?"

"When you add it all up a certain picture emerges," Donnelly replied. "He gets bailed-out by the father of the woman he killed; that father may not have gotten to him while he was out on bail, but now charges have been dropped," she explained. "He's got to be in fear for his life."

"Holy crap!" Nash blurted-out as she had a disturbing thought, "I may have inadvertently provided Spencer with both a motive, and a defense, to kill Gary Copeland."

"What do you mean?" said Brogan.

"Spencer could turn the tables on Copeland by hunting him down, kill him, set the stage by planting a weapon on him if he didn't already have one on him, and claim, 'The guy was coming after me; I killed him in self-defense'."

"Shit, I hadn't thought of that."

"And if that happens," Nash sighed, "I've got blood on my hands."

"But you had no choice except to warn Spencer," Donnelly responded to Nash.

"A frickin' Catch-22, that's for sure," Nash lamented.

"And if Sheriff Clarke has someone surveilling Gary Copeland, wouldn't they intervene before a tragedy occurs; either by him going after Spencer or vice-versa?"

"It's not like we'll have a dedicated twenty-four-seven tail on the guy."

"Oh," said Donnelly.

"Anyway… enough about that," Nash said. She gestured toward the whiteboard's list of open items, "Did you two make any progress while I was gone?"

"Quite a bit, actually," Brogan responded as he approached the board. "I compared the photos we took in and around Greg Wilson's cabin with those from the case file," he said. "And, as we surmised, it appears that no one had set foot inside the cabin from the time authorities released the scene until we showed up."

"Other than whoever spewed the vomit," Nash said.

"Do we know that it wasn't from Samantha or Wilson?" Donnelly asked.

"No," Nash replied. "Since Lowell only received the samples from me last night… I was merely speculating."

"Understood," said Donnelly. "Another thing we found out is that a number of news outlets across the state covered the Samantha Dalton murder, including the Slaughter County Journal."

"So, Spencer could have gotten his plan from what he read in one of these news articles," Nash commented.

"That's one option," Brogan responded. "The other being that he has some tie to Greg Wilson," he added. "On that note, any idea when we'll get DNA results from that case?"

"Not a clue," Nash replied. "Hey, did you get anything from Spencer Dunn's neighbors in regard to Natalie's car?"

"Yep… but no."

"Okay… what does that mean?"

"Yes, I talked to them; but none of them saw a car matching the description of Natalie's that night."

"I guess I'm not surprised," Nash responded.

"But on a related subject," Donnelly interjected, "We struck pay dirt on our expanded cab and Uber search zone." She grabbed her memo pad and continued, "A driver picked up a guy in 'Joker' makeup at twelve-thirty-seven over near the R&L Market… you know, the little Mom and Pop store with the reader-board that advertises Chicken Gizzards on a Stick, a few blocks from where Spencer ditched Wilberforce."

"Yeah, I'm familiar with the store."

"He… the driver… said he took the Joker to the Quonset Hut," said Donnelly, "Dropped him off at twelve-fifty-three."

"The Quonset Hut?" Nash was surprised. "The same place he had come from just an hour or so earlier."

"Probably because that's where Natalie's car was parked," said Donnelly.

"Twelve-fifty-three would give him enough time to dump Natalie's car at the Thriftway," Brogan chimed in. "Hell, Belfair's only what, fifteen-to-twenty minutes from the Quonset Hut?"

"Did he call from a pay phone at the R&L?" Nash said to Donnelly. "Do they have surveillance cameras?" she added before Donnelly could respond.

"Actually, the Joker flagged-down the cabbie," Donnelly replied, "And I couldn't tell you about surveillance cameras; I'll have to check."

"Make that a priority," Nash said.

"Yes, ma'am."

"I don't suppose there's any chance he paid for his ride with a credit or debit card?"

"Cash."

"What about from the Thriftway back to Spencer's place?" said Nash, "Any taxi or Uber activity in that direction?"

"Nothing that we've dug up as of yet."

"Well, you know what that means…"

"Keep digging."

"Correct," Nash responded. "I can't believe we've made this much headway today," she added and then glanced at the board. "What about Spencer being in the area of Greg Wilson's cabin at any time in the past year or two?"

"Pretty darn close," Donnelly replied, "The Hoquiam Castle Bed & Breakfast."

"Bed & Breakfast?" said Nash, "I thought the Hoquiam Castle was a tourist attraction museum sort of place?"

"Maybe back in the day, but it's a Bed & Breakfast now."

"When did Spencer stay there?"

"A year ago this past August."

Nash grew wide-eyed, "Just a few months before Samantha Dalton's murder."

"Correct."

"Was Spencer with anyone when he stayed at the Castle?"

"Their records show two guests."

"I think we could be onto something," Nash crossed her arms and stared at the board.

47

Detective Mackenzie Nash and Deputy Coroner Valerie LaGrange were among the few attendees paying their respects as the Coroner's Office held a public burial for the remains of twenty-one indigent people. LaGrange was in attendance in an official capacity. For Detective Nash: although her oath to serve and protect her community, to be a champion of the downtrodden, and to be a voice for the abused and neglected generally determined her actions; her reasons in this instance were primarily personal.

Nash leaned in toward LaGrange. "Twenty-one people who were destitute with no known family or funds for a proper burial service at their time of death?" she sighed. "Such a sad state of affairs," she added.

"I agree," LaGrange replied. "I tend to think of them as casualties of misfortune," she said. "Some of them in the literal sense, some of them merely figuratively."

"In either case, they died penniless and all alone," Nash shook her head.

For these unfortunate individuals Detective Nash could no longer be their voice or champion; but she could provide them a dose of dignity in their final moment, and honor the memory of what they once had been: sons and daughters, perhaps brothers or sisters, perhaps husbands or wives. Somehow those whom they loved, those who loved them, had lost touch. 'Gone but not forgotten' is the honored phrase, but it appeared that these lost souls had sadly become 'The forgotten'.

As Nash stood in quiet reverence throughout the service her own reality began to manifest itself within her thoughts. She had to face the fact that she had not been in attendance for her father's funeral.

She'd had no choice in that decision as she had not been informed of his passing—one of the painful lessons of being estranged from a loved one. Pride has a way of taking its toll on a relationship, and you often don't realize it until it's too late.

The last name had been read, the public burial concluded, and the small gathering had dispersed. Heading toward their respective vehicles Nash and LaGrange passed by another memorial service—it was a stark contrast to the solemn occasion they had just attended. People were smiling, hugging, and sharing a laugh or two. Curiosity having gotten the best of them, Nash and LaGrange stopped in their tracks. Not wishing to encroach upon the service Nash scanned the area and noticed an empty gazebo back and away from the formal event. She nudged LaGrange and nodded. LaGrange got the hint and the two of them strolled over to the gazebo.

A gentleman in a casual suit approached the podium and addressed the gathering, "If everyone would take your seats, please."

Once all were seated the gentleman began, "Thank you all for coming to celebrate the life of Verdanelle Blair."

He extracted a piece of paper from his inner coat pocket and placed it on the podium. "I'm sure it will come as no surprise that Verdanelle composed her own eulogy," he smiled. Subtle laughs rang out amongst the audience.

"With that in mind," the gentleman continued, "The following are Verdanelle's own words addressed to all of you," he pointed to the crowd.

"Let there be no tears shed today; no proclamation of a life gone too soon; no attempted explanation by a minister stating, *"We can never know, or expect to understand, God's will."* I mean, come on people, I'm almost one-hundred-three; God's will, if there is a God... Good God I hope there's a God..."

The gentleman paused as the audience began to chuckle. He smiled and then continued... "God's will was to provide me a long... some might say too long… life filled with the love of family: my children, grandchildren, and great grandchildren. And the love of my many friends… none of whom are here today because… well… because I guess I won the bet." The gentleman, and the audience, broke out in laughter. The gentleman provided a commentary as he held up the paper, "You're not going to believe this," he said, "but she actually followed the line about winning the bet with 'LOL,'" he pointed. The audience erupted even louder.

The gentleman waited for the laughter to subside and then read the final words from Verdanelle, "I'm sure many of you have a funny story or two to share; or in Jimmy's case, a half-dozen to a dozen. So get up and share a laugh; it's what life's all about. Love you! V," the gentleman folded the paper and returned it to his coat pocket.

Per Verdanelle's wishes, the gentleman relinquished the podium to anyone who might want to share a funny story about their friend, mother, grandmother, and great-grandmother. What followed was an assembly-line of hilarity, of silliness, of shared memories. It was truly a celebration of a life lived to the fullest.

When the service ended LaGrange turned to Nash and said, "Now that's what I'm talking about."

"She set an example for all of us," Nash responded, "That's for sure."

After returning to their respective vehicles Nash extracted her cell phone, scrolled through the contacts, and hit 'Send'.

"Hello?" echoed through Nash's phone.

"Hi Mom," Nash spoke into her phone, "Long time no chat."

48

Detective Nash was staring at the whiteboard when Brogan and Donnelly entered the office. She turned to acknowledge them, "Are you two carpooling, or is there something going on that I don't want to know about?"

"Uh, no," Brogan glanced at Donnelly and then back to Nash. "We just happened to arrive at the same time."

Nash grinned. Not that she thought that there might be something going on between Brogan and Donnelly, but she enjoyed making them sweat a little. "So, I trust you all had a nice day off?"

"Yep," said Brogan with a thumbs-up.

"It was a sleep-in, lounge-around-and-relax, kind of day," Donnelly added. "I hope you took the day off as well."

"A quasi-official attendance at the Coroner's Office's public funeral for indigent folks," Nash replied, "but otherwise… yes."

"Since we were all off yesterday I guess that means there's nothing new to report?" said Brogan.

"Actually, I just got some big news from Sheriff Clarke," Nash replied. "Spencer Dunn has flown the coop to Arizona."

"Wait a minute," Donnelly responded. "He can't do that, he's jumping bail."

"Charges were dropped," Nash reminded Donnelly, "he can go wherever he wants."

"Do you think he took off in order to evade justice?" Brogan asked, "Or was it because he was afraid that Gary Copeland was going to hunt him down and kill him?"

"Your guess is as good as mine… it could be a combination of the two," said Nash.

"And if we get sufficient evidence to reinstate charges, then what?"

"Then we'll have to hope that the State of Arizona extradites his ass back to Washington."

"I guess that means we've got a lot more digging to do."

"That's a fact," Nash replied just as her cell phone was buzzing–it was Forensic Scientist Evan Lowell. "Hey Evan," Nash spoke into her phone.

"Hey Kenz, I've got some updates for you," Lowell responded.

"Go for it," said Nash.

"The metal shavings from the eyebolts in Wilson's cabin were likely from a chain–the kind of heavy-duty chain you can find at almost any hardware store."

"In other words," Nash said, "You cannot specifically tie them to the shavings found in Natalie Copeland's wounds?"

"Correct," Lowell said, "but not at all surprising."

"Why do you say that?"

"My guess is that both women were restrained by some kind of shackle connected to a chain," Lowell replied. "In this case, with the other end of the chain looped around an eyebolt and secured with a padlock."

"So, you're saying that the shackles and the chain are likely two different metals?"

"That's exactly right."

"Understood."

"The next batch of items is a bit more intriguing," Lowell said. "The DNA results from Grays Harbor County."

"Really?" Nash replied. "Hang on while I put you on the speaker," she added. She set down her phone and then said, "Okay, go ahead."

"The first item is no surprise, at least not a *major* surprise," said Lowell. "The vomit did not come from either Samantha Dalton or Greg Wilson."

"Since you haven't given us a name as to whom it DOES match that must mean that the person is not in the system?" said Nash.

"Correct."

"So, it could have been from Greg Wilson's wife Madelyn, or another family member, for example?"

"Correct again," Lowell replied. "The second item also falls into the 'no surprise' category; at least from my perspective."

"What's that?"

"Greg Wilson's DNA does NOT match the 'unidentified male' DNA in Spencer's trunk."

"So, Wilson and Spencer weren't accomplices after all?" Brogan chimed in.

"I wouldn't jump to that conclusion based on one small data-point," Lowell responded.

"Nor would I," Nash glared at Brogan.

"Got it," Brogan responded.

"Besides," Lowell continued, "Remember that the unidentified male DNA populated the same area of the trunk as the three unidentified female specimens."

"In other words," Brogan said, "More likely to be a victim than an accomplice?"

"Ahh… you're jumping to another conclusion."

"Well, crap," Brogan tossed up his hands.

Nash turned to Brogan, "What Evan's trying to say is that we don't have enough information to draw a conclusion one way or the other, all we know is that there's a consistency with the various DNA samples— they all could be victims, or they all could be innocuous for one reason or another."

"We couldn't have some from a victim, some from a killer?" asked Brogan.

"We could," Nash replied. "But right now we don't have enough evidence to determine if such is the case."

"Understood," Brogan responded.

"And now I'm about to throw a wrench in everything," Lowell commented.

Nash, Brogan, and Donnelly stood in quiet anticipation.

"One of the unidentified female specimens from Spencer's trunk is a match to Samantha Dalton," said Lowell.

"Holy shit!" Brogan blurted-out.

"Wait… what?! How is that even possible?!" Donnelly chimed in. "Samantha Dalton and her killer, Greg Wilson, are found dead in Wilson's cabin near Hoquiam a *year* ago," she continued, "and yet Samantha's DNA is found in the trunk of Spencer Dunn's car some eighty miles away *two weeks* ago?"

"No shit; how do you even wrap your head around that?" Brogan added. "Not to mention that the exact same car trunk contained the body of another victim, Natalie Copeland."

"And how do we reconcile the fact that we have these crazy evidentiary ties between Samantha Dalton, Greg Wilson, and Spencer Dunn," said Donnelly, "but we've uncovered zero evidence that Wilson and Spencer even knew each other?"

"I think we just uncovered some," Brogan responded.

"Don't forget that we've also placed Spencer near Wilson's cabin just months before Samantha's murder," said Nash.

"That's right… the Hoquiam Castle," said Brogan. "And, according to their records, he had someone with him."

"That's got to be Samantha Dalton, right?" Donnelly replied.

"I don't mean to interrupt your discussions," Lowell chimed in, "but it sounds like you all have come up with some potential leads to follow?"

"Uh… yeah," Nash responded while still trying to come to grips with the news. "You got anything else for us, Evan?"

"That was it for now," Lowell replied.

"Got it; thanks," Nash said and ended the call.

"Whew," Nash exhaled, "I did *not* see *that* coming."

"Damn, I wish we had this before Spencer went on the lam," said

Brogan.

"Technically, he's not…" Nash started.

"I know…" Brogan interrupted. "Technically, he's not on the lam."

"So, what do we do now that Spencer's in Arizona?" asked Donnelly.

"We continue to build the case," Nash replied.

"But we've got the new evidence of Samantha Dalton's DNA in Spencer's trunk," Brogan responded. "Can't we get the Prosecutor to extradite Spencer's ass back to Washington based on that?"

"There are two problems with that," Nash replied, "The first being that all evidence from the trunk of Spencer's car has been ruled inadmissible."

"Damn; I forgot about that," Brogan lamented.

"The second is that Samantha Dalton is not part of our case," Nash replied, "At least, not as of yet."

"So we need to try to make the Samantha Dalton case fit within ours?"

"Excluding the DNA from the trunk, yes… that's one possible avenue," Nash responded. "I mean hell… someway, somehow, these two cases merge; and a couple of items jump out at me right off the bat."

"Finding any ties between Spencer and Wilson?" Brogan said. "And discovering the identity of whomever Spencer was with at the Hoquiam Castle?"

"Yes," Nash replied. "In fact another one comes to mind." She turned to Donnelly, "Laura, now that we have a tie to Hoquiam, we need to look at the entire state of Washington for similar crimes."

"Yes, ma'am," Donnelly responded. An additional thought emerged, "Hey, what about the fact that we've still got two unidentified female DNA samples along with the unidentified male?"

"If we're able to solve those mysteries it could crack this case wide open," Brogan commented.

"Well, our statewide search for similar crimes could help with that," Nash replied. She paused in thought, "Hmm… another idea just hit me."

49

Negotiating the highways, byways, and country roads that meander toward the city of Westport, this would be the second trip to Grays Harbor County in a matter of days for Detective Nash. The first had been primarily a crapshoot: the curious nature of a lone similarity between Natalie Copeland's injuries and a year-old closed-case some eighty miles away. A visit to that crime scene yielded nothing of substance in regard to Detective Nash's case. Or so it seemed. But homicide investigations have a habit of unearthing clues from sources beyond the immediate focal point, and a simple request to run DNA from the Grays Harbor County case took Detective Nash's investigation in an entirely new direction. Next stop: the parents of homicide victim Samantha Dalton.

Detective Nash pulled her cruiser up to the curb outside of the home of Frank and Louise Dalton. She killed the engine and glanced toward the home—a subtle movement of the front curtain caught her eye. She exited her vehicle, trod along the home's walkway, and stepped onto the landing. Reaching for the doorbell, the door opened to reveal the curious gaze of an early-fifties couple.

"Mr. and Mrs. Dalton?" asked Nash as she held up her badge, "I'm Detective Nash with the Slaughter County Sheriff's Office."

A sense of unease gripped the couple. "Yes," Louise Dalton replied, "What can we do for you?"

"It's about your daughter Samantha," Nash replied. "And let me begin by saying that I'm very sorry for your loss."

Although Nash's statement was sincere and heartfelt, Frank Dalton became defensive, "Why are you dredging up the worst moment of our lives?"

"I apologize, Sir," Nash replied. "I'm following leads in a case that not only bears a striking resemblance to that of your daughter's, but it also includes direct evidence tied to her."

"Wait a minute," Frank responded. "What exactly are you saying here; that there's evidence in yet *another* case and our daughter is the common thread?"

"In a sense, yes; but not in the manner that you might think," Nash replied. "What we're dealing with is a similarity in M.O between the two crimes, and we've discovered evidence tying your daughter to our prime suspect."

"What; you're working some cold case and you're trying to implicate our daughter in it?!" Frank snarled.

"No Sir; this is a current case… the victim was killed just a couple of weeks ago," Nash responded. "There is absolutely no implication in regard to your daughter whatsoever; but somehow, some way, she crossed paths with both suspects."

Frank took a breath as he processed Nash's statement. "Are you implying that Samantha might have known the suspect in your crime?" he asked.

"That's correct," Nash replied. "A more troubling possibility is that the two perpetrators knew each other."

"And that the suspect in your murder was an accomplice in our daughter's attack?"

"We have no evidence to that effect thus far, but it is an avenue we are pursuing."

"Good God; I thought this nightmare was over," Louise pleaded to her husband as she grabbed his arm.

"I'm so sorry to put you through this, but any information that you're able to share might help our case," Nash stated. "And it may also provide some answers in regard to your daughter's case."

"That case is closed," Frank huffed.

"I'm aware of that, Sir; but I also understand that because of the demise of the perpetrator you were left with many unanswered questions."

Louise turned to her husband, "We never could understand how that monster crossed paths with Samantha. Was she a victim of opportunity? Had he been stalking her? Did she know him somehow?"

"Do you think Samantha knew this guy in your homicide?" Frank asked Nash. "And that he, in turn, knew the monster that took her from us?"

"That's one theory I'm investigating," Nash replied.

Louise jumped in, "How can we help?"

Nash held up a photo, "Do you recognize this gentleman?"

Frank and Louise stared at the photo and then replied in tandem, "Nope… not at all."

"How about the name 'Spencer Dunn'?" said Nash.

The couple glanced at each other, nodded in the negative, and then Frank replied, "No; is he the…?"

"Yes," Nash interrupted. She held up another photo, "How about this woman, Natalie Copeland; any chance that Samantha knew her?"

The couple eyeballed the photo. Louise responded, "I'm sorry, but no."

The three stood silent. Nash thought for a moment and then continued, "Do you know if Samantha stayed at the Hoquiam Castle Bed & Breakfast a year ago this past August; specifically, the weekend of the eighteenth?"

"It's possible," said Louise. "She was spending a lot of time with a guy she was seeing, at least that's how it seemed to us, so she could have stayed there with him."

"But you don't know for sure?"

"No; she was kind of invisible that summer," Frank interjected.

"Different from the norm?" Nash asked.

"Yes and no," said Frank. "She was always busy when summer rolled around; but in the past she'd mention what she was doing, where she was going, who she was with… like one or more of her girlfriends, what a great time she had, that sort of thing."

Louise chimed in, "But that summer we could barely get a peep out of her other than the fact that she was busy."

"With this guy?"

"That was our guess," said Louise. "To be honest, she didn't talk about him much. You know… little to no details."

"Any idea why she was so secretive about this guy?"

"This may sound silly, but I think she had developed a feeling that if she got all giddy and talked-up a new man in her life, that it would jinx the relationship."

"I can understand that perspective."

"She always said that there was nothing worse than having the post-traumatic-conversation… that's what she called them… of her friends asking *'How are things with Mister Wonderful?'* and her having to fess up that *'it was over'*. And then of course you get bombarded with the *'What happened?'* questions."

"I can definitely relate," Nash nodded. "She must have given you the guy's name though, right?"

"Nope," Frank responded. "She always downplayed him, saying he was just some guy whose company she enjoyed, and if things got serious then she'd fill in the details."

Nash exhaled, "This is a familiar story."

"With your guy… this, uh… Spencer Dunn?" Frank responded.

"Correct," Nash replied. She paused in thought, and then broached a sensitive subject, "I hate to ask, but do you think there's any possibility that the guy Samantha was seeing was, in fact, Greg Wilson?"

Such an implication drew Frank's ire, "Absolutely not!"

"Um, okay then," Nash responded. "Did the local authorities happen to look into Samantha's movements, phone records, or computer activity?"

"They didn't do a damn thing," Frank replied. "Nothing resembling any kind of investigation anyway–it was pretty much 'we have the victim, we've got the perp, case closed'."

"In that case, I'd like to have your permission to look into her phone records, her activities, her computer…"

"Absolutely," Louise replied. "Her cell phone and her laptop are in her bedroom… well, her old room that she had before she moved out," she added.

"That would be great," said Nash, "thank you."

50

Officer Clarence Wilberforce sat at his desk inside the Bennington Police Station. He was mired in the doldrums of being a chairbound, pencil-pushing, keyboard-punching administrative assistant courtesy of his own dire actions that fateful morning two weeks prior. Considering the circumstances that dictated his current situation, he realized that things could be worse; at least he was still wearing the badge and uniform of a police officer and not the orange jumpsuit of an incarcerated criminal.

Wilberforce's focus on administrative minutia was broken by Captain O'Rourke entering the area. The Captain walked through the space as he addressed the squad, "There's a massive, multi-vehicle accident in town. Dispatch has requested all available units report to the scene," he yelled. "It's all-hands-on-deck, people!"

A throng of uniformed officers popped-tall and scattered out of the area–Officer Wilberforce quietly remained seated at his desk.

"You too, Officer," O'Rourke said to Wilberforce.

"But Sir, I'm on desk duty," Wilberforce replied.

"Actually, you're on modified duty," O'Rourke responded. "Which means staying away from your normal police duties, but you can sure as hell get out there and direct traffic."

"Yes, Sir," Wilberforce jumped up, grabbed the keys to a patrol car, and bolted out of the office.

-*-

Officer Wilberforce stood at the intersection of 11th Avenue and Spruce Street–positioned in front of two police cruisers that were blocking traffic from proceeding eastbound along 11th Avenue. A fellow Officer and he were directing vehicles around the accident scene. It was a simple yet mundane task: rerouting drivers either north or south away from the bottleneck; but it was a welcome reprieve from Wilberforce's remedial desk-bound assignments.

The majority of the Officers' interactions with drivers were nothing more than pointing in the direction of the detour; however, occasionally a curious driver would stop and ask in regard to the situation. One such vehicle pulled up next to Officer Wilberforce and rolled down his window.

"Sir, you're going to have to detour over to Sixth Avenue," Wilberforce said to the man.

"What's going on?" the man replied.

"There's a multi-vehicle accident up ahead; the road is completely blocked-off."

The man took notice of the Officer's nametag, "Officer Wilberforce, is it?"

"Yes, Sir," Wilberforce replied.

"The name sounds familiar," the man responded. "Aren't you the cop who shot that unarmed guy?"

"I umm…" Wilberforce stumbled.

"Shouldn't you be on desk duty or something?" the man continued. "Or locked up behind bars, perhaps?"

Wilberforce remained silent while his face turned red—not with anger, but with embarrassment.

"And I see you've been neutered," the driver added with a smirk while nodding at Wilberforce's lack of a weapon.

The man's taunting voice rang familiar with Wilberforce. "Have we met before?" he asked.

"Do you mean like 'on a dark and stormy night'?" the driver once again smirked. "Of course not… *Officer.*"

"Wait a minute," a chill ran down Wilberforce's spine. "Is it…" he stammered, "Is it you?"

"Come again?"

"You don't know what I'm talking about?"

"Not a clue," the man shook his head.

"License and registration, please," Wilberforce said.

"Why?"

"Are you refusing my request?"

"No problem, Officer," the man replied. "I'm going to reach into my wallet, and then my glove box. We wouldn't want you to get all freaked-out now, would we?" the driver grinned.

Wilberforce's heart began to race, "See… right there… you're doing it again."

"I don't know what you're talkin' about," the man replied as he handed his license and registration to the Officer.

Wilberforce scanned the man's driver's license, looked at him, back to the license, and then back to the man. "This is you?" he held up the license.

"Who else would it be?"

Wilberforce handed the documents back to the man and said, "How about you pop the trunk?"

"No thanks."

"That wasn't a request."

"It sounded like one to me," the man replied. "Besides, it's not like there's a body in there," he added.

"Okay," Wilberforce was getting frustrated, "you need to get out of your vehicle, Sir."

"Or what, you're going to shoot me with your… uh… pointer-finger?" the man attempted to push Wilberforce's buttons.

Judging by the beads of sweat accumulating on Wilberforce's forehead the taunts were working. In a slow and deliberate manner, over-enunciating each word, Wilberforce directed, "Sir, get out of your vehicle."

The man extricated himself from behind the wheel and stood next to the door.

"Excuse me," Wilberforce nudged past the man, leaned into the car, and reached toward the trunk release.

"Hey, you have no probable cause to conduct a search," said the man. "Nor do you have permission to do so."

Wilberforce popped the trunk.

The man turned to a nearby fellow driver, "Sir, can you please be my witness that I did not give the Officer here permission to conduct a search?"

The fellow driver remained silent, but a woman in another vehicle chirped, "I'll be your witness, I heard the entire conversation."

"There you go, Officer," the man said as Wilberforce was walking toward the vehicle's trunk, "I have witnesses."

Wilberforce lifted the trunk lid and observed nothing more than the usual suspects: a jack, a first-aid kit, jumper cables, and a fire extinguisher. He looked back toward the man, "What happened to your trunk mat?"

"A gas can toppled-over and drenched it," the man replied. "The fumes were overwhelming; not to mention that it was a fire hazard; so I tossed it."

"I don't smell any gas."

"Like I said; I got rid of the mat."

"How long ago was that?"

"A couple of months," the man replied.

"I'm thinking that you and I need to talk," said Wilberforce.

"Isn't that what we've been doing?"

"You know what I mean," Wilberforce replied.

51

Captain O'Rourke exited his office at the Bennington Police Station and did a double-take when he passed one of the station's Interview Rooms: Officer Wilberforce was seated at the table in the midst of a discussion with some unknown gentleman.

O'Rourke stopped in his tracks, opened the door to the Interview Room, popped his head inside, and directed to Wilberforce, "Officer… a word, please."

"Excuse me," Wilberforce said to the gentleman and then exited the room, shutting the door behind him.

"You're supposed to be out directing traffic," O'Rourke said to Wilberforce. "Who is this guy?" he thumb-pointed toward the room, "and why is he here?"

"I brought him in for questioning," Wilberforce replied.

"About what?"

"About being the Joker… you know… Spencer Dunn," said Wilberforce, "I'm sure it's him."

"What the hell are you talking about?!" O'Rourke began to rip into Wilberforce. "Charges were dropped against Spencer Dunn and he's currently in Arizona."

"Yeah, well, he's back and using an alias."

O'Rourke glanced into the Interview Room and then back to Wilberforce, "That is NOT Spencer Dunn."

"But the voice…" Wilberforce pleaded, "He was taunting me just like the Joker did that night."

"So, some jerk reads about you in the paper, happens across you directing traffic, decides to screw with your head, and you determined that was sufficient to bring him on for questioning?" O'Rourke replied.

"Well, there's also the thing with his trunk."

"What thing?"

"Detective Nash said that Spencer Dunn's car had an extra trunk mat."

"Yeah... so?"

"So this guy's car is *missing* its trunk mat."

"And how do you know that?"

"I looked."

"On what grounds did you have to look into the trunk?"

"He was talking and acting all suspicious."

"Are you frickin' kidding me?!!" O'Rourke exploded. "Do you know why charges were dropped against Spencer Dunn even though the Prosecutor has scads of direct physical evidence in hand?!!" O'Rourke said in a hushed yet direct voice. "I'll tell you why... because of your procedural misconduct!! And here you are doing the exact same thing!!"

Wilberforce slumped his shoulders.

"And what were you expecting to get from him in your interview?"

"A confession."

"To what?!"

"To killing the woman found in his trunk," Wilberforce replied. "You know... the trunk of his other car... the one in the CSI garage."

"How many times do I have to explain to you that this guy is NOT Spencer Dunn?!"

Wilberforce remained silent.

O'Rourke continued, "You're allowing the fact that you only saw your nemesis in the dark of night, wearing some crazy-ass Joker makeup, to skew your reality."

"How do you mean?" Wilberforce responded.

"Look; I'll cut you some slack here because your memories of that night are wrapped in the post-traumatic stress of shooting a painted-up monster," O'Rourke replied. "But I guarantee you that this guy is not

Spencer Dunn."

"I understand, Sir."

"Good; then get your ass back out on the street directing traffic," O'Rourke thumb-pointed, "I've got some damage control to take care of."

"Yes, Sir," Wilberforce mumbled and walked away.

O'Rourke entered the Interview Room and said to the man, "I'm Captain O'Rourke and I apologize, Sir; my Officer mistook you for someone else and had no authority to bring you in for an interview. Rest assured that he will be dealt with accordingly."

"I understand, Captain," the man replied. "No harm, no foul."

"I appreciate that," said O'Rourke. "If you hang on just a moment I'll have one of my other Officers get you back to your vehicle."

"No need, Captain; my car is right outside."

"Great," O'Rourke replied, "And once again… my apologies."

The man exited the Interview Room and proceeded out of the police station.

O'Rourke began to head back to his office when he noticed Wilberforce still inside the station. "What the hell, Officer?" he said to Wilberforce.

"Sorry, Sir," Wilberforce began to scramble toward the Interview Room, "I just wanted to grab the bottle of water I left in the room."

"Make it quick," O'Rourke huffed.

52

Detective Nash entered the Sheriff's Office to the sight of Brogan and Donnelly jotting on the whiteboard. She glanced at her watch. "You two got an early start; what's up?" she said.

"Got a few nuggets while you were in Westport yesterday afternoon," Donnelly responded.

"How did that go, by the way?" Brogan asked Nash.

"If you're wondering if I came away with any ties between Spencer Dunn and Samantha Dalton," Nash replied, "the answer would be, 'no'."

"So, Samantha wasn't the person who stayed with Spencer at the Hoquiam Castle?" said Donnelly.

"I was unable to make that determination one way or the other," Nash replied. "I even stopped by the Castle myself, but everyone said it was too long ago to recall."

"Why don't you just get on the horn with Spencer and ask him who he was with?" said Brogan.

"For one, do you really think he'd agree to talk with me?" Nash responded. "And for two, even if he did we don't want to show our hand."

"What do you mean?"

"If we let him know that WE know about his stay at the Castle then he could get a friend or family member to say that *they* were his guest."

Brogan connected the dots, "In order to avoid him being tied to Samantha Dalton."

"Bingo."

Donnelly was perplexed, "Forgive me for asking, but what exactly were you hoping to get out of your trip?" she said. "To be honest, I'm not seeing how a tie between Spencer and Samantha could help our case."

"Since we're being honest," Nash winked, "I wasn't sure if there was anything to uncover, either. I mean heck, even if Spencer had been with Samantha at the Castle, what would that have to do with Natalie Copeland? But one thing I DO know is that the trunk of his car has DNA from both Natalie and Samantha, so there's some crazy-ass tie between them… we just haven't found it yet."

"Ahh…" Brogan jumped in, "You weren't necessarily looking for a tie between Spencer and Samantha, you were looking for a tie between Samantha and Natalie," he concluded.

Nash gave Brogan a thumbs-up. "Samantha's parents did not recognize a photo of Natalie or her name, but…" she held up an evidence bag, "they did give me Samantha's cell phone, along with permission to review her call records," she said while handing the bag to Donnelly. "I also dropped off her computer at the CSI lab," she added.

"We're working the Samantha Dalton case now?" Donnelly asked.

"Not exactly," Nash replied. "But apparently Grays Harbor County authorities didn't dig into too many details as part of their investigation since they had an open and shut case staring them in the face."

"So, Lowell's team is looking for any digital activity that might help us connect the dots?" said Brogan.

"Precisely," Nash responded.

"Another avenue that might help us just hit me."

"Oh yeah? Let's hear it."

"If we're unable to find evidence tying Greg Wilson and Spencer Dunn together, how about seeing if we can place Spencer's *car* at the scene?"

"The scene of Samantha Dalton's murder?" Nash replied.

"Correct," Brogan replied. "After all, we know the car is tied to both Samantha and Natalie."

"So, if we can place Spencer's car at the scene we've got a strong piece of circumstantial evidence tying Spencer to Wilson," Nash nodded.

"Yes, ma'am."

"Good point," Nash replied. "And on that note," she glanced between Brogan and Donnelly, "what else do you two have?"

"Mostly dead ends, unfortunately," Brogan responded.

"R&L Market has surveillance cameras," Donnelly chimed in, "but no 'Joker' showed up that night around the time that Spencer ditched Wilberforce."

"Do we know if Lowell's search team included the area near the market?" Nash responded.

"Yes they did," said Donnelly, "with a particular focus in and around the nearby dumpster–nothing."

"We've been scouring the entire state for crimes involving similar injuries to those suffered by both Natalie and Samantha, but have come up empty thus far," Brogan said.

"And there's no taxi or Uber activity from the Thriftway in Belfair back to the vicinity of Spencer's house that night," Donnelly added, "So our best guess is that Spencer hitch-hiked or got a ride from a friend."

"And since his cell phone remained at his house, we're assuming he called from a burner?" Nash remarked.

"There's a pay phone at the Thriftway, but he would have been caught on camera," Donnelly replied. "So yes… a burner is the likely option."

"Hmm…" Nash pondered the information. "I usually say that potential leads that go nowhere tend to help us narrow our focus," she said, "but this doesn't seem to be helping."

"I agree," Brogan responded.

Nash's cell phone rang. She glanced at the screen and said aloud, "It's Lowell; maybe he's got something of note." She answered her phone, "Hey Evan; we've got nothing but dead ends here this morning, so I hope you're not calling to add to our misery."

"I've got some good news, actually," Lowell replied, "DNA results from the water bottle."

"Water bottle?" Nash's face scrunched up, "What water bottle?"

"The one that Officer Wilberforce dropped off."

"What're you talking about?"

"You didn't send Wilberforce here with the bottle?"

"Not at all," Nash replied, "He doesn't work for me; he works for Captain O'Rourke at the B.P.D."

"That's weird," Lowell responded. "I mean yeah, I knew he was with B.P.D. and not the Sheriff's Office, but he specifically said to contact you with the results."

"What about Captain O'Rourke?"

"I assumed that the Officer was proceeding under Captain O'Rourke's direction, but I didn't ask."

"Did Wilberforce say why he wanted this info to go to me and not his Captain?"

"He said that he thought it might be relevant to the Natalie Copeland case, which is under your jurisdiction."

"But why?" said Nash. "Where did he get this sample? Who is this person and why did Wilberforce think they might have some relevance to my case?"

"Can't answer you on that one; I guess you'll have to talk to Wilberforce himself," Lowell replied, "but I CAN tell you that you will be very interested in the results."

"Hmm… okay," Nash resigned herself to not getting any more answers at this time, "what've you got?"

"A match to the unidentified male from the trunk of Spencer's car."

"Holy crap; let me put you on the speaker," Nash replied. She set her phone down and then said, "Okay… go ahead."

"To reiterate for everyone else to hear," said Lowell, "I've got a DNA match for the unidentified male."

"So, he wasn't another victim after all," Nash concluded.

"Or, unlike Natalie Copeland, he managed to get away from his attacker," Lowell responded.

"Since we didn't get a match earlier I assume this guy's not in the system?"

"Correct; but Officer Wilberforce had a name to go with the water bottle," Lowell replied. "After some research we matched it to the guy from whom Wilberforce obtained the sample… according to Wilberforce anyway."

"What's the name?"

"Clayton Metcalf."

"Clayton Metcalf??" Nash was taken aback, "Really?"

"Yeah," Lowell replied. "Why do you sound surprised?"

"It happens to be my father's name."

"Quite the coincidence I'd say, but it's definitely not your father."

"Don't I know it; my father died about a month ago."

"Wow, I had no idea; my condolences."

"I appreciate that."

"Anyway… this guy's thirty-eight years old," said Lowell. "I'll email you his Driver's License photo as soon as we're done here."

"Sounds good," Nash replied, "Anything else?"

"That's it for now."

"Roger that," Nash ended the call. She scurried over to her computer and opened the email from Lowell. Her heart began to race, "What the hell; you've got to be shitting me?!" she said as she stared at the image. "How… how is this even possible?!"

"What is it?" asked Brogan.

"It's… uh…" Nash stumbled. "It's Lyle."

"Lyle?"

"Casey," Nash replied. "He's um… uh… a ghost from the past."

"Lyle Casey?" Brogan responded. "Do you mean the guy that disappeared twelve years ago and was presumably dead?"

Nash jerked her head around to face Brogan, "How the hell do you know…?" she stopped herself and glared at Donnelly. Donnelly's face turned the color of guilt. Nash returned her focus to Brogan, "Since you seem to know certain aspects of my past personal life…" she glanced at Donnelly and then back to Brogan, "Yeah, that's the guy; and for some reason he's using my father's name, even though he never met the man."

"Coincidence?"

"I don't see how," Nash replied, "but who the hell knows; the guy's a frickin' chameleon."

"You think he's trying to make some kind of point… trying to get into your head, perhaps?"

"I wouldn't put it past him, but it seems rather ridiculous after a dozen years," said Nash. She thought for a moment and added, "Let's find out how long he's been using this alias."

"Got it," Brogan replied.

Donnelly finally got the courage to come out of the shadows and lean in to take a look at Nash's computer screen. "Wait a minute," she pointed at the screen and then looked back at Nash with disbelief, "That's Lyle?"

"Yes," Nash tried to get a read on Donnelly, "Why?"

"That's the guy who was at Natalie Copeland's funeral," Donnelly explained, "The one I was telling you about."

Nash looked at Donnelly and then pointed at the screen, "*That's* the guy?"

"Yep… I'm sure of it."

"What the damn hell?!"

"And like I was saying, he looks familiar," Donnelly said. She eyeballed the screen, "Now where the heck have I seen him before?" she said to herself aloud.

✵✵ 17 Days Ago: Saturday, October 26th, 8PM ✵✵

Driving along Mason-Slaughter Highway he was lost in his thoughts among the hypnotic repetition of darkness, to glow of a street lamp, to darkness, to glow of a street lamp.

A hint of anxiety kicked in when he spied an intersection up ahead with a Slaughter County Sheriff's Department cruiser rolling up to the associated stop sign. He instinctively eased off of the gas pedal as he cruised past the cross street.

He glanced at the rearview mirror. "Go straight through the intersection, do not turn onto the highway behind me, do not pass 'Go', do not collect two-hundred dollars," he attempted to telekinetically speak to the Sheriff or Deputy or whomever was behind the wheel of the cruiser. It didn't work; the headlights from the cruiser appeared in the mirror.

Cross streets, various mile-markers, a county maintenance road, and an intersecting highway came and went; the cruiser stayed the course.

In the midst of miles of nothingness he noticed signs of life up ahead to his left. "Okay, time to flip the script," he said aloud as he engaged his blinker and steered into the parking lot of the Quonset Hut Pub & Ale House.

The cruiser wheeled in behind the man and rang out a "whoop" on its siren. The man rolled to a stop and lowered his window. "Ma'am?" he said to the Deputy when she approached.

"Halloween party?" the Deputy asked when she noticed the man's painted-up face.

"Yes, ma'am," the man replied.

"You made an illegal left turn here," the Deputy nodded toward the roadway.

"Really?" the man glanced back and then returned to face the Deputy.

"Yes, Sir; this would be a dangerous spot to make a left during a high-traffic time of day," the Deputy turned her head and pointed, "thus there's a roundabout up ahead in order to safely get back here to access the parking lot."

"I apologize, ma'am; I was just following the directions from my GPS."

"I see," the Deputy replied. "Understand that those devices can help you get from here to there, but they don't take into account the traffic laws."

"Yes, ma'am."

"In the future, please play it safe and utilize the roundabout."

"I will, ma'am."

The Deputy returned to her cruiser, spun around, and disappeared into the night.

The man exhaled a sigh of relief. He paused in thought and then scanned the lot. "Well, time's a wastin'," he said as he began to slowly motor his car through the parking lot. Something caught his eye, "Ah… here we go."

❋ ❋ ❋

"I've got it!" Donnelly proclaimed, "He was the Joker I pulled over that night at the Quonset Hut!"

"Wait… what??" Brogan responded.

"Yep," Donnelly nodded.

"Holy frickin' crap!" Nash remarked. The wheels began to turn inside her head as she processed this revelation, "So Lyle, or Clayton…" she stopped herself, "I am NOT calling him Clayton," she iterated, "was at the Quonset Hut around the same time as Spencer, was dressed up as the Joker… just like Spencer, and his DNA was found in Spencer's trunk?"

"Not to mention that Spencer's trunk also contained a bound-and-gagged Natalie Copeland," Donnelly added. "AND this guy attended her funeral."

"This is frickin' crazy!" Brogan proclaimed, "How do we connect all of these puzzle pieces?" he began to gesture, "One from over here, one over there, another over yonder," he said, "all converging in the trunk of Spencer Dunn's car??" he tossed up his hands.

"It may feel like we're suddenly trying to drink from a fire-hose," Nash responded to Brogan's quandary, "but we do what we've always done: gather the evidence, determine what's relevant, throw out what's not, and build the case."

"What do you think, Kenz," said Donnelly, "he was Spencer's accomplice?"

"Maybe he's the doppelganger that Spencer's been yelling about?" Brogan chimed in before Nash could respond.

"Spencer's got you buying into that load of crap?" Nash said to Brogan. She pointed at the computer screen, "You're telling me that you could mistake Mister… I hate to say it… Tall, Dark, and Handsome… with…"

"Barney Fife," Brogan interrupted. "Yeah, I guess not."

"Precisely," Nash responded. "But Laura's idea about an accomplice is not out of the realm of possibilities."

"I was thinking," said Donnelly, "If he was still at the Quonset Hut when Spencer returned after ditching Wilberforce, he could have followed Spencer in Natalie's car to Belfair, and then taken Spencer home before Wilberforce and his Sergeant showed up."

"That fits into our theory of a friend being involved such that the timeline works," Brogan remarked. "And would explain why Spencer took a cab to the Quonset Hut instead of going straight home."

"Something just hit me," Donnelly said. "If he and Spencer were accomplices, then why wasn't he in the car with Spencer when Wilberforce pulled him over?"

"Obviously we need to pull the string on all of that," Nash said while staring off into space, appearing to be lost in thought.

Brogan and Donnelly noticed the change in Nash's demeanor. They glanced at each other, then to Nash, then back at each other. Brogan broke the silence, "Something on your mind, Kenz?"

Nash turned her gaze to Brogan, "What the hell is Lyle Casey doing up here in Slaughter County?"

"Trying to find you?" Donnelly responded.

"After twelve years?"

Donnelly shrugged–she had no answer.

"So hey," Brogan directed to Nash, "Lowell said that Officer Wilberforce was the one who obtained this guy's DNA?"

"That's correct," Nash replied.

"Well, how did he and this guy cross paths? What made him decide he needed to get the guy's DNA in the first place?"

"Good questions," Nash responded. "That's something I'm going to have to delve into with Wilberforce."

Brogan nodded. He glanced back at Nash's computer screen and something caught his eye, "Whoa, check this out," he said, "The guy's home address is Aberdeen."

"Holy crap… right next to Hoquiam," Donnelly looked to Nash.

"So, what the heck is this telling us?" Brogan said.

"If you're thinking it's telling us that Lyle, or Clayton, or whatever name he's using, is somehow tied to Greg Wilson or Samantha Dalton, we need to sit back, relax, and take a deep breath," Nash replied.

"But the three of them lived within just a few miles of each other," Brogan pleaded, "two of them, Wilson and Samantha, were found dead in Wilson's cabin, and Samantha's DNA was inside the trunk of Spencer's car along with that of this Lyle or whatever guy?"

"And then you add the fact that Spencer's car trunk also throws himself and Natalie Copeland into the mix," Donnelly chimed in. "How do we make sense of five people, with seemingly no connection whatsoever, all converging together someway… somehow?"

"The stuff that you two just verbalized…" Nash said as she grabbed her jacket, "Put it on the board and let's see if a picture begins to emerge."

"Roger that," Brogan replied. "Where're you headed?"

"To find out how Officer Wilberforce crossed paths with Lyle," Nash replied. She thought for a moment, "A visit to the CSI garage is likely on the agenda as well."

53

Detective Nash departed the Bennington Police Station with mixed emotions. Admittedly, she was as wrapped up in the emotional impact of a personal nature as she was in regard to the case she was investigating. How ironic that the two had intersecting lines. Why had Lyle Casey, Nash's abusive former lover, seemingly disappeared off of the face of the earth twelve years ago only to resurface, under an alias, here in Slaughter County, a thousand miles north of his last known whereabouts? Why had he chosen the assumed name of Nash's father, a person he had never met and knew little about?

Something dawned on Nash: an aspect of her father which Lyle *was* aware is the fact that he had walked away from Nash at the tender age of six, never to be seen or heard from again, and that this was a particularly painful memory for her. Is that why Lyle chose the name… to rub Nash's nose in it if they ever crossed paths again? Was his sojourn to Slaughter County a purposeful move to do exactly that? If so, how was he able to track Nash to the area; after all, she had her own little secret that should have kept him from doing so?

Nash snapped out of her focus on the past and transitioned to those of the present: the Natalie Copeland homicide. But she couldn't escape an equally perplexing conundrum tied to Lyle, aka 'Clayton': how did his DNA end up in the trunk of Spencer Dunn's car? She had gotten answers from Officer Wilberforce as to the coincidental nature with which the Officer had crossed paths with Lyle, but the Officer's actions in regard thereof were, for the most part, suspect. His nonchalant way of obtaining Lyle's DNA was a smart move; his other actions… not so much. From Nash's perspective Wilberforce seemed almost obsessed with Lyle; an assessment shared by the Officer's boss, Captain O'Rourke.

Another aspect of the conundrum: Lyle's car missing its trunk mat. It was an item that would normally be a piece of information with a handful of reasons for rendering it meaningless, but existing circumstances had the potential of proving otherwise. With that in mind Nash would seek out the help of the CSI lab and garage; the location with which she was now rolling her cruiser to a stop.

Entering the CSI garage Detective Nash was met by Forensic Scientist Lowell. "Hey, Kenz," Lowell said, "I had a feeling you might be stopping by after I tossed that bombshell your way."

"You have no idea," Nash replied. "There's a lot more to this Clayton Metcalf character than you could have imagined."

"How do you mean?"

"I'll get to that in a minute, but first of all I've got a priority item for your team to look into."

"What's that?"

"Officer Wilberforce said that this guy's car was missing its trunk mat," Nash said. "Which of course jumped out at me since Spencer's car has an extra mat," she thumb-pointed.

"And you're wondering if…?"

"You've got to admit it's quite a coincidence," Nash interrupted. "Do you think your team can determine if Spencer's extra mat is an aftermarket item, or if it originated from another vehicle?"

"Absolutely," Lowell replied. "What make and model are we looking for?"

"A 2010 E-series Mercedes."

"Got it," said Lowell. "And while we're talking about vehicles, we got nothing from Natalie Copeland's car; in fact it was almost 'too clean'."

"Like it had been wiped down?" Nash replied.

"Exactly."

"Well, we know that the Joker was wearing gloves when he

encountered Wilberforce."

"Why did you say 'the Joker' and not 'Spencer'?" said Lowell.

"I don't know… I guess because that's who Wilberforce kept referring to," Nash responded. "The Joker this… the Joker that. I mean hey, he made a great call with the water bottle, but other than that I'm not sure what to think."

"Maybe that's his coping mechanism… you know, how he's dealing with shooting Spencer Dunn at point-blank range?" Lowell replied. "Maybe it's easier for him to have gunned-down a phantom rather than a living, breathing human being?"

"You make a great point," said Nash. "So, back to Natalie's car; you found no evidence of Spencer Dunn or maybe this Clayton Metcalf character?"

"Nope. The peripheral places where you would've expected Natalie's prints, like the radio, the console, the cup-holder, did in fact have her prints," Lowell replied. "But the primary places… the steering wheel, blinker, door handle… were devoid of prints."

"One more piece of evidence that she was not the last person to have been in her car," Nash concluded.

"Correct," said Lowell. "And whoever *that* was obviously wanted to make sure they left no such evidence of being there."

Nash nodded.

"So hey," Lowell continued, "you were going to fill me in on this Clayton Metcalf guy."

"Oh yeah," Nash replied. "Get ready to have your mind blown."

54

Having returned to the Sheriff's Office Detective Nash noticed a new entry on the whiteboard: 'Clayton Metcalf (Lyle)'. She threw out a comment to Brogan and Donnelly, "I appreciate you appeasing me by identifying Lyle's name within his ridiculous Clayton Metcalf alias."

Brogan and Donnelly nodded. "Adding his info to the board helps us visualize everything," Brogan said, "but as you can see, there's nothing really to visualize at this point."

"Here's an addition that might help," Nash responded. "Lyle's car is *missing* its trunk mat, and Spencer's has an *extra* trunk mat."

"You don't think…?" Donnelly started.

"Not a clue at this point," Nash interrupted, "but Lowell's running down the source of the extra mat just in case."

"Is that the extent of what you got from Wilberforce?" Brogan asked Nash.

"From an evidentiary perspective that's about it," Nash replied. "But the nature of how he encountered Lyle is rather interesting."

Nash educated Brogan and Donnelly as to Wilberforce's exchange with Lyle. "Wow, what are the odds that you happen across some guy while you're directing traffic and his DNA has ties to a crime scene?" Brogan commented.

"Not that it necessarily implicates Lyle in the crime," Nash reminded, "but it is certainly one crazy-ass coincidence."

"On a side note," Donnelly commented, "How is Wilberforce dealing with all of this? You know; him shooting an unarmed suspect, his actions being presented to a Grand Jury for possible indictment?"

"That's a whole separate issue," Nash shook her head. "The guy seems so confused about the events of that night that he doesn't know what-the-hell."

"How do you mean?"

"All I can say is that he's not someone I would put on a witness stand."

"That bad, huh?" Brogan interjected.

"I'm afraid so," Nash replied. "Anyway…" she returned her attention to the whiteboard, "what else do we have?"

"I looked into Samantha Dalton's phone records," Donnelly responded, "and there were no direct ties to her abductor, Greg Wilson, or to Spencer."

"The word 'direct' sounds like a caveat?" Nash replied.

"Of sorts… yes," said Donnelly. "Since I *did* find calls between her phone and a burner."

"The same burner that Natalie was calling?"

"No such luck," Donnelly shook her head.

"Well, here's another coincidence of sorts," Nash commented.

"What's that?"

"Samantha's parents mentioned that she had a new boyfriend that she had shared little to nothing about; not even his name," Nash replied.

"Whoa… just like Natalie," said Brogan.

"Now that I think of it," Nash said, "she didn't even refer to this guy as a boyfriend, but actually downplayed whatever their relationship was."

"Do you think she was hiding the fact that she was seeing a married older man–Greg Wilson?"

"I broached that possibility with them and Samantha's father about exploded," Nash replied. "He would have none of that sort of talk."

"Deniability," Brogan said, "the common thread when it comes to close friends, and even more so… family."

"Yep," Nash responded. "The other item of coincidence is that both Natalie and Samantha were communicating with their individual unnamed person via burner phone."

"Any chance we can dig into Greg Wilson's financials to see if he purchased such a phone?"

"Hmm… I'm not sure how much Grays Harbor County would agree to us digging into their closed case."

"But they've been providing us info thus far?"

"Only in attempt to seek out a tie to our case," Nash replied. "It would be hard for me to make an argument that Greg Wilson's financials would have any tie to the Natalie Copeland case."

"Well, crap," Brogan responded.

"What else have you two got?" Nash said to Brogan and Donnelly.

"Another item related to Grays Harbor County," Brogan replied. "I talked to Candace Olsen, you know… Spencer's friend who did his Mad Hatter makeup… and she said that she was the one who was with Spencer at the Hoquiam Castle."

"Hmm… you don't think she'd lie for him, do you?"

"Considering that she made a point of emphasizing that the room had two beds gave me an indication that she was being forthcoming," Brogan replied, "but I guess you never know for sure when it comes to close friends."

"Good point," said Nash. "So, it's sounding like a dead end; at least for now."

"I concur," said Brogan. "Oh, and I also found out that it's Candace's birthday tomorrow," he added.

"Okay… good for her," Nash tried to comprehend the purpose of Brogan's statement.

"It's a milestone… her thirtieth."

"I'm assuming there's a point you're trying to make?"

"I'm thinking that Spencer will be back in town to attend; after all, she's one of his closest friends."

"I like the way you think."

Donnelly was concerned, "We're not going to crash someone's birthday party, are we?"

"Having recently attended my sister's thirtieth birthday bash I know how important those moments are," Nash responded. "So no, we will not be raining on her parade; but you've got to figure he will be staying at his own place while he's here."

"What are you planning on discussing with him?"

"For one, seeing if he gives us the same story about the Hoquiam Castle that Candace gave us; and for two, throwing a little 'Clayton Metcalf'," she said with air-quotes, "at him."

"Hey, one last little item regarding Grays Harbor County," Brogan commented. "This one's in regard to Lyle."

"Go for it."

"For starters: apparently he no longer lives in Aberdeen," said Brogan. "He moved ten months ago—left no forwarding address."

"A familiar theme rears its head," Nash responded.

"Here's another familiar theme," said Brogan, "There was no 'Clayton Metcalf', as we know him, before six years ago."

"Do we have anything on that alias during that time?"

"Not yet; I literally just got this piece of info."

"In that case I'll let you get back at it," Nash replied. "Unless you two have anything else?" she added.

Brogan and Donnelly both nodded in the negative.

Nash strolled over to her desk, retrieved her cell phone, and made a call. "Hey," she spoke into the phone, "I know we haven't talked in a while and I was thinking tonight would be a good time." She listened for a moment and then added, "Great. And bring your laptop; along with all your notes about Lyle Casey."

55

Brogan and Donnelly were adding notes to the whiteboard when Detective Nash strolled into the office carrying a portfolio. Nash headed directly to a nearby table, opened the portfolio, and extracted a stack of papers.

"What's up?" Brogan queried Nash.

"This is part of the research that Ian was doing on Lyle Casey," Nash responded.

"You and Ian have patched things up?" Donnelly asked Nash.

"To some extent," Nash replied. "Heck; after he found out that Lyle was alive, that I hadn't bludgeoned him to death a dozen years ago, he felt like a complete and total ass for even considering such a thing," she added. "Truth be told, I may have overreacted a bit a week or so ago when I found out what Ian was up to. Go figure that I'd subsequently ask to see his research."

"What's your plan with all this?" Brogan asked.

"To be honest, I'm not sure yet," said Nash. "Hopefully we can take this as a starting point, add Lyle's recent *Clayton Metcalf* persona, and perhaps fill in the missing years."

"I don't mean to sound like *Negative Ned* here," Brogan responded, "but how does this help us with the Natalie Copeland case?"

"It might not," Nash replied, "but a few things that we DO know is that his DNA was found in the same trunk as Natalie, he was making 'body in the trunk' jokes to Wilberforce when he got pulled over, his car's trunk mat is missing, Spencer's trunk has an extra mat which is the same type as Lyle's car… a 2010 Mercedes," she glanced at Brogan, "I just got that info from Lowell," she clarified. "And according to

Laura," she nodded at Donnelly, "Lyle attended Natalie's funeral. So some crazy crap is going on here, and I want to know what and why."

"Roger that," Brogan grew wide-eyed. "Are you thinking accomplice?"

"Beats the hell out of me," Nash replied. "Hence the 'what' and 'why'."

"Understood."

Nash glanced at the board, "So, what new items-of-note do we have?"

"I've been able to fill in some of Clayton Metcalf's past six years," Brogan replied. "Before Aberdeen he lived in Healdsburg, California."

"Healdsburg?"

"Yeah; he was living there at the same time you were down there on your 'unofficial working vacation' in support of the Wagner case."

"That's one hell of a coincidence," Nash crossed her arms.

"Yep; he had lived there for three years," said Brogan. "Before that he lived in Petaluma, California; which is about thirty miles south of Healdsburg. That was the first known existence of this version of the guy."

"Hmm… so twelve years ago he was south of San Francisco in the Monterey area as Lyle Casey," Nash responded. "Then six years ago he ends up north of San Francisco in Petaluma, then up to Healdsburg, and then continued moving north; this time to Aberdeen, Washington."

"And now he's in Slaughter County, but we don't know exactly where," said Donnelly.

"Unless this was just a weigh station and he actually lives in Jefferson, or Pierce, or Mason, or some other county in the state," Brogan responded.

Nash turned to Brogan, "Any police reports on this Clayton Metcalf version?"

"Not officially," Brogan replied.

"What does that mean?"

"Some Domestic Violence complaints, but charges were never filed."

"So, the leopard hasn't changed his spots," Nash responded. "No surprise there."

"His line of work has been as a sales rep for a furniture company," Donnelly chimed in. "He has the Northwest Pacific territory, which covers both Oregon and Washington from the Pacific Ocean to the Cascade Mountains."

"Same line of work," Nash commented. "You might be able to use that as a way to figure out whatever alias he used between six and twelve years ago."

"Assuming a geographical area from Monterey to Petaluma?" said Donnelly.

"You may have to expand your boundary, but that's a great place to start."

"Got it."

Nash looked at her watch, reached into her portfolio and extracted a thumb-drive. She handed the drive to Brogan, "More research info on Lyle or Clayton or whoever." She grabbed her jacket and headed for the door.

"What's up?" Brogan asked Nash.

"You two have your marching orders," Nash responded. "Wish me luck," she said as she walked out the door.

※ ※ ※

Detective Nash pulled her cruiser up to the curb in front of Spencer Dunn's home. The yard and the path to the front door were all covered in leaves—it appeared that there had been no activity at the home in some time. A glance at the driveway determined otherwise: the associated leaves revealed two lines of flattened vegetation the width of the track of a vehicle.

Nash exited her cruiser and trekked to the garage door. She pressed her ear up close to the door and could hear the tick-tick-tick of an engine that had been recently turned off. She proceeded to the home's front door.

Rap-rap-rap Nash knocked. She heard footsteps approaching from the other side of the door. The door swung open to the sight of Spencer Dunn—a furrowed brow and clenched jaw defined his face. He glanced up and down the street and then back to Nash. "I flew into town solely to help a dear friend celebrate their birthday," he said to Nash. "How about showing a little respect?"

"I apologize, Mister Dunn; I only have a couple of questions and I'll leave you be," Nash replied.

"I don't have to talk to you."

"That's true," said Nash. "How about I talk, and if you want to respond… great; and if you don't… that's fine, too?"

Spencer crossed his arms, but remained silent.

Nash extracted a photograph and held it up, "Do you know this gentleman; he goes by the name of Lyle Casey or Clayton Metcalf?"

"The guy has an alias?" Spencer responded. "What is he, some kind of con-man or something?"

"Some might consider that to be an accurate description, but that's not why I'm here."

"Don't recognize him, and I've never heard either name; why do you ask?"

"If you'll bear with me, I'll get to that."

Spencer took a deep breath of displeasure.

Nash extracted another photo, "How about Samantha Dalton?"

"Nope."

"I understand you stayed at the Hoquiam Castle a year ago this past August?"

"You're kidding me, right?" Spencer was becoming frustrated, "What the hell does that have to do with anything?"

"You prefer not to answer," Nash responded, "okay."

"Yes, I was there with my friend Candi," Spencer replied with a glance at his watch. "And we had separate beds," he added, "in case you're trying to imply something."

"Not at all," said Nash. She extracted another photograph, "Do you happen to know this gentleman–Greg Wilson?"

"Nope," Spencer shook his head. "Who's he?"

"He has a cabin not too far from the Hoquiam Castle."

Spencer had had enough, "This is the second time you've tried to throw a bunch of cloak & dagger B.S. at me; either explain yourself or get off of my property."

"DNA from both the Lyle Casey, aka Clayton Metcalf, guy; and Samantha Dalton," Nash explained, "was found in the trunk of your car."

"What, you're trying to pin more murders on me?"

"I never said that," Nash replied. "In fact, I didn't even say that both of them had been murdered."

"Well, I don't have a damn clue as to why DNA from these people would be in the trunk of my car," Spencer said. "Did you ever consider that it could be from the guy who owned the car before me?"

"We're investigating all possibilities."

"Doesn't sound like it to me," Spencer replied. "And what about the other dude… that Wilson or whatever guy?"

"He's been tied to Samantha Dalton," said Nash.

The wheels were turning inside Spencer's head. "Oh, I see where you're going with this," he said, "I was in Hoquiam and this Wilson guy has a cabin nearby. This Wilson guy has ties to this Samantha chick, and her DNA was found in the trunk of my car."

Nash nodded in the affirmative. "You can see why we might be asking questions of you now, correct?"

Spencer shook his head, "You people just don't give up, do you?"

"It's not in my nature," Nash replied.

"Well, you all need to take a look at the previous owner of my car then because I had nothing to do with this stuff, not ANY of it," Spencer responded. He thought for a moment, "Wait a minute; what about the other dude, the one with the alias?"

"We have nothing tying him to Samantha Dalton or Greg Wilson;

only that his DNA was found in your trunk," Nash replied. Her response was accurate, yet purposefully incomplete. She didn't want to provide Spencer with a possible alternative to Natalie Copeland's death, especially since the so-called tie between Lyle and Natalie was solely the fact that he showed up at her funeral. The two other items of note regarding Lyle: that both he and Spencer were made up as 'the Joker' that night, and both were at the Quonset Hut, were nothing more than coincidental; but Nash knew that a good Defense Attorney might try to make 'something' out of these two 'nothings'.

"Are we done here?" Spencer asked.

"Yes," Nash replied. "Thanks for your time."

Spencer glared at Nash, but provided no response.

Nash turned and walked away. Spencer remained at the doorway until Nash drove out of sight.

56

"It's a good thing you're here," Brogan said to Nash when she entered the office.

"Why? What's up?" Nash replied as she glanced around the space.

"Sheriff Clarke was looking for you."

"Did he say why?"

"Not exactly; but he was asking about the Natalie Copeland case."

Donnelly chimed in, "I got the impression that he thinks perhaps we're dragging our feet in regard to finding new evidence."

"Either that or he's getting pressured by the Prosecutor," Brogan added.

"We said you were out following a possible lead," said Donnelly, "And then we went over a few things from the board."

"Crap, I was having a chat with our prime suspect," said Nash.

"Spencer's back in town?" Brogan responded.

"Yep; just like you suspected," Nash replied. "I threw everything except the kitchen sink at him and he feigned ignorance at all levels."

"Considering his behavior thus far, that didn't really surprise you, did it?"

"No; but sometimes you learn something from what would appear to be nothing."

"And this time?" asked Donnelly.

"I'm not sure yet."

"So hey, Deputy Prosecutor Dansby is here as well," Brogan said. "He's in with the Sheriff," he nodded toward the Sheriff's office.

"That's probably why Clarke was asking about the case," Nash commented, "Dansby's likely trying to micromanage the situation."

"Which means he's probably going to want an update?"

"Yep; so we'd better be prepared to provide all that we have thus far."

"Roger that," Brogan responded.

"With that in mind," said Nash, "do we have anything new?"

"I've got a name that could be another alias for Lyle Casey during those missing years, but it's a longshot," Brogan replied. "And of course, it has nothing to do with the Natalie Copeland case."

"What makes you think this could be one of Lyle's aliases?"

"He's another furniture sales rep, and his digital footprint disappeared around the same time that the Clayton Metcalf persona showed up," said Brogan. "But this guy was in the Reno-Tahoe area and not the San Francisco Bay Area."

"That seems pretty far-fetched."

"Like I said… it was a longshot."

"What's the name?"

"Andrew Brooke."

"You got a pic?"

"Not yet."

"How'd you come up with the name?"

"Actually, it's a name that Ian came up with; I dug it out of his research."

"Hmm…" Nash pondered. "Feel free to keep digging, but make it a low priority."

"Got it."

The discussion was interrupted by the office door opening. In walked Officer Wilberforce with a handcuffed Lyle Casey, aka Clayton Metcalf, in his custody.

Lyle caught sight of Nash and gave her a wry smile. Nash's heart sank—a gut-punch that transported her back in time. She did her best to hide the emotional impact, but found herself overwhelmed by a montage of moments from the past – memories that had brought forth nightmares on more than one occasion, including recently.

"Hey Mac," Lyle said to Nash, "Long time no see."

57

Lyle Casey stood handcuffed in the custody of Officer Wilberforce of the Bennington Police Department, just inside the entryway of the Slaughter County Sheriff's Office. Detective Nash hadn't seen her abusive former lover since she had escaped his wrath a dozen years earlier and went into hiding. She had pieced her life back together over that time; but now, with the demon standing before her, it was all crashing down upon her as if it had happened only yesterday.

Struggling to keep herself from reverting back to the helpless victim of days gone by, she took a deep breath and reminded herself of the courage it took to escape this monster, of the person she had subsequently become… a champion for victims; and that no one was going to force her back down that rabbit hole.

Nash crossed her arms and gave Lyle the once-over, "That's a nice look for you," she said.

"You must be referring to my bracelets here," Lyle gave a head nod. "No worries, it's only a temporary thing."

"Oh really?"

"Yep."

Nash remained silent.

"I read about you in the Healdsburg Herald: *The hero detective from Seattle who took down the killer of a local icon*," Lyle emphasized. "It took me a while to figure out that the article misspoke when they said 'Seattle'; maybe they just didn't know what or where the heck Slaughter County was, or perhaps they merely defaulted to the known big city?" He pondered for a moment. "Now if *I'm* a news editor I'm playing up the name 'Slaughter' for all it's worth," he added. "I mean hell; what a frickin' headline: Slaughter!"

Nash maintained her silence.

Lyle continued, "I had no idea you were in my neck of the woods. In fact, I didn't even realize it was YOU the paper was talkin' about at first; you know… the last name of 'Nash'. I guess that means you're married now, huh?" He glanced at Nash's hand, "But hey… where's your ring? You and *Mister* Nash on the outs, are you?"

Nash turned to Brogan, who was standing next to her. "Detective Brogan, can you please escort our guest," she nodded toward Lyle, "to the Interview Room?"

"My pleasure," Brogan replied. He walked over to Lyle, took custody of him from Officer Wilberforce, and led him into the nearby Interview Room.

Nash gestured to Wilberforce while simultaneously moving to position herself at the viewing glass outside of the Interview Room. She watched as Brogan had Lyle take a seat at the interview table, Lyle's hands cuffed in front of him on the table, and then Brogan exited the room. Lyle clasped his hands and began to tap his thumbs together—he was smiling.

Nodding toward Lyle through the glass Nash asked Wilberforce, "What's the story?"

"Ma'am?" Wilberforce responded.

"There has to be a reason you brought him here?"

"I just happened across him and he was acting all suspicious; and I couldn't just ignore it."

"Suspicious?" Nash responded, "In what way?"

"I was in my cruiser heading to lunch when I noticed him just sitting there parked in a residential area of town," Wilberforce replied. He paused and clarified, "I recognized his car from the other day." He then continued, "And then, on my way back from lunch, the guy was still there—as if he was staking-out one or more of the homes."

"Where was this?"

"On Marine View Place."

"Marine View Place?"

"Yeah; the 1600-block."

"That's just up the street from my sister's place," Nash responded under her breath.

"Really?" Wilberforce commented. "Anyway, I stopped and asked him what he was doing and he said he was lost, and then he held up a map."

"A road map?"

"Yep."

"The guy's car has Nav, yet he was using a road map like those you get from a gas station mini-mart?"

"Suspicious, right?"

"Did you ask him why he was using a road map instead of his car's GPS?"

"Yes, I did; and he said his GPS sent him to the wrong place."

Donnelly jumped in, "He used his car's GPS as an excuse when I pulled him over at the Quonset Hut that night."

Nash continued her questioning of Wilberforce, "What did he say he was looking for?"

"The 1600-block of South Marine Drive."

"Hmm… close enough to seem legit," Nash responded.

"You think he was lying?" Brogan asked Nash.

"I don't know, but I don't trust the S.O.B.," Nash replied. She then turned to Wilberforce, "You handcuffed and brought him in solely because he was acting suspicious?"

"Not at all," Wilberforce replied. "You told me about his DNA being in the trunk of Spencer Dunn's car, and Mister Lowell told me about the extra trunk mat that matched the same type of car as this guy's," he thumb-pointed. "And then there was all the stuff I shared with you earlier… his missing trunk mat and how he was talking and acting," he took a breath, "and then this suspicious stuff just now."

"You realize that it is *not* normal for a Bennington Police Officer to bring a person of interest to the Sheriff's Office, correct?"

"Yeah, but since the case is under your jurisdiction I didn't know what else to do."

"Okay," Nash glanced between Brogan, Donnelly, and Wilberforce. "You all wait here while I go have a chat with our guest."

Nash walked over to the door of the Interview Room and grabbed the handle. She took a breath, opened the door, and entered the room. Lyle glanced Nash's way and grinned as Nash pulled up a seat at the table across from him.

"Well, well, well… Officer Mackenzie," Lyle said, "Who'd a thunk it?"

"Actually, it's Detective," Nash replied.

Oh, gee… my bad," Lyle replied in a manner that sounded condescending. "To be honest, I would've never imagined you making such a career choice; what led you to this line of work?"

"The opportunity to put away abusive assholes and murderers," said Nash.

"It's that gratifying, is it?"

"Very much so," Nash nodded.

"Well, it's obviously working for you," Lyle scanned Nash over.

"You're trying to flirt with me?" Nash glared, "Really?"

"What can I say?" Lyle grinned.

Nash shook her head, rolled her eyes, and decided that it was time to get down to business. She held up a copy of Lyle's driver's license photograph, "Clayton Metcalf?"

"So it says."

"You stole my father's identification?"

"Not his identification; just his name," Lyle responded. "But you can call me 'Clay'," he grinned.

"Because you mold women into subservience?" Nash replied, "Or did someone mold you into… whatever it is you are?"

"I see you haven't lost your sense of humor."

"So, why 'Clayton Metcalf'? What happened to 'Lyle Casey'?"

"Lyle Casey was dead to me…"

"Like Natalie Copeland?" Nash interrupted.

"Hey, you've got nothin' on me," Lyle gestured.

"I beg to differ."

"Don't beg, Mac… it's unbecoming of you."

"Nonetheless…"

"And before you so rudely interrupted me…" Lyle continued, "Like I was saying, 'Lyle Casey' was dead to me… I needed a fresh start, to become a whole new person."

"To evolve from someone who *batters* women to one who *murders* them," Nash nodded, "I get it."

"You're pretty quick with the comebacks, I can see why you'd be a good cop, but you're out of your league, my dear."

"We'll see."

"By the way, that was not very nice of you to just up and walk out on me like you did… you know, back in Penngrove."

"Penngrove?"

"I meant Pacific Grove," Lyle corrected. "Anyway; no one had ever done that to me before… or since, for that matter."

"I wasn't looking to set a precedent."

"In fact, after that I vowed that no one would ever leave me again," Lyle said, "except on MY terms."

"In other words, you murder them if they try?"

"There you go again, trying to get me to admit to something I didn't do."

"I think some of the women back in Sonoma County might say otherwise."

"Hey, I've got no blood on my hands there."

"Oh really?" Nash replied. "How do you explain reports of Domestic Abuse?"

"Nosy neighbors making something out of nothing," Lyle responded. "I'm sure you noticed that no charges were ever filed; not even by *you* back in the day," he grinned.

"Something I've regretted every day since," Nash replied.

"Regret?" Lyle shook his head. "A life lived with regret is a life not lived at all."

"So, your mantra is 'no regret – no remorse'?"

"Life's too short for that garbage."

There was a moment of silence, and then Nash resumed her line of questioning, "So, back to your aliases," she said, "What about the in-between years; who were you then?"

"What do you mean?"

"Lyle Casey ceased to exist twelve years ago, yet your Clayton Metcalf persona only showed up six years ago," Nash responded, "so who filled in the gap?"

"Sounds like you've got data issues," Lyle replied. "That sucks."

"I take it that means you're not going to tell me?"

"Hey, you're the detective."

"Fine," Nash responded. "So, how do you know Spencer Dunn?"

"Who says I know the guy?"

"Your DNA was found in the trunk of his car."

"Really? Is that the guy who attacked me at the Brewpub place?"

"Attacked you?"

"Yeah; I pull into this place and park my car, making the mistake of parking in a dimly lit area of the lot, it turns out," Lyle explained. "This joker flags me down saying he's having some kind of car problems. He's got the trunk lid open and I go over to see what's up, and the next thing I know the guy smacks me in the head with a friggin' crowbar," he pointed to his head. "I stumbled back, regained my senses, knocked him on his ass, and got the hell out of there."

"What did you mean by 'this joker'?"

"The guy's face was made-up like the Joker."

"And you too, I heard."

"Who told you that?"

"One of my deputies pulled you over at the Quonset Hut that night."

"And she could recognize someone wearing Joker makeup?" Lyle responded, "That doesn't seem very likely."

"Sounds like you just admitted to being made-up as the Joker?"

"I was merely making a point."

"Oh yeah? You said 'she', but I didn't state that the deputy was female," Nash replied. "Besides, you don't think she called-in your license plate number when she pulled you over?" Nash fudged the truth.

"Yeah, well… there were a bunch of us dressed up as the Joker that night."

Nash paused in thought; wondering why Lyle had attempted to hide the fact of his Halloween disguise. She decided to attempt to test him on a somewhat-related item, "That same deputy also saw you at Natalie Copeland's funeral," she said. "Why were you there?"

"I don't know who or what you're talkin' about."

"You didn't question Natalie's name when I mentioned it a minute ago."

"That's because I was responding to your allegation, not to the name of the person you were trying to link me with."

"So… the funeral?"

"I'm afraid your deputy is mistaken."

"I see," Nash replied; realizing she had no direct proof that Lyle had actually been there, and that she was unable to come up with a subterfuge to get him to admit to being in attendance.

"How about we go back to the trunk of Spencer Dunn's car?"

"What about it?"

"Was there anything in the trunk?"

"Like that woman's body?"

"That's exactly what I mean," Nash replied.

"I don't know… maybe, I suppose."

"Now that's interesting," Nash crossed her arms.

"Why do you say that?"

"If there was a body in the trunk, and you got hit over the head, how did your DNA end up on the mat that was *under* the victim?"

Lyle started to respond, but Nash cut him off, "And if you saw a body in the trunk, why didn't you call the police and report it?"

"Ooh, you're good at this."

Nash grinned, "So, do you have an answer?"

"Maybe I got a concussion from him hitting me over the head and I'm remembering it wrong?"

"That's all you've got?" Nash responded to Lyle's explanation.

Lyle shrugged.

"How about you show me this alleged head wound?" Nash pointed toward Lyle's noggin.

"It's all healed-up now."

"That was less than three weeks ago."

"Apparently I'm a quick healer," Lyle grinned.

Nash wasn't buying Lyle's explanation, but decided it wasn't worth pursuing at this point. "So, here's another little nugget for you," she continued, "Your car is missing its trunk mat while this guy's car has an extra trunk mat which just so happens to match that of *your* car."

"How would you know that?"

"Forensics."

"I see what you're doing," Lyle replied. "You're trying to get me to admit that his mat came from *my* car when in reality your forensics geeks can surely only stipulate that it came from a car *similar* to mine."

"Not yet."

"Oh, you assume someone's going to analyze the contents of *my* car's trunk?"

"That would be the normal process," Nash replied.

"That won't do you any good."

"Why not?"

"Ask Officer Overeager out there," Lyle thumb-pointed.

Nash remained silent. She had a sinking feeling that Officer Wilberforce may not have shared a crucial piece of information with her that Lyle was obviously privy to.

"Come to think of it," Lyle continued, "aren't there issues with the evidence associated with this Spencer Whoever guy's trunk mat... the one that allegedly has my DNA on it?"

"What gives you that idea?" Nash responded.

"Maybe I heard about it on the news?"

"Those details have not been shared with news agencies."

"The fact that charges were dropped against the guy has," Lyle replied, "and maybe I just connected the dots?"

"Or maybe you got the info from your buddy Spencer?"

"He's my buddy now?"

"Buddy, accomplice, cohort in crime, whatever," said Nash.

"Nice try," Lyle responded.

"So, tell me about your current residence."

"Changing the subject are you?" said Lyle, "Is that some kind of 'cop trick' to try to throw me off my game?"

"Your residence?" Nash pressed.

"What does my DMV photo there say?" Lyle pointed.

"Aberdeen."

"There you go."

"Our records indicate that you moved a number of months ago and left no forwarding address."

"Sounds like more data-issues on your end," Lyle replied. "If I were you I'd look into getting my I.T. guys squared away."

"You're telling me that if I show up at this Aberdeen address you'll be there?"

"Sure; we can chat over coffee and scones," Lyle grinned.

"So, why are you here," Nash said.

"You'll have to ask Officer Wilber-doofus," Lyle thumb-pointed,

"He's the one who's so obsessed with me he keeps dragging my ass into your police stations."

"No; I mean why are you here… in Slaughter County?"

"Maybe it's to catch up with you?" Lyle replied, "To talk about old times… the good ol' days?"

Nash decided not to play Lyle's game of attempting to personalize the conversation, "According to the Officer you were looking for an address on South Marine Drive."

"Yep; that's what I said."

"And what's there? Who were you going to see?"

"Mister and Misses 'None of your business'."

The door to the Interview Room suddenly opened. Both Nash and Lyle glanced over to see Sheriff Clarke poke his head inside the room. "Detective," the Sheriff said to Nash while head-nodding toward the door.

"Yes, Sir," Nash replied.

The Sheriff shut the door.

"Uh oh… looks like someone's in trouble," Lyle grinned.

Nash got up from her seat. "Excuse me," she said to Lyle.

"Don't mind me," Lyle replied, "I'm not going anywhere… at least not yet," he added with a wink.

58

Detective Nash exited the Interview Room and almost bumped into Sheriff Clarke standing just outside the door. The Sheriff gave Nash a 'follow me' gesture and proceeded to the viewing area adjacent to the Interview Room—Nash followed. Deputy Prosecutor Dansby was standing near the viewing glass; Brogan, Donnelly, and Officer Wilberforce had migrated to an area of the room that provided them with a buffer-zone of sorts from the Sheriff and Prosecutor.

"Detective," Dansby acknowledged Nash.

"Prosecutor Dansby," Nash returned the acknowledgment.

Sheriff Clarke looked to Dansby, with Dansby providing a 'go ahead' nod.

Clarke turned to Nash, "So, who is this guy and why is he here?" he said while nodding toward the Interview Room.

"Clayton Metcalf; also known as Lyle Casey," Nash replied. "He's a person of interest in the Natalie Copeland case."

"How does he fit in?"

"It's sort of complicated."

Dansby jumped in: "Un-complicate it for us," he said to Nash.

"Yes, Sir," Nash replied. "For starters, his DNA was found in the trunk of our prime suspect's vehicle—the same trunk where Natalie Copeland was discovered."

"Unlike Natalie Copeland," Clarke interjected, "he's obviously not a victim."

"Actually, he's trying to portray himself as one, but I'm not necessarily buying it," Nash responded.

"Yeah, we gathered that," Clarke gestured toward Dansby.

"Sir?"

Prosecutor Dansby clarified, "We caught almost the entirety of your interview."

"I see," said Nash.

"Very impressive interrogation," Dansby commented. "And I can see why you might consider him to be a person of interest, but you're going to have to cut him loose."

Nash looked dejected, "I understand, Sir."

"You understand the reasons?" Dansby probed.

"Not completely," Nash admitted, "but I have an idea as to the issues of concern."

"Well, let's go through it with your team so that we're all on the same page," Dansby gestured toward Brogan, Donnelly, and Wilberforce.

Nash gave Brogan, Donnelly, and Wilberforce the 'come hither' finger wave—the trio joined the group.

"Alright, Detective," Dansby said to Nash, "Go ahead."

"Well, 'big picture'-wise," Nash responded, "I'm sure you noticed that Lyle seemed to know a lot about the circumstances surrounding this case?"

"To a certain degree one could say that," Dansby replied, "but he could've learned various aspects from news reports, and other items could merely be speculation on his part. Don't forget that if someone *guesses* the right answer it doesn't mean that they *know* the right answer."

"Understood," said Nash. "On another note, I caught him in a contradiction."

"Are you referring to him saying that perhaps the victim was in the trunk of Spencer's car when he got hit over the head, and then recanted that statement when you pointed out his DNA was *under* the victim?"

"That's correct," Nash replied. "And note that he never did say why he didn't call the police after reportedly seeing a body in the trunk of a car."

"My take was that his *'maybe I got concussed and remembered it wrong?'*

response was his way of answering that item."

"Ah, but remember that HE is the one who offered the 'body in the trunk' statement–I merely followed-up," Nash replied. "And something with which you are probably not aware: When Officer Wilberforce pulled him over a few days ago he was making 'body in the trunk' jokes with the Officer."

Dansby turned to Wilberforce, "Officer?" he prodded.

"Yes, Sir," Wilberforce responded. "When I asked the gentleman about the contents of his trunk he replied, *"it's not like I have a body in there"*."

"Interesting," Dansby commented. "Please continue, Detective," he said to Nash.

"And of course there were the trunk mat disparities," Nash said.

"Not to get ahead of you on this," Dansby responded, "But are you suggesting that perhaps the trunk mat in question originated in Lyle Casey's car, and was subsequently transferred to Spencer Dunn's?"

"That scenario would make sense if the two men are, in fact, accomplices," Nash replied. "Perhaps Lyle felt that the heat was on after Deputy Donnelly pulled him over, so he convinced Spencer that they needed to switch vehicles before dumping Natalie's body?"

Brogan jumped in, "Which would also explain why the box of rugby outfits was tossed out of Spencer Dunn's trunk into the parking lot: to make room for Natalie's body," he explained to Dansby.

Dansby glanced between Brogan and Nash, "Are you postulating that Lyle Casey was the person who was originally on the hook to dump Natalie Copeland's body, but circumstances dictated Plan B: transferring that responsibility to Spencer Dunn?"

"That's one possibility, Sir," Nash responded.

"And what's your theory as to Mister Dunn's actions after he escaped Officer Wilberforce?"

"A cab driver picked up a 'Joker' a few blocks from the scene a matter of mere minutes later," Nash replied, "and dropped them off at the

Quonset Hut."

"The same location where he and Lyle Casey met earlier," Dansby recognized.

"That's correct, Sir," Nash responded.

"But with half the county in makeup and costumes that night I suspect that the cab driver cannot positively state that *his* Joker is *our* Joker?"

"Unfortunately," Nash replied.

"And if it *was* Spencer Dunn whom the cabbie dropped off at the Quonset Hut?"

"One of the two men could have driven Natalie's car to Belfair while the other followed," Brogan jumped in. "At that point they dump her car, and Lyle drives Spencer back home where Officer Wilberforce once again encountered him soon thereafter."

"That all sounds reasonable," Dansby responded, "but can you tie these two men together in order to fit your theory? Do you have a motive?"

"Not yet, Sir," Nash replied.

"Even if you manage to meet those criteria you have major issues in regard to presenting such a case in court."

"Sir?" said Brogan.

"Virtually all evidence discovered in Spencer Dunn's car has been ruled inadmissible," Dansby replied. "So, for all intents and purposes Lyle Casey's DNA is NOT on the trunk mat."

Nash provided a counter argument, "But if we get a Search Warrant for the trunk of Lyle Casey's car, and the same DNA evidence shows up in areas of his trunk that matches the extra trunk mat in Spencer's car..."

Dansby interrupted as he saw where Nash was going, "And you're able match *that* trunk mat to Lyle Casey's car?"

"Yes, Sir."

"Therein lies another problem," Dansby responded. "The discovery of Mister Casey's missing trunk mat is pursuant to an illegal search...

there's no way a Judge will grant a Search Warrant, nor would any evidence obtained be admissible in court."

"You're telling me that if Natalie Copeland's blood and DNA are found in the trunk of Lyle Casey's car that evidence cannot be used?" Nash replied.

"That's correct."

Nash turned and glared at Wilberforce. Wilberforce slumped his shoulders and looked down toward the floor.

"The bottom line is that you have zero evidence against this guy," said Dansby. "And the evidence you were hoping might materialize does not exist… even if it does," he added, "if you know what I mean?"

"Yes, Sir," Nash sighed.

"Do you have anything else that can point to Lyle Casey?"

Something dawned on Brogan, "Wait a minute," he blurted out, "the car seat positions of both Spencer's and Natalie's vehicles."

"What about them?" Dansby replied.

"They were too far back for Spencer to have been behind the wheel," Brogan explained, "but were right in line for Lyle, who is three to four inches taller."

"Now you're changing your theory that Spencer was the perpetrator, and instead you're saying that it was Lyle Casey?" Dansby responded. "Did you forget that you've got your guy on video?"

"Well…" Brogan stammered.

"A good Defense Attorney would use that piece of info to push an alternate theory… to attempt to cast a reasonable doubt as to their client's guilt," Dansby responded. "And now that I know about the seat position issue I'm going to have to share it with the Defense as part of the Discovery Process," he huffed.

Brogan looked as if he was about to crawl into a hole and never return.

Nash jumped in, "Actually, Sir," she directed to Dansby, "we are ready for such a defense tactic."

"Let's hear it," Dansby replied.

"We can argue that Spencer purposely manipulated the seat positions in order to throw investigators off."

Dansby pondered Nash's statement, "Okay; I can use that," he said.

Brogan exhaled a sigh of relief.

"If you're going to attempt to push this 'accomplice theory'," Dansby said with air-quotes, "you need to find a way to tie Spencer Dunn and Lyle Casey together outside of the evidence that you currently have but cannot use."

"I understand, Sir," Nash responded.

"And if I were you," said Dansby, "I'd see if the cab driver has any hard evidence that Spencer Dunn was in his vehicle."

"Yes, Sir," Nash replied.

"And if there's nothing else…" Dansby started.

"Actually, there *is* something else," Nash interrupted.

"What's that?"

"We DO have a possible thread between Spencer and Lyle."

Dansby seemed perturbed, "I thought you said, or at least implied, that you didn't have anything?"

"Well, it has to do with a separate case," Nash replied, "In another jurisdiction."

Dansby gave Nash a 'just out with it,' gesture and associated glare.

"The DNA from a homicide victim in Grays Harbor County was also found on Spencer Dunn's trunk mat," Nash explained.

"The trunk mat in question?"

"That's correct, Sir," Nash replied. "And Lyle Casey was living in the area at the time of the murder."

"Are you working with Grays Harbor County authorities on this?"

"They have been cooperative… yes; but their case is closed," said Nash. "The victim and the perpetrator were both dead at the scene," she added. "And this all occurred almost a year ago."

"Son of a…" Dansby stopped himself as something dawned on him, "If the perpetrator was dead at the scene, how does Lyle Casey fit in?"

"We're not sure yet," Nash replied. "Hell, this gal's DNA being in Spencer's trunk is just as baffling as Lyle's being there, but there's got to be a connection one way or another."

"Well, considering what little evidence we have that's admissible it sounds like you need to pull the string on this issue in an attempt to find some way to tie Spencer Dunn and Lyle Casey together."

"One thing they have in common," said Nash, "Out of the various DNA specimens we've identified thus far, they are the only two people still alive."

"Hmm… that's something to consider," Dansby responded. "If you need any help in getting Grays Harbor's cooperation, you let me know."

"I will, Sir."

Dansby looked at his watch, "If you have nothing else I'm going to get out of here and let you all get to work."

"That was all, Sir."

Prosecutor Dansby exited the building. Sheriff Clarke turned to Nash, "I concur with the Prosecutor," and then turned and exited the space.

Detective Nash let out a large exhale and addressed the team, "Well, we obviously have a lot of work to do." She turned to Wilberforce, "Can I borrow your cuff key?"

"Oh, uh… sure," Wilberforce replied as he handed Nash the key.

Nash walked over to the Interview Room, entered, and approached Lyle—not uttering a word as she gestured toward his wrists.

Lyle extended his arms to expose the key slot of his handcuffs. Nash inserted the key, unlocked, and released Lyle's wrists from the handcuffs.

Lyle looked at Nash and waved his un-cuffed hands around, "Told ya," he grinned.

Nash stepped back while remaining quiet.

"Wow, the silent treatment," Lyle said. "Must have had a rough go of it out there?"

Nash gestured for Lyle to get up. He rose to his feet and Nash escorted him to the doorway where Officer Wilberforce was waiting.

Before Lyle reached Wilberforce he stopped, leaned in toward Nash, and whispered, "And remember what I said."

"What's that?" Nash replied.

"No one walks away from me."

"Is that a threat?"

"I don't need to make threats," Lyle responded, "the facts speak for themselves."

Wilberforce took charge of Lyle and the two began to walk toward the office doorway.

"Yes, they do," Nash mumbled under her breath.

When Wilberforce and Lyle reached the doorway, Lyle turned back around to face Nash. "Ah, c'mon, Mac," he pleaded, "We've got a lot of catching up to do."

Wilberforce grabbed Lyle's arm and directed him out of the office. "Oh Maaac," could be heard as Lyle dropped out of sight.

Nash made her way toward her desk; Brogan and Donnelly were there to greet her.

"Mac?" Brogan said to Nash.

"Yeah, that's what he called me," Nash rolled her eyes. "And the name makes me cringe, so you two need to stick with Mackenzie, or Kenzie, or Kenz."

"Of course," Donnelly responded.

"Speaking of names," said Brogan, "You used to be married?"

Nash looked at Brogan with surprise. Suddenly it dawned on her what he was suggesting, "Oh, uh… that," she responded. "Nope… 'Nash' is my mother's maiden name; but now I know how Lyle discovered me: that news article in Healdsburg."

"So, you're given surname was…" Donnelly started.

"Metcalf," Nash interjected. "After I escaped Lyle I had a feeling he'd try to track me down; so 'goodbye Mackenzie Metcalf – hello

Mackenzie Nash',￼" she said. "Besides; my father hadn't been in my life for almost twenty years by then, so his last name meant very little to me at that point."

"Wow; sorry to hear all that," said Donnelly.

"I appreciate that," Nash replied. "But enough about me; we've got a shitload of work ahead of us."

"Roger that," said Brogan.

59

It was a restless night for Nash. She'd been able to maintain her composure while interviewing Lyle, thanks to her decision that the best defense when dealing with an egotistical manipulator was to go on offense; but in the quiet solitude of the comforts of home the reality of it all sank in…

How did Lyle's DNA truly end up on the trunk mat of Spencer's car? His declaration that Spencer attacked him for no apparent reason seemed highly unlikely, unless Lyle had discovered Spencer holding Natalie Copeland captive and Spencer's response was to try to kill the witness. But if that was the case why wouldn't he have stated as much, and moreover, why wouldn't he have called the police? On the other hand, if Spencer and he were accomplices why would he be throwing Spencer under the bus with such a statement?

Why did he initially hide the fact that he was wearing Joker makeup that night? Was it an attempt to try to distance himself from other Joker-faced individuals that evening, like Spencer, perhaps?

And why was he in Slaughter County in the first place? Could it have anything to do with Nash and his 'no one walks away from me' remark? After all, he not only mentioned it during the interview, but made a point of reiterating it as he was departing, as if it was more of a threat than a statement.

beep-beep-beep-beep Nash sprung to life at the repetitive annoyance. She silenced her alarm, rested her head back on the pillow, and stared at the ceiling. The scenarios that had been running through her head when she drifted off to sleep began to repopulate her mind.

After a couple of minutes of contemplation she turned her head, took note of the time, and emerged from her cocoon.

Detective Brogan entered the Sheriff's Office to the aroma of fresh brew wafting throughout the space. He scanned the surroundings–no Detective Nash in sight. Shedding his jacket and placing it on a nearby coat hook he spied Detective Nash emerging from the shadows with coffee mug in hand. "Where's your partner in crime?" Nash said to Brogan.

"You mean 'partner in *solving* crime'?" Brogan grinned.

"You're pretty quick with a comeback this early in the morning," Nash replied, "You been saving that one?"

"Maybe," Brogan replied. "And she was just pulling into the lot," he added, "the aforementioned crime solver that is."

Nash responded with a head nod, and took a sip of java.

Brogan parked himself in front of the whiteboard–he looked perplexed.

"Something on your mind?" Nash probed.

"What if we're out-to-lunch trying to tie Lyle to Spencer, you know… as accomplices?" Brogan responded.

"Because we have no evidence beyond Lyle's DNA on the trunk mat found in Spencer's car," Nash replied, "and Lyle says it's because Spencer attacked him?"

"Well, yeah… we told a good story to the Prosecutor, but in reality we've got bupkis."

"Truth be told; I've been having similar thoughts," Nash remarked just as the office door was opening.

"Similar thoughts about what?" Donnelly commented as she entered the office.

"The whole 'accomplice theory'," Brogan replied to Donnelly.

"Such as…?" Donnelly asked.

Nash proceeded to discuss all of the issues and concerns she had surrounding Lyle and his associated actions.

"Hmm… I hadn't considered that Spencer might have attacked Lyle because he was attempting to silence a witness to Natalie's abduction," Brogan responded to Nash's input.

"Me neither," Donnelly added.

"Who knows if that's the case," said Nash, "but based on what we know of Spencer Dunn at this point it was the only reason I could come up with in regard to an attack."

"Do you think it's plausible?" said Brogan.

"Plausible… yes; but likely…?" Nash pondered, "Not really."

"I agree."

"You know what's been gnawing at me?" said Donnelly.

"What's that?"

"Motive," Donnelly responded. "I mean really; what could possibly be the motive for Spencer and Lyle to work together to attack Natalie?"

Brogan turned to Nash, "She's got a point," he nodded toward Donnelly.

"Can't argue with that," Nash responded.

"That notion hit me when I stopped by the Quonset Hut yesterday after work," said Donnelly. She extracted an evidence bag filled with receipts, "These are all of the receipts that have 'Joker' scribbled on them from that night," she said. "There were no purchases made under the name of Clayton Metcalf or Lyle Casey; so this is it," she added.

"Maybe he schmoozed one or more women into buying him drinks?" Brogan responded.

"I'm sure that's possible," Donnelly shrugged. "I also showed them his picture, but no one recognized him," she added. "And yes, I did remind them that he would have been wearing Joker makeup."

Brogan started flipping through the receipts, "What exactly are we looking for?"

"For one: to determine how long he was at the pub," Nash responded. "And for two: to see if he might have been with someone."

"Like Spencer?" Brogan replied. "You know… before he skedaddled and got pulled over by Wilberforce?"

"There's probably no way to tell for sure who he might have been with, if anyone; but overlay the timestamps of Spencer's receipts with these."

"Will do."

"And remember; just because those receipts identify *some* Joker, it doesn't mean that the person is *our* Joker."

"When you put it that way it sounds like this is potentially an exercise in futility."

"You could be right, but I'd rather look and find nothing than ignore it and miss something that might be relevant."

"Try to find some way to tie Spencer and Lyle together outside of a damn trunk mat," Brogan sighed, "Roger that."

"The less-than-exciting details of investigative minutia," Nash responded, "Sorry about that."

"Hey, wait a minute," Brogan had an epiphany. "Spencer Dunn works at a used car lot, and has done so for years," he commented. "What if that's the tie between the two of them… maybe even between the three of them, you know… Greg Wilson?"

"Are you thinking that perhaps Lyle or Wilson purchased their vehicle from Spencer?" Donnelly responded.

"That's one option," Brogan replied, "but heck, they could've simply been in the lot to check out a car or take it for a test drive."

"I can see how that would be a way for them to meet, but they'd still need to hatch a plan around some kind of motive," Donnelly responded. "And what, why, and how could that have happened out of some 'chance meeting'?"

"Those are great questions, but I have an idea that would make them moot," Brogan replied.

Nash jumped into the conversation, "We're all ears."

"What if there's a tie between Wilson and Spencer that proves there's not really a tie between the two of them?"

"Okay, now *you're* the one speaking in riddles," Donnelly said to Brogan.

"It might seem that way, but hear me out," Brogan responded. "What if Samantha Dalton's DNA got on the trunk mat because a year ago Greg Wilson owned that car?"

Nash saw where Brogan was going, "And the car was subsequently sold to Spencer; which would mean there is no nefarious tie between him and Wilson?"

"Correct," Brogan replied. "And same example for Lyle's car; if that's where the trunk mat in question originated."

"True; but in that scenario we're still looking at Lyle and Spencer being accomplices of some sort."

"I don't disagree; I'm merely pointing out a scenario where we can explain Samantha's DNA without getting all tied up in enough knots to earn an Eagle Scout's merit badge."

"Well, it shouldn't be too hard to follow the trail of ownership for both vehicles," said Nash.

"Got it," Brogan replied. "Anything else on the agenda for today?"

"I'm sure there'll be plenty, but go ahead and start with your vehicle-thing," Nash responded. She then turned to Donnelly, "and those receipts."

"Will do," Brogan replied. "Got it," Donnelly added. The two of them proceeded to their respective desks.

Nash sat down at her desk, grabbed her cell phone, scrolled through the contacts, and hit 'Send'. "Hey Evan," she said when Forensic Scientist Lowell answered, "Has your team gotten anywhere with Samantha Dalton's computer?"

"We haven't even touched it yet," Lowell replied.

"What? Why not?"

"Because it's a closed case in another county and I've got higher priority items here in Slaughter County," Lowell said. "We're talking stuff from Port Sydney, Scandia, Silver City…"

"I get that, but Deputy Prosecutor Dansby is pressing for us to see if we can tie anything from the Grays Harbor case to ours," Nash explained. "I'm not implying that you should make it your top priority, but if you can move it up the list I'd appreciate it."

"I'll see what I can do."

"Thanks," Nash replied and ended the call. She logged onto her computer and brought up the footage from her interview with Lyle.

60

Detective Nash sat at her desk dissecting video footage from two separate interview sessions with Lyle Casey. She began with the footage from the interview that she had conducted the previous afternoon, realizing that when you are the interrogator your focus can be too direct and subsequently miss certain subtleties that might prove relevant. She also realized that her guard was up during the entirety of the interview, whereas experiencing the event from the position of observer should provide her a more objective perspective of the exchange. Her review had just transitioned to focusing on the footage provided by Captain O'Rourke of Lyle's interview with Officer Wilberforce when her cell phone rang. The number was familiar, but the hour of the morning was curious.

"Hey Sis," Nash said as she answered her phone.

"Sorry to bother you," Katelyn replied.

"No problem at all," said Nash. "What's up?"

"I'm sure this sounds crazy; but I could have sworn I just saw Lyle, you know, Lyle Casey, that guy you were seeing way back in the day."

"Where was this?" Nash replied.

"Just down the street from my place."

"You're shitting me?!"

"I was making breakfast, looked out the kitchen window, and noticed this car that I didn't recognize," Katelyn responded. "I didn't think too much about it at first, but then I realized there was someone in the car just sitting there. I thought maybe they were waiting for someone, you know, like a ride to work. Anyway, I finished my breakfast, went and got dressed, did my makeup; and when I walked out the door he was still out there."

"You could see him well enough to determine who it was?"

"Not at first," Katelyn replied. "It was after I got in my car and started heading down the street."

"You passed right by him?"

"Oh yeah; he looked directly at me, like he recognized me or something, and gave me a weird look," Katelyn responded, "It really creeped me out."

"Son of a bitch," Nash replied.

"But it couldn't really be him; could it?"

"It might be," Nash responded. "He showed up here at the office yesterday."

"What? Why… what did he do?"

"I'll stop by tonight and give you the details," Nash replied. "In the meantime, if he shows up again I need you to call me right away."

"Umm… okay," Katelyn responded and ended the call.

"Son of a damn bitch!" Nash yelled.

Both Brogan and Donnelly scurried over to Nash's vicinity to see what had drawn her ire.

Nash began to vent, "Frickin' Lyle Casey is hanging out just down the street from my sister's house!"

"What??" Donnelly responded.

"You know how Wilberforce said he caught Lyle on Marine View Place yesterday acting suspicious?"

"That's near your sister's place?"

"Yep."

"But he said he was there by mistake," Brogan interjected, "Claimed that he was looking for South Marine Drive?"

"Another frickin' lie, obviously."

"Didn't he say that he still lives in Aberdeen?" said Donnelly.

"Add that load of B.S. to the list," Nash replied.

"Do you think he's purposely stalking your sister?"

"Do you have another explanation?" Nash continued to vent.

Donnelly had no response. Brogan jumped in, "Any idea what he might be up to?" he asked Nash.

"Trying to screw with me, at the very least," Nash responded. "Do you remember where he made a point in the interview that no one ever walks away from him?"

"Yeah."

"When we were cutting him loose he pulled me to the side and reiterated it… like a threat."

"You think he'd try to get back at you through your sister?"

"If he tries anything…" Nash began and then stopped herself mid-sentence.

Brogan and Donnelly stood silent within the tension. Nash's computer screen caught Brogan's attention, "I… uh…" he attempted to break the tension, "You're going over footage of his interviews?" he said to Nash.

Nash broke out of her fog. "Both mine and the interview he had over at B.P.D. with Wilberforce," she replied. "That's what's on the screen right now," she pointed.

"What're you looking for?"

"Inconsistencies and mistakes."

"Any luck thus far?"

"I'm not sure yet," Nash crossed her arms. She almost jumped out of her chair when her cell phone rang. Her heart raced as she fumbled to grab it, "Oh no… not Katelyn," she murmured aloud. "Whew," she exhaled as the Caller I.D. identified Forensic Scientist Evan Lowell.

"Hey Evan," Nash answered her phone. "You got something from Samantha Dalton's computer?"

"No, we haven't jumped on that one yet," Lowell replied, "I'm calling because our illustrious Officer Wilberforce stopped by…"

Nash cut him off, "You've got to be kidding me; what the hell is he sticking his nose into this time?"

"This is something that is better seen than explained."

"Can you email it to me?"

"You'll want to see this in person," Lowell replied.

Nash looked at her watch. "Alright," she exhaled, "I should be there within the half-hour."

"See you then," Lowell replied and ended the call.

Nash rose from her desk chair.

"Some important news from Lowell?" Brogan asked Nash.

"So he says," Nash replied as she grabbed her jacket.

"Any idea what it is?"

"Not a clue," Nash said as she headed toward the door.

61

"Hey Evan," Nash said to Lowell as she entered the CSI garage, "What's this super important item you've got for me?"

"Hey Kenz," Lowell responded. "It's all tied to our infamous trunk mat," he head-nodded and began walking toward Spencer Dunn's car. Nash followed suit.

Lowell stopped at the trunk of Spencer's car. Nash peeked in and commented, "That looks too clean to be the trunk mat."

"That's the one that was underneath," Lowell replied, "the other one's over on the large table," he thumb-pointed. "I wanted to start here because the blood and DNA on this mat is consistent with that found on the other areas, such as the edges, corners, and over the wheel wells."

"I take it that means you've got Spencer's blood or DNA on this mat, unlike the other mat?" Nash responded.

"Correct," Lowell replied and began walking toward the table featuring the other trunk mat. "Which makes sense if you get a new mat and just place it over the old one," he added while he walked.

"Officer Wilberforce pointed this out?" Nash said as she followed Lowell.

"No," Lowell responded, "I'll get to that in a sec."

Lowell stopped at the table and donned latex gloves. Nash donned gloves as well. Lowell began pointing out details within the trunk mat, "See this scrape mark here that continues to, and seemingly beyond, the end of the mat?"

"It doesn't continue anywhere within Spencer's trunk?" Nash replied.

"Nope," Lowell said and then began pointing out other indicators on the mat. "Here we've got a stain that goes to the edge, this here's a blood droplet, over here's a rip," he said. "None of these are consistent with Spencer's trunk."

"So, this mat came from another vehicle," Nash concluded.

"That's my assessment."

"Okay, but I don't see how this helps us."

"And that's where Officer Wilberforce comes in," Lowell responded as he pointed to a nearby large screen. He manipulated a computer keyboard and brought up a number of photographic images on the screen. "The Officer took multiple pictures of the trunk of Lyle Casey's car when he pulled him over the other day."

"Son of a…" Nash responded.

Lowell began to point out specific areas of Lyle's trunk on the screen, "Scrape mark… stain… droplet."

"They match the trunk mat?" said Nash.

"They do when you put them together," Lowell replied as a photo of the trunk mat emerged on the screen and was digitally-positioned to the area corresponding to Lyle's missing mat.

"Holy shit!" Nash commented as the mat matched up perfectly. "There's the continuation of the scrape, there's the completion of the stain," she pointed-out.

"Yep," Lowell replied. "It's a shame that none of this is admissible in court," he added.

"Yeah… dammit," Nash responded. She thought for a moment, "Hmm… just because it can't be used in court doesn't mean that the evidence is nonexistent."

"You've got a workaround?" said Lowell.

"In one way or another," Nash replied, "I believe so."

"Knowing you, I have no doubt."

"Speaking of evidence," said Nash, "Have you submitted Lyle's DNA to CODIS?"

"No, we haven't."

"Why not?"

"I don't believe it meets the requirements for submittal because, as of the moment, Lyle is not considered to be the putative perpetrator," Lowell replied.

"Putative?" said Nash.

"It means 'supposed'."

"Why didn't you just say that?"

"I was using the verbiage directly from the FBI's database concerning CODIS."

"Well, crap."

"If we'd discovered his DNA on Natalie herself that would be a different story," Lowell replied. "But with nothing more than a small amount of DNA on a trunk mat, well…"

"I get it," Nash sighed.

"But I figured out a minor workaround of sorts," Lowell said.

"Yeah?" Nash perked up.

"I have some connections in Northern California, and have provided his DNA to select counties therein."

"That's great," Nash replied. "You'll keep me posted?"

"Absolutely."

❊❊❊

Detective Nash's mind was racing a thousand miles-per-hour as she negotiated the city and county roads that marked the way back to the Sheriff's Office. With the knowledge that the trunk mat from Spencer Dunn's car had originated from Lyle Casey's vehicle, had that strengthened the case for the two men being accomplices? But how? And why? And did this all lend credence to Prosecutor Dansby's notion that perhaps it was Lyle whom had originally planned to dump Natalie's body but his exchange with Deputy Donnelly had caused Spencer and him to implement Plan B? Then again, Donnelly had made a great point; what could possibly be the motive for the two of them to work together to attack Natalie Copeland? And what about

Samantha Dalton; was Brogan correct in the possibility that Lyle's car had been previously owned by Greg Wilson and the presumed tie between the two homicides was merely a one-in-a-million coincidence? As she reflected upon the variables Nash was feeling as if the more she learned the less she actually knew.

Approaching the city limits a thought hit Nash—she took a detour from her planned path and ventured onto Old Kitsap Highway. After several blocks she turned onto Marine View Place.

"Son of a bitch," Nash said as she spied a white Mercedes parked less than a block from her sister Katelyn's house. She pulled in behind the Mercedes, exited her cruiser, walked up to the driver's-side door, and rapped on the glass.

Lyle glanced over at Nash and smiled as the window rolled down. "Look who's here… Officer Mac is back," he said.

"It's 'detective'," Nash replied.

"A little testy about the whole Officer-Detective thing, aren't you?"

"What are you doing here?" Nash got to the point.

"Just sittin' around minding my own business," Lyle responded, "You should try it."

"And why here?"

"It's as good a place as any," Lyle replied. "Besides; I kind of like the view."

"Of what?"

"The tree-lined street, the mid-century homes, and not to mention the interesting people coming and going," Lyle said. He looked directly at Nash, "By the way, how's your sister?"

Nash just about exploded, "Excuse me?! What kind of question is that?!"

"Just making small-talk," Lyle shrugged.

Nash stuck her finger in Lyle's face, "You leave my family out of this; if anything happens to her you're a dead man!"

"Is that a threat?"

"I don't need to make threats," Nash smirked as she threw Lyle's own words right back at him, "the facts speak for themselves."

"Touché," Lyle responded.

"Remember how you told me yesterday that I was out of your league?" Nash leaned in. "Well, guess what... I know that the trunk mat is from YOUR car."

"What trunk mat is that?" Lyle feigned ignorance.

"You know exactly what trunk mat I'm talking about."

"Too bad you'll never be able to use that in court," Lyle replied.

"Maybe not, but I WILL nail your ass."

"Good luck with that," Lyle grinned. "Can I go now?"

Nash responded with a deep exhale and stern glare. She would've liked nothing more than to drag Lyle to the Sheriff's Office, toss him in the slammer, and throw away the key; but circumstances dictated otherwise... unfortunately. "Get the hell out of here," she head-nodded. "And remember what I said."

"Yes ma'am, Officer Detective," Lyle replied with a condescending salute. He started his car, pulled away from the curb, and drove out of sight.

62

Arriving back at the Sheriff's Office Detective Nash shared the information she had learned from Lowell with Brogan and Donnelly. She also provided details of her exchange with Lyle.

"You're telling me that you had just found out that the trunk mat is actually from Lyle's car, and then you saw him hanging out near your sister's place?" Donnelly said to Nash. "How were you able to maintain your cool when you saw him there… especially with what you had just learned?"

"Believe me, it wasn't easy," Nash replied.

"What are you going to do about him?"

"I'd like to keep an eye on him; but between his secretive ways, and the fact that we don't have enough on him to consider him to be a suspect, our hands are pretty much tied," Nash responded. "Hopefully our little chat causes him to crawl back into whatever hole he crawled out of."

Brogan entered the conversation, "I'm still blown away by the trunk mat info," he said, "I wish I could've seen how Lowell's team pieced it all together."

"You're in luck," Nash replied to Brogan as she manipulated her keyboard, "Lowell sent me the images and associated animation."

Nash ran the footage for Brogan and Donnelly to view.

"Damn those forensics folks are good," Brogan responded to the feed. "And you've got hand it to Wilberforce for getting those shots of Lyle's trunk," he added.

"That's a double-edged sword," Nash replied. "His overzealous actions have one, if not two, killers walking around free while we have to ignore overwhelming evidence and try to piece together bits and chunks from out in the periphery to attempt to build a case."

"True; but if not for Wilberforce we may have a homicide with zero clues, or maybe that has not yet even been discovered, depending on where Natalie's body was intended to be dumped."

"Like I said… a double-edged sword," Nash responded. "So, did you two happen to come up with anything while I was out?" she asked Brogan and Donnelly.

"Our possible tie between Greg Wilson and the trunk mat went 'poof'," Brogan gestured.

"I take it that means he was not the owner of the Mercedes before Lyle?" Nash concluded.

"Nor Spencer's Beemer," Brogan responded, "Which is a moot point at this juncture of course."

"And the 'Joker' receipts from the Quonset Hut yielded nothing," Donnelly added. "So we have no idea if Lyle was there long enough to follow Spencer to Belfair or not."

"Understood," Nash responded. "With our new trunk mat revelation, you two see what you can build around that slice of knowledge; I'm going to take a fresh look at all of the video footage we have on this case."

"Roger that," Brogan replied.

Nash sat down at her desk and got back to where she had left off before her trip to the CSI garage: the video footage of Officer Wilberforce interviewing Lyle. She then began to take a fresh look at the dash-cam and body-cam footage of Wilberforce and Spencer's interactions the early morning hours of October 27th. Bouncing between the various video feeds provided her a perspective not seen within each individual piece of footage. "Hey you two," she called out to Brogan and Donnelly, "if you've got a minute, how about providing me a second opinion?"

Brogan and Donnelly rambled over to Nash's desk. "What's up?" Brogan said.

"I'm going to play snippets of four videos: mine and Wilberforce's interviews with Lyle, and the dash-cam and body-cam videos of Wilberforce and Spencer," Nash responded. "Let me know if anything jumps out at you, or at least begs a question."

"Uh… sure," said Brogan.

Nash ran through the portions of footage and then asked, "Anything grab you?" she glanced between Brogan and Donnelly.

"Umm… not really," Brogan replied.

"Well…" Donnelly thought for a moment. "When Spencer was talking to Wilberforce when he got pulled over, he was talking like Heath Ledger's 'Joker'… you know… like he was playing a role."

"Well, yeah… I got that," Brogan interrupted as if to defend himself.

Nash scowled at Brogan and then nodded for Donnelly to continue her thought.

"So, if someone's manipulating their voice you can't really try to match it to the specific person," Donnelly continued. "But to me, the voice inflections seem more like Lyle than Spencer."

"My thoughts exactly," Nash nodded.

"Wait a minute," Brogan turned to Donnelly, "You talked to him when you pulled him over that night; nothing jumped out at you when you first saw the 'Joker' footage?"

"A dozen words in a normal voice compared to the breathy 'Joker' voice?" Donnelly responded, "Nope; not at all."

"Hmmm," Brogan mumbled, "Can you play that again?" he asked Nash.

"Sure," said Nash, "but let me play a portion of Lyle's interview followed immediately by the Joker and Wilberforce interaction so you get a direct comparison."

Nash ran the two video feeds.

"I see what you mean," Brogan noted. "But I don't think we can call that conclusive," he added, "especially since we aren't voice experts."

"I agree," Nash responded, "but it certainly makes one wonder."

"What if we send it to Lowell for analysis?" said Donnelly.

"That's precisely my plan," Nash replied.

"Now that I think of it," Brogan said, "The way the Joker was screwing with Wilberforce was exactly how he was interacting with you," he nodded to Nash. "Smug, cocky, smart-assed…"

"Whoa; you're right," Donnelly noted.

"Bingo," Nash responded.

"Well, shoot; now that we're looking closer I just noticed that Spencer never moved his seat back before getting out of the car," noted Donnelly.

"Yeah, but he could've moved it back before Wilberforce got up to his car door," Brogan responded.

"That's true," Donnelly realized. Something else dawned on her, "Hey wait a minute; can we run through the dash-cam footage in its entirety?" she said to Nash.

"Sure," Nash replied and then ran the footage.

Upon completion of the run Donnelly asked, "How tall is Wilberforce?"

"Around 5'10" I believe," Nash responded.

"The camera angle, the poor lighting, and the distance all prevent us from making an accurate comparison," Donnelly noted, "but doesn't it seem like the Joker might be slightly taller than the Officer?"

"Yeah," Brogan interjected. "Spencer's around the same height—maybe a tad shorter, but Lyle's a couple-three inches taller."

"Uhh… maybe," Nash replied, "But like Laura said, there's no way for us to tell conclusively if that is the case."

Donnelly was perplexed. "Where exactly are we going with all this?" she said. "Are we now considering that Lyle is the Joker and not Spencer?"

"That's a bit of a leap," Nash replied. "Right now we are merely identifying oddities. And don't forget the primary piece of evidence we have in this case—the lipstick match between Natalie's frown and Spencer's Joker smile."

"Oh yeah," said Donnelly.

Brogan exhaled, "We were starting to sound like defense attorneys."

"Well, one aspect of being an effective prosecutor is the ability to anticipate the defense team's strategy and be prepared to counter their argument," Nash responded.

"So, now what?" said Donnelly.

"I'm going to send this to Lowell and see if they can make anything of it."

"Oh, hey…" Brogan started, "You said that if I found anything on the Andrew Brooke guy I should let you know."

"The guy from the Tahoe area whose digital footprint disappeared around the same time that Lyle's 'Clayton Metcalf' persona showed up?"

"Yep," said Brogan. "This is probably nothing, but I dug up a photograph of the guy," he said as he produced a DMV photo.

"I suppose he bears *some* resemblance to Lyle," Nash viewed the photo, "but it's definitely not him."

"From the perspective of someone who knows him as well as you do… sure," Brogan replied. "But if he just showed up, new guy in town, flashing this I.D. around…"

"What are you implying?"

"What if Lyle assumed this guy's identity?"

"It sounds like you're grasping at straws," Nash replied. "Think about it; if that was the case then what happened to the supposed REAL Andrew Brooke? And if people were concerned about this guy when he allegedly disappeared at the time his digital footprint stopped six years ago, friends or family would have filed a Missing Persons Report, and law enforcement around Tahoe would have investigated. Did any of that occur?"

"I couldn't really tell you," Brogan responded.

"I appreciate your investigative curiosity, but right now we don't have time to waste attempting to figure out Lyle's alias from six-to-twelve years ago, we need to focus on his recent history."

"Understood."

"If you don't have anything else I need to give Lowell a call."

Both Brogan and Donnelly nodded in the negative and retreated to their respective desks.

Nash made a call to Lowell, "Hey Evan," she said. "I'm sending over some videos tied to the Natalie Copeland case. There are three items I'd like your folks to assess if at all possible, realizing that the quality of the footage might provide nothing more than 'three strikes you're out'."

"What are we looking for?"

"A potential voice match, a height comparison, and probably the least likely of the three considering the makeup..." Nash said, "...possible facial recognition."

63

Pouring her morning cup of coffee in the Break Room, Detective Nash reflected upon the previous evening. It was more than the simple matter that restless nights had become an all-too-common occurrence, it was the reasons therein. Not that an active case running through her head twenty-four-seven would be an abnormality, but this one introduced an entirely new variable: the angst of circumstances hitting too close to home. How do you explain to your younger sister that an abusive lover from your past had suddenly shown up, twelve years and a thousand miles later, using the alias of your father? And even more concerning: What was he doing just down the street from that sister's home? Nash had received responses to such questions, but she had no faith in the reliability of the source… the former lover and abusive manipulator himself, Lyle Casey. Nash had refrained from sharing details about the case which had ensnared Lyle in some not-fully-understood way. With the knowledge that Nash had confronted Lyle, and that Katelyn had orders to notify her if she caught sight of him again, Katelyn had placed complete trust in her big sister. Nash, on the other hand, was still on edge—not in fear for her own safety, but for that of her sister. She couldn't shake the notion that Lyle was up to something. She took a sip of coffee and headed toward her desk.

"Hey, you two," Nash said as the sojourn to her desk was interrupted by the sight of Brogan and Donnelly adding notes to the whiteboard, "What're you working on?"

"With the info we received concerning Lyle Casey yesterday, I figured it would help to lay out a timeline as to his whereabouts over the past several years—those encompassing his Clayton Metcalf alias,"

Brogan replied.

"Good plan," Nash responded. "What's the breakdown?"

"As we've discussed, the genesis of 'Clayton Metcalf' occurred about six-and-half years ago in Petaluma, California," Brogan said as he pointed to the associated entry on the whiteboard.

"He lived there a couple of years and then moved up to Healdsburg," Donnelly chimed in. "Some three years later he got the territory that covers all the way up to Western Washington, which is when he moved to Aberdeen."

"And that was just over a year ago?" Nash responded.

"Correct," Brogan replied. "And I've got an update on that," he added. "It turns out that he rented a room from some couple, and as we already know he moved out ten months ago, so he was only there a few months."

"But here's a new piece of info," said Donnelly. "He still receives some mail there; and he stops by every so often to pick it up—most recently about a week ago."

"That's good to know," Nash replied. "If he transitions to 'suspect' at some point they could be key to capturing him if he shows up there."

Both Brogan and Donnelly nodded concurrence with Nash's statement.

Nash's cell phone rang. "Hey Evan," Nash spoke into her phone as she answered.

"My connections in Northern California paid off," Lowell replied, "We got a DNA hit tied to two crime scenes in Sonoma County."

"You're kidding?" Nash responded.

Lowell went on to provide details. When he was finished Nash hung up, momentarily stared off in space, and responded, "Holy crap!"

Both Brogan and Donnelly grew wide-eyed. "What's up?" Brogan said to Nash.

"Lyle Casey's DNA matches a person of interest from two homicides in Sonoma County," Nash replied.

"What the hell?!" Brogan responded.

"Lyle's a suspect in these crimes?" said Donnelly.

"Not officially," Nash replied. "Lyle's DNA was found inside the homes of the victims, not on the victims themselves, so he is merely someone that authorities wanted to talk to."

"What's the story on the victims?" said Brogan.

"Kristin Atwater was found along the shores of the Russian River near Healdsburg just over a year ago. Her case is still active, but had essentially gone dormant," Nash replied. "Olivia Bissett was reported missing four years ago. Her body was found near Penngrove two years ago. The M.E. determined that she was killed around the time she disappeared."

"Damn," Brogan responded.

Donnelly turned her focus to the whiteboard, "If our timeline is correct, Lyle moved from Petaluma to Healdsburg soon after Olivia Bissett disappeared," she said, "And he moved again, this time from Healdsburg to Aberdeen, right around the time that Kristin Atwater was killed."

"Shit; you're right," Brogan commented.

Something dawned on Nash, "And he blurted-out the town of Penngrove when I was interviewing him," she said. "He tried to walk it back by saying that he meant Pacific Grove, but now I'm wondering if it was a Freudian slip."

"If we really want to think outside the box," Brogan said, "Lyle got the heck out of Aberdeen right after Samantha Dalton was killed."

"You're trying to make him an accomplice with Greg Wilson now, are you?" Nash responded.

"Nah..." said Brogan. "Just recognizing the odd coincidence." Something struck him, "Hey, back to those Sonoma County cases; were the injuries similar to our victims?"

"Lowell didn't have that info."

"I hate to say it," Donnelly commented, "but I don't see how this has any tie to our case."

"You're right," Nash replied. "It doesn't. But if there is anything to these occurrences, then it helps us establish a pattern."

"Well, shit… now what?" said Brogan.

Nash's cell phone rang–she did not recognize the number. "Detective Nash," she said as she answered the phone. She perked up as she listened. "Wait… what?" she commented; listened some more, and finished with, "Whoa; thank you very much."

Nash hung up her phone and relayed to Brogan and Donnelly, "Shit just got real."

"Who was that?" Donnelly responded.

"Grays Harbor County's Crime Lab," Nash replied. "Due to our requests, they performed additional testing from their crime scene; specifically, the clothing of both Samantha Dalton and Greg Wilson," she said. "And this will blow your mind," she added, "Neither one had the other's DNA on them."

Brogan was dumbfounded. "Wait a minute," he said. "We all saw the crimes scene photos and visited the cabin itself… how the hell is that possible?"

"Here's how," Nash responded. "Guess who's DNA *was* there?"

"Spencer Dunn?" Donnelly said.

"Lyle Casey," Nash replied.

"What the hell?!" Brogan responded.

"Like I said," Nash commented, "Shit just got real."

Nash's cell phone rang. "What the heck is the deal this morning?" she commented with a tinge of frustration before seeing the identity of the caller. "Oh, it's Lowell," she changed her tune. "Hey Evan," she looked at her watch, "Something new for me to go along with the bombshell I have for you?"

"You have a bombshell for me?" Lowell replied. "Well, I guess that goes both ways; we got a major find in our search of Samantha Dalton's computer," he added. "We just got started, but I wanted to share this info right away." He went on to provide details to Nash.

"Holy crap; this is a game-changer," Nash responded at Lowell's news. "And it dovetails with news I just got from Grays Harbor County," she added, and then went on to relay the info concerning Lyle's DNA on the clothing of Samantha Dalton and Greg Wilson.

"Holy shit," Lowell replied. "It sounds like Grays Harbor County needs to reassess their case?"

"I concur," said Nash, "As do I."

"Agreed," said Lowell. "Keep me posted," he said and ended the call.

Nash turned to Brogan and Donnelly. "It's time for another road trip," she said.

"What's up?" Brogan replied.

"Lowell's team just uncovered a direct tie between Samantha Dalton and Lyle Casey."

"More than the tie we just learned about his DNA on her clothing?" Donnelly responded.

"Yes," said Nash, "Communication between the two of them via the website Affluence-dot-com."

"What the heck is that; some Sugar Daddy kind of website?" Brogan responded.

"According to Lowell the site says that its aim is 'to connect women with successful men seeking a relationship of substance'," Nash said with air-quotes.

"Holy crap," Donnelly commented.

"And the destination of our road trip?" said Brogan.

"The Wilson family cabin," Nash replied. "Assuming I'm able to obtain Madelyn Wilson's permission." A thought hit her, "But first I need to put my sister on High Alert," she added as she grabbed her cell phone.

64

Detective Nash had shared minimal information with Madelyn Wilson regarding her request to take a second look at the Wilson family cabin. As tempting as it was to reveal the fact that new evidence could shed a fresh light on the incident that had involved Madelyn's husband, Greg; Nash realized that such a revelation would be premature. Instead, she kept the focus on her own case, stressing that the newly-uncovered information which had prompted her request had zero implications toward Madelyn's husband.

The subsequent drive to the cabin was both brief, and wrapped in silence. Brogan and Donnelly had noticed that Nash appeared to be in deep contemplation, and the two opted not to inquire as to Nash's demeanor.

As the trio approached the cabin's door, Nash took a breath and broke her silence, "Madelyn Wilson provided some information that was not in Grays Harbor County's official report," she said. "According to Madelyn, the reason her husband Greg went to the cabin that day was because a nearby property owner had concerns about possible trespassers, maybe even squatters. Madelyn went on to say that she had shared this information with the investigators, but they assumed it was merely Samantha's vehicle that had been seen, and that Greg Wilson's trip to the cabin that day was to meet up with her… Samantha."

"Did the authorities actually question the other property owner?" Brogan responded, "Or did they merely make an assumption regarding Samantha's vehicle?"

"Since none of that was in their report we have no way of knowing without asking them directly."

"With what we now know about the DNA evidence, I'd say it's likely they never pursued it," said Brogan.

"Another option is that the investigators assumed that Greg Wilson lied to his wife," Donnelly chimed in, "that he made up the story about trespassers."

"Well, here's another wrinkle that might affect your line of thinking," Nash glanced between Brogan and Donnelly. "According to Lowell, Lyle's correspondence with Samantha mentioned 'his cabin in the woods'."

"Wow; that tells a story in and of itself," Brogan responded.

"Yes, it does," Nash replied as she inserted the key into the lock. She opened the door, "Okay, let's do this," she said.

Crime scene photos in hand, the trio entered the cabin. They walked to each area of the cabin depicted in the associated photograph. One-by-one they compared the physical location with the images in-hand: Greg Wilson's body here, Samantha Dalton's body there, the knife next to Samantha's hand, and the details of their injuries.

Scanning the cabin, taking in all of the evidence, a story began to emerge for Detective Nash. She took a deep breath and ever-so-subtly shook her head.

"Got a theory?" Brogan said to Nash.

"Lyle had been communicating with Samantha via the Affluence website before he moved to Aberdeen," Nash replied.

"While he was still in Healdsburg?" asked Donnelly.

"According to the digital timeline… yes," said Nash. "He portrayed himself as this successful professional who was being transferred to the area and, unfortunately for Samantha, she fell for his *Mister Smooth Talker* routine."

"So, once he was here the two of them met up, and subsequently started communicating via Lyle's burner phone?"

"Correct," Nash replied. "At some point Lyle happened across this cabin which, I'm guessing, probably appeared to be unused or abandoned. It likely began as a romantic escape for the two of them, but soon became a 'House of Horrors' for Samantha."

"Installing the eyebolts?" Brogan gestured toward the bolts, "And then connecting what we assume were chains and shackles?"

Nash nodded in the affirmative.

"Are we assuming it was a one-time thing?" said Donnelly, "Or was it ongoing?"

"I don't think we have enough data to make that determination," Nash replied.

"How could it have been ongoing?" Brogan commented. "Why would Samantha continue to see the guy after he had chained her up?"

"Knowing Lyle the way I do, he started out as Mister Wonderful, but once he knew he had Samantha under his spell he began to whittle away at her self-esteem," Nash replied. "Belittling and verbal abuse would enter the picture, maybe the first sign of physical abuse. He'd follow those with his *I'm so sorry I'll never do it again*' routine, and eventually convince her that no one else would ever want her-—that she was nothing without him."

"Wow," Brogan responded.

"Back to my theory as to the events here at the cabin," said Nash. "Greg Wilson comes out to the cabin based on his neighbor's concern. He walks into the cabin to the sight of Samantha chained-up and gagged. Unbeknownst to Wilson, Lyle had positioned himself such that he was hidden when Wilson opened the door. Lyle ambushes Wilson from behind and slashes his jugular before Wilson even has a chance to defend himself."

"You don't think there was a struggle?" Donnelly asked.

"Greg Wilson had zero defensive wounds," Nash replied. "He never knew what hit him."

"And Samantha?"

"I can't speculate if Lyle had planned to kill Samantha that day or not, but her fate was sealed when Wilson showed up," Nash shook her head.

"Lyle then unshackles Samantha and stages the scene to make it appear that Wilson had killed her. He continues his scheme by placing the knife near Samantha's hand to make it appear that she had managed to grab it and slash Wilson's throat before succumbing from her injuries."

"Geez," Donnelly sighed.

"Yeah," Nash took a deep breath, crossed her arms, and stared off into space.

Brogan and Donnelly glanced at each other and then back to Nash, "Something else on your mind, Kenz?" Brogan asked Nash.

"I, uh… it's just…" Nash stammered through a response. "The guy is a notorious abuser, both verbally and physically," Nash started. "However, it's one thing to beat someone to a pulp without realizing you could be killing them, but it's another thing altogether when you deliberately murder someone," she added. "It's a transformation I never would have considered."

"But maybe it's like you said," Donnelly responded. "Maybe murder wasn't part of the plan, but when Greg Wilson showed up Lyle felt his only recourse was to silence Wilson. And now that Samantha was a witness to Wilson's murder, Lyle reasoned that he had to silence her as well?"

"Perhaps; but even if his attack on Wilson was a reactive response due to getting caught, his subsequent killing of Samantha was a deliberate act."

Donnelly nodded concurrence with Nash's statement.

"And if Lyle had something to do with Natalie Copeland's death, how do we explain Lyle's mindset in regard to that?" Nash responded.

"I see what you mean," Donnelly responded.

"One thing is perplexing, though," Brogan chimed in. "If Lyle does have anything to do with Natalie's murder, and perhaps even those in California, he always made sure to avoid leaving his DNA at the scene, so why is this one different?"

"Best guess…" Nash replied, "He figured that he had staged the scene so perfectly that authorities would have an open and shut case against Wilson and would not look any further."

"So, if we didn't have the Natalie Copeland case, and our M.E. didn't attend the symposium, he would have been right?" Brogan responded.

"It sure looks that way," said Nash. "Especially since Lyle made another mistake that the authorities never questioned."

"What's that?"

"Samantha had fresh wounds on her wrists and ankles, but Lyle had taken the chains and shackles with him when he left the scene."

"They never tried to explain those injuries, and thus how she got them?" said Donnelly.

"Not according to the report," Nash replied.

"So, now what?" Brogan asked.

"I think it's time to let Madelyn Wilson know that her husband was a victim, not a killer."

"What about Samantha's parents?" said Donnelly, "You know... letting them know who her real killer was?"

"Do you really want to tell them that their daughter's killer is still out there?" Nash replied.

"I guess not," Donnelly responded.

"And how about Lyle?" said Brogan. "I mean hell, it looks like we've got him dead-to-rights, don't we?"

"For Samantha's murder, which is outside of our jurisdiction, I agree," Nash replied. "We need to get our assessment to Grays Harbor County authorities."

"And then?"

"We work together to find his ass."

65

Departing the Wilson family cabin, the sojourn through Grays Harbor County took two more turns for Nash, Brogan, and Donnelly. The first was the Grays Harbor Sheriff's Office where Detective Nash shared her theory of the deaths of Samantha Dalton and Greg Wilson. Following Nash's presentation, Grays Harbor County authorities agreed to revisit the case and revise their findings based on the new evidence uncovered via Nash's prompt.

The second stop was Madelyn Wilson's home to return the key to the cabin. Detective Nash also had some news to share with Madelyn, but reconsidered her initial instinct and decided to limit the extent of information to the fact that Grays Harbor authorities had agreed to reopen the case. With Lyle still at-large Nash did not want to risk word getting out about him being a suspect in the deaths of Samantha Dalton and Greg Wilson. From an investigator's perspective it was best for the alleged perpetrator to believe they had successfully pulled-off their frame-job and thus, hopefully, let their guard down. Madelyn was appreciative of Nash's efforts-–her eyes becoming glassy as she shook Nash's hand.

Returning to Slaughter County, Nash dropped Brogan and Donnelly at the Sheriff's Office, and made what she hoped would be her final trip of the day-–to the home of Gary and Nancy Copeland.

Rap-rap-rap Detective Nash knocked on the door of the Copeland residence. The door opened to reveal both Gary and Nancy standing side-by-side.

"Detective," Gary acknowledged Nash.

"Sorry to bother you; I merely wanted to provide you an update on our case," Nash responded. "We've uncovered a fair amount of new evidence, including a second person of interest."

"What does that mean?" Gary replied, "Are you implying a possible accomplice?"

"It's too soon to say for sure; but yes, that is a possibility," Nash responded. "And this may be a bit troubling to hear, but we believe this person may have attended Natalie's memorial service."

"Oh my God; someone involved in our daughter's death might have actually attended her service?" Nancy replied. "What kind of sick monster does that?!"

"We don't know for sure if he's involved, ma'am," Nash replied, "He's only a person of interest at this point."

"What has you looking at this guy?" said Gary.

"You know I am unable to share that information with you, Sir," Nash responded.

"So, that's it?"

"I'm afraid so."

"Okay… got it," Gary responded as he began to shut the door.

Nash held up her hand. "But I do have a request," she said.

Gary gave Nash a 'let's hear it' gesture.

"The Guest Log from Natalie's service…" Nash started.

"My God… noooo!" Nancy shrieked as her mind envisioned the name of a person involved in Natalie's death enshrined in such a cherished keepsake meant to honor the memory of her dear daughter.

Nancy buckled to her knees as the tears began to flow. Gary wrapped his arms around his wife and escorted her out of sight. Nash's heart sank at the sight of Nancy's despair.

Gary reemerged at the doorway. "I, uh… how about if I take some photos of the pages and email them to you?" he proposed.

Nash extracted her card and handed it to Gary. "That would be fine," she said, "Thank you."

❋❋❋

Detective Nash slowly trod into the Sheriff's Office; the events of the day had taken its toll, punctuated by the distressing breakdown of Nancy Copeland. She walked directly to her desk without uttering a word. Brogan and Donnelly looked at each other, "That can't be good," Brogan whispered to Donnelly and then head-nodded in the direction of Nash's desk.

Brogan and Donnelly approached Nash. "How'd it go?" Brogan asked Nash.

"Not good," Nash replied. "Imagine your child has been murdered and then you discover that the murderer had signed the Guest Log at her memorial service," she sighed.

"Lyle signed the log?" Donnelly responded.

"I don't know," Nash shook her head, "Gary Copeland is supposed to be taking some snapshots of the log and emailing them over, but when I mentioned that a person of interest had been seen at Natalie's Memorial Service, and then asked to see the Guest Log… well, Nancy Copeland immediately imagined the worst." Nash took a breath and added, "And I can't blame her."

"Any idea when you'll be getting the email?"

Nash glanced at her computer screen. "Actually, it just showed up. Hang on a sec," she replied as she manipulated her mouse and keyboard. "Okay, I just forwarded it to you," she said to Donnelly.

"I'll let you know what I find," Donnelly replied.

"Needless to say I am not looking forward to having the same conversation with Samantha Dalton's parents," said Nash.

Donnelly gestured toward Brogan. "Dirk and I have been looking into Lyle Casey, or as everyone else knows him, Clayton Metcalf," Donnelly said to Nash. "We talked to his last known place of work and they said he was essentially an independent entity."

"What did they mean by that?" said Nash.

"They were pretty much hands-off as long as he gave them results."

"Which he did," Brogan chimed in. "They said that the guy was a machine. They deposited his commission checks into an account quarterly, and had little communication with him."

"Wait a minute," Nash responded. "Why are you speaking in the past tense?"

"He resigned several months ago," said Brogan.

"His last known address according to their records is the place in Aberdeen," added Donnelly, "However; they refused to provide any financial information without a warrant."

"We certainly don't have enough to get a Judge to sign-off on one," Nash responded, "but Grays Harbor County likely can."

"I hate to say it," said Donnelly, "but it looks like Lyle is once again 'in the wind'."

"You're probably right," Nash replied. "When I told him that I knew the trunk mat came from his car he had to realize that we're onto him."

"Well shit, there's got to be some way we can hunt him down," said Brogan.

"His financials should help," said Nash. "I'll get on the horn with Grays Harbor County as soon as we're done here," she added, "Anything else?"

"For what it's worth, I've got an update on Andrew Brooke," Brogan responded.

Nash was skeptical, but curious, "Okay, what've you got?"

"An interesting side-note to his digital footprint disappearing," said Brogan. "Up until recently he's been a 'John Doe' in a Santa Cruz County morgue."

"Not to rub it in, but I suggested that you were grasping at straws on this one," Nash replied. "Obviously Lyle didn't assume this guy's identity after all."

"Actually, the murder of this particular John Doe has been a cold case," Brogan responded. "His body was discovered eleven years ago."

"Eleven years ago??" Donnelly grew wide-eyed. "What the…"

"So, *someone* was posing as this guy in Tahoe," Nash concluded.

"You don't have anything that points toward Lyle, do you?" she asked Brogan.

"Not at this time," Brogan responded.

"An intriguing piece of info for Santa Cruz County," said Nash, "but immaterial to our case."

"Understood."

"If there's nothing else," Nash glanced between Brogan and Donnelly, "I need a jolt of coffee."

"I'll go through the Memorial Service Guest Log," said Donnelly.

Nash extracted her cell phone as she started walking toward the Break Room.

Brogan turned to Donnelly, "Mind if I take a look at that Guest Log with you?"

"Not at all," Donnelly replied. She opened up the email and associated attachment of photographs.

After a few minutes Nash returned with coffee mug in hand. "Okay," she said to Brogan and Donnelly, "Grays Harbor County is working on a Search Warrant, and I've given Sheriff Clarke an update."

"I went through the Guest Log," Donnelly said to Nash, "and there's no 'Lyle' or 'Clayton' entry in there."

"On one hand it's a shame since it doesn't help us," Nash responded. "On the other hand it's a good thing for Nancy Copeland." She paused in thought, "Now I wish I'd never said anything about it to her," she sighed.

Nash's cell phone rang. "Hey Evan," she said as she answered the phone, "What've you got?"

"Hey Kenz," Lowell responded. "Our experts have gone through all of the video footage you provided and a one-word summation would be: 'inconclusive'," he said. "Uh… let me revisit that," he added, "Perhaps 'not conclusive' would be a better description."

"Most people would say you're mincing words, but I think I know what you're getting at," Nash replied. "Inconclusive would imply that you can't make anything out of it one way or another, whereas 'not conclusive' would tend to imply that it points a certain way, but not enough to positively conclude as much?"

"You're spot on," Lowell responded. "If we work together much longer we'll be reading each other's thoughts."

"Now that's a scary notion," said Nash. "So, what are the specifics?"

"You were right about the camera angles, the dark of night without a nearby streetlamp, and the quality of the videos," said Lowell. "In other words, depending on which side of the argument you wanted to make you could say that it appears the Joker might be taller than Officer Wilberforce, but on the other side you could easily argue that it is inconclusive."

"I had a feeling that particular one might go that way."

"The other two items fall into the 'not' conclusive category," said Lowell. "Concerning the voice comparison: the role-playing, modified-voice aspect definitely made it more difficult to assess. But according to our voice expert, the pattern of speech and the voice inflections are very similar to Lyle Casey."

"So, I wasn't just hearing what I wanted to hear?"

"Not at all," Lowell replied. "And with facial recognition: We don't have a clean shot of the Joker due to all of the aforementioned technical issues, but the facial structure is, once again, similar to Lyle Casey."

"Holy crap!" Nash responded.

"Before you get all excited here; or maybe dumbfounded, depending on one's desired outcome," said Lowell, "You need to take into account the bottom line."

"Which is?"

"None of this is conclusive in regard to identifying a specific individual," Lowell replied. "But I'd put it this way: if Spencer Dunn has a good defense attorney he or she would probably want to use this as a means to cast doubt as to their client's involvement," he said. "And for Lyle Casey: his defense attorney's argument would be that the evidence is inconclusive."

"Understood," Nash responded.

Nash hung up the phone and provided the latest news to Brogan and Donnelly.

"So, what exactly are we saying here?" Donnelly responded. "I mean… if it's more likely that Lyle is the guy that Wilberforce pulled over that night, what was he doing driving Spencer's car? And how do we explain everything else that we knew, or thought we knew?" she commented. "Our theory of the events that night has gotten completely blown up."

"Not if we go back to our 'accomplice' theory," Brogan replied to Donnelly's statement.

Nash was about to provide a response when her cell phone rang. "What the heck?" she said as she grasped her phone. "Lowell again?" she mumbled when she saw the Caller I.D. "Hey Evan, you forgot something?" she said as she answered her phone.

"No, that's not it," Lowell responded, "Our Cyber folks just uncovered a major new piece of evidence."

Nash listened in almost disbelief as Lowell detailed his team's findings. "You've got to be frickin' kidding me?!" she responded to the news, "This changes everything."

66

Detective Nash's exclamations throughout her phone call with Forensic Scientist Lowell had stopped Brogan and Donnelly in their tracks. Their eyes darted between Nash and each other as they anxiously awaited the cessation of Nash's call.

"Everything just went sideways," Nash commented as she hung up her phone. "Or, now that I think of it," she reconsidered, "Everything WAS sideways and now it's right in front of us, but scattered around like pieces to a puzzle or tiles from a mosaic."

A voice rang out, "What went sideways?" Sheriff Clarke commented as he approached.

"The Affluence-dot-com website where Samantha Dalton met Lyle Casey," Nash started, "Natalie Copeland was on the site as well."

"Communicating with Lyle?" Donnelly responded.

"As Clayton," Nash replied, "but yes; their initial conversations, Natalie talking about the family trip to the Oregon coast, the two of them subsequently meeting up at Cannon Beach… it's all in there."

"Ho-lee crap," Brogan responded. He suddenly realized what he had just said and turned to the Sheriff, "Sorry, Sir."

"No worries, Detective," Clarke replied, "I had the same thought myself." Clarke turned his attention to Nash, "I assume there are additional conversations between these two after Cannon Beach?"

"No, Sir," Nash replied. "Presumably they exchanged phone numbers at that point and had no further need to communicate via the website."

Donnelly added to Nash's statement, "Natalie started making calls to a burner phone shortly after her trip to Cannon Beach," she said to Clarke.

"Have you been able to tie this burner phone to Lyle Casey?" asked Clarke.

"The phone never turned up," Nash responded. "But Natalie's friends stated that this particular phone number is the one they used to communicate with her just a few weeks before her death."

"That speaks volumes," Clarke replied. "Uh… no pun intended," he added. "I don't suppose you have a new theory regarding this crime?"

"I've been kicking around a few ideas ever since Lyle Casey entered the equation," Nash responded. "They revolved around him being a potential accomplice, but…" her voice trailed off as she contemplated possibilities.

"But you need more time?" Clarke attempted to finish Nash's statement.

"Uh… no, actually," Nash replied. "I believe that Natalie was in the trunk of Lyle's car when Deputy Donnelly pulled him over at the Quonset Hut that night," she nodded Donnelly's way.

Donnelly looked bewildered, "You mean I could have stopped him right then and there?"

"You had no way of knowing," Nash responded.

"Nor did you have probable cause to access the trunk of his car," Clarke added for reassurance.

Nash continued… "After that close call, Lyle felt he needed to change-up his plan, and saw an opportunity when a stumbling drunk Spencer Dunn walked up to him and asked if he was his Uber driver."

"He thought Lyle was his Uber driver?" said Donnelly.

"Think about it," Nash replied, "We know Spencer called an Uber; and he has never wavered from his insistence that he got a ride home."

"But how did Spencer's car get to be the one that Wilberforce pulled over?"

"I'll get to that," Nash pointed.

"And you think Spencer was stumbling drunk at this time?" said Brogan.

"According to his blood-alcohol level," Nash responded. "We thought that he must have drunk himself into a stupor after he got home, but if the lucid smartass in his car was Lyle and not Spencer…"

"Got it."

Nash continued… "Based on where we found the box of rugby uniforms, we know that Spencer's car was at the far end of the lot where there are no streetlamps. Lyle probably asked him where his car was and suggested he make sure it was locked or to get anything he needed out of it. He gave him a ride to his car and, while Spencer was rummaging through it, Lyle moved his car to the other side of Spencer's. Lyle walked Spencer over between the two cars and helped him into the passenger seat. Spencer was so out-of-it, possibly even passed out at this point, that he didn't realize that he's in his own car and not that of 'his Uber driver'. Lyle opened the trunk of Spencer's car, tossed the box of rugby outfits, and transferred Natalie from the trunk of his car, trunk mat and all, to Spencer's."

"That's a lot of conjecture," Sheriff Clarke responded.

"Perhaps, but it fits what we know, Sir," Nash replied. She then continued, "Since he got pulled over by a cop," she nodded at Donnelly, "and was painted-up as The Joker, he drew a Joker smile on Spencer to set him up as a possible patsy."

"Why would he need a patsy?" Brogan chimed in.

"Spencer's car is now the crime scene," Nash said. "So if he ditched the car, with or without Natalie's body inside, it's chock full of evidence."

"Which is essentially what happened," Brogan recognized.

"Correct," said Nash. "Lyle then dropped Spencer off at home and proceeded toward his planned dump site. Unfortunately for him, he got pulled over by an overzealous Officer Wilberforce."

"He escapes Wilberforce, flags down a cab, and gets a ride back to the Quonset Hut?" Brogan stole the last part of Nash's thunder.

"Precisely," Nash responded. "At some point, either that night or sometime later, he dumped Natalie's car at the Thriftway lot in Belfair."

"Any idea why he chose that location?" Clarke asked Nash.

"Unfortunately… no," Nash replied.

"What about Natalie's frown?" Donnelly asked.

"Either Lyle's a disgusting sick bastard," Nash responded. "Or he added Natalie's frown as a means to tie her to Spencer; which is exactly what we all did when we analyzed the lipstick on the two of them."

"I hate to say it," Brogan started, "but if you're right, this sick bastard is frickin' brilliant in the way he set up Spencer."

"Oh my God," Donnelly had a disheartening realization. "That would mean an innocent, clueless Spencer Dunn was awakened by pounding on his door in the wee hours of the morning, and was subsequently gunned-down by Wilberforce the moment he opened the door."

"And if Spencer didn't recover from his gunshot wound," said Nash, "Lyle would have gotten off scot-free… everyone would've assumed Spencer killed Natalie… case closed."

"Just like the Samantha Dalton – Greg Wilson case," Brogan added.

Nash thought for a moment, "It also means that I owe Spencer Dunn a major mea culpa."

"Not near as much as the mea culpa Wilberforce owes him; I mean hell, he gunned-down and almost killed the guy," Brogan responded. "What's Wilberforce's status anyway?"

"The Grand Jury returned an indictment this morning," Sheriff Clarke replied.

"Damn," Brogan responded.

"So, what's your next move, Detective?" Sheriff Clarke said to Nash.

"Based on Lyle Casey's previous history, he is likely in the wind; thus I've got a BOLO out on him," Nash replied. "Grays Harbor County authorities are drafting a warrant for his financials," she added, "That might not only help us find him, but we could likely track his activity: credit or debit card usage and such."

"Grays Harbor is drafting the warrant based on him being tied to their case?" said Clarke.

"Yes, Sir."

"Well, hell; with what you've just learned we've got sufficient evidence to draft our own in lieu of waiting for them."

"I'll get right on that, Sir," Nash replied. She turned her focus to Brogan and Donnelly, "You two need to go through everything we've got and reassess it all from the perspective of Lyle Casey being our killer."

"Roger that," Brogan and Donnelly responded in unison–-the two of them scrambling to the whiteboard.

"If you need anything from me don't hesitate to ask," Clarke said to Nash.

"Actually, Sir; if you can contact a Judge with whom I can deliver the warrant?"

"Got ya covered," Clarke replied.

67

The dreary overcast day had given way to dusk, which had given way to darkness. Shocking new evidence had flipped the script in the Natalie Copeland murder case, and Detective Nash and her team found themselves revisiting their data from an entirely new perspective. Brogan and Donnelly were reconfiguring the murder board in support thereof, while Nash was drafting two warrants. The first warrant was to obtain the financial records of Lyle Casey, aka Clayton Metcalf, which would be delivered to a Judge sometime that evening. The second was an Arrest Warrant for the same individual. Nash would need to outline sufficient probable cause in support of this warrant, which was currently a matter of debate due to portions of their evidence having been previously ruled inadmissible. This warrant would remain on standby until Nash had completed amassing the additional evidence necessary in support thereof.

The first warrant completed, Nash rose from her desk, threw on her jacket, and started toward the office door when her cell phone range—-it was her youngest sister Bella.

"Hey, Sis," Nash answered her phone, "What's up?"

Bella was frantic, "I think something happened to Katelyn."

"What are you talking about?"

"We were talking on the phone when Katelyn said, *Hang on a sec, someone's at the door*. A couple of seconds passed and I heard her say, *What are you doing here?* followed by, *Wait… what… get out!* It sounded like some kind of scuffle and then her phone went dead. I tried calling her back, but she never picked up."

"Did she mention the person's name? Did you hear their voice?"

"No; but I got the impression she knew them."

"I agree," Nash responded, "I'll get over there right away."

"Thanks, Sis. Call me when you know something."

"I will," Nash ended the call. She immediately called Katelyn's cell phone--no answer.

With warrant in hand Nash dashed to Sheriff Clarke's office, "Sir, I have a problem and I may need some help."

"What's the issue?" Clarke responded.

"I think my sister Katelyn may have been attacked, in her home, and I need to get over there right away."

"Do you have any idea who…?" Clarke started.

"Lyle Casey had been seen near her house on more than one occasion," Nash interrupted.

Clarke held out his hand, "I'll take care of the warrant," he said, "You get over there."

"Yes Sir."

Nash's heart and mind were racing faster than her cruiser was skirting the traffic laws as she forged her way toward Katelyn's home. Visions of her sister fighting for her life were running through her head: *Could it truly be Lyle whom had shown up on Katelyn's doorstep? Or was it someone else that Katelyn recognized: an ex-boyfriend, a secret admirer, a stalker?*

Turning onto Marine View Place the first thing that caught Nash's eye was that Katelyn's home was drenched in darkness as if no one was home, yet Katelyn's car was in the driveway. The other oddity: the porch light was out. Home or not, Katelyn always had the porch light on once dusk had overtaken the light of day.

Nash wheeled up to the curb, grabbed her flashlight, exited her cruiser, and drew her weapon. With a heightened sense of caution she trekked along the home's pathway and stepped upon the landing. She stopped and listened--not a peep from within the home.

She rang the doorbell and yelled, "Katelyn, it's Kenz!"

No response.

She pounded on the door and yelled more loudly, "Katelyn!!"

Silence.

She grasped and rotated the doorknob and then nudged the door slightly off of the jamb. She readied her weapon.

Positioned away from the opening, she pushed the door open. A quiet clanging thud hit the upper quadrant of the opposite side of the door causing her to flinch. She took a breath, spun around and, while still standing on the entry mat, swept the immediate area with her flashlight–nothing. She reached inside and flicked on the entryway light while moving back out of the doorway. All remained quiet.

She bolted into the entryway and scanned her surroundings via the sightline of her weapon—a cell phone lying on the living room floor caught her eye.

"Katelyn?" Nash said while her eyes darted around the room. The coffee table and nearby wicker chair were askew—as if someone had fallen into them. She looked back at the door and spotted the source of the previous clanging thud–the chain security-latch had been ripped off the wall and was dangling from the connection slot on the door. "Shit!" she groaned.

Slowly and methodically progressing through the house and garage yielded no sign of Katelyn. Nash holstered her weapon, grabbed her cell phone, and made a call, "Sir, all indications are that my sister's been abducted," she reported to Sheriff Clarke.

"I've got a team on the way," Clarke replied.

Nash hung up and immediately jumped into investigative-mode.

Within mere moments Forensic Scientist Lowell and his team arrived, followed by Detective Brogan and Deputy Donnelly. Nash flipped ON the porch light and positioned herself in the entryway so as to be seen by the team.

Descending on the scene, the various investigators reported to Nash. "Katelyn would have been yelling and fighting like a banshee… she must have been knocked out," Nash stated as she gestured toward the coffee table and chair. Forensic technicians began to dissect the area.

"I've got a couple of techs going through the front yard in event that's the route the perpetrator took when he abducted her," Lowell said to Nash.

"Considering the porch light was out and there are no nearby streetlamps?"

"Correct," Lowell responded. "Do we have any idea who it might have been?"

"Oh, I've got an idea alright," Nash replied.

"You're not thinking…?"

"Yep," Nash responded. She turned to Brogan and Donnelly, "Canvass the neighbors," she said, "Find out if anyone saw or heard anything."

"On it," Brogan replied.

Something dawned on Nash. She turned to Lowell, "The safest route out of here to avoid being seen…" she started.

"The backyard is a non-starter, so with the porch light out the front yard was almost pitch black," Lowell interrupted.

"Ah, but the porch light also illuminates a portion of the driveway," Nash said as she headed toward the door that leads to the garage from within the home—-Lowell followed suit.

Nash and Lowell entered the garage and scanned the contents, paying particular attention to the floor. There was a damp area on the concrete that ran from a corner of the garage door to approximately six feet, and covered a three-foot swath.

Nash proceeded to the garage door, being sure to avoid the damp area, grasped the inner handle of the garage door and lifted. "The door has been manually released from the garage door opener," she said to Lowell.

"It's quieter to open the door manually than the noise of the opener," Lowell concluded.

"Yep," Nash replied. The door now fully open she looked to the right of Natalie's car. "Tire tracks in the grass here," she pointed. "He backed his car onto the far side of Katelyn's, away from the porch light," she continued. "The driver's-side tires on the pavement, the passenger-side on the lawn."

"And that would hide his car initially, while also providing easy access to get her to his car through the garage," Lowell determined.

"I concur," Nash replied, "That would minimize his risk of being seen." She then continued, "He carried her from the living room, through the kitchen, and into the garage near the door. He manually disengaged and opened the door, opened the trunk lid of his car, returned and picked up Katelyn, and placed her in the trunk. He came back and scuffed through whatever footprints he had left, manually closed the garage door, jumped in his car, and sped away."

"I agree," Lowell responded. "And I hate to say it, but with all of the lights out I have a feeling we're going to find that the neighbors didn't see a thing."

"You're probably right," Nash sighed. "Dammit, I should have done something more than just give that stinking bastard a warning when I saw him down the street yesterday!"

"You didn't really have any other options, did you?" Lowell replied. "Besides, we don't even know if it's him."

"Who else could it be?!" Nash railed. "I failed her… my own sister… dammit!!"

Lowell stood silent, realizing there was nothing he could say to alleviate, what appeared to be, a disconcerting reality.

"And to make matters worse," Nash continued, "we have no frickin' clue as to where this guy is," she stared off into space. "Every time we turn around he vanishes into thin air like a ghost… shit!!"

68

Detective Nash looked at her watch–it was 5:07 in the morning. Her alarm would be going off right now… if she was home. The overnight hours had produced nothing of note: Katelyn's neighbors had not seen anything out of the ordinary, and the tire tracks at Katelyn's home were nothing more than flattened grass and leaves––no tread impressions had been left behind.

Nash had provided a photograph and the physical details of her sister Katelyn to all Washington state law enforcement agencies. Assuming that Lyle had her held captive in the same location he had also held Natalie Copeland, Nash figured that no news was better than a report of a body being discovered.

The conversation with her sister Bella had been difficult. Knowing that Katelyn had been abducted, Bella feared the worst. Nash did not share that she suspected Lyle to be Katelyn's abductor; she merely stated that they were following leads.

Sheriff Clarke entered the office to the sight of Detective Nash, "Have you been here all night?"

"I can't work the case from home," Nash replied, "and I couldn't just sit around staring at the walls and twiddling my thumbs."

"You're probably already aware," said Clarke, "but our BOLO on Lyle Casey, his alias, his car, and your sister, went statewide. It also included ferry terminals and the Canadian border."

"Yes, Sir," Nash replied. "A few vehicles matching Lyle's were inspected at ferry terminals and the border, but they were dead ends, obviously," she added. "Since Katelyn was on the phone when he abducted her, he had to know we'd be on the scene right away, so I'm assuming he's lying low for now."

"Are you sure that Lyle Casey is her abductor?"

"I wish I could say for sure, but honestly I don't know," Nash replied, "and I'm getting concerned that we may be having tunnel vision and could miss clues that would point us in a different direction."

"I've been having that same thought."

Nash's cell phone rang—it was an unfamiliar number. "Detective Nash," she said as she answered. "What? You're kidding?" she turned white as a ghost, "I'm on my way."

Nash turned to Sheriff Clarke, "That was the Mason County Sheriff's Office," she said. "A body was just discovered in Dewatto Bay," she took a breath, "The description matches Katelyn."

<h1 style="text-align:center">69</h1>

Detective Nash arrived at the estuary at the head of Dewatto Bay and pulled up alongside two Mason County official vehicles: a Sheriff's Department SUV and a Coroner's Office van.

Nash exited her cruiser and caught sight of a Sheriff's Deputy—she recognized the Officer. "Deputy Myers," she extended her hand.

"Detective," Deputy Myers shook Nash's hand. "I wish circumstances were different," he said. "Especially since… well… the reason we called you."

Nash responded with a nod and a sigh.

A woman standing nearby clad in a jacket that read 'Coroner', and wearing latex gloves, introduced herself, "Detective Nash, I'm Mason County Coroner Maria Blanco."

"Ma'am," Nash replied with a head nod.

"She's right over here," Blanco began to walk. Nash followed behind while donning a pair of latex gloves.

A body covered by a plastic sheet soon came into view. The trio surrounded the body.

"Where exactly was she found?" said Nash.

"Right here in the estuary," Myers replied. "See the little flag marker?" he pointed.

Coroner Blanco grasped the sheet near the head of the victim. "Are you ready?" she said to Nash.

Nash took a deep breath, "Uh… yeah."

Blanco pulled back the sheet just far enough to reveal the victim's head. Nash gasped.

70

"It's, uh… it's not Katelyn," Nash breathed a sigh of relief followed by a gut-wrenching feeling of guilt.

The scene was interrupted by the arrival of Slaughter County Deputy Coroner Valerie LaGrange. "Hey Val, what brings you out here?" Nash said to LaGrange.

"Sheriff Clarke called and, umm, well…" LaGrange stumbled through a response.

"Understood," Nash got the picture.

"Oh, hey Maria," LaGrange noticed Coroner Blanco.

"Hey Val," Blanco replied.

"Mind if we get a closer look?" LaGrange said to Blanco while head-nodding toward Nash.

"Not at all," Blanco replied. She pulled the sheet back to reveal the entirety of the victim.

LaGrange got up close and made an initial observation. "Similar wrist and ankle injuries to Natalie Copeland and Samantha Dalton," she said, "and the neck like Natalie as well."

"Same killer?" said Blanco.

"I would certainly lean in that direction," LaGrange replied. "One aspect is slightly different, however," she added.

"What's that?" Nash responded.

"Natalie, and Samantha to a lesser extent, had a mixture of older and newer injuries; but this gal's injuries are all recent."

"Which would tend to imply either a recent abduction," Nash replied. "Or, if he had been seeing this gal, then perhaps we're looking at a fresh transition to physical abuse."

"That's much more your area of expertise than mine, but I concur with such an assessment," LaGrange said. "And of course none of these injuries are the cause of death," she added.

Coroner Blanco pointed to the victim's eyes, "I'm sure you noticed the petechial hemorrhage," she said to LaGrange.

"Yes, I did," LaGrange replied.

"So, she was strangled," Nash jumped in.

"Correct," said Blanco.

"Which is a difference in M.O.," LaGrange noted.

"Does that change your opinion as to whether we're looking at the same killer?"

"Not necessarily," Nash responded to Blanco. "The first two victims were silenced by cutting their throat; this one was silenced by grabbing her by the throat and choking the life out of her."

"So, the objective was the same, but the manner differed somewhat?" Blanco replied.

"Correct," said Nash. "If she was a short-term captive he may have just lost patience and strangled her in a fit of rage," she added. "We may not have the answer until he's captured."

"But it still could be a different killer, right?"

"That's true; the last thing we want to do is predetermine the perpetrator and potentially miss relevant clues," Nash replied. "And I realize this case falls under your jurisdiction, but can you keep Val and me in the loop?"

"Absolutely," Coroner Blanco replied.

"Yes, ma'am," Deputy Myers chimed in.

"And of course we'll share any and all info from our case that might assist in yours," Nash said.

"We appreciate that," Blanco responded.

Nash and LaGrange walked back to Nash's cruiser. "How're you holding up?" LaGrange asked Nash.

"I don't know," Nash sighed. "Right now I feel like a horrible human being."

"What? Why?"

"That poor gal lying under that sheet," Nash responded, "And here I was not only relieved, but actually elated, when I saw that it wasn't Katelyn."

"Anyone under these circumstances would have felt the same way."

"Yeah, well…" Nash's voice trailed off. She grabbed her cell phone and made a call. "Hey Dirk," she said after Brogan answered, "Grab a map and highlight the following three locations: Dewatto Bay, Belfair, and the Quonset Hut Pub. Let's see if it tells us something," she said and then added, "I'll be back at the office in a half-hour or so."

❀❀❀

"So, what have we got?" Nash asked Brogan and Donnelly as she entered the Sheriff's Office to the sight of a large map adjacent to the whiteboard.

"As you can see," Brogan thumb-pointed at the map, "Dewatto Bay, Belfair, and the Quonset Hut give us a nice triangle of an area. If you were looking to traverse the route you've got two main roads, intersecting with each other, that gets you from A, to B, to C," he added. He then began tracing it out, "Dewatto Bay Road connects to Bear Creek - Dewatto Road, which runs past Panther Lake and Tiger Lake, and continues until it ends at Old Belfair Highway. If you head north it becomes Mason-Slaughter Highway and runs you right past the Quonset Hut. If you head south it takes you to Belfair."

"So, we can reasonably assume that Lyle's hideout could be somewhere within this path?" Nash replied.

"That's our assessment," Brogan nodded toward Donnelly.

"Note that this path alternates between Mason and Slaughter Counties, FYI," Donnelly added.

"I'll be sure to get this info to Deputy Myers," said Nash.

"Actually, we already have," said Donnelly. "And I must say that these Mason County officials are Rock Stars," she added, "They've already

334

gotten an I.D. on the victim."

"Kayleigh Durst," Brogan chimed in. "Age twenty-seven, lives in Bennington, works as a stylist at the salon *To Dye For* in Silver City."

"A Missing Persons Report was filed with B.P.D. Monday night," said Donnelly. "She was supposed to catch the 4:40AM ferry from Bennington to Seattle, but wasn't there at the terminal in Seattle when the ferry docked an hour later," she added, "according to her girlfriend who was there to meet her."

"Is that all we know?" asked Nash.

"The Starbucks near the ferry terminal has her on video purchasing a latte at 4:17; that's the last known sighting of her."

"So, we can assume she was abducted soon thereafter."

"You think she was abducted and not one of those 'abused girlfriend' scenarios like Natalie and Samantha?" said Brogan. "You know... if we believe Lyle Casey might be the perpetrator?"

"Good question," Nash replied. "Do we know if there was a guy in her life that she was being all secretive about?"

"She had a steady boyfriend who was initially a person of interest," said Donnelly.

"Someone other than Lyle, correct?"

"Correct," Donnelly replied. A thought hit her, "This may sound a little crazy; but the victim has very similar looks, is around the same age, and has a similar name as Katelyn," she said. "You don't think...?"

"Shit, I hadn't even considered that," Nash responded. "Lyle was first seen near Katelyn's house on Wednesday; this gal was abducted on Monday, I suppose we could come up with a scenario..." she stopped herself. "The reason this gal was abducted is not going to help us find Lyle or Katelyn at this juncture, so let's dispense with such speculations for now, shall we?"

"Understood," Donnelly said.

"Speaking of Lyle," Brogan chimed in, "Sonoma County, California authorities have upgraded our 'otherwise known as Clayton Metcalf'," he said with air-quotes, "from person of interest, to suspect."

"In both homicides?" Nash replied.

"Correct."

"Well, shit!" Nash responded and began to stare off into space as if she'd just been sucker-punched.

"Uh… is something wrong?" Brogan said to Nash.

"It's all my fault," Nash replied in a disheartened tone.

"What's all your fault?"

"Six people are dead, maybe more, because I did *nothing.*"

"What're you talking about?"

"Twelve years ago," Nash sighed and paused in reflection. "If I would've called the police, pressed charges, filed an order of protection… something… *anything,*" she took a breath, "instead of just disappearing."

"You can't blame yourself," Donnelly responded. "You were what, in your early-to-mid-twenties, being emotionally and physically abused by this guy. You know better than anyone how much courage it takes to get the hell out of a situation like that."

"But if I would've gone to the authorities he'd have a record, he'd be in the system," Nash responded. "One way or another he would've been nailed a long time ago."

"And what if you went to the police and they said there was not enough evidence to charge him? What do you think his response would have been?" Brogan chimed in.

"If you didn't get away when you did…" Donnelly inferred.

"But he has my sister!" Nash screamed. She took a deep breath and wiped her eyes.

Sheriff Clarke entered the area. He took one sight of Nash and asked, "Everything okay here?"

"Yes, Sir," Nash replied as she regained her composure.

"Lyle Casey, as Clayton Metcalf, closed all of his bank accounts a few days ago," Clarke said. "My guess is that he knew you were onto him and he's on the run."

"Probably under a new alias," Brogan commented.

"And Kayleigh Durst was a loose end he needed to tie up, perhaps?" Clarke added.

"Or she was a case of mistaken identity that he needed to silence," Nash responded.

Clarke looked confused.

"Just an idea we've bantered about," said Nash.

"Got it," Clarke replied. "I'll let you get back to work," he said and departed the area.

Nash's cell phone rang. "Detective Nash," she answered. "What? You're kidding?" she responded to the news. "And I've got something for you as well," Nash said and went on to detail the potential search area her team had determined. She ended the call and scrambled to her computer.

"That was Deputy Myers from Mason County," Nash said to Brogan and Donnelly while manipulating her mouse and keyboard. "You know how walk-on passengers on the ferry only pay in the Seattle-to-Bennington direction?"

"Uh, yeah," Brogan replied.

"And how must of us, if we're going round-trip, pre-purchase that ticket from the Bennington terminal before we board?"

"Sure."

"Well, Kayleigh Durst purchased a ferry ticket that morning for her subsequent return trip from Seattle," Nash said, "And her ticket was used that evening on the 7:50 to Bennington."

"So, she wasn't abducted around 4:30 that morning after all?" Donnelly responded.

"I have video footage from the ferry terminal at the moment her ticket was used," Nash replied. "Take a look," she stepped back from her monitor.

"You've got to be shitting me," Brogan responded. "Lyle Casey?"

"Why the heck would he have gone to Seattle and then returned by using Kayleigh's ticket?" Donnelly said. "Trying to fabricate some sort of alibi that he was in Seattle when she disappeared?"

"I'm not overly concerned with his reason," Nash replied. "All that matters to me right now is that we've finally got the bastard!"

"Uh, yeah," Brogan responded. "As soon as we find him," he tossed up his hands.

Nash grabbed her jacket and headed toward the office door.

"Where're you going?" Brogan asked Nash.

"Hunting," Nash replied and exited the office.

71

The search was on. No matter how much of an ill-fated endeavor it might be Detective Nash could not sit and wait for someone else to provide the answer, for Katelyn to suddenly walk through the door, for Lyle to make a mistake, or for karma to intervene. She knew full well that time was of the essence when your prime suspect has a history of being a chameleon… a ghost. But the odds were against her: the search area was large and relatively remote, covering hundreds of acres of woods and forests; numerous lakes, creeks, and streams; with little more than a smattering of one and two-lane country roads meandering in and around the sea of evergreens. As the miles began to rack up, and the trail seemed to run cold, a thought came to the forefront: Was she seeking to bring Lyle to justice? Or was she seeking to bring justice to Lyle?

Exhausted from her search and all that it had entailed she pulled her cruiser onto the gravel shoulder of a county maintenance road. With rapid breaths and trembling hands she realized that the gravity of it all was taking its toll. Her stomach tied in knots, her mind racing, her heart pounding, she wondered, "What now?"

Bzzz…bzzz she fumbled to grab her cell phone. "Detective Nash," she spoke into her phone.

An anxious voice responded, "Yes ma'am, Deputy Myers here."

"Yes Deputy, what can I do for you?" Nash replied.

"An anonymous caller reported seeing a white Mercedes matching the description of our suspect's vehicle near Panther Lake."

"Panther Lake?"

"Yes, ma'am; Deputy Conway and I responded to the call," Myers replied. "I don't know how quickly you can get here, but you're gonna wanna see this."

"I actually happen to be in the area; I'm over near Tiger Lake," Nash responded.

"Tiger Lake?" Myers said. "Yeah, you're only a few minutes away."

"I've been independently working through the search-zone I relayed to you," Nash replied, "I can't believe I didn't come across the Mercedes."

"It's not visible from the main road."

"No wonder," said Nash. "Do you have an address or milepost marker?"

Nash raced toward the scene, headed down a long gravel driveway, and pulled up behind a Mason County Sheriff's Office cruiser outside of a small cabin. She exited her sedan and was flagged-down by a Sheriff's Deputy standing in the doorway of the cabin.

"Detective Nash, I'm Deputy Conway," the Deputy greeted Nash.

"Deputy," Nash acknowledged.

"Once we got here we realized this location is actually under *your* jurisdiction, so we haven't touched a thing," Conway said as Nash followed him into the cabin.

Nash entered the cabin to the sight of Deputy Myers standing over a body.

"Holy…" Nash's heart raced as she took in the scene—a body lying on the floor with a heavy-duty chain wrapped around their neck. One end of the chain was attached to an eyebolt anchored to the wall of the cabin; the other end of the chain included a shackle-like device.

"This is your guy, correct?" Myers asked Nash.

"Yep, that's him alright," Nash exhaled as she attempted to process the depth of the vision before her.

"From our perspective it looks like he had someone held captive and restrained by the chain, and somehow the victim turned the tables on him," Myers said.

"No sign of the person who was held captive?" Nash glanced around the cabin. "They weren't out on the road flagging you down?"

"No, ma'am," Myers shook his head.

"Well, shit!" Nash responded. "Have you searched the area at all?" she said as she donned a pair of latex gloves. "Note that his M.O. has been to slit the throat of his victims, so they could be stumbling around out there in dire need of medical attention."

"Understood," Myers replied and gestured toward Conway.

"Copy that," Conway bolted out of the cabin.

The sound of an approaching vehicle caught Nash and Deputy Myers' attention. Nash glanced out the window––it was the Slaughter County CSI van.

Deputy Myers posed a question as Nash returned her focus to the body, "What do you make of the frown drawn on his face?" Myers said to Nash. "It seems like someone was really trying to make a statement."

"He had drawn a similar frown on his victim, Natalie Copeland," Nash replied.

"Whoa; talk about payback," Myers responded. "Wait a minute," something dawned on him, "Was that information made public?"

"Uh… no, it wasn't."

"So, this person must have known about the frown somehow?"

"Or he…" Nash gestured at the body, "drew a frown on his captive and once they turned the tables on him they returned the favor in a 'take that, sucker' response."

Myers nodded.

Forensic Scientist Lowell and Deputy Coroner LaGrange arrived on-scene.

"Perfect timing," Nash said to Lowell and LaGrange as they entered the cabin.

"Yeah, we…" LaGrange started when the sight of the victim stopped her cold. "Whoa; is that who I think it is?"

"Yep," Nash replied.

"Holy shit; someone got him good!" Lowell remarked. "And a lipstick-frown to boot," he added, "Talk about karma."

LaGrange approached Nash and quietly asked, "How are you feeling about this?"

"Conflicted," Nash responded. "Of course I wanted to stop him, and even had dreams, literally, of him getting his comeuppance," she continued, "so why do I feel sad when I see the wretched look of death upon his face? Why do I suddenly recall the rare good times from back in the day and not the vicious beatings he inflicted upon me?" She took a breath and proclaimed, "It sucks to feel this way."

"It's called being human… having compassion."

"It feels more like being a stupid idiot," Nash exhaled. "Anyway… I was just starting to get an up-close look at his injuries," she said, "but of course I'll let you take over."

"What say we get some as-found photographs?" LaGrange commented.

"Got it," Lowell stepped forward with his camera and took numerous shots of the victim and the surrounding area.

LaGrange focused immediately on Lyle's throat—manipulating the chain ever so slightly. "Whoever did this was either in drastic fear for their life, or embroiled in rage," she said. "The petechial hemorrhage is the first sign," she pointed at Lyle's eyes, "but also, due to the thickness of the chain and the degree of pressure applied, the thyroid cartilage… his Adam's apple… has been fractured."

"Damn," Deputy Myers responded.

LaGrange looked at Nash, "Any news on Katelyn?"

"Unfortunately… no," Nash sighed.

"Do you think she could have done this?"

"I hate to sound cruel, but I hope so," Nash responded, "It would mean she's still alive."

"Assuming that Lyle Casey was her abductor," LaGrange pointed out.

"True," Nash exhaled.

"And if so, then the overriding question is: Where is she?"

"A Mason County Sheriff's Deputy is searching the area for whoever was held captive, which we assume turned the tables on Lyle."

"Was Katelyn aware of the frown drawn on Natalie Copeland?"

"To be honest, I don't remember if I mentioned that detail to her or not."

Lowell jumped into the conversation, "I'll get started on forensic evidence," he said as he began to inspect the eyebolts. "These anchors are virtually identical to those of the cabin near Hoquiam," he commented.

"We're gonna need to dissect the shit out of this place to figure out the extent of what exactly went on here," Nash said, "And to determine if Katelyn was, in fact, at this location… or if someone else has her."

"I'm all over it," Lowell replied.

Deputy Conway entered the cabin. He was red-faced and breathing heavily. "Not a sign of anyone in the nearby area," he relayed to the crowd between breaths.

Nash grabbed her cell phone and made a call. "Hey Dirk, I need you and Laura to get out here," she said, and then informed him of the situation.

"I'll get some more of my folks to help search the area," Deputy Myers offered to Nash.

72

Nash, Brogan, and Donnelly slogged into the Sheriff's Office. Darkness had overtaken dusk hours ago, and the search for whoever had escaped Lyle Casey's captivity had been called-off for the night. The prevailing notion, or more accurately, the hope of all involved, was that Nash's sister Katelyn was the escapee; but there was no direct evidence to support such an idea. Had she gone into hiding in fear for her life? Was she injured and unable to cry out for help? Or was Katelyn's disappearance unrelated to the events that took place at the cabin which had resulted in the death of Lyle Casey? The latter had two perplexing possible scenarios. The first begged the question: *Who was the escapee, and where were they? Had they flagged-down a motorist? Were they in the hospital somewhere?* The second scenario was more unsettling: *If Lyle had not abducted Katelyn, who did? Why was she abducted? And where was she being held?* The team was holding out hope for a positive outcome, but Katelyn had been gone for over twenty-four hours now and the prospects were growing increasingly grim with each passing tick of the clock.

Neither Brogan nor Donnelly had wanted to broach the 'what next?' question with Nash. Brogan decided to break the tension via a semi-related item. "While you were searching the Tiger Lake – Panther Lake area I got some updated info about that guy Andrew Brooke if you're interested," he said to Nash.

Nash had started to remove her jacket, but suddenly stopped herself.

"Heading back out?" Brogan said.

"Uh… I'm not sure," Nash replied. She seemed to be either in deep thought, or somewhat perturbed—-at least from Brogan's perspective.

"Just thought I'd throw it out there," Brogan commented, "About the Andrew Brooke guy."

Nash took a breath and responded, "Okay… let's hear it."

"As we know, he was a furniture sales rep," Brogan began. "He lived in Salinas, California, and his territory covered all of Monterey County, which included the store where Lyle Casey worked back in the day."

"At the same time that Lyle worked there?" Nash inquired.

"Yep," said Brogan. "He… Brooke… abruptly left that company and subsequently showed up in Tahoe," he continued. "And get this: that happened just a few months after the last known sighting of Lyle."

"But the REAL Andrew Brooke was actually a 'John Doe' in a Santa Cruz County morgue, correct? And someone else was masquerading as him in Tahoe?"

"Correct," said Brogan. "I'm not saying that Tahoe-guy was Lyle Casey, but the timing fits."

"Have you shared any of this with Santa Cruz County authorities?"

"Since all I've got is my own personal hair-brained idea and nothing definitive, I didn't want to waste their time."

"You've got a point," Nash responded.

Brogan glanced at Donnelly and then back to Nash. "Anyway; that's all I had."

"Got it," Nash replied. She paused in thought and added, "So hey, there's no need for you two to stick around and burn the midnight oil," she said to Brogan and Donnelly.

"Well, what about you?" Donnelly responded.

"Lowell thought he might have something for me tonight, so I'm going to ride it out for a while."

"Then I'm staying a bit longer as well."

"Ditto," said Brogan.

The door to the Sheriff's Office opened and in walked Forensic Scientist Lowell. He scuffed his feet on the entry mat. "Pretty thick mist out there," he said as he glanced around the space. "I had a feeling you all might be here," he added.

"Good news I hope?" Nash responded.

"The cabin was a treasure trove of evidence," Lowell replied. "We found a lipstick tube whose contents matched Natalie Copeland's frown and Spencer Dunn's Joker smile," he said. "And yes…" he added before receiving the question he knew was coming, "…the frown drawn on Lyle Casey."

"So, Spencer Dunn really was an unfortunate patsy?" said Brogan.

"So it appears," Lowell replied. "I swabbed the eyebolts and the chain–the metal shavings matched that from the Wilson's cabin. And the shackles match the injury patterns on Samantha Dalton, Natalie Copeland, and Kayleigh Durst."

"I guess I can finally let Samantha's parents know what really happened to their daughter; and that Greg Wilson had nothing to do with her death." Nash commented. "And Madelyn Wilson will be especially glad to know her husband was not a murderer," she added, "Even though it means he was a cold-blooded killer's collateral damage—an unfortunate victim of stumbling onto the scene of a crime."

"The owner of the cabin lives out of state," Lowell continued with his information. "He identified the lessee as a guy named Brock Andrews; whoever the hell he is."

Nash was dumbstruck. "Brock Andrews?" she said.

Lowell looked at his notes, "Yep."

"Son of a bitch," Nash responded, "That name was listed in the Guest Log of Samantha Dalton's memorial service."

"Oh my God," Donnelly jumped in, "That name was in the Guest Log of Natalie Copeland's service as well."

"Crap; we never compared the Guest Logs, did we? We only noted that there was no Lyle or Clayton listed," Nash said to Donnelly.

"It looks like we've discovered Lyle's latest alias," Brogan said.

"Damn," said Nash as a distressing thought hit her. "I am NOT telling the Copeland's and the Dalton's that the monster who murdered each of their daughters attended their funeral and signed the Guest Log."

"Wait a minute," a thought hit Brogan, "The name Brock Andrews is almost the inverse of Andrew Brooke. You don't think...?"

"Son of a..." Nash responded. She turned to Lowell, "Hey Evan, you need to provide Lyle's DNA to Santa Cruz County. In fact, I'm thinking it's time to get his DNA into CODIS—who knows how many more victims are out there?"

Nash's statement about more potential victims hit everyone like a ton of bricks, but no one wanted to mention Katelyn's name.

"I uh… I agree," Lowell said as he could feel the tension in the room. "And speaking of DNA," he continued just as Sheriff Clarke entered the area, "The cabin had both Natalie Copeland's and Kayleigh Durst's DNA; including on the chain and the shackles."

"That was it?" Sheriff Clarke jumped into the conversation.

"Uh… no Sir," Lowell responded, "There is a familial match to Detective Nash."

"Katelyn," Donnelly responded in a breathy whisper and a look of despair.

All eyes were trained on Nash as silence overtook the room.

73

The door to the Sheriff's Office slowly opened. In trudged a beaten and disheveled Katelyn. Nash rushed over and gave her sister a hug. She stepped back and looked her over. "Are you okay?" Nash said.

"I am now," Katelyn choked out a gravelly response.

Donnelly's eyes began to well up from a mixture of relief and joy.

"Hey guys," Katelyn exhaled to the group.

"You're a sight for sore eyes," Brogan responded with a smile.

"Your hands," Nash said to Katelyn as she continued to look her over. "They're all ripped up."

"Uh, yeah," Katelyn rotated her hands over and back.

"Can you tell us what happened?" Sheriff Clarke asked Katelyn.

"Lyle stormed into my house and knocked me out before I had a chance to defend myself," she pointed to a bruise and welt near her left eye socket and temple. "I have no idea how long I was out, but I woke up at the cabin with my wrists and ankles shackled, and my mouth duct-taped," Katelyn gestured. She turned to Nash, "He said he abducted me to get back at you."

Nash's face bore the expression of anger encased in guilt.

"Did he say what he ultimately had planned," Clarke asked Katelyn.

"No; he really didn't do much talking," Katelyn replied. "He seemed pretty out of it, just kind of sat there in a daze, constantly nodding-off, mumbling about having been awake for a couple of days straight 'taking care of business'."

"Did he say what he meant by 'taking care of business'?"

"No," Katelyn replied. "And I didn't want to know."

"Understood," Clarke replied. "But you somehow got the drop on him?"

"I did," Katelyn replied.

"How did you manage that?"

"I, uh…" Katelyn's hands began to shake. "Well, there was a lot of slack in the chains," she began to explain. "He removed the duct tape from my mouth under the promise that I wouldn't yell out. He said if I did he'd gag me and would tighten the chains such that I could barely move; so I complied," her eyes darted around the room. "Like I said, he kept nodding-off, and when it looked like he was totally out-of-it I asked for a drink of water. I had positioned myself so that the chains were as loose as possible. He walked over with a water bottle in hand and gave me an initial drink, but he was pouring too fast and I started to gag. He stopped while I took a breath. At this point his guard was down and I lunged at him with my arms and wrapped the chain around his neck. I gripped as hard as I could for what seemed like forever, until he fell limp. Once he had slumped to the floor I reached into his pocket, grabbed the key to the padlocks on the shackles, freed myself, and got the heck out of there."

"Where did you go?"

"I ran through the woods, figuring he'd be coming after me."

"You didn't just follow the driveway out to the main road?"

"I had no idea where I was, or when a car might drive by," Katelyn replied. "I would have been in plain sight on the driveway and the road; I just kept running until I found a small garden shed on a piece of property and hid inside."

"What about finding some neighbors and ask for help?"

"And put their lives in danger?" said Katelyn. "Not until I was sure it was safe for me and anyone else; which is what I did," she explained. "Once a fair amount of time had passed and it was dark, I found a house and they called the Mason County Sheriff's Office. One of their Deputies dropped me off here."

"Wow," Brogan responded.

"You managed to turn the tables on Casey and get away all by yourself?" Sheriff Clarke said to Katelyn, "I'm impressed."

Katelyn briefly glanced at Nash and then back to the Sheriff, "Umm… yes… yes, I did."

"Well," Nash started, "What say we get Katelyn to the hospital to get checked out?"

"By all means," Sheriff Clarke responded.

"You've got him in custody now, right?" Katelyn asked.

"Umm… he's gone," Nash replied.

"He escaped?!" Katelyn began to tremble.

"No… no he didn't," Nash responded.

"Oh," Katelyn's eyes grew wide.

Nash grabbed Katelyn and headed toward the door. Katelyn stepped through and, just before Nash disappeared, Lowell gestured her way and said, "Hey Kenz."

Nash stopped and looked back at Lowell.

Lowell leaned in and whispered, "Your DNA was there, too."

The End